# ADVANCE PRAISE

"In *Tales of Ming Courtesans* Alice Poon masterfully brings to life three fascinating women who had a lasting impact on China's culture and history. This beautiful telling of their turbulent lives and devoted friendship is a reverential testament to their memories."

— *Kelli Estes, bestselling author of* The Girl Who Wrote in Silk

"*Tales of Ming Courtesans* is a poignant and captivating exploration of the lives of three extraordinary women. As with her courtesans, Poon handles the tumultuous fall of the Ming Dynasty with grace and nuance that evokes the underlying beauty beneath the violence of this period of Chinese history. Ultimately an enduring tale of the power of sisterhood and the bonds between women."

— *Jeannie Lin, USA Today bestselling author of* The Lotus Palace

"*Tales of Ming Courtesans* is a brilliant, 'ownvoices' alternative to Memoirs of a Geisha. Readers will love seeing 17th century China through the eyes of the young courtesan-poet Liu Rushi. An exquisite reading experience. Highly, highly recommended."

— *M. H. Boroson, author of* The Girl with Ghost Eyes

"Alice Poon's excellent *Tales of Ming Courtesans* follows the intertwined lives of three seventeenth-century courtesans. Poon's real achievement is to create believable depth to her characters' known histories, thereby undermining the way that these women – rather like those in Victorian Britain – have so often been measured solely in terms of their men. She has clearly written *Tales* from the heart."

— *David Leffman, author of* The Mercenary Mandarin

# TALES OF MING COURTESANS

Alice Poon

EARNSHAW
BOOKS

Tales of Ming Courtesans

By Alice Poon

ISBN-13: 978-988-8552-67-2

FICTION / Historical

EB128

Published by Earnshaw Books Ltd. (Hong Kong)

# CONTENTS

# Notes

Liu Rushi (1618 – 1664), Chen Yuanyuan (1625 – 1681) and Li Xiangjun (1624 – 1653) were famous courtesans of Qinhuai, Nanjing in the transition period between the Ming Dynasty and the Qing.

Qinhuai is the name of a glitzy pleasure district that thrived in the city of Nanjing for centuries, and which stood at the apex of prosperity in the late Ming era.

Liu Rushi was a poetry prodigy whom her biographer, an iconic historian, lauded as embodying the nation's spirit of independence and liberal thinking.

Chen Yuanyuan, a peerless beauty, was maligned as the jinx who brought down the Ming Dynasty.

In the masterpiece historical drama *The Peach Blossom Fan*, Li Xiangjun came alive as the heroine who dared to fight oppression.

This novel tells the story of their sisterhood and their respective destinies.

In Chinese names, the surname precedes the given name.

# TALES OF MING COURTESANS

# PART ONE

## Girl Prodigy

# TALES OF MING COURTESANS

# ONE

JINGJING, ever since you came into our lives, our one obsession, as with all parents, was to give you a happy home, sheltered from all cares and miseries. I have never told you about my past, for no reason other than to spare your young mind any trace of gloom. But, you see, there is a truth about you that we've kept hidden all these years, and it will be hard to explain it fully without going into my painful history. I thought it best to put my story on paper, so that you can access it when you are mature enough, and just in case I'm no longer around to tell it. You will probably find it an unpleasant read, but I know your sweet and compassionate nature will not let you turn away from it.

Some women are condemned for life just because ill fate afflicts their childhood. My woeful journey began when, having lost both parents, I fell into the hands of a thin horse breeder from Yangzhou.

Thin horse breeders are procurers of beautiful slave girls, commonly called "thin horses". Girls are bought and sold like fillies by these breeders. If you are a girl orphaned or born to a poor family who cannot feed you, it is very likely you will end up in one of those breeders' herds. These procurers run establishments that train and prepare young girls for sale as concubines, house maids, and brothel sing-song girls.

It was no coincidence that this trade in slave girls thrived in Yangzhou. This city had been living off its colony of brothels since the Tang Dynasty. Surely you remember how the Tang poet Du Mu mocked himself in his poem *Dispelling Sorrow*. He gave a good sense of the degenerate place in these lines:

Waking up from a ten-year Yangzhou dream,
I found myself styled a dallying brothel prince.

My father left home when I was three, to try to find work in another town, as his craft of fishing tool repairs was no longer in demand in Songjiang. That day when he departed, I was standing on the threshold of our thatched cottage, crying and holding tightly onto Mother's leg, fearful that she might leave too. The last image of him was his stooping back, wrapped in a dark patched robe. Since then, Mother and I had to fend for ourselves. That image was all that remained of him in my memory.

Mother, who was good at needlework, somehow scraped a meager living by offering sewing services to our neighbors. She toiled away silently during the day; at night, her muffled sobs told me that she felt sad, but tried not to draw my attention. I didn't know how to comfort her, except to crawl into her bed to sleep beside her. She would then quiet down, probably consoled by the thought that she still had me.

When I was five, I began to learn to read and write from a poor scholar who lived next door. He taught me Tang and Song poetry and calligraphy. Mother could not afford to pay him, so in return for his tutoring, she cooked and brought him daily meals.

His teaching inspired me to start my own scribbles even at that early age. This art would eventually become my obsession and escape. Through contriving the music and dance of words, I seemed able to drip fear and sorrow into verses. After writing a verse, my heart would feel as if a knot was loosened. But as I grew up, I would find that new knots tended to flourish in their place.

The lessons lasted until I was nine. That year, my kind teacher left Songjiang for Nanjing to sit for the civil service examination. It was common knowledge that the examination results could make or break a scholar's future, especially those with limited means. I thought my teacher was the wisest person in the world. There was not a shred of doubt in my mind that he would pass the exam. Sadly, as things turned out, I was wrong. Mother said, "The heavens can be very unfair." At that time, I had no clue what fairness or unfairness meant, much less whether it was the heavens or the humans who dished out unfairness. We never heard from him afterwards.

A year after my teacher's departure, chronic coughing began to plague Mother. Her sickness quickly went downhill, as there was no money to buy herbal medicine. Her face, which to me looked so beautiful, hollowed out, and her once-smooth white skin turned waxen. In a matter of months, she was reduced to a mere bag of bones. By this time, she began coughing out sputum streaked with red.

A few days after my eleventh birthday, one morning the Emperor of Ghosts came for her. With her last breath she said in a stutter,

"Daughter, don't forget..... you have.... special gifts. I hope better fortune.... awaits you. Live with courage.... and be kind."

As her drooping eyelids closed for the last time, I kept tugging at her blood-stained sleeve, "Mother, please don't die. I'll be a good girl. Please don't leave me...."

My wails, no matter how loud, were not going to bring her back. Panic was grabbing me by the throat. In the morbid silence, a voice whispered from the walls: "You have to take care of things now. Fretting won't help."

That day is still raw in my memory. It was the day that forced me to suddenly grow up. By mid-afternoon, instinct compelled me to fish through Mother's large sewing basket. It was stuffed with spools of white and gray threads, all shapes and sizes and colors of cotton cloth, thimbles, needles, pair of scissors and a few finished pieces. I picked out three sets of newly sewed children's clothes and wrapped them up in a small bundle. With this, I headed to her clients' homes in the neighborhood in the hope of exchanging them for a pittance.

One of her clients directed me to the nearest funeral home to buy a tombstone. "How do you want the inscription to read?" the man in the shop asked. I shook my head, emptying all the copper coins from my sleeve pocket. There was no extra money even for a coffin.

When I got home, I used scissors to cut out a lock of her hair to save as keepsake. Feeling the softness of her hair, still breathing warmth, I could not hold back my tears.

In the backyard storage shed I found a frayed straw mat and an old hemp cape. I wrapped the body in the cape and then rolled it up in the mat.

When it was dark and the streets empty, I slipped out through the postern gate, carting the bundle along with the tombstone and a rusty shovel, and headed to a small copse in the vicinity to complete the burial. This was where poor people came to bury their dead. Mother had brought me here several times at night with a lantern, to catch fireflies.

For all I knew, burying a body was a crime, and the last thing I wanted was to get caught in the act. I thought better of lighting a lantern. Feeling my way along, I came to the clearing near a large mulberry tree. There were no fireflies, not even a sliver of moon. A part of me yearned to see Mother appear in spirit form. But the darkness stoked my innate fears, and my heart rumbled. While digging a pit, I recited under my breath the longest poem I had learned.

Having finally covered the pit with loose earth and embedded the tombstone, I was breathless and my palms were blistered. When I raised my head, the first glimmer of dawn was poking through the black foliage. Never had morning light looked so grim. I took one last look at the gravestone and dragged myself home.

As the rice in the earthenware pot gradually depleted, anxiety and hunger taunted me. When you go empty-stomached for days, your foggy brain sometimes plays tricks on you with illusions. Steamy bowls of rice cooked with preserved sausages would appear on the table and then disappear when you moved closer.

The landlord soon found out about my mother's death and, without one moment's delay, he marched in with a pack of scavengers, to swoop down on the last bit of furniture.

Being thrown out of the only home I had ever known, I dwelled on the streets. You could never imagine what begging was like until you experience it. Most people would just amble past, their neck stiff, eyes looking straight ahead as though you were not there.

Common sense told me to stay clear of quiet alleys and lanes, because rough street urchins would converge in such places. I always chose to move around the busy street shops by day, and sleep near a main street shop front by night.

But whenever I paced near the shops in daytime, the owners, just by one peek at my messy look, would shoo me away. One time when gnawing hunger drove me to filch a handful of peanuts from a large sack placed near a store entrance, the owner, with disgust hewn on his craggy face, barked obscenities at me as if I were pestilence.

Before long, a thin horse breeder spotted me. I had no clue how long he had been spying on me, being completely ignorant of the existence of such people. The man's chin vaunted a black mole with a single hair sticking out. Other than that feature, and his oil-slick voice, nothing of him stayed in my memory. But our very encounter was going to carve my fate in stone.

"I see potential in you. You should count yourself fortunate, because I don't easily pick a girl. You'll have a new life in Yangzhou, with free food and lodging, plus you get free training in the arts."

In no time he convinced me that he was my fortune-bearer. Since I began living on the street, he was the first person to utter to me any words that were remotely kind. I couldn't discern his hidden motive, if he had one. Besides, it was easy to let the pangs of hunger persuade you. What could possibly be worse than a griping stomach, day in, day out?

On the boat ride from Songjiang to Yangzhou, the man asked me repeatedly if I had any relatives, and my answer was always a resounding no. When he asked the same question for the fourth time, I thought he was hard of hearing. But later I would see that he had good reason to be doubly sure about that detail. Orphaned girls with no relatives meant no one would ever come to claim them.

Both my parents in their younger days had been rootless vagrants who had to flee famine in their respective home villages, and they never talked about any relatives. Growing up, I had always wished I had siblings and uncles and aunts and cousins. People with big families must feel that much more secure.

Before the Qing army turned Yangzhou into a ghost town, it used to be a prosperous trade center for salt, rice and silk. Its preeminent fame, though, was for producing beautiful and well-trained slave girls. It was by far the favorite destination for men with wealth and power who wanted to purchase concubines and maids. Pleasure seekers also loved to dally in the countless music salons and brothels. Those men flocked here like bees attracted to flower nectar. Blissfully ignorant of this, I set foot on the banks of the decadent city.

Mutely I followed the man through a warren of crisscrossed streets thronged with shoppers from far and near. Once inside the city gates, catching my eye was a flare of shop banners flapping gaily in the light breeze. The burst of colors was almost blinding.

Dapper merchants and well-groomed scholar-officials gleefully sauntered in and out of textile shops that overflowed with bolts of fabrics, herbal apothecaries that oozed fragrance of dried herbs, dainty tea shops that offered an inviting nook of peace, and pet bird shops which spilled waves of cheery warbles. Elsewhere, locals and visitors swarmed through restaurants, teahouses, gambling salons, opera singing parlors and story-telling salons. In the din of the throbbing marketplace, house servants and maids busily haggled with curbside hawkers and peddlers, each trying to drown out the others.

I could not desist from dragging my feet when we passed by a peddler who sold pork buns in a large bamboo steamer, but when the man turned back to give me a scowl, I lifted my legs to keep up with him.

We turned off into a squalid lane lined with open, rank ditches, and a drab neighborhood, made up of a straggle of unkempt streets and alleys, greeted us. Two main intersecting streets were flanked by rows of two-storey wooden houses that breathed decay. Our destination, one of the largest procurer houses in Yangzhou, splayed out at the intersection.

For the next two years, I was to live in the shelter of this procurer house, sharing with five other girls an allotted loft chamber fitted with a single lattice window on the east side.

Against the north wall were lined six bamboo pallets stuffed with straw. The glued-on oil paper on the window lattice had several slits through which wintry gusts could brazenly whip.

The adjoining chamber and two others on the opposite side of the courtyard were similarly furnished, all opening onto a girdling verandah that looked into the courtyard, where a couple of chicken coops were kept. The front hall was on the south-side ground level, with a training hall above. The dining lounge and guardians' quarters filled up the ground and upper north-side levels, while servants' quarters and the kitchen hid in the backyard.

On the day of my arrival, I was handed two plain grey cotton robes and one dark grey quilted jacket with torn patches sewn back on, which was to double as a blanket for cold weather. A tall girl with fair skin came to the front lounge to greet me. She led me into the courtyard to take the stairs up to the loft chamber. The coops caught my interest and I stopped to take a peep at the fluffy chickens. She said to me in a half-joking, half-serious manner, "Don't expect to have eggs or chicken meat in your meals. It's too fattening for us."

A middle-aged woman with a wattle, whom we called Madam Yi, was our designated guardian. Her job was to ration our food and plan our daily training lessons.

There was really not much planning for her to do. Usually we would spend the morning learning singing, dancing and *pipa*, the four-stringed lute, from two instructors. The afternoon was devoted to working on calligraphy and ink painting, and the evening to needlework and reading.

Each day we were served three meals: congee for the morning, sweet potatoes for lunch and a small bowl of rice with salted fish and vegetables for supper. The portions were always stingy. At times, I would muster enough courage to ask for a little more, but such requests were routinely dismissed out of hand. Sometimes my chamber mate, Xu Fo, who was ten years older and a small eater, would spoon some of her portion into my bowl. She was the tall girl who had spoken to me on my first day here.

The Zhou household was, and still is, one of the wealthiest in Songjiang. Master Zhou Daodeng was a learned Donglin Academy scholar and a retired senior ministry official. I had heard Mother mention that he owned a huge red brick mansion with a green ceramic-tiled roof and a large beautiful garden. The lush property crouched haughtily amidst a cluster of smaller but equally ornate mansions on the northern bank of the White Dragon Lagoon. The moon gate at the arched entrance, glazed in maroon, was guarded by a pair of stone unicorns set on plinths.

At that time, he was already a white-haired old man who lived in opulent retirement with one aging wife and five concubines. For all his status and wealth, he was visited with the great misfortune of not having a single male heir to carry his name.

My mother used to tell me that my almond-shaped, agate dark eyes and high cheekbones betrayed wisdom, and my tapered fingers were made for artistic craft. But she had also warned me that my watery gaze and luscious pink lips might attract bad fortune. She said, "A beautiful face is a curse. Girl, you have to tread with extra caution." Now looking back, perhaps the procurer had reason to pick me up.

The year I turned thirteen, on one late autumn day, Master Zhou took a special trip to Yangzhou for the purpose of selecting a girl from one of the thin horse breeders to be his sixth concubine. The news had run way ahead of his arrival.

An unusual buzz of excitement rattled the house that morning. While we were having our morning congee, Fo announced with an air of authority, "Madam Yi will soon tell us to prepare for a parade." She had apparently eavesdropped on a conversation among the guardians the previous night and concluded that an important customer would be coming by. It was only then that I found out that the six of us were considered the prettiest of all the trainees in the house and we were reserved for the wealthiest of the gentry and the classiest of brothels. Only moments later, Madam Yi came in and commanded in her hoarse voice:

"Girls, go quickly and change into the white robes that I have laid out on your pallets. Comb your hair and tie it neatly with the red ribbons I'm going to hand out now. Then remain in your chamber." She paused for breath, then resumed, "When your name is called, walk slowly down the stairs and into the front hall and do exactly as you are told there."

I was starting to fidget when the other five girls had been called out and come back. They said the man was really old, but he wore expensive silk garments and embroidered velvet shoes. Just as I strained my ears to listen to the girls' chatters, my name was called. I descended the stairs and stepped inside the hall in as natural a gait as I could manage.

The old man was seated in a red wood chair with armrests, flanked by two of his house servants standing quietly on either side. He had piercing eyes despite his old age and his intense stare made me feel a bit uneasy.

"Lady, step forward and lift up your robe to show your feet," Madam Yi hollered. I did as she ordered.

My mother had insisted on having my feet bound when I was four. She meant well, as a girl with bound feet was considered refined, and more likely to find a good family to marry into. For her, following traditions and submitting to the fate of her lot was as natural as the change of seasons.

As you know, Jingjing, both your father and I were always

opposed to the obnoxious tradition of foot-binding. Naturally we could not bear to let you go through the crippling ordeal, notwithstanding fierce objections from his bigoted concubines and female relatives. Jingjing, my precious, I've told you this before and it bears repeating: it is never wise to follow senseless traditions blindly.

Smugness crept across Madam Yi's face, which seemed to say that she knew exactly what the customer wanted. The old man nodded approvingly as she continued to direct the show.

"Lady, roll up your sleeves to show your arms." I did so. I thought I heard a light gasp.

"Now lift your head and let the Master see your face." I slowly raised my head, but kept my eyes down.

"Now dance a few steps of the water sleeve dance." I did as I was told, struggling with awkward minced steps and focusing on my circular arm movements. Dancing was and would always be a problem for me because of my broken feet. When I finished the dance, I was perspiring profusely from the exertion and pain. Madam Yi turned to the customer, who was leering at my feet, and flashed her secret weapon, "This girl can do excellent calligraphy too."

"Is that true? Show me her work then," the old man's face brightened.

Madam Yi called out to a servant to bring out my work. The old man took a quick glance at my writing and rose from his chair. He came near me, took hold of my hands and examined the long slender fingers as if they were pieces of jade.

"What fine hands these are. These are the hands of a born artist. Girl, what is your name?"

"Rushi. My surname is Liu," I replied in a barely audible voice.

"How old are you?" he asked. Before I could answer, Madam

Yi sprinted forward to whisper something into his ear.

"Do you like poetry?" he asked, continuing his quest for answers.

"Yes, I like reading poetry very much, particularly Tang poetry," I became bolder and answered with confidence.

"Can you recite Bai Juyi's *Song of Everlasting Sorrow*?"

"Yes, I can."

Then he stepped back to his chair and eased himself into it, quite incredulous of my positive answer. I calmly proceeded to recite the whole narrative poem for him, building emotion into my voice where appropriate. His wrinkled face showed apparent awe when I finished the long recital. Still not satisfied, he asked,

"Can you tell me what the poem is about?"

"It is about the tragic love affair between Emperor Xuanzong of the Tang dynasty and his favorite Consort Yang Guifei." I told him what I had learned from my scholar teacher, "But in the poem a Han dynasty emperor is used as a substitute for Xuanzong."

The old man clapped his hands heartily. Madam Yi opened her mouth wide in disbelief. Then the old man signaled for one of his servants to put a pearl hairpin into my hair, at which gesture Madam Yi cackled a torrent of thankful words and obsequious remarks about the forthcoming concubine adoption ritual.

She then took out a long list of items that would be needed for the new bride and the wedding ceremony, and scribbled the cost of each in the margin, never forgetting to add a surcharge to the subtotals. Realizing that I was peeping over her shoulder, she shooed me away, now in a much gentler tone.

Four days later, a bridal sedan chair came up to the procurer house to take me to the Zhou mansion in Songjiang.

I was sold to him for three hundred silver taels. The price was considered high. Some plain-looking girls were sold as house maids for only thirty to fifty silver pieces each. The transaction was in writing and the parchment sealed my fate. I was now a bonded concubine, belonging in the lowest caste of females. From that moment on, I became a chattel that could be resold to another household or a brothel, or given for free, unless my new master saw fit to tear up the bond contract.

Dressed in a light pink embroidered satin robe and a full-length skirt of the same color, and my head covered with a pink veil with tassels hanging down the edges, I climbed onto the back of a house servant to be carried to the sedan chair. When I peered out from the sedan, I saw my chambermates trailing behind and waving me farewell, some sniffling and sobbing. Fo, my best friend, wailed the loudest.

During the time we lived together, we often heard stories of the miserable fates that had befallen slave girls sold by the house. For some, beatings by the wives and favorite concubines were a daily routine. Among those unfortunate enough to be sold to brothels, forced abortions were common after they were used by customers. We always cringed at hearing those terrible stories, but found enough courage to make jokes and to comfort each other. Deep down in our hearts, though, we were aware that our fates would turn out the same. We would always be looked down upon as worthless slaves.

I said a silent prayer wishing them good fortune in their future, uncertain as I was about mine.

Madam Yi was standing at the front entrance. Her wattle neck trembled in mirth when she saw the man with the black mole leading a scrawny, fine-featured girl in bedraggled clothes towards her.

I slumped back onto the seat inside the sedan chair and tried to think positive thoughts. At least I was returning to the place of my birth. Looking on the bright side, perhaps I could look forward to decent meals, or at least more generous portions of each meal. But I just couldn't push away one haunting thought: my fate was at the mercy of my new master and others in his household. He had bought me on contract and I was his slave.

# TWO

Songjiang in Jiangsu Province was as beautiful a place as I remembered it. As a child, I used to like walking from my home to spend time in my refuge on the serene southern shore of White Dragon Lagoon.

There, I could loiter among the fragrant osmanthus bushes and magnolia trees embedded in the sweeping wave of green willows, and daydream to my heart's content. Losing myself in the lilting warble of thrushes, larks, finches, nightingales and magpies was the sweetest pastime I could ever ask for. The songbirds were my poetic fairies who could coo me into a trance. It was at those times that I discovered the magic of finding peace in Nature. It helped me to allay miserable questions like why my father never came home to us, and why my teacher just disappeared.

Across the glinting mirror of water, plush crimson mansions with green glazed-tile roofs skirted the opposite riverbank. The fact that one day I would have the fortune, or misfortune, to live in one of them, was far away from my scope of imagination.

The lagoon is the widest part of the Songjiang River and the most scenic. Here the shimmering pool hums, hemmed in by a vast mantle of vivid green mottled by dazzling white, against distant tiers of amethyst hills cloaked in mist. Sometimes at sunset, the sky above the lagoon would float through fluffs of gilded clouds, dappled in vermilion, rose pink, steel grey and purple.

The upper stream, branching off from the main river, rushes forward until it loses speed at this wide spot, and then the water collects into a waterway that snakes downstream. I would sometimes venture as far as the spot where pleasure boats fitted with brightly painted cabins moored, with colorful silk curtains fluttering like flowers caught in the wind. The quaint boats were called flower boats. They were the floating venues of entertainment, where courtesans performed music and songs for their customers.

Some of my earliest poems, inspired by the glorious sunset, the wistful murmur of willows, the dreamy sigh of the pool and the sob of falling leaves, were created at that time, as were some of my inchoate sketches of landscapes, flowers and songbirds. Sometimes I would mock myself for daring to fantasize of myself as a poet and painter.

In those days, I often used to picture in my head a little girl living inside one of those huge mansions. In my mind's vista, her hair was impeccably coifed into two plaits adorned with ribbons and she looked daintily pretty dressed in a silk robe with flowery patterns. She had kind and learned parents who doted on her and taught her to read, write and paint. Her father would make her laugh by mimicking her pet parakeet, which she kept in the garden. Her mother would make festoons of flowers and catch butterflies in nets and would surprise her with gifts of them.

But such spells of self-deception always left a bitter aftertaste.

When the bridal sedan stopped at the front gate of the Zhou mansion, the procurer house servant carried me on her back and went round the huge residence to the postern gate at the back. On reaching the porch landing of the rear lounge, she set me down and held my hand to lead me forward. The silk veil prevented me from seeing anything other than the hem of my skirt and the tip of my embroidered slippers.

As I stepped over the threshold, I heard a shrill voice say: "She has to pass under six sets of underpants."

At the time I did not know what that meant. Later I would find out from the house maids that the underpants belonged to the Old Mistress and the five concubines. The ritual was to teach me that I had to be obedient to all of them.

Madam Yi had repeatedly instructed me what my duties would be, the most important of which was to bear Master Zhou a son. The sooner I was able to do that, the less misery I would have to suffer at the hands of the concubines, she had counseled.

After the humiliating ritual, I was led to do the rounds of tea-offering to Master Zhou and all his women who were present. Old Mistress was the only one who bade me a warm welcome to the household. She also gave me a gold bracelet carved with the surname Zhou as my wedding gift. Even though I could not see her face, I sensed she was smiling. Touching my hand, she said gently, "Now that you are a member of this household, I'm giving you the new name Yulan. Do you like it?"

As much as I did like magnolia ("yulan"), I could not help feeling like I was being branded like livestock. My name was my true identity, and they had to strip me of it. Sullen and helpless, I grudgingly mumbled my reply: "Yes, I do, Venerable Lady."

Fourth Mistress, named Gold Flower, seemed the most peeved about my joining the concubines' ranks. I could hear her acerbic hiss through the nostrils. Later I would find out that the shrill voice was hers. She accepted the cup of tea without saying a word, and put it down on the side table without drinking it.

First, Second and Third Mistress each drank the tea and gave me a red packet, conveying auspicious wishes with thinly-disguised contempt. Fifth Mistress, named Orchid, discreetly slipped a white jade bracelet onto my wrist after drinking the tea. My instincts gave me a good hint of what to expect in this new home in the days ahead.

Then Master Zhou instructed the servant, "Take the bride to the bridal chamber on the west upper level. She probably needs a rest before banquet time." As the servant and I exited the rear lounge, I heard him tell a maid to take the Old Mistress back to her chamber, and order his concubines to go to the front reception hall to welcome guests.

At the wedding banquet, which was served on the plush upper level dining lounge, I was treated to the most scrumptious meal of my life. Not knowing the required etiquette, I thought it safest to just wait to be served. I did not know the name or ingredients of any of the dishes, but they all looked so enticing. As Master Zhou heaped helpings of each dish into my bowl, I lost no time in working my way through the food. Each dish tasted heavenly to me, certainly not things I had ever eaten before. My best guess was that they were some kind of expensive seafood and fowl, cooked to perfection with flavorful sauces and condiments.

Seated at the host table, the five concubines looked garish with their excessively made-up faces and bedizened garments. It struck me as strange that none of them looked attractive in their adorned attire, or in the least happy about the sumptuous fare spread out on the table. Without my wedding veil now, I could see clearly their looks of disgust as they watched me gorge the delicious food to my fill. Master Zhou looked on a little amused, and he cheered me on good-naturedly by putting second helpings of every course into my bowl.

That night, when Master Zhou and I were alone at last inside the candle-lit bridal chamber, he told me something that came as a complete puzzle, way beyond my power of reasoning.

"When I saw you that day at the procurer house, I felt a

strong affinity for you, as if I had previously known you. When they showed me your beautiful writing, I knew you have special talent. Your poem recital and interpretation was further proof that you are a natural that should not be laid waste. I made up my mind there and then to take you in as my student."

He paused, as if to observe my reaction. I must have looked blank, though not on purpose.

"You are probably wondering why I went through the charade. Indeed, my initial plan was to get a concubine just to please my nagging old wife, but I changed my mind on the spot. Then I considered that if I said I wanted to take you in as my student, Madam Yi would certainly have become suspicious, because no teacher would ever take a strange girl as a student, and she might think I was some kind of a sneaky go-between trying to land a bargain, thus she would have an excuse to spike up the price. So I thought the quickest and simplest way to get you out was to stick with the original plan. And I also want my wife to believe I have kept my promise."

I listened to him patiently, and slowly let down my guard. My instinct advised me that at the very least he did not mean any harm, even though my doubts were not completely dispelled.

"I am far advanced in age and frankly I don't expect a new concubine to give me a son, even if that's what my wife hopes for." Pausing, and for a brief moment he closed his eyes and shook his head almost imperceptibly, as if regretting his accidental candor.

Then he looked me in the eye and spoke as if he meant every word.

"On the other hand, I've been thinking that it would be a terrible waste if I let all the literary knowledge that I had acquired over a lifetime to go with me to the grave. I have no children or grandchildren, and only had one nephew, but he sadly died in his youth. My five concubines are all shallow and indolent, with the exception of Orchid perhaps, but she is totally engrossed in her embroidery. My judgment is that you would be an ideal acolyte to inherit my knowledge. You would be like a granddaughter that I never had. Your young age means that you could be a fast and voracious learner. Yulan, would you like to be my student?"

As I tried to let this surreal proposition sink in, I remained uncertain of what I was expected to say. Was it all too good to be true, or did my wretched fate just turn the corner? I stared into Master Zhou's weathered face and could find no trace of malice. But emotions were obviously absent from his eyes. How I wished my mother was with me. There was now no one to ask advice from. After a long moment, I spoke with a stammer, "Yes, Master, I think…. I would love…..to be your student."

"That's good. Then it's all settled. Now go to bed and have a good night's sleep. Tomorrow you can take a tour around the house and browse my library. Lessons will start the day after tomorrow in the library. Meanwhile, for your own good, just try to keep out of the way of my concubines. But always be courteous to them, because I don't want to hear any squabbles among you. There's already enough bickering as it is. And keep everything that I just said to yourself. To everyone in this house, you are still my concubine. Do you understand me?"

"Yes, Master," I replied with a mix of relief and nagging doubt.

That whole night I tossed and turned between the smooth silk beddings in the canopied bed, thinking about my chamber mates at the procurer house. I was missing them terribly, Xu Fo most of all. I wondered what was happening to her at that very moment. Yet they all felt so far away. If I were in any kind of danger, none of them would be aware, let alone come to my rescue.

For hours, I wavered between wakefulness and slumber. Every little sound, be it the slight creaking of floorboards, or the wind brushing on the lattice window, was enough to startle me out of quietude. It must have been near dawn when deep sleep finally caught up with me.

A housemaid named Peony came into my bed chamber to wake me up. She said it was my duty as the new concubine to serve morning tea to Old Mistress and the five mistresses. So I quickly got out of bed, washed my face using a wet cloth that I found in the porcelain basin, ensconced in a mirror stand near my bed, and hastily coiled my hair into a bun. Then I slipped into the pink silk robe and skirt that Peony had taken out from the camphor wood chest for me.

She had ready for me a lacquered tray with six cups of hot tea. I followed her guide to deliver the tea to the mistresses' chambers.

"Who will serve tea to Master?" I asked Peony when the final cup of tea was served. "Fourth Mistress, always," she said in an irritated voice. Peony was supposed to serve Gold Flower, Orchid and me, but was noticeably unhappy with her last assigned mistress. I couldn't blame her, as I was bought on a contract, not any different from her.

According to her, Gold Flower came from a wealthy local cotton merchant family, and Orchid's father was one of the richest old-moneyed Suzhou silk kerchief manufacturers. The other concubines were all from scholar-official families.

The sheer opulence of the Zhou mansion was like a dream to me. The contrast between what came into view now and the squalor I had been used to struck me dumb.

Behind the front gate on the south was a large garden decorated with a man-made fish pond in the center. On the east side, porcelain stools and a round marble table huddled under the shade of a large willow tree, behind a cluster of artificial sculpted rocks. I could almost imagine myself playing hide and seek there. Rows of trimmed hedges and fragrant rose bushes enlivened the west wall.

A two-storey building wrapped around a spacious central courtyard, fringed on the inside with porches on the ground level and verandahs above. A square pond filled with late-blooming pink lotuses graced the center of the courtyard. The main reception hall with a wide porch on a step-up platform faced the garden. Above the hall was the formal dining lounge. On both the east and west side of the courtyard lay two bed chambers on upper and lower levels, connected by staircases, totaling eight bed chambers in all. The rear lounge, with Master Zhou's library above, sat on the north side of the courtyard. Hidden away in the backyard were a busy kitchen, a deep well shaded by a gnarled banyan tree, and servants' and maids' quarters.

The bed chamber I was assigned used to be a guest chamber, and was on the south side of the west upper level. Orchid occupied the one adjacent to mine, while First and Second Mistress took up chambers beneath us. Opposite, Master Zhou's chamber was on the north side of the east upper level. Next to him was Gold Flower, and beneath them were Old Mistress and Third Mistress.

Age-wise, I was the youngest. Both Orchid and Gold Flower were twenty-one, eight years my senior, while the other three concubines were in their late thirties to early forties.

I knew that I looked more mature than my age, but I never thought of myself as pretty. Of the two younger women, Gold Flower looked to be the prettier and smarter one, and she seemed to believe she was the favorite. Orchid was naturally her one and only adversary, real or imagined, before my arrival. I just wished I could say aloud that she could safely dismiss me as not worthy of attention.

After taking my first tour of the plush mansion, I explored the library. Its massive collection of classic books, literary imprints and endless painting scrolls made my head spin. Totally exhausted from the cursory browsing, I was on my way back to my chamber, when Orchid called out to me. On her invitation, I stepped inside her chamber for a chat.

"Yulan, do you like the bracelet I gave you?" she asked me gently with an expectant look.

"Yes, I love the precious gift, Fifth Mistress. I should have come here earlier to thank you. Please forgive my lack of manners," I said.

"Oh, let's do away with the formalities. You can call me Orchid. So, how did you sleep last night?"

"I slept well, and thank you for asking, Fifth... Orchid," I thought I'd be cautious, being a total stranger in this house.

"I heard that you've been trained at a procurer house. Can you play the pipa?"

"Yes, but I don't play it well. I like calligraphy better," I said modestly, not wanting to show off.

"Peony told me she found you alone in bed this morning.... So, didn't Master sleep in your chamber last night?"

"Umm, he said he had a headache and went back to his own chamber," I felt I had better be careful with my words, not knowing her well.

"Oh, I see. Master's health is far from good these days. I hope it's nothing serious. There will be other nights...." She paused to wait for my response, and when I kept silent, she went on circumspectly, "Yulan, I feel so lonely here and have been longing to have someone to talk to. You seem to be a nice person and look like you could use some company..... I did try to be friendly to Gold Flower, as she is my age and from a similar background, but she chose to ignore me," she said in a plaintive voice.

"I understand the feeling of loneliness. I am the only child in my family and have always wished I had sisters." I began opening up to her.

"Maybe it is the gods who have brought us together. We are in fact sisters in this household!" A smile lit up her face as she responded to my disarming words.

"Yulan, just between you and me, I've wanted so much to give Master a son, but no matter how hard I try, with the help of precious herbs and all, nothing comes of it. Old Mistress has been quite disappointed with both Gold Flower and me. But you see, we are both from good families and we can't possibly act like courtesans...." She blushed as she blurted out what seemed to be her deep-seated concerns.

I could sense the desperation in her quavering voice, and began to see what kind of pressure concubines were often under.

Master Zhou, in an oblique way, had slipped out his secret to me: that his seeds were no good. Normally he would never covertly make such a confession, because that would be a grave solecism, one that would impair his image of mastery and manhood. His senility could never be blamed. These poor women did not understand that they could be as seductive as they wanted, but it would not make a smidgen of difference to the end result.

Yet they were not wrong in assuming that trained slave girls possessed the skills to satisfy their masters' desire or fantasy in bed. At the procurer house, my mates and I received special training to become enchantresses. Besides taking dancing, singing and pipa lessons, we were also taught how to throw away our inhibitions and to give men bed pleasures. The illustrated version of *Jin Ping Mei*, which boldly displayed carnal acts, was required reading for us.

"Orchid, thank you for entrusting me with your troubles. We can only do our best to fulfill our duty as concubines. If a child is not meant to be, it may not be due to our fault. There are many reasons if a woman cannot produce one." I tried to console her, but at the same time I was careful not to let slip my secret. She seemed to have caught my meaning and relaxed a little. She bade me sit down on a carved redwood stool at her work table.

Then something caught my attention and I couldn't help exclaiming, "What beautiful kerchiefs! Such fine work!"

She had apparently been engaged in her embroidery before I entered. Two piles of white silk squares were loosely scattered on her table, one finished and one waiting to be worked on, along with a big box containing numerous spools of colorful threads.

I leaned over to take a closer look. Each kerchief in the finished pile was embroidered in a different flower design: a light pink blooming peony, a vivid yellow sunflower, a dainty bunch of lilacs, a pastel purple lotus mottled with dew drops, a ruby-red rose with green leaves and a vermilion hibiscus. The stitching and the meshing of color threads were exquisitely executed. The one she was working on was mounted on a wooden tambour and the half-finished work was a bough of pearly white magnolia.

"Oh, Orchid, your work is sublime! I've never seen anything so lovely," I said with earnest admiration. Then on impulse, I took the chance to make a request, "Orchid, may I ask for a favor? Would you mind teaching me to embroider? I was taught some stitching basics, but I really want to learn the craft. Please don't say no."

I could never resist beauty, whether in nature or in art. The effect beauty had on me was like alcohol on men. It was addictive.

"Yes, Yulan. It would be my pleasure to teach you. It's not that difficult, if you know the stitching basics," she responded with alacrity. "These designs were sketched on paper first by our neighbor Master Dong, who is a famous painter and a good friend of our Master's. My work would not have been possible without his beautiful creation."

Her enthusiasm put me at ease. I was so glad that I had asked. Not only did I get a new teacher, but I also won a friend that day. Already I was trying to visualize sketches of birds in my head. I knew I could sketch with flair. Once I learned this handicraft, I would be able to apply my own designs to it.

There was no way I could foresee that the renowned painter and I would later have an ill-omened encounter.

# THREE

MASTER ZHOU did keep his promise. I spent the next year taking daily lessons in classical literature and calligraphy in his library. I found out that he was quite an expert in calligraphy and it was he who helped me correct my earlier flaws in handling the brush pen. He told me that a serious calligrapher must focus on one of the five writing styles and work it to perfection.

Discovering that my style leaned towards the wild grass script, also known as the cursive script, he suggested that I try to work at that. This particular style, if correctly executed, should show forceful strength belied by tender, fluid strokes. I loved the spontaneous and graceful flow of brushstrokes, which was very close to creating an impressionist image out of a character. Each character was like a painting in itself. Just like a painting, the brushstrokes in a character could evoke imagination in the viewer.

Along with calligraphy and literature, he also taught me how to write formal poetry in the classic Tang style, with strict rules on form and rhyming. With my basic training in poetry from my former neighbor, I lapped up with ease the writing techniques as shown to me.

Master Zhou was a well-known calligrapher specializing in the cursive script. He was also an avid collector of ink paintings. As I made progress in my calligraphy, I developed a desire to learn ink painting as well.

Aware of my eagerness, he kindly agreed to invite Master Dong to dinner and sound him out on taking me as his apprentice. I was ecstatic.

During that first year in the Zhou household, I was careful not to rub any one of the Mistresses the wrong way, while they, with the exception of Old Mistress and Orchid, continued to treat me with icy disdain. It was really fine with me.

Shortly after that first conversation with Orchid, she gifted me with her latest finished product: the magnolia kerchief. It made me really happy.

She also kept her promise and started to teach me the craft of embroidery. Within three months, I was able to apply my own sketches of birds to the craft.

But when she heard that Master Zhou had invited Master Dong to come for dinner on my account, she did not seem pleased. Alas, I was too wrapped up in myself to detect her displeasure, and didn't know better than to gloat in front of her.

Meanwhile, Gold Flower kept up her belligerence and was in the habit of nitpicking my table etiquette flaws at mealtimes, as if wanting to provoke a fight with me. I knew better than to fall into her trap, and always kept my peace.

I heard from Peony that Master Dong's wife had passed away many years ago and that he had seven young concubines aged between twenty and thirty. She even whispered a rumor in my ear: that one of his concubines had been forcibly snatched from a poor family on the day she was to become a bride to her betrothed. That family had owed him a large debt and could do nothing about the brazen kidnapping. I didn't know whether to believe Peony's story or not.

On the appointed day, Master Dong came over for dinner. As Master Zhou had instructed, only Orchid and I were to attend.

When Peony came to announce the guest's arrival, I went to

Orchid's chamber to see if she was ready. When I was about to knock, she opened her door and emerged looking like a blooming flower in her newly-made peachy satin robe and skirt.

"Did Peony tell you anything about Master Dong?" I asked her gingerly as we headed to the dining lounge.

"Don't you believe anything that nosy maid tells you," she snapped, apparently quite peeved. So I dared not utter another word.

At the dinner table, Master Zhou introduced me to Master Dong and then did all the talking. Master Dong put in an occasional polite rejoinder.

The guest looked younger than our Master by a few years and physically more robust. His attire was impeccably put together and his demeanor pleasant. I had not seen any man up close except the scholar teacher, the procurer and Master Zhou, and thought that Master Dong, with his trimmed goatee, carried a certain artistic air.

After the third round of rice wine, he appeared more relaxed and began gushing about painting techniques. Orchid hung on his every word and blushed from time to time when the guest's eyes met hers. The two of them seemed to be connected on some level, but I thought that was only because they had a working relationship.

When at last Master Zhou broached his request, the guest replied with unexpected zeal.

"I couldn't ask for a more ideal student, knowing that you've already taught her the wild grass script. As you must know, I've always been a big fan of your calligraphy. You're doing me an honor with your kind invitation."

When he flicked his gaze to me, a shiver ran down my back. His narrow eyes gleamed like those of a hungry leopard. But as soon as he began citing names of great painters of the Song and

Ming dynasties, that momentary unease all but dissipated.

It was thus arranged that Master Dong would come to the library on the first, tenth, fifteenth and twentieth day of a lunar month to give me painting lessons. Orchid pouted her lips and her eyes glistened with held-back tears, but I was too beside myself with joy to take note. That image would only come back to me much later.

The next six months sailed by as I poured my heart and mind into learning wild grass script and formal Tang-style poetry writing from Master Zhou, and ink-and-wash landscape painting from Master Dong.

During the first painting lesson, my teacher told me that as I had already mastered the brush in calligraphy, there was no need for me to go through the usual basics with plum blossom, orchid, chrysanthemum and bamboo. I was to learn landscape firsthand from him. One essential was that I had to learn to master the skill of placing real life objects and scenes in the foreground while leaving the background as a vast and abstract space, where mountain contours, for example, could disappear into distant high clouds and mist. This style had its origins in the Northern Song dynasty.

Earlier I had had the chance to study Master Zhou's collection of landscape paintings and I loved the misty and abstract feel of those paintings. My favorites were *Early Spring*, *Deep Valley* and *Snow Mountain*, the famous ink-wash landscapes by Guo Xi, the Northern Song great master who was famous for his "floating perspective" techniques.

As much as Master Dong sometimes gazed at me with a watery glint in his eyes, he never gave me reason to suspect any improper intent during my lessons. On a professional level, he did show mastery and deep knowledge in the field of landscape painting. Slowly I began to let down my guard, thinking that that was just men's way of looking at young women.

By this time, I had in fact come to accept as normal such kind of leering glances from Master Zhou, even his caresses at times. The only thing I could do was to freeze my emotions against such lewdness, because he was my master, and he could do whatever he liked with me. When I was alone in my chamber though, I would weep and weep, feeling angry with myself for believing that he meant what he said; that he only wanted to teach me. It was something too good to be true.

One hot summer day in the sixth lunar month, I was supposed to have a painting session with Master Dong.

That day, Master Zhou had gone away to Nanjing to enjoy a boat cruise with an old friend for a couple of days and was due back the next day. Gold Flower was on a home visit to her parents' residence, accompanied by Peony, while the Old Mistress and other mistresses were gone to an out-of-town Guanyin temple for a praying session and vegetarian food feast. I was usually barred from such temple visits because of my low status. Master Zhou never saw fit to tear up my bond contract, and so I was still legally a slave.

I had just finished my assigned painting work in the front garden and was walking up the west courtyard stairs to head for the library for my lesson. When I was on the verandah, I heard laughing noises coming out from Orchid's bed chamber. I stalled my steps. The voices I heard were unmistakably Orchid's and Master Dong's.

While I dithered on whether I should retreat into my own bed chamber, or walk past Orchid's chamber, all of a sudden Master Dong bolted out through the doors, with Orchid right at his heels, both half disrobed, barefooted and hair in disarray. They were flailing their arms about and singing aloud with abandon, obviously both very drunk.

All the servants were bantering and enjoying the cool under the banyan shade in the backyard and were most likely out of earshot. But the accidental discovery of this gross impropriety came as a complete shock to me, especially as I always assumed Orchid to be of a timid and mild nature, someone who would never risk breaking any rule of etiquette.

Before I could react, Master Dong was staggering towards me, slurring words that sounded like: "I want you too... you beautiful thing! I've wanted... you..... for so long. Don't put on any airs now..."

The next thing I knew, he was lunging at me and grabbing at my chest. I gasped in alarm, short of screaming aloud. Then with one hand he pulled me close, and with the other, fumbled with the waistband that held my robe and tried to rip it off. I yanked myself with the last shred of strength from his clasp and lurched away, almost falling flat on the floor. Finding my feet, I scampered away as quickly as they could take me.

When I looked back, Orchid shot a glance my way. Her face froze. Then some sense returned to her and she urged Master Dong to put his robe and shoes back on. In a blink, I woke up from my stupor and scrambled to the library.

I waited in the library and thought to myself how I should behave when Master Dong showed up. There was in fact little choice but to act as though nothing had happened. Reason told me I had to keep my lips sealed about the whole thing, because it would be best not to stir up any trouble. After all, Master Dong was Master Zhou's good friend. Also, my heart was set on protecting Orchid, my only friend in the household. Still, anxiety and fear was stalking me. I just hoped that none of the servants had heard anything.

Master Dong never appeared. It was just as well that he didn't. Now calmer, I then recalled the strange expression on Orchid's

34

face when Master Dong agreed without a thought to give me painting lessons when asked. It was sour jealousy.

The next evening, at the dinner table, Master Zhou told us to gather in the library afterwards, as there was something he wanted to announce.

He had just returned from the trip that morning and had looked tired all day. Orchid had been in his bed chamber for a long time in the late morning. I had busied myself with my painting in the library all morning and afternoon.

During dinner, Orchid looked inordinately pale, while Gold Flower wore a nastier-than-usual smirk on her face. The Old Mistress drew her face into a scowl and did not speak one word. An air of evil foreboding filled the lounge.

I was guessing that Orchid had come clean with Master Zhou about her indecent conduct and was waiting for a verdict. From what I gathered, a concubine who committed adultery could be banned from the master's house forever. She would most likely not be accepted back in her own parents' house because that would bring shame and disgrace on their household. I began to feel worried for her sake. The meal was like a never-ending chore.

Inside the lamp-lit library, Master Zhou was pacing the length of the room, walking from the oblong writing table at one end to the bookshelves on the other, and back, his hands tucked behind him. I had never seen him with such a grave expression. The Old Mistress was seated in his chair, while the other women were fanned out in front of the table. I huddled behind my usual work table in the nook next to the bookshelves.

Standing beside the Old Mistress, Master Zhou withdrew a piece of paper from his sleeve, and said in a stern voice,

"This note was found in Yulan's bed chamber this morning. I'll read it to you and you will see what it's about.

'My lovely Yulan, please don't make me wait any longer. I have yearned to put my lips on your soft skin, as no doubt this is what you've been pining for too. Tomorrow is our perfect chance. I know Orchid will join the women in their temple visit. Nobody will be around except the servants. I'll come straight to your bed chamber. Your adoring teacher.'"

As soon as I heard the name Yulan mentioned, my heart sank almost to my feet. With Master Zhou's utterance of each subsequent sentence, my head throbbed a little harder. Where on earth did Master Zhou get this vulgar note from? Was it really Master Dong who wrote it? Why would he do this to me? Questions kept raining down on me. In a dark fog I heard Master Zhou's voice again:

"Yulan, Orchid found this note under your pillow and she has told me everything. This note is irrefutable proof of your misconduct, as I recognize Master Dong's handwriting. Have you no shame? How can you try to seduce your teacher? You are such a disappointment. To think that I have taught you so much about literature and the arts...." He shook his head, appearing to be as incredulous as disgusted. The way he chastised me felt very much like he was stoning me in public.

"But there's no truth in that note. It is a big lie," I retorted desperately, vexed, hurt, and humiliated. He was someone who appreciated my talent and character, despite his lust for me. This sudden vicious denigration was like gagging me and parading me naked on the streets. I could not believe that Master Zhou bought the lie.

I turned to Orchid, asking with my eyes what ridiculous yarn she had spun for our Master. The moment our eyes met, she recoiled, shrinking into her shell. There lay my answer on her flushed, guilt-laden face. The truth was that she feared I would tell on her, so she moved first to pre-empt me, colluding with her lover to frame me. When it came to a matter of her word against mine, she knew very well I would be the ineluctable loser.

"If you ask me, I would totally believe Orchid's words," said Gold Flower, spitting out her judgment with perverse delight, like flinging darts at a hated target. "After all, she is from a respectable family. Old Mistress, you will probably remember that I had voiced my reservations about accepting a slave girl into the family as a concubine. I wouldn't blame her, though. Nobody had ever taught her what dignity is."

Like never before, the remaining mistresses came together in unity to side with Gold Flower and joined in the belligerent chorus. "Master, shouldn't she be punished by flogging?" "Yes, she deserves it!" "It is in our house rules!"

The Old Mistress flicked her hand to stop the squabble. She asked Master Zhou to approach her and whispered something into his ear. Then she instructed First Mistress to call in her maid.

When she and her maid had stepped out of the library, Master Zhou declared in a bland and icy tone, his eyes averted from mine,

"Yulan, you have brought disgrace to our family and you are no longer fit to stay in this house. Based on your bond contract, I have the right to sell you to a brothel. Until arrangements are finalized for the sale, you are to live in the servants' quarters. Peony will help you move your belongings there. Old Mistress is kind and has convinced me to spare you your corporal punishment."

That night, I lay in bed with my eyes wide open, running through every scene that had led to this. When basic trust was at stake, it was a lost cause for us slaves.

After giving the incident some more thought, lucidity began to emerge from a tangle of facts. At last, I figured out why there was no other way this could have unfolded.

If Master Zhou had pursued the matter, regardless of whether I or Orchid was the adulterer, he would have to call out his old-time gentry neighbor, an act he would certainly try to avoid at all costs, because the gentry would always watch each other's backs; it was the unspoken rule. Besides, even if he had suspected Orchid of being the real culprit, having to confront his wealthy in-laws would be the last thing he would want to do. The easiest way out was obviously to make a scapegoat of me, someone entirely expendable, and sweep the dirt under the rug.

This conclusion made me feel a little better. I could even forgive poor Master Zhou. As for Orchid, I understood she did what she did in a desperate attempt to save herself from disgrace, and she would have to live on with her warped conscience. I only felt sorry for her for loving an incorrigible womanizer, who was bound to hurt her one day.

As regrettable as it was, this brief chapter of my life was at an end, and I must force myself to look with all the hope I could muster to my future, however bleak it might seem. The biggest lesson I had learned was that my slave status was a real curse. Still, I was grateful for the opportunity to learn calligraphy, poetry writing, painting and embroidery. The bright side was that I could ditch the name Yulan and resurrect my real name Rushi.

# FOUR

AT ALMOST FIFTEEN and feeling utterly morose, I was in a dive into the abyss of ominous fate, the fate of prostitution. I could imagine what names people would be calling me by. An outcast. A fallen woman. Or other even worse names.

That greyish morning, I was summoned to the library for the last time. Master Zhou told me in a frosty voice that I had been sold to a brothel owner surnamed Xu, who ran a riverside brothel on the bank of a stretch of waterway downstream from White Dragon Lagoon. My new owner would soon be arriving to fetch me and I was ordered to pack my things and get ready.

Too dejected for words, I glumly stepped out of the library. A sudden pang erupted inside me. Having lived in denial of the wound in the past few days, I suddenly felt crushed by the egregious wrong done to me. Those who are able to inflict the deepest cut are those you once trusted. Repressed tears found their escape as soon as my former master was out of sight.

Peony had already gathered my belongings and was waiting for me outside the maids' quarters. She walked me all the way to the front entrance gate in haughty silence, with the corners of her lips turned up in a smirk, as if to say, "I knew you would come to this." Her heartlessness was chilling and made me want to scream at her, "I don't need your pity!" Swallowing the words, I wiped my tears with my sleeve and snatched from her the cloth sack and wicker basket containing my belongings.

Stung by my brusque move, she sniggered with spite, "Did you really think you had risen above your slave status? You are so naïve. Master Zhou was going to give you away as a *jiaji* to his old friend at court, in return for a past favor. He took the trouble to teach you because he wanted to impress his friend." Her words cut me like a sharp knife, drawing blood.

A *jiaji* is a household slave courtesan who is classed above a maidservant and below a slave concubine and is required to entertain her master's guests at banquets and offer bed favors to them. Any illusions about Master Zhou now blazed into cinders. The hair on my skin stood up at the thought of his hypocrisy.

I squatted there for I didn't know how long on the cold stone steps in front of the maroon moon gate. The cloth sack slung over my shoulder, I held in my clammy hand the basket filled with the essence of my life: brush pens, ink-stick and stone mortar, scrolls of paintings, sheaves of poetry and calligraphy, and embroidery pieces. My mouth was bitter and dry.

After days of scorching heat, the heavens had to choose this moment to dump a deluge. On any other day, I would have welcomed the rain. It could clean the roads, cool the roof tiles, nourish the growing crops, feed the thirsty lagoon and give a drink to the willows. But on this day, I felt like it was playing a bad joke on me. My heart sank and sank and I started seeing things.

Just at this moment, a mule-drawn cart stopped in front of the entrance. Out stepped a neatly dressed lanky young woman carrying a brown oil paper umbrella. When she saw me, she waved vigorously. I dashed up to her, trying clumsily to cover the basket with the cloth sack to keep the rain off my precious belongings. When I raised my head and tried to make out the woman's face, I couldn't believe my eyes! Xu Fo was wearing a wide smile on her face, as she stepped up to usher me into her canopied cart. I had to wipe my eyes again and again to make sure it was indeed my beloved former chamber mate.

"I knew I would surprise you. They didn't allow me to contact you in the house until this day. Those petty people! I'm sure they didn't let you know my full name. Never mind that. Don't you worry about a thing now. I'm going to take good care of you. You poor girl! You look like you haven't slept for days!" Xu Fo gushed just like she used to in our days together at the procurer house. It was a huge comfort to hear her voice again.

"What happened to you since I left the procurer house?" I couldn't help noticing the fine fabric of her dress and the jade hairpins in her hair and I surmised that she must be doing quite well. But I was really eager to hear her story.

"The strangest things! A few days after you left, a senile scholar official came looking for a mature woman to fill the place of his diseased wife. Even Madam Yi was surprised when he chose me. Within four months of our formal wedding he passed away, having been ill for a long time. In those four months, I nursed him with my whole heart, which moved him deeply. With his dying breath he wrote my name in his will, as he was childless. He bequeathed to me his big mansion, seven hundred taels of silver, some priceless antiques and a few pieces of jewelry that had belonged to his first wife."

She paused for breath and looked at me to see if I was following her story. I bobbed my head slightly to signal my full attention.

Then she went on with renewed zest:

"But naturally his blood relatives would never let me take his mansion, which their ancestors had passed down, and they threatened me with my bond contract. I knew I had no legal defense regarding property, because a slave has no such right, but I brandished the written will in their face, reminding them that I was his proper wife. In the end, a compromise was reached. They reclaimed the mansion and antiques, let me take the seven hundred silver taels and jewelry, and tore up the bond."

It took me a while to let my vexed brain take in what she was saying. She didn't look as if she was making this up. To me, the story did sound a little too good to be true, especially after my bitter experience. But I chose to believe her words. When she paused again, I managed to put in a question.

"How did you find out that Master Zhou was putting me up for sale?"

"Ah, that was chance, I guess. Ten days ago I had gone to visit Madam Yi to see if there were girls with music potential that I might recruit. She told me that Master Zhou was seeking a buyer for you. When I heard that, I was really excited and two days later made a trip to his White Dragon Lagoon residence to seal the deal. Anyway, I've torn up your bond contract and you can deem yourself a free girl now."

At hearing that last sentence, my tears erupted like water bursting a dam. While waiting at the gate, I had been hallucinating myself drowning in a deep murky lake with no help in sight; then in a lightening flash, Guanyin levitated in a brilliant aura of light, and with a flick of her tasseled wand she lifted me to her side.

I noticed the warm and kindly glow that lit up Fo's oval face. It was the most beautiful face I had ever laid eyes on since my mother's death. Then I remembered that the Chinese character of her name Fo meant Buddha! Bless her parents for giving her such a fitting name. And, like Guanyin, she appeared in the nick of time to lift me from dark peril. My voice stuck in my throat and all I could do was to circle my arms around her, and let my tears flow. What she said next sounded almost like a chant of sutra to me.

"Having been through the nasty experience at the procurer house, I made up my mind to use the new found riches to do some good for slave girls. So I bought this riverside villa and set up a music salon on the bank of the Songjiang waterway downstream from the Lagoon. I then recruited slave girls from Yangzhou procurer houses to train in *guqin* * [* a seven-string zither ] and singing. We have attracted a steady stream of scholar patrons who have such a predilection."

When my tears dried, I told her all about my days in the Zhou household.

"The ending of your story doesn't surprise me at all. When it comes to a matter involving saving face, what wouldn't they do?" she said ruefully. Patting my hand tenderly, she made a mordant remark, one which burned on my memory, and which I will never forget it for as long as I live.

"Don't be fooled into thinking that the tearing up of your bond contract will give you back your dignity. Even now, after I have made myself known as a charity champion and salon owner, people still look upon me and my girls as no more than lowly courtesans. You can strive all you can to change a condition, but people can choose to ignore the facts and cling to their bigoted views."

In the depths of my soul I knew she was right in her judgment. For the moment though, I was content to lose myself in my new-found freedom. After all, things could have been so much worse. To move forward, I needed somehow to purge my memory of the nightmarish parts of my Zhou household days.

Xu Fo's riverside villa was a modest two-storey house about one-third the size of Master Zhou's grand residence, with more or less the same layout. She occupied one of the four bed chambers on the upper level; another two on this level and four others on the lower level housed her six recruits. She led me to the spare upper level chamber, right next to hers.

"I was hoping you could help me by giving the girls poetry and calligraphy lessons. I know you can do it well. You see, if the girls are more cultured, they can communicate better with patrons as escorts. It would help them find a spouse eventually. The most idealistic thing for them is ultimately to become concubines of older men. The next best thing would be for them to stay with me through old age, I guess." She was helping me lay out my scant belongings. I could sense a twinge of sadness in her words and I said softly,

"Fo, doing good deeds is one thing. But you shouldn't give up your own happiness."

She made a face at me, and, with habitual levity, said, "I'm happy enough. Now I have you to take care of. What more do I need?" Then she turned and fussed with setting up the gauze net over my bed.

As the villa was near the river, mosquitoes were a constant nuisance, and thus all the beds needed to have gauze nets draped over them. At night, sandalwood incense sticks would be left burning as a repellant in all occupied bed chambers. She had especially instructed a maid to leave a burning stick in my chamber the previous night. Having gone through a tempest of enervating emotions that day, I was content to indulge in the soothing fragrance.

Remembering the proposal she had just made, I said:

"I would do anything you ask, Fo. You are my only family in this whole wide world now. How can I ever repay you for what you've done for me? If only you knew how much I missed you while I was at the Zhou's..."

"Stop being so long-winded, Rushi! Your Master Zhou told me you are a prodigy. Of course you are! Unbelievable that he would want to let you go. Serves him right, his loss is my gain," she said, laughing her usual care-free laugh.

At the mention of my former master, my heart sank again. While telling my story, I had deliberately left out the part about the caresses and the secret plan that Peony had slurred out. That stultifying pain now stirred of its own accord.

"Aiya, don't be so miserable, my good little girl! Fate let our paths cross and we should always treasure that. We belong together. I had always had a strong feeling that some day we would be reunited. It may sound stupid, but I had kept this chamber especially for you, waiting for this day. Tonight we must celebrate our reunion." She paused to take a breath, then went on,

"Listen, I have a *guqin* master coming in every other day to train the girls to play the instrument. If you are interested, you can join in the lessons. I'm sure you'll pick it up in no time."

At hearing this, I almost squealed with delight, "I would love to. It's always been my dream to play this instrument!" I couldn't help pecking her on the cheek like a child. The *guqin* was customarily reserved for the literati and gentry ladies. Very few courtesans could play it.

"Fo, I know I can never repay your kindness to me, but I would like to at least repay you the cost of buying my bond contract, and to earn my food and board here."

"Food and board for all my other recruits is free, and you will be no exception. As for their bond contract repayments, they pay me back in tranches from their performance and escort earnings. Don't let this bother your mind too much for now. You will earn some income from tutoring my recruits, although I can only afford to pay you a small fee. But, my little one, I have a great idea for you: I've noticed that some of our richer scholar patrons who plan to sit for the Nanjing civil service examinations really lack finesse in their writing. I was thinking perhaps you could take on the job of critiquing and editing their essays and poetry for a fee. How would you like that?"

"That sounds like an ideal job for me! You always have magic up your sleeve, don't you? It seems I'm running into greater debt over your kindness to me."

"Well, don't think that you owe me anything for my help. I believe in Buddha and karma. Good deeds in this life will only help me reach Nirvana earlier…"

Fo was right when she said it was fate that had brought us together, and we should always treasure our friendship. She was an orphan and I was an orphan. There was a kindred bond between us as natural as blood ties. I considered myself extremely fortunate to have crossed paths with her.

The next morning, as soon as dawn broke, I went out through the small gated front yard to take a stroll down the riverbank, which was about fifty steps from the villa's front entrance. I was in need of taking in some fresh air to rejuvenate myself. A new lease of life stretched before me. The promise of freedom felt like catching a rainbow in my hands after a deluge.

The sky had cleared from the previous day's downpour and wore blue and pink with thin wisps of grey cloud streaked across. The sandstone path leading to the bank, with tufts of grass and tiny, defiant white flowers sprouting in the crevices, was strewn with reflective puddles. At the end of the path, a wooden jetty stretched a short way out into the water.

Two early bird fishing enthusiasts were sitting on the edge of the jetty, with fishing rods thrust out and their eyes fixed on the gently wavering water. Both banks of the waterway couched in the shades of swaying willows. Speckles of raindrops on the willow leaves, played upon by the waking sun, were spun into webs of glimmering stars. A string of ducks was sliding cheerily across the river in one curvy line.

Against the mossy embankment just a few feet away from me were moored two flower boats, each fitted with a canopied cabin, with balustrade railings on both sides, and the back enclosed by boards. Beautifully crafted silk lanterns hung on all four corners of the cabin and on poles at the bow and stern. Pink silk curtains fluttered idly over the cabin front and the railings. I wondered if these were the same ones I had seen when I was a child. A sudden desire to capture the scene on paper engulfed me. I turned and darted ahead, wanting to make a dash for the villa to fetch my paint brushes and ink and paper. In my haste, I bumped right into someone who had been standing not far behind me.

"I'm so sorry. Please forgive me." I was flustered. The young man appeared dazed by the close contact and he just kept staring at me, seemingly lost for words.

When I tried to move out of his way, he also tried to swerve, thus blocking me. I careened to the other side, and he did the same. Then we both broke into a giggle. I noticed in spite of my confusion that he was sprucely dressed and had a dapper look. Tension now relaxed, he regained his cool and spoke with courtesy.

"I'm sorry to block your way. I thought you were enjoying the scene as I was, and wasn't expecting you to turn so suddenly. This scene takes my breath away, and I was going to ask my servant to bring me my painting utensils."

"Oh, I see. So Master…is a painter?" I asked, pleasantly surprised by his revelation.

"May I introduce myself? My name is Zhengyu, surnamed Song, and my residence is on the north shore of White Dragon Lagoon. I am a poet and I dabble a bit in painting."

"It is my honor to meet you, Master Song. My name is Rushi, surnamed Liu. I teach calligraphy at Madam Xu's villa just over there. I, too, was just going to fetch my painting tools." I immediately regretted my lack of reserve in front of a total stranger.

When I took a good look at him, I found that he was a handsome young lad with a high forehead and smooth skin, possibly about my age. His robes were made of the finest silk and his shoes of embroidered felt. All the signs betrayed he was from a wealthy family.

"I have been to Madam Xu's villa several times to listen to the girls' performance, which I enjoy a lot. But I don't remember ever seeing you there. Maybe you were engaged with your teaching."

"Oh, actually I only arrived yesterday, from Nanjing." I told a little lie, wary that he might somehow be linked to the Zhou household.

"I see. Nanjing is a mesmerizing city. I've been there many times to visit friends and for pleasure and shopping. Are you a Qinhuai courtesan?"

That question hit a raw nerve in me. Why would he assume I was from the pleasure district? Did I look like a courtesan to him? I didn't paint my face, nor was I dressed in bright color satins.

Sensing my longer-than-normal silence, he knew he had made a clumsy gaffe and at once tried to clarify, "Lady Liu, please do not take offense. I didn't mean to make an assumption. It's just that you... you are so beautiful and.... from Nanjing, and you are associated with Madam Xu..." He had no idea that his explanation incensed me even more.

Ah, so Fo was right when she said that people still looked upon her and her girls as courtesans, notwithstanding the fact that they were not. Everyone knew that courtesans, high-class or low-class, were just a cover for prostitutes. What else would these wealthy lads go to Nanjing for, other than to seek pleasures of the flesh?

"Master Song, can you not tell the difference between performers and courtesans? Did any of Madam Xu's girls offer bed chamber favors to you at any time?" I asked him a bold straight question, which had the desired effect of ruffling him. He blushed a deep red.

Bristling with anger at his insult of me and Fo, I stormed off towards the villa without waiting for his reply.

As I stepped inside the front gate, Fo waved at me from the porch saying that breakfast was ready. Her beckoning sounded so sweet as it reminded me that I was famished. I headed straight for the dining lounge at the rear to fill an empty stomach, my earlier urge to paint having evaporated.

I told Fo everything that had just happened, and she giggled. "I never knew you could talk like a man!"

I was surprised at myself too. Much as I had never cared two coppers about Gold Flower's nit-picking at my lack of lady-like manners, I had still behaved properly like a demure maiden in the Zhou household, never daring to say anything out of line. Perhaps it was the new-found freedom that emboldened me to say exactly what was on my mind.

Also, a strange idea spurted in my mind at that moment. If I were to take up the job of an editor, would it not be better for me to dress like a Confucian scholar, to give an air of scholarly authority? Such a cover would have the added benefit of never having to face the humiliation of being mistaken for a courtesan again. The more I thought about this idea, the more I liked it.

After eating my fill, I sounded Fo out about my idea, and to my astonishment, she voiced enthusiastic support.

"The Song dynasty female warrior Liang Hongyu had a habit of dressing like a man," she said with a mischievous glint in her eyes. "I'll start sewing some men's robes for you right away."

Looking at my little feet, she wrinkled her nose and chuckled. "Luckily you don't have to do battle as she did." As she laughed, she broke into a fit of hacking cough. Then she said good-humoredly, "I'll make the robes longer to hide those three-inch golden lotuses of yours. Rushi, did you ever realize that your name is a pun of the term *Rushi* for Confucian scholar?"

"It never occurred to me... What a keen observation!"

Then my mind turned to more practical matters. How on earth was I going to find my clients? As if she could read my mind, Fo tilted her head and smiled.

"Thinking of how to get clients? Well, I know someone from the Revival Society who can help you. His name is Li Wen. He is one of the 'Three Geniuses of Songjiang' known for their outstanding poetic and literary talent, and he is a senior member of a prominent poetry club. He told me that many of the club members had at one time or another failed the civil service examinations. Oh, what did you say that young man's name was?"

"Song, something like Zhengyu," I said disinterestedly.

"Oh, he is the youngest one of the Three! And the richest! The third one is Chen Zilong, the most senior, and he is the leader of both the poetry club and the Revival Society! He's a good friend of Wen's."

I was wondering how my poetry would compare with the esteemed works of these men. By now I had written a bunch of fifty five-character and seven-character regular verses and quatrains, all of which Master Zhou had given high praise to. The theme of this collection centered on landscape, flora and nature. Would I ever become a published poet? One could always dream!

The next day, I began giving daily lessons in calligraphy and poetry reading to Fo's six apprentices. It warmed my heart to see that they were all young and eager learners. I noticed on the first day that the girls were all marred by some kind of physical imperfection. One girl had a cleft upper lip, one was cock-eyed, one walked with a limp, one was pockmarked, one had a mole on the chin and one spoke with a stutter. All were plain-looking except the one with a stutter, who had the lovely face of a girl flowering into a young woman.

Fo told me that this girl was named Dong Xiaowan and she could sing like a lark, but whenever she spoke, she stammered to the point of being unintelligible. She sighed.

"When Xiaowan was fourteen, her mother passed away. Her father is a compulsive gambler and owes a lot in debt and sold her to a thin horse breeder. Soon after I bought her out, her father sold her on a new contract to his creditors. Even now, he comes here from time to time to extort money from her. She has expressed a wish to go to Nanjing to work in one of the Qinhuai brothels, where she can earn more money. I'm hoping she will change her mind, but her father's pile of debts is a huge problem."

I understood why Fo had selected these girls. They were those who were the least "marketable" on a thin horse breeder's roll. The most likely path for them would be to end up being sold as lowly maidservants to frugal households or as prostitutes to cheap brothels. A maidservant was usually required to take up the foulest and most menial of household chores like cleaning chamber pots and spittoons, cleaning kitchen pots and woks, chopping up fire logs for kitchen stoves, fetching pails of water from wells and such other labors. A low-class prostitute was often subjected to physical abuse by customers and mistreatment by brothel owners. By taking them in, Fo had delivered them from wretched fates. In the unfortunate case of Xiaowan, it appeared that she would soon jump right back into the fire.

"Is there nothing that we can do for her?" I asked. Something about the girl strummed my heartstrings.

"The best I can do is to recommend her to my friend Jingli, whom people call Madam Li in the Qinhuai district of Nanjing. She operates a profitable opera and music salon and is the only salon owner in Qinhuai whose girls are not forced to serve patrons in bed."

As it happened, several years would lapse before Xiaowan would leave us for a more lucrative prospect at Jingli's famous Villa of Alluring Fragrance.

The tutoring sessions, which would begin at sunrise each day and end in mid-morning, quickly settled into a routine. I would spend late mornings taking long strolls along the waterway, sometimes venturing upstream as far as my favorite childhood refuge on the south side of the Lagoon. Try as I might to avoid brooding over my past, on these visits, I tended to dwell on the painful loss of my mother and the sad disappearance of my father. Like a spectral shadow, the deep sense of loss always lurked around every bend, keeping peace at bay.

Releasing my sorrow into poetry seemed a good way to give cathartic purge in those moments. At the same time, I realized that the craft of words needed practice for it to be perfected, just like any other form of art. My poetry at this stage was taking on nuances of pathos, listlessness, loss, and death. These poems quickly grew into a new collection.

The afternoons were spent either taking *guqin* lessons with the girls or engaging in my painting or embroidery. The salon's *guqin* and singing performances were held in evenings. Occasionally I would dress in the pale green, loose-fitting Confucian scholar cotton robe that Fo had custom made for me, hide my long hair inside a square cloth cap with two streaming bands, and join the audience of scholars and officials. More often, I would retire to my chamber to avail myself of Fo's large collection of books, which she had inherited from her deceased husband. Reading voraciously was the only way to hone my writing craft.

By now, Fo was well educated enough to spar with any scholar patron on the arts. Under Li Wen's influence, she was well trained in lyric poetry writing, which was complemented by her fame in orchid painting.

It was during one performance session that Fo introduced Scholar Li to me. He was a tall man, mature and genteel in his disposition. I had learned from Fo that Li was an expert in lyric poetry and was inspired by the Song poet, Su Shi. Our conversation quickly drifted into comparing Song and Tang poetry.

In our second meeting, I invited him to have tea in the rear lounge, and showed him my two poetry collections and mounted calligraphy and painting scrolls. An enraptured look rippled across his face when he finished reading my poems. By the time he rose to leave, it was well into the late evening.

Apparently I made a good impression on him that night, as three days later, he brought with him four poetry club members who were eager to employ my editing service. Thus started my new job as an editor. It was a delightful job that I easily fitted into my afternoon schedule.

From time to time, Scholar Li would come by to see how I was getting on with my work. If there were any questions about the texts I was editing, he was always happy to give me guidance on his visits. During his visits, he liked chatting with me and Fo about history and current events. From him, we learned a lot about the precarious situation our nation was now in, plagued at once by internal woes and external threats. I was particularly distressed by the news that our valiant General Yuan Chonghuan had been unjustly executed, thanks to the eunuchs' dirty wiles. These discussions disquieted me a lot and sent me into deep meditation for long spells.

On more than one occasion he said to me, "There is a person I would really like you to meet. His name is Chen Zilong. I'm sure Fo has mentioned him to you. He is a man of noble ideals and is a renowned poet and Tang classicist."

Having learned from Master Zhou, I had some idea that one essence of Tang poetry was the profuse usage of literary allusions, which involved deep knowledge of Chinese history and classic literature appreciation. I was guessing that Scholar Chen must be a very learned and upright man. A palpable outline of him was taking shape in my head.

# FIVE

TWO CALM MONTHS spun past, and just as my memory of Scholar Song was starting to fade, I caught sight of him in the audience at a *guqin* performance. Seated in one of the second-row chairs, he turned his head left and right, as if in search of someone. I was sitting in the last row, four rows behind him. Even if he chanced to see me, I was certain he wouldn't be able to recognize me in my scholar disguise. As I was still feeling annoyed, I chose not to greet him.

At the end of the session, he walked up to one of the performers. It looked like he was asking her a question. To my frustration, the girl pointed her finger to where I was sitting. Alas, there was no escape. For a brief moment he seemed to hesitate. Then he walked briskly towards me. On his approach, I noticed his mixed expression of disbelief and awe. He scanned my face in amazement and appeared elated by what he saw.

"Lady Liu, I'm so pleased to see you again. I've come to offer my sincere apologies for my uncouth words that morning. I am begging you for your forgiveness," he said, bowing deeply to me and bringing his delicate white hands together.

I was taken aback by his candor and couldn't find words to say to him. When I kept my silence, he suddenly flopped onto his knees and wailed like a woman:

"I've taken this long to come to you because I fell sick and was bedridden for over a month. It took me another month to recuperate. I will not rise until you say you accept my apologies."

His unseemly gesture immediately drew everyone's attention towards us, which sent me into a flush. Looking at his distraught face, I couldn't but lean down and try to help him back onto his feet. "Master Song, please, please rise," I said. "I accept your apologies."

For a month thereafter, he showed up every other evening to attend the salon's performances.

Fo remarked one day: "It is clear as day that he is attracted to you, Rushi. How do you feel about him?"

I would be lying if I said I wasn't flattered. My concern, though, was that he was from an extremely wealthy family, which to me was an impediment. But he seemed pleasing and congenial and I did not dislike his company.

He fell into a habit of staying after each performance to chat with me. We talked about Tang poetry and Song paintings. Whenever he looked into my eyes, he had a dreamy expression on his face, full of ardent admiration and childish wonder. If I were completely honest with myself though, he and I were not of the same ilk and there was hardly any spark between us.

Another month passed, and one day he did something with calculated pomposity. He came to the salon in mid-morning to catch me before my usual stroll. I was in my chamber taking a short rest after the tutoring session. Having changed into a white skirt and a light grey cotton robe under a long vest, I went out to the reception lounge to meet him. He said with barely concealed excitement, "Please come with me. I have something to show you."

He took hold of my hand and led me down to the riverbank. It was a deep autumnal day, the air was crisp and fresh, imbued with the delicate fragrance of sweet osmanthus. When we reached the spot where we had met the first time, he directed my eyes to a boat parked behind the two stationery flower boats. It was similar in size and trimmings to those two boats, except for the colors. The hull, cabin boards and railings had a fresh coat of dark green paint; the couches were purple; the canopy, silk lanterns and silk gauze curtains were all light violet. The color scheme gave an ethereal feel to the boat, making it look exotic. Then I remembered telling him on one occasion my favorite colors.

"How do you like that boat?" he asked sheepishly.

"Why, you want to give it to me?" I asked a question that I knew the answer to.

"Yes, if it pleases you. It would make me very happy... if you accept it as a gift from me," he said as if he were awaiting punishment.

I didn't know what to say. If I said yes, it could be taken to mean I was committing myself to the relationship. If I said no, it would be such a pity, as, truth be told, I loved the boat at first sight. I was already envisioning the kind of freedom I would enjoy: sailing it to faraway places that I had never been to before, or just cruising in it on the river in the full moonlight. I could even hold literary parties in the boat. My mind ran wild with scenarios, until a fake cough from him brought me back from reverie.

"Well, I was hoping you might consider it as recompense for your hurt feelings over my inappropriate remark at our first encounter."

I loved the boat too much to let it slip through my fingers. But I knew that somehow I had to dissociate my acceptance of it from anything that might even hint at a commitment to him. I came up with an idea and said softly,

"Master Song, may I thank you for your generosity. But I cannot accept such a valuable gift from you, lest people may mistake it for a token of love between us. I was wondering if this idea might work: I am indebted to Madam Xu for the payment of my bond contract. If you insist that you want to use this gift to make amends, could you not use it to repay my debt owed to Madam Xu? She will then become the owner of the boat and would be entitled to sell it any time to recover the debt I owe her. With her permission I get to use the boat for my purpose. Would this not be good for all parties?"

"That is a brilliant idea, Lady Liu! I'm so happy that you've come up with a perfect solution. It will be my pleasure to help you pay off your debt. I will have Madam Xu sign the papers tomorrow for the transfer of ownership."

I was a little surprised that he agreed so quickly to my suggestion. It was an extraordinary generous gesture on his part. The boat was probably worth three hundred silver taels, and I owed Fo two hundred and fifty. It was an obvious bargain from which I would benefit the most.

That evening at supper time, I told Fo about the agreed deal. She said with an expression of concern mixed with joy.

"Zhengyu is the only son in the Song family," she said. "He was born with a silver spoon in his mouth and his mother is known to have pampered him like a prince since birth. Buying a boat as a gift is nothing to him. However you look at it, he is doing you a great favor. The way I see it, it won't be long before he proposes marriage to you. I would hate to see you leave me so soon. But if you and Zhengyu are meant to be a couple, I couldn't be happier for you both."

"Don't be silly, Fo! I would hate to leave you and I won't get married any time soon. I've just started a job that I love and I have every intention of carrying on with it. Would you mind if I use the boat as my study?"

"Of course not. Use it as you wish, sweet dumpling. You

know I get seasick on boats, so don't count on me for company."

"Fo, have you taken any herbal medicine to treat your cough?" It suddenly struck me that Fo had been coughing a lot lately.

"I've been taking a potion made with brined kumquat. It has helped. It's just the recent changes in weather that have brought it on."

I was relieved to hear her say that. Maybe I just chose to believe what I wanted to believe. I pushed aside the thought that Fo's complexion was losing its luster and she was getting noticeably thinner.

In late summer, Zhengyu and I took the boat for cruises on a couple of occasions. From late autumn to early winter, I used the boat as my workplace. Then came winter, and when nature finally stirred from its long deep slumber, I was so looking forward to setting out for a boat ride in the lovely spring.

Shortly after the New Year, one afternoon, Zhengyu came to see Fo to ask her for my hand in marriage and to seek her advice on the formalities to follow.

His mother had already made plans for him to wed a girl from a wealthy scholar official family as his primary wife in the coming month. He was hoping to take me as his concubine shortly thereafter. Fo said to him,

"Rushi is a free girl. She's like a little sister to me, but I don't know her mind. It would be best for you to speak to her directly."

The boat had been moored alongside the riverbank in the depths of winter, but a few days earlier, I had asked Ah Luk, one of Fo's servants, to move it out to the jetty for easy boarding. The invigorating early spring scent and flood of bird songs were just too tempting, and I surrendered to their call.

I was doing some editing work inside the boat cabin, snugly trussed up in a thick quilt. I had a small brazier burning near the low table, to keep out the early spring chill. A pot of jasmine tea was brewing on the brazier grille.

Taking a moment to relax on the couch, I was lost in the glitter of the reflective river, in relief against the distant folds of dark green mountains wreathed in ribbons of white mist. When I glanced at the jetty, I saw Zhengyu there pacing back and forth, as if undecided as to whether to come on board or not. I waved to him and beckoned him to join me.

After sitting himself down on the couch opposite me, he said timorously, "Rushi, I've come to… ask for your hand… in marriage. Mother insisted that I first take a wife next month. I told her that I wanted… to take you… as my concubine, but she gave me no answer. I thought I would ask you anyway, because you are the one I love. She will come around somehow to accepting you."

His proposal came as no surprise, as I had been expecting this moment. I looked him straight in the eye for a while, and said with firmness,

"You wealthy lads all want concubines. You will already have a wife. How am I to know that you will treat me kindly after marriage? What will prevent you from taking more concubines after me? You say you love me. But words are not reliable. Would you be willing to do something that I specifically ask, as proof of your love?"

"Yes, yes, I will do anything you ask. What would you have me do? You must accept my proposal if I comply with your request." A look of partial relief spilled across his face. He was probably betting that my request had something to do with literary challenges or gifting of valuables.

"Jump into the river now," I pronounced the words slowly with a serious look, fully expecting that he would back down. Any sane person would have done, especially someone who couldn't swim, like him.

He looked hesitantly at the icy water, with patches of the azure sky in its depths. He turned his face to me. I kept up my impassive expression. Baffled to see I was not joking, he reluctantly rose from his seat and walked to the deck at the stern. My bet was on him coming back to wheedle me into changing my mind. I didn't even bother to follow him with my eyes and turned my attention back to the papers I was working on.

A few moments passed. Then a loud splash jerked me out of my smugness. I jumped up and scampered to the stern, shouting for help. His boy servant, who had stayed on the jetty, heard my frantic screams and sprang into the water. Like an agile frog, he propelled himself towards his struggling master and pulled him ashore.

After Zhengyu and his servant had dried themselves, I invited him to stay for dinner, at which I got an earful from Fo. Not only that, the worst thing was realizing that my outlandish idea had now landed me in a bind. How was I to get out of my side of the bargain?

Up to this time, I had not allowed intimacy between myself and Zhengyu. After dinner, I hinted for him to follow me into my bed chamber. As a reward for his brave act and the boat, I allowed him to kiss my mouth and run his hands over me, with my outer robe off. But I drew the boundary there, as I just could not bring myself to offer my virginity to him. Fortunately, he knew better than to force me.

Then things took another twist. A twist less surprising than it was humiliating.

By the end of the second lunar month of the New Year, Zhengyu was wedded to the wealthy and well-born girl. "A perfect spousal match of wooden doors with wooden doors," as the saying went. But her mother adamantly refused to let him take me as a concubine. He was too craven to come and tell the truth to my face. Instead, he wrote me a short letter to convey his deep regrets and begged me to accept the role as his kept mistress.

When I showed Fo the letter, she said with a sigh,

"Old Madam Song has always been known to be a strong-willed and imperious old lady. I thought there was little chance that she would accept you as her secondary daughter-in-law. The Song family is a well-known scholarly family in Songjiang. For such families, face always comes first. My only bet was on Zhengyu. I was hoping he would try to convince his mother that you never joined the ranks of courtesans and that you hold a respectable job. But it seems I made a bad wager."

"It shows what a coward he is. He had the nerve to ask me to be his kept mistress! How deluded could he be? I'll bet Madam Song is also one of those who would rather cling to their prejudices than see things as they really are. Frankly, I never expected her to look past the fact that I am a fallen woman cast out of the Zhou household. Anyway, this doesn't upset me at all. I never had any urge to be his concubine to begin with."

"Sometimes we can only see a man's true face after a critical event forces him to make a choice. His mother drives him like a puppet on strings and he gladly follows her commands. If this man is not even willing to fight for the woman he claims to love, what kind of love is that? I'm glad that you never had feelings for him." As usual, Fo was sharp in her observation.

As the spring season charm was at its most irresistible, I invited Li Wen and his friend Chen Zilong to a boat cruise. It was Wen's remark that had nudged me to send the invitation to Scholar Chen. "I've spoken to Zilong about your poetry, and he said he would love to meet you in person, if you would grant him the pleasure."

It was one of those picturesque late spring afternoons. I wouldn't accept Fo's excuses and insisted she come along on the boat cruise. Wen, Fo, the boatman Ah Luk and I embarked on the boat a little after noon. Wen told us that Zilong was running a bit late and asked us to wait for him.

Fo took out from the basket plates of glazed walnuts and dates, roasted peanuts, red bean cakes and jasmine tea leaves and spread them on the low table in the cabin. She set the large pot of water on the brazier to bring to boil.

I had donned a lilac silk robe with dark green borders at the collar and sleeve cuffs, matched with a dark green skirt. This pretty outfit was one of Fo's creations and was my favorite. She herself was wearing a pale blue silk robe and dark blue skirt, and looked very pretty. A proud and knowing smile lit up her face, and something told me that she was in as buoyant a mood as I was.

It looked like a perfect day for a boat cruise. Feathery clouds wheeled across the pale blue sky. The sun's warm rays gilded everything they touched, dappling the crystal clear water with silvery patches. The murmur of waves lapping against the sides of the boat was in chorus with the sonorous rustle of willows. The landscape strummed in harmony.

At long last, Zilong appeared in a distance. Looking svelte and upright in posture, he moved with an elegant gait. As he glided nearer, his eyes lingered on the river vista for a long while, seemingly rapt with wonder, yet deep thoughts showed in his crinkled forehead. Waking from his reverie, he moved like mercury towards the embarking plank.

When he was seated, his deer-like gaze swept around and then nestled on me. Almost paralyzed by his fervid stare, I couldn't but lock my eyes on him. He had a broad brow, sharp around the chin, a straight nose and clearly defined eyebrows perched high above a pair of gentle eyes. Entrancement and inquisitive wonder chased each other across his face as he kept up his impassioned gaze.

Bewildered beyond words, I saw a bizarre familiarity in the forlorn but handsome visage.

"Did he appear in one of my dreams, or had I seen him in my previous life?" I asked myself quietly.

He dazzled me to blindness.

# SIX

"THIS IS LADY LIU; and this is my good pal Chen Zilong!" Wen made the introduction as he put jasmine tea leaves into the teapot and poured hot water into it. I smiled from my heart, eyes glued on him. He bowed his head to me.

Fo said to Ah Luk, "We are all here now. You can start rowing."

After a brief exchange of pleasantries, our conversation drifted to the pressing issues facing the nation. I had often heard Fo and Wen talk about drought and famine afflicting peasants in Henan, Shanxi and Shaanxi. On top of that, they were also crushed by the punitive taxes, exacted by the court for the upkeep of the imperial army.

"Li Zicheng has now rallied twenty thousand rebels in Shaanxi after a mutiny. Provincial officials have become their assassination targets. At the same time, bad news arrives everyday from the northern border. It won't be long before chaos will overwhelm us," said Wen with a downcast look.

"People blame drought and famine for the peasants' discontent, but I would say the crux of the matter goes deeper than that. Rampant corruption in officialdom is the root cause, inherited from previous reigns. For decades the court hasn't lifted a finger to correct this venal culture. Little surprise that it has fallen afoul of the grassroots!" He paused and bored his eyes into mine, as if knowing he would find rapport there.

"The Manchus have long been prowling the borders like

vultures, waiting for the right moment to swoop down on us. And our Emperor has chosen to place his trust in a new cabal of eunuchs, some of whom are remnants of the notorious Wei Zhongxian clique from the prior reign." He breathed a long sigh, waiting for my response.

I returned his gaze and, slowly, found words to express thoughts that had long been burrowed in the back of my mind,

"If he is a wise Emperor, he would look to the Revival Society for advice instead of to the groveling eunuchs," I said. "Eunuchs are self-serving toadies, but I understand the Society to be full of learned scholars who are prepared to give their all to help the nation get back on its feet. If he can't see which of the two groups is the more reliable, then he is not fit to be the supreme leader. Of course, sincere advice is always unpleasant to the ear, just like effective medicine is always bitter to the tongue. Master Chen, as a leader of the Society, what advice would you give our Emperor?"

He was watching me closely as I spoke. A look of mystified awe descended on his face, as if he had just stumbled on his long-lost twin. Quiet amusement also lurked behind his alert gaze.

"Before I answer your question, Lady Liu, please allow me to say this. I have never heard a more sincere and sagacious piece of advice. I bow to you for your keen perception, and I hurry to thank you for commending the Society. Well, my advice is very simple, as Wen here and others know it well. First, it is necessary to abolish the eunuch system. Castration is inhumane and turns innocent boys into twisted monsters. This poisonous system must stop. Next, the Emperor needs to set up an advisory council consisting of scholars selected on a competitive basis. This could be done with an open call for essays on policy reforms and defense strategies. Writers of the best essays would be invited to serve on the council. This way, the Emperor can be assured of

# ALICE POON

sound advice."

"You make a good point on the ban of eunuchs!" I exclaimed. "If the Emperor is so afraid of becoming a cuckhold, he might as well ban his harem of consorts. Cruel customs are the festering bed of bitterness and poison, and must be put to an end."

I was a bit carried away in my response, hardly mincing words. But then I wouldn't have voiced my visceral thoughts if I hadn't felt comfortable with the company. At the same time, I saw the brilliance in Zilong's advisory council idea and didn't shy from giving him due credit:

"Yes, you're so right in saying that ideas on policies are best generated from among educated commoners, because they are the ones who are in touch with all levels of society and everyday life. Scholars who live near the border should be able to formulate the best defense strategy because they know the terrain inside out. Courtiers and noblemen at the top live in another world and would never be capable of such insights. Look at how the Manchu Emperor Hong Taiji respects and values the military advice of our Han scholar Fan Wencheng! I wish our Emperor had the same open mind in choosing and treasuring talent."

"Wen, didn't I tell you that our Rushi is no less a thinker than you scholars? Now you see what I mean?" Fo chimed in with a proud grin, as she poured jasmine tea into serving cups and served everybody refreshments.

"I have always believed in your judgment of character, Fo. You yourself are as wise as a sage, I think," Wen said gently, his admiring gaze never straying from Fo. She blushed a deep pink.

"You flatter me, Wen," she demurred shyly. "I believe in Buddha, that's all. My greatest wish is to see the thin horse trade banned, and the *jianmin* caste system abolished. No man or woman, no matter how lowly his or her birth is, should be labeled as *jianmin* and be abused for life. Courtesans, actors and performers are humans, just like any other commoner. But that's just the dreamer in me talking."

"You're so right, Fo! I admire you for your passionate cause in trying to save the slave girls. Yes, those thin horse breeders are shameless parasites. The world would be better without them. If I had any savings, I would donate it to your cause!" Wen blushed. It must have been hard for him to draw attention to his lack of means. He was just a teacher who could barely scrape by with his meager pay.

I just couldn't make out why Fo had been avoiding this nice man. There was an unmistakable affinity between the two. I wished so much that they would eventually commit to each other.

"Unfortunately, there is not much we poor scholars can do to bring about change. It is sadly an industry that exists to serve the rich and the powerful. The cities thrive on commerce and trade, and wealth and power breeds lust. Try as I might to push for a ban to the thin horse trade, there is stiff opposition from the gentry, who are the customer base. Another high wall is, of course, the corrupt government officials; the perpetrators know who to bribe." Zilong released a deep breath, his eyes betraying careworn fatigue. Suddenly he looked much older than his age. He struck me as one who struggled hard to lug a heavy boulder uphill, and midway, to a fanfare of sneers, saw it roll back down. I wanted so much to reach out to and comfort him.

At this point though, I thought I should try to change the mood before it moved too far into the gloom.

"Today is such a beautiful day, let's not dwell on such serious matters," I said. "Why don't we move to the open deck to enjoy the sunshine and the river scenes?"

By this time, the boat was gliding towards the junction of Songjiang River and Green Brook, and the river traffic was getting

68

more congested. So Fo asked Ah Luk to turn the boat around and head back to White Dragon Lagoon, where the setting was a lot more tranquil and pleasant.

When we passed by the northern shore, Zilong pointed to a large mansion with red brick walls and blue roof tiles and said that was where Song Zhengyu lived. Ah, so Zhengyu's residence was just two houses away from Master Zhou's mansion. Something was pricking my mind but I couldn't tell what it was.

The strange feeling of having previously met Zilong made me feel relaxed and at ease in his company. I told him about my days in the procurer's house and then in the Zhou household, skipping the unseemly parts. Pointing to my favorite childhood refuge on the south bank, I let him in on the spontaneous whims and dreams of my girlhood. He appeared totally absorbed in my story, and his eyelashes glistened with tears.

In response, he told me how he had been orphaned as a child and been brought up by his grandmother. He had had to fend for himself and had worked as a jack-of-all-trades to survive. A good twist of fate called when he met Wen, who encouraged him to study for the civil service examination, and even helped to support him until he passed. From there, he went on to build a literary career and was now a well-known published poet and literary icon, not to mention his leader status in the influential Revival Society.

He asked me about my poetry and we began talking about the unconventional mix of ethereal beauty and realism in Bai Juyi's and Du Mu's poems, and the flaming passion of illicit love in Li Shangyin's untitled poems. I promised to let him read my work if he would pay us a visit some day at the riverside villa.

"Would you let me borrow your two collections so that I can savor them at my leisure?" he asked.

"Certainly. Just be sure you return them to me, with your

honest comments!" I said flippantly, reeling with delight.

Three days after the boat cruise, Zilong and Wen came by to have dinner with us on Fo's invitation.

After dinner, Wen disappeared discreetly with Fo into the garden. I fetched my two collections of poetry and some calligraphy and painting scrolls from my chamber and showed them to Zilong in the rear lounge. He unrolled the paintings and pored over them as if drawn by magnet, nodding his head from time to time.

In the soft, flickering candle light, his manly face emitted kindly warmth mixed with child-like curiosity. When his eyes riveted on me, my defenses dissolved into a puddle. Sensing my kindled desire, he bent down to kiss me lightly on the lips. A quiver of shameless pleasure rushed down my spine and my breathing quickened. I had a sense that my fate was going to irredeemably be intertwined with his from that moment on.

His doleful eyes, the open window into his tortured soul, held me dazedly captive. The way he always wore his wearied heart on his sleeve was like an invitation to me to coddle him. So I tried hard to imprint his wistful, careworn visage on my memory, in order that I could always carry him with me, like a wounded bird in my bosom.

Instinctively I was convinced that Zilong and I were made of the same fiber.

On the spiritual plane, he was an incorrigible dreamer, always reaching for the unreachable, burying his head inside mirages. He believed he could change the ways of the world for the better even if it was evidently a feat beyond his power. In a similar way, I was trapped in the illusory pursuit of freedom, freedom from the shackles of discrimination, from condescending attitudes, and from gross injustices. We were both destined to meet with snide excoriation in the end.

Artistically, we both breathed, sensed and experienced life through the filter of our poetic imagination. Our passion for poetry was beyond mind, heart, or measure. Maybe in our past lives we had indeed been twins.

When he said farewell, he didn't forget to take away with him my poetry collections.

For the next few days, I sailed through the motion of daily routines as if floating on a cloud. Restless and pensive, I sometimes blushed for no reason. At other times, I felt moody and maudlin. Fo took it all in. One day, she said to me,

"You and Zilong are a perfect pair. I am really happy that you've found each other. But I have to warn you: he has a grandmother who is protective to the point of possessive, and his wife is known to be difficult to get along with."

The way I was falling for this man, no warning of any kind could possibly hold back the wild horses of my passion, which I had to let loose in a long prose poem. I would later title this poem *Ode to the River God*, meant to invoke the ancient poem that extolled the magical love between a mortal and an immortal, called *Ode to the Goddess of the Luo River*. The poem was written by Cao Zhi, a prince of the State of Wei and younger son of King Cao Cao during the Three Kingdoms period.

Cao Zhi fell madly in love with a beautiful girl whom he could not marry, because his father had schemed to betroth her to his elder brother, just to fire up the sibling rivalry. The girl, out of lovelorn despair, sought death by jumping into the Luo River. In Cao Zhi's fantasy, she turned into a river fairy. He loitered by the river tirelessly day after day, calling out her name in desolation. At last the fairy appeared to him in all her unworldly splendor, and he took her home and never let her out of his sight again. His poem sketched a make-believe world in which his impossibly beautiful immortal love became real for him.

My prose poem borrowed that fantastical notion and portrayed Zilong as the inimitably beautiful river god, my immortal love, molding in verse that indelible image that I had captured on our first encounter on the Songjiang River.

Two months sailed past almost unnoticed, as happy times often do. Then unexpected trouble paid a visit.

One day, Fo received a municipality notice of eviction with a one-month deadline. It turned out that Zhengyu's mother had sent in a complaint that Fo's villa was being run as a brothel and that it sullied the respectable image of the White Dragon Lagoon community. She had managed to gather evidence of the two flower boats having previously been used as a brothel and thus made the case that Fo's riverside villa couldn't but be associated with the sleazy trade .

The underlying reason would appear to be that she didn't want my presence anywhere near her son, having heard gossip about me from the Zhou household. The whole idea was to exile me from the district once and for all. Now I recalled that twinge of unease while passing by the Song residence on the boat cruise.

Poor Fo slumped helplessly into the chair after reading the notice. With such little time, how could she possibly find a suitable place for her business? It broke my heart to see her in such a bind. So I offered to go to see Zhengyu and ask him if he could persuade his mother to retract the complaint. He knew better than anyone that the villa was run as a music salon and not as a brothel. My nagging anxiety was that he and I had not seen each other since my rejection of his brash offer to keep me as a mistress.

Ah Luk ferried me across the river. On my way to the moon gate of the Song residence, I felt a knot in my stomach. I knocked the polished brass ring two times on the door. A man servant peered through the slightly ajar double-doors. I told him my name and asked to see Master Song. His face hardened into a stony masque, told me gruffly to go to the postern gate, and banged the door shut.

I did as I was told. After waiting for what seemed like forever, the postern gate creaked open and Zhengyu poked his head out. Without inviting me inside, he said with a pinched brow, "What is it, Rushi? Please tell me quickly. I'm in the middle of something…" His voice sounded icy, as if he couldn't get rid of me fast enough.

"Zhengyu, it's about the eviction notice sent to Fo. Your mother filed a complaint with the authorities against Fo, accusing her of running the villa as a brothel. You know the truth… it's never been run as a brothel…" I tried to tell him the situation in as concise a manner as possible, but before I could finish, he held up his hand to stop me, saying with unconcealed ire,

"I know, I know. But please try to understand. My mother believes the rumor about your banishment from the Zhou household. I know you told me otherwise. But she is now convinced that you are a bad influence on me. There's little I can do to change her opinion. I am her only son and I must respect what she says. My advice to you would be this: just persuade Fo to take the girls elsewhere to start anew. I could help you with some money, but not much…"

"What makes you think that we want your money, Master Song?" I said curtly. "It is truth and justice that we are seeking!"

I was infuriated by his spineless recoil from doing the right thing. He said nothing. Even in the faint moonlight I could see him blushing. I then added, "Don't you know me, Zhengyu? Are you saying that what I told you was a lie?" He had previously accepted my version of the story with not so much as a hint of doubt, and had shown profuse sympathy. Somehow the truth did not matter now.

"Rushi, I just don't want to engage in an endless argument with my mother…. I can't fight both her and my wife."

I had nothing more to say. Exasperated, I turned my back on him and walked away, never wanting to have anything more to do with this person. Losing his friendship did not hurt half as much as the fact that my supposed notoriety, baseless as it was, was going to cause unnecessary and stressful disruption to my best friend's life.

It sickened me to realize that Zhengyu was one of those people who could turn their back on a good friend just because standing up for the truth would inconvenience them. As Fo had remarked previously, it often took a critical incident to reveal the true nature of a person. Time and again he had shown himself to be a self-indulgent prig, for all his proclamation of love.

# SEVEN

BY THE TIME I arrived home, I had worked up my anger into an explosive fury. I stomped up to my bed chamber and snatched from the bookshelves the new *guqin* that Zhengyu had earlier gifted me. In a fit of rage, I used a pair of scissors to cut all the strings, and flung the instrument with all my strength on the floor, smashing it to pieces. Fo came in, saw what I had just done, and wrapped her arms round me and rocked me like an infant. When at last I stopped shaking, she said,

"Don't worry, Rushi. I've been thinking... those two flower boats seem to have been left unused for a long time. I know the owner. Perhaps we could rent them and use them along with the boat that Zhengyu gave us as the new performance venue..." A fit of coughing cut her short, and when she recovered, she contined, "*Guqin* performance on boat cruises could be an attraction for both our existing and new patrons. My villa will then only be living quarters, and this should not contravene any rules. The only downside would be that we have to close during the winter months."

Once again, Fo was showing her cool-headedness in a difficult situation. I was so relieved to hear her suggestion, and added my own thought, "We could always charge higher fees for the boat performances to make up for the winter loss."

"Higher fees are a must, because there is the boat rental to offset. It may take some time for this model to be tested out. A small loss is likely at the beginning. It means that I may not be able to buy out Xiaowan's bond contract any time soon. I've already used up all my savings buying out contracts for the other girls and you. We'll see how the new model works out."

I was beginning to see the kind of financial pressure that Fo had to contend with. I at once offered to give her all the fees that I received from editing to help sustain the salon's operations. I didn't allow her to say no.

Zilong heard about our new plan and volunteered to promote our new "Music Cruise" program to the Revival Society members.

But our first major argument erupted when he tried to put in a good word for Zhengyu, his fellow genius. He had always had a high regard for Zhengyu's poetic talent. After I filled him in on the whole story, he came round to seeing why I was so put off. At length he said, "Talent is no excuse for betraying a friend's trust. As a scholar, Zhengyu evidently failed on both counts of integrity and decency."

Zilong's help did boost our business a little. A few scholars from the Society came looking for tickets to the new mid-summer evening program. At last, our financial crisis seemed to be over, as a slight profit was recorded in the spring, after the first winter lull. We could not be happier with the general state of things at the salon.

Meanwhile, the feelings of love between Zilong and I deepened with the passing of every day.

About one year after we had first met, one spring evening, he appeared in the front lounge and asked a servant to announce him. I hastily dressed in my favorite lilac robe with dark green collar and cuffs paired with the dark green skirt and went down to the lounge. He had been served tea and was seated on a redwood stool. I saw on the table an exquisite lacquered black box, rectangular in shape with a copper lock on the side.

"What's in the box, Zilong? Why are you smiling like a fool?" I couldn't help asking.

"It is a gift from me to you, Rushi. I hope it will please you. Why don't you open the box and see what's inside?"

I carefully unlocked the box and looked inside. There was a beautifully bound printed book with a dark blue soft cloth cover, on which was printed the vertical title *Anthology of Poems by Liu Rushi*. I drew in a sharp breath! Never had I dared to pretend that my silly dream was anything more than wishful thinking. Barely seventeen and here I was: a published poet!

Seeing that I was lost in ecstasy, he gently cheered me on.

"I remember you asking for my comments. Open the book and read the preface for yourself."

I quickly flipped to the opening page. Zilong's writing at the front of the book completely sucked me in. It was a long and flattering piece, written with equal doses of insightful commentary and charming accolades, in luminous and erudite prose. My heart throbbed with such wild excitement that I felt faint. No one had ever honored me with such praise before, let alone in such a flamboyant manner. And to be acclaimed by Chen Zilong, the literary prodigy and icon! This made it all the more surreal! Any words would have been false and frivolous. My tear-filled eyes conveyed to him my silent gratitude.

"Today marks the first anniversary of our first encounter, and I thought of giving you this to remember me by. I had asked my publisher in Hangzhou if he would be interested in publishing the work, and he gave his immediate consent upon reading the draft. I kept quiet about it as I wanted to surprise you. It makes me happy to see you so moved."

Quietly he rose from his seat, came up behind me and encircled his arms tightly round my waist, whispering: "Would you consider coming to live with me at my villa?"

I turned around to face him. His complexion glowed with fervid anticipation. Trembling with emotions, I nodded my consent with a twinge of shyness. Fo's earlier warning surfaced briefly but quickly submerged.

"I'm afraid I don't have much to offer you. But I can still give you a comfortable life. The only thing is that my wife is not happy about my taking a concubine. Yet I managed to persuade my grandmother to allow me this pleasure. Her one condition is that you have to give her a great grandchild, preferably a male, within a year of our living together. I don't see that as a problem for us."

Hearing that untoward statement, I was jolted back into harsh reality. The security of my future happiness would hinge on whether I could produce an offspring for the Chen family. And he didn't even mention marriage. It was a bit like throwing dice. Yet in the consuming blaze of our passion, I was content to let blind optimism sway me. A man like Zilong didn't come by every day. I must seize happiness with both my hands.

"Now, can I take your silence as a yes?" he said, while pressing his lips on mine, confident he had chosen the right moment to ask. I whimpered weakly in surrender. He swept me up in his arms and carried me upstairs to my bed chamber. I yielded to him, body, soul and heart, as passion matched passion. For a climactic moment I felt my soul winging from me. Was this how Lady Du in *The Peony Pavilion* felt in her erotic dream in the garden?

The next day I told Fo of my wish to live with Zilong, and she hugged me, tears both happy and sad rolling down her cheeks. She then trudged up to her chamber to fetch something. When she appeared again she held in her hand an exquisite green jade hairpin, which she handed over to me. "This is the last piece of jewelry that I have in my possession. I saved it as a wedding present for you. But wedding is just a formality. I might as well give it to you now. With this I wish you and Zilong a long and happy life together."

Words escaped me as hot tears flooded my eyes. It pained me to leave my dear Fo.

Knowing the ways of his wife and certain she would not allow me in the family residence, Zilong had secretly made ready a small two-storey villa in the quiet southern suburb of Songjiang as our temporary abode. It was called "South Villa". His plan was to get me pregnant first, and then he would try to persuade his grandmother and his wife to accept me formally into the Chen household as a concubine, with a proper wedding.

So, effectively my status now was just a kept woman. But I was so looking forward to enjoying life with Zilong that that thought didn't even bother me. I knew his love for me was from the heart, as was mine for him, and the heavens were our solemn witness. That seemed good enough for me.

I quickly settled down in our new sweet home. It was a quaint little villa, with a small front garden filled with peach trees.

When I moved in, spring was almost over, and the fallen petals blanketed the ground like a thin layer of snow, evoking a sad wintry mood. Denuded branches, flicked by the breeze, seemed to be singing a dirge to mourn fleeting beauty. My wistfulness did not escape Zilong. He took me into his arms and whispered into my ear, "The next spring will come before you know it. By then, the peach blossoms will bloom in time to welcome our newborn son." I smiled, and allowed his sweet words to swaddle me.

For the next year, Zilong and I were drunk with our own passion. He could not let a day pass without seeing me in South Villa. During that time, he wrote a copious amount of poetry to express his feverish sentiments. I also wrote a new collection of lilting lyric poems about my love for him, to which I added the long prose poem *Ode to the River God*. He suggested to his publisher to publish a revised edition of my works to include this new collection. His publisher agreed.

With the publication of the new edition, I began to make a name for myself among the literati, and came to know many famed poets through attending meetings of the Songjiang poetry club, attired in scholar robe and cap. That was when I first noticed the acclaimed work of an old poet and scholar official named Qian Qianyi, who was a deputy minister in the Ministry of Rites, living in Changshu of the Suzhou Prefecture.

During our time together, Zilong continued to be engaged as the chief editor in the compilation of a monumental tome: the voluminous *Anthology of Statecraft Writings of the Ming Dynasty*. This work touched on every aspect of administration in every reign throughout the Dynasty, shedding light on why some reigns were more successful than others. It would certainly become a gem of reference works when the editing was completed. I felt deeply proud of him for his dedication to such a great cause.

Whenever he took a break from his engrossing work, he would talk with me on light-hearted topics, like the erotic love stories in the novel *Jin Ping Mei*, and the folktales in Tang Xianzu's famous collection of plays, *Four Dreams*. At other times we would debate on more serious subjects. One time he asked with a somber face,

"If you were to choose between sacrificing yourself for our country and saving yourself, what would your choice be?"

I mulled on the question for a while, and then replied,

"When we say our country, we actually mean the imperial court. So, I think it's a matter of whether the court is worth sacrificing oneself for. Civilian subjects owe their allegiance to the court as long as it is benevolent and worthy of respect."

Zilong looked surprised at my answer. After a long pause, he

ALICE POON

said,

"But we as scholars owe a duty to the incumbent imperial court, even if it is not perfect."

"Duty is duty. Duty is not life. I don't object to scholars doing their utmost to support the court and improve on the administration. But scholars don't owe it their lives. Dynasties can be replaced, and should be replaced if they are rotten and incorrigible," I argued heatedly.

"You do have a fresh perspective, Rushi. But we have always been taught that as Confucian scholars we must, when the need arises, sacrifice our lives for the Emperor. It is not for us to differentiate between court and country."

"That's the traditional dogma. Not all traditions are worth preserving. In fact, I applaud Fan Wencheng's prudence in choosing the Qing Emperor as his new master, because he respects Fan and treasures his advice. By contrast, our Chongzhen rewarded patriotic General Yuan Chonghuan with cruel death by slicing. Confucius had said: 'The ruler must treat his ministers with propriety; the ministers then pledge him their loyalty.' (君使臣以禮, 臣事君以忠). So it is in effect a two-way relationship. There is a precondition to loyalty."

I knew that Zilong, in face of the current tumult and chaos, had been bothered by this question for a long time. He and other scholars were yoked to a rigid belief in civilian duty and loyalty to rulers. I was not sure that he would come round to accepting my viewpoint.

After a moment of contemplation, he said ruefully, "Rushi, if we lose our country to the Manchus, we civilians will suffer collectively as a defeated people." His argument was sound, I would admit, and somehow I could not get it out of my mind.

In order to lift Zilong's downbeat mood, I suggested we take a leisure trip to Suzhou City in the spring.

On that trip, I came upon Fo's good friend Li Jingli at a teahouse. She was bidding for two slave girls to add as performers to her music salon. Those girls were Chen Yuanyuan and Li Xiangjun, who would later become my lifelong kerchief sisters. The sisterhood would change my life forever.

At that time, they looked so miserably wan and pinched in their drab rags. The innocent smile on Xiangjun's face revealed her unearthly sweetness, while dainty Yuanyuan promised to grow into a peerless beauty. Their singing and pipa performance showed they were both extremely gifted in music.

Just looking at them brought back memories of that day when I had been dangled like a piece of meat in front of Master Zhou in Yangzhou. It broke my heart to see resignation bordering on despair in their vacuous, sunken eyes.

Without a second thought, I went up and offered to Jingli to be their sponsor. Knowing their immediate need for a good sprucing-up, I gave each of them five silver taels to help them start on a solid footing as new performers, and promised to visit them in Qinhuai, Nanjing the following Lantern Festival.

Zilong was supportive, and he asked me to remind him to write another memorial to the provincial government urging a ban on the thin horse trade.

After that trip, Zilong appeared a little reticent. With some effort, I coaxed it out of him. The problem at hand, as I found out to my dismay, was that his grandmother and wife were pressuring him to take a new concubine from the gentry, and to banish me from South Villa. They had given me a chance, and I had failed to deliver.

As hard as I tried to live life to the full each day, I could not shake off the feeling that evil gloom was waiting for us. Happiness filled to the brim was a natural invitation to ill fortune, which was forever prowling on the doorstep.

Time crept along for another three months, and my womb was still tragically barren. Then mischance finally stepped over the threshold.

One summer morning, Zilong told me he had to go home to see his wife at her repeated requests.

Not long after he left, a group of seven or eight rough-mannered women holding long rods and posters in their hands broke into the villa, leaving the front gate wide open. They gathered menacingly in the front garden. Some went round the outside fence wall and pasted slandering posters all over, came back in and pasted more on the inside walls of the garden.

Two of them started accosting passers-by and telling those who would stop to listen the story of how I had lured a husband away with my foxy wiles, pointing out that I was a fallen woman cast out by the Zhou household.

I watched this terrifying scene unfold from the upper level verandah, hiding behind the bamboo shades. The stoutest of them looked up and shouted in a croaking voice,

"Liu Rushi, you shameless bitch! What kind of witchcraft are you using? Master Chen and his lovely wife were happy until you came along. You bring shame on all women! Why don't you show your foxy face? What are you afraid of? Yes, you deserve a good beating, don't you? Let us teach you a good lesson, you cheap whore!"

The whole gang repeatedly shouted: "Cheap whore, Liu Rushi!"

They seemed to want people in the whole neighborhood to hear their message. Recalling the harsh demands that Zilong's grandmother and wife had made, there was no doubt in my mind that they were behind this show. At that moment though, I was so scared that I could only think of hiding. There was no one in the house, as our maid Ah Lan had gone out to the town market to buy foodstuffs.

I quietly slipped down to the ground level and sneaked into the kitchen in the backyard. The only sensible hiding place was under the kitchen stove, where the fire logs were stored. So I moved the pile of logs from the recess and climbed into the back of the nook, placing the logs in front of me.

I stayed crouched in the nook a long time, like forever, trembling and praying for Zilong's return. My head was too addled to think clearly. Never in my life had I faced such overt humiliation and prostrating fear. I heard some of the women coming inside the front lounge and wrecking things. There was little chance my painting scrolls that were hung on the walls could escape their indiscriminate wrath.

After a long while the commotion died down. But I was still too frightened to come out. Another long stretch ensued. When I finally heard Zilong's voice calling out my name, tears burst forth like water through a broken dam.

He came into the kitchen and found me clambering out of the nook. By nature I was not a squeamish person. But this time, all my nerves snapped. I threw myself into his arms and wailed like an infant.

"I know, I know. I should have come back sooner. My wife was deliberately trying to delay me, and I sensed something was wrong. I never imagined they would go to such extremes... Please, please don't cry, my sweet love. You are breaking my heart..." He coddled me as he inspected my face carefully, and asked, "You're not hurt, are you?" I shook my head, and said between heaving sobs, "They wanted to beat me up. If they found me.... I would not be in.... one piece now. I really feared for my life..."

"How barbaric of them! That was uncalled for. Don't worry

now, Rushi. Let me take care of things. I'll try to talk some sense into my family. Would you like to stay with Fo for a short while, just until things calm down? I'll come every day to see you."

Even in my distress, I knew that was the most sensible thing to do. I simply could not stay in this place for one moment longer. He looked around at the wreckage of broken vases and vandalized furniture and paintings, and shook his head in deep dismay.

Then he walked me up to our bed chamber and packed a few clothes for me. Our only consolation was that the bookshelves were untouched. As soon as Ah Lan returned, we set out for Fo's villa.

After hearing what I had just gone through, Fo went to the kitchen, and moments later, came back with a bowl of ginger tea for me to calm my nerves and a cup of jasmine tea for Zilong. Pinching her already furrowed brow, she said in a low voice, "I was always afraid that something like this would happen." Turning to Zilong, she said, "I have to ask you a straight question, Zilong. If your grandmother and wife won't be persuaded to let you keep Rushi, what will you do?"

Zilong was obviously not prepared for such a piercing question. His face crumpled into a deep frown, as he stammered, "I have to.... think about this. Right now, I don't... have an answer. Please give me some time..." I understood completely the quandary he was in. Even if he could ignore his wife's tantrums, he would find it hard to handle his grandmother, who had had to scratch and scrimp to bring him up. As the only male heir in the Chen family, he carried the burden of having to ensure the family's posterity, and he was not getting any younger, being then almost thirty.

After Zilong left, I went to my bed chamber to lie down. The whole night I was wide awake, turning the matter over and over in my confused mind. Even in my fuzziness, I could see one thing clearly, and that was that Zilong's grandmother would never welcome me into the Chen household. Her earlier concession in letting me stay in South Villa was just a bargain chip to use later.

I would say that even if I had born Zilong a son, that wouldn't have made a trace of difference. For her, to have a great grandson born of a fallen woman would be unthinkable; it would be worse than having no great grandson at all. Her idea had always been to get Zilong a proper concubine from the gentry. Now that he had enjoyed his fling with me, it was obviously his turn to show good faith by returning home and doing his duty. At least that was what she was expecting from Zilong.

The clear message that I was no longer welcome was, without doubt, from her. The drama was most likely something that Zilong's manipulative wife had concocted.

For my part, I would hate to see Zilong forever torn between myself and his grandmother, who singlehandedly raised him and whom he loved dearly. At the same time, if I were to tear myself away from my eternal love, it would be like cleaving out a chunk of my heart. Yet, what kind of a life would Zilong and I have, if there could never be one moment of peace in the Chen family? I could not ask him to give up his filial piety just to satisfy my selfish needs.

I realized then that our love affair had come to its natural end. In my naivete I had thought that Zilong's love would be enough to set me free. I could not be more wrong. My cage was a cage of social scorn. There was no breaking it. But for now I would just try to collect myself and ease back into my work routine, while thinking through how to conduct myself.

I stayed at Fo's villa all through the rest of summer and autumn. One late autumn evening he came to see me, and told me that his new concubine was three months pregnant. I looked him in the eye and said,

"Zilong, would you elope with me to some faraway place, and start a new life?" I was bracing myself for a final slash. He looked at me with deep pain written on his face, wounded by my apparent ridicule. Yes, my question was meant to induce him to say the inevitable. I was handing him a sword to make one last deadly cut on me. That would be better than for me to suffer a festering wound.

He flinched, not saying a word. The twilight streaming through the lattice window brushed the chamber a dusty, macabre yellow. The grieving notes of a blackbird suffused the space. Was it expressing sympathy for a caged bird, bereft of love?

Suddenly seized with emotions, he kissed me with burning intensity. "My sweet love, you've brought me the most pleasurable moments," he murmured, "Never will I have such joy again. I don't know how to go on without you…"

A big drop of tear slid from the corner of his eye down his cheek, and he said in a wearied voice, "Rushi, I'm asking you to forgive and forget me… I'm not strong enough to rebel against traditions. I hate myself for failing to protect your honor, but I can't bear to hurt my grandmother. I hate these times that we live in… all hypocrisy and bigotry. You're still so young, and you are a rare talent. I am not worthy of you. Find your own happiness with someone who can love you with an open mind. But please don't ask me to forget you, ever!"

Pain was eating into my bones, as I pretended to understand the sense of it all. We locked ourselves in each other's embrace until total darkness palled over us, unable to stanch our grief.

I knew the only way to love him was to let him go.

# TALES OF MING COURTESANS

# PART TWO

## Kerchief Sisters

# TALES OF MING COURTESANS

# EIGHT

*ESCORTED BY HER half brother Qian Sunyi, Jingjing had arrived at Anfu Garden in the outskirts of Kunming seven days ago. He had helped her carry two large cloth sacks filled with sheaves of writings and painting scrolls that her mother had left to her. Upon arrival, Sunyi had said farewell and returned home to Changshu.*

*Aunt Yuanyuan had given her an emotional welcome and had done everything she could to make her feel at home. The stinging shock of her mother's suicide, only three months after her father's death, had seared her heart and left an open gash.*

*At dawn this morning, she pulled out a stitch-bound sheaf from those bundles of papers. It had a dark blue cloth cover. The title page was marked "My Past". Affixed on top was a loose note with a few hastily jotted lines, which she had read numerous times.*

*"My precious Jingjing: I wrote this memoir when you were thirteen and meant for you to read it when you are old enough. The time has now come for me to lay down my worldly burden to join my beloved in the other world. I have only this personal tale, my poetry and paintings to bequeath to you. I would urge you to go and find Aunt Yuanyuan and Jingli Po Po in Kunming. They will take good care of you.*

*I chose death to shame the people who scorn and bully women whom they call 'jianmin' and regard as inferior and worthless. Please try to spread my message of protest. Lastly, I thank you for giving me and your father sixteen years of happiness. Farewell. Your doting Mother."*

*Since her mother's funeral a month earlier, she had started to read*

*the memoir and had reached the point where she had left Chen Zilong.
What she had read so far deeply unsettled her. She had grown up in
a care-free gentry world of familial love and literary immersion. Her
mother's wretched girlhood was simply shocking to her.*

*The year she turned thirteen was the year when Zheng Chenggong's
anti-Qing campaign was utterly crushed. Her parents had been staunch
supporters of the campaign. She didn't understand the reason behind
their actions but only knew they had acted in honor of Chen Zilong.
Since that year, chronic illness beset her father, and her mother hardly
wore a smile any more. Her father died three years later.*

*After reading the sad note again, she stepped out to get some air.*

*Yuanyuan had reacted calmly when she heard the heart-wrenching
news. Then, as if trying to hide her pain, she had turned all her attention
to fussing over Jingjing. Perhaps at her mature age of thirty-nine, she
had tasted enough bitterness in life to be able to look at death with
resigned detachment, inspired by years of Taoist immersion.*

*"Were you able to sleep last night, Jingjing? Is the quilt warm
enough? Sometimes the night mountain air can be quite chilly in
spring."The moment she saw Jingjing, who just came in from her stroll,
she smiled from the heart. In deft motion she removed the limp flowers
from the vase on the side table and put in the fresh bunch of lilacs she
had brought in.*

*"I slept better last night than previous nights, thank you, Aunt
Yuanyuan. The quilt is warm and light and comfortable," Jingjing said
politely with a voice hoarse from lack of sleep.*

*Sensing that the girl was in better spirits this morning, Yuanyuan
decided to stay and chat with her.*

*"If you need anything at all, don't be shy, just tell me. I want you
to know that your mother was my dearly beloved sister and best friend,
and there's nothing I wouldn't do for her daughter." She paused, and
then gave a long sigh.*

*"The last time I saw you, you were only two, and such a pretty toddler,"* she said. *"Your mother brought you along to our farewell dinner. That was the year your Aunt Xiangjun, Jingli Po Po and I retreated to the Temple of Three Sages just up the hill. I can't believe you're sixteen already."*

*When Jingjing had first laid eyes on Yuanyuan seven days earlier, her aunt struck her as resplendent and dewy, like a flower in full bloom. Nothing betrayed her real age of almost forty.*

*Ever since she had read the first half of her mother's sad memoir, a question had been hovering in her mind. The three kerchief sisters seemed to share a common background; what kind of life had Aunt Yuanyuan and Aunt Xiangjun experienced?*

*"Aunt Yuanyuan, I've read a good portion of Mother's memoir and was wondering... How did life treat you and Aunt Xiangjun in your younger days?"*

*No sooner had the words left her lips than she saw melancholy pall over the older woman's lovely face. Second thoughts now reined in her eagerness. For a moment she feared it might be rude to pry. After a spell of strained silence, Yuanyuan started to speak in a low voice, her face clouding over with nostalgic sorrow.*

*"Each of us kerchief sisters had her own kind of tragedy in life. If not for the strong bond of our sisterhood, we could easily have given up all hope. That bond kept us going in our darkest moments. But now I'm the only one left.... Xiangjun passed away eleven years ago."*

*"Aunt Yuanyuan, can you tell me how the three of you came to be kerchief sisters? In what way exactly did the sisterhood help each of you?"* Jingjing ventured with a different approach, unable to quell her curiosity.

*Then, crimping her smooth forehead, Yuanyuan stared into space and slowly unwrapped her past, layer by layer.*

It was twenty-six years ago, the Eleventh Year of Chongzhen

Emperor's reign, when we swore our oath of sisterhood on the day of the Lantern Festival. The festival falls on the fifteenth day of the first moon of the lunar New Year. As you well know, some people call it the Festival of Love.

Two years prior to that memorable event, when Xiangjun was twelve, and I eleven, we were paraded in front of potential buyers in a Suzhou City teahouse. The sale was done by way of bidding. The one who offered the highest price would end up as the buyer. We had both been orphaned in childhood and had been sold to the same thin horse breeder. That was how I had first come to know Xiangjun. We had since become inseparable mates.

As it happened, a music/opera salon owner named Li Jingli, then known to your mother through her best friend Xu Fo, was there to take part in the bidding. Madam Li, as she was known, was seeking two young girls to train as performers for her salon in Qinhuai, Nanjing. She spotted Xiangjun and me singing and playing pipa, and put in vigorous bids for us.

Rushi was on a leisure trip to Suzhou City with her lover Chen Zilong and they happened upon the teahouse when our procurer was about to close the deal with Jingli.

When Rushi saw us, she was at once reminded of her own woeful experience in Yangzhou. She went up to Jingli and asked her if she could become our sponsor. Jingli was more than happy to take up her offer, being always shrewd about cost-cutting.

Cold and hungry, Xiangjun and I must have looked like willow sprigs trembling in the wind. The thin horse breeder who had picked us up was debt-laden and couldn't even properly feed or clothe us.

Rushi came up quietly and handed each of us five silver pieces, and spoke to us like an elder sister, "My dear girls, please allow me to help you. A performer would need a pipa, decent clothes and shoes, and some rouge and face powder. You can use this money to get started. Always remember that you are talented. Don't ever let anyone tell you otherwise. May Guanyin bless you with good fortune as you turn a new page at Jingli's salon."

Before she left, she promised to visit us the following Lantern Festival at Jingli's Villa of Alluring Fragrance in Nanjing. She also gave us her Songjiang address and made us promise to write to her if we had any further needs.

Sadly, just before the appointed meeting date, Rushi was separated from Zilong and, being totally crushed, she was not up to making the trip to Nanjing as promised. She wrote to us pledging to come the following Lantern Festival.

So it was two years after our teahouse encounter that the three of us were finally reunited in Jingli's Villa.

During those two years, Xiangjun and I learned to sing under *kunqu* master Su Kunsheng, whom Jingli hired to teach the two of us. Xiangjun made great progress with the opera songs of *The Peony Pavilion*. I took pipa and singing lessons along with her for the first year-and-a-half. Our teacher often showered praises on our efforts, which spurred us to work even harder.

After Jingli took the two of us in, I thought for the first time in my life that good fortune was descending upon me. She was at heart a caring and generous woman, as well as astute about business. She knew all too well about courtesans' pitiable lives, as she had been one from the age of thirteen.

The Qinhuai pleasure district in Nanjing was renowned for the exquisitely beautiful and talented courtesans and performers who resided in brightly furnished brothels that hugged the willow-fringed southern shore of the Qinhuai Canal. After the Manchu invasion, though, the place was reduced to only a shadow of its former glamorous self; just a sorry relic for the nostalgic few. But in those more prosperous times, it was like a pilgrimage site attracting young scholars and officials from all over the country.

The Nanjing Examination Court, where scholars took civil service examinations, was located on the opposite shore. Examinations were highly stressful for scholars, as results would determine their career future. Many of them paid visits to the pleasure quarters to find distraction and relief from stress.

The ornate two-storey Villa of Alluring Fragrance, with its signature jasmine-scented verandah and billowing lilac silk curtains, stood out among the crowd of luxury brothels and salons. Perched in front of Wu Ding Bridge, it overlooked colorful flower boats that thronged the waterway. With its back on bustling Bank-Note Vault Street, the villa sat amidst a constant clamor escaping from the crowd of teahouses, restaurants, story-telling salons, pet bird shops and cock-fighting booths that packed the street.

Jingli always encouraged her girls to properly learn opera singing, pipa playing, painting and poetry writing. To any new apprentice she would say right from the start:

"I would never expect you girls to sell bed favors. I believe in free love, and we can help each other out. As you will see, scholars love to meet here at my villa. They come here for the opera singing and for inspiration to write poetry. If you cultivate yourselves, your skill in the arts and your charming company will help to make them regular customers, and I can charge them for shows and dining to support the operation. Of course, there's nothing to prevent you from hooking up with the man of your fancy."

So Xiangjun and I threw ourselves into learning music, poetry and classic literature. Jingli is a cultured lady who had studied under her benefactor Chen Zhenhui, and she taught us to read

Tang poetry and the works of famous playwrights, such as Tang Xianzu's *Four Dreams (The Peony Pavilion, The Purple Hairpin, A Dream Under the Southern Bough* and *The Handan Dream)*, and Wang Shifu's *Romance of the Western Chamber*.

From Master Su, we learned pipa playing and *kunqu* singing. After half a year's intensive training, we were able to perform excerpted opera songs on stage.

On my debut night, I met a handsome and learned nobleman named Mao Xiang, a frequent patron of the salon. He fell in love with my singing and pipa playing, especially the opera songs from *Romance of the Western Chamber*.

From that night on, he never missed any one of my bi-nightly performances. In truth, my singing was nothing like Xiangjun's silver-bell voice, although I could play the pipa better than anyone else in the salon, but somehow he was attracted to my velvety, emotion-laden vocal. He would write verses to honor me and would hand me his beautifully brushed love letters on the nights when I performed. We were falling deeply in love. His first-ever gift to me was a beautifully crafted pipa made of the finest wutong wood, with ivory turning pegs. Jingli said he must have spent a fortune on it.

One-and-a-half years drifted past like the airy brush of a spring breeze.

Then one day, an evil gust, when it was least expected, struck from nowhere. The chief eunuch from the Imperial Palace, followed by a band of his minions, paid an unexpected call on Jingli one afternoon. At that time, I was rehearsing a pipa tune alone on stage, getting ready for my performance that evening.

Flopping his wiggly bulk on a chair, the eunuch flicked his white fat hand like brushing off a fly. One of his underlings promptly went and fetched Jingli. He gruffly told her that he was under orders from the Empress to buy a girl from her brothel.

"That girl playing the pipa, is she a virgin?" he asked in a loutish manner. When Jingli answered yes and politely told him that her girls would not offer bed favors, he cleared his throat noisily in contempt and spat into a spittoon at his feet. In a guttural voice he said, just loud enough for me to catch: "I take it you are her owner. Draw up a bond contract. I'll give you five hundred taels of silver."

The air in the hall stretched taut. My right eyelid fluttered uncontrollably, portending something sinister.

Jingli had no alternative but to comply with his demand. She couldn't possibly fight the Imperial Court.

At that time, Empress Zhou was embroiled in a feral fight with the young and beautiful Consort Tian, who had captured the Emperor's heart. The Empress ordered the chief eunuch to search for the prettiest and youngest virgin courtesan from Qinhuai. She wanted a courtesan because she had heard of how courtesans were trained to seduce men, just as her father had often boasted of taking Qinhuai courtesans as his concubines. She was going to fight fire with fire.

The next thing I knew was that the eunuch's men were bundling me out of the Villa. I turned and saw Xiangjun drowned in tears at the garden gate, slumped to the ground. Before I could utter a word, they shoved me inside a waiting sedan, which carried me to the Peach Leaf Pier. From there, I was taken to the capital by boat.

Upon arrival in the Imperial Palace, the chief eunuch at once delegated his charge to a minion, who promptly locked me into a small, windowless chamber in the retreat house of the inner court, a place to which aging consorts retired to spend their fading years.

Except for the old palace maid who came in twice a day to

deliver my meals and buckets of water for washing, I never saw another soul. In the first few days, I wept from morning till night, couldn't eat, couldn't sleep. Then I sank into depression.

Informants had early on reported to Consort Tian of my arrival. An Emperor's favorite habitually held indomitable power within the realm of the inner court. As things stood, Consort Tian had the Chongzhen Emperor wrapped around her little finger and at times she even dared to flout the Empress's orders. Empress Zhou had never been subjected to such overt humiliation and vowed to use me to lure the Emperor from Consort Tian's clutches. That was all very well, except for the nagging question: who would take me to the Emperor?

With the Emperor's frequent bestowing of gifts and grants, Consort Tian clearly had the upper hand in the contest. She could bribe his chief eunuch into pandering to her wishes as easily as she could coax a parrot into repeating her words.

So bribe the eunuch she did, and the Emperor never heard of a girl named Yuanyuan, not to mention ever having even a cursory glance at her person. When Empress Zhou asked the chief eunuch about me, he told her in a straight face: "Venerable Highness, I regret to tell you that the girl has unfortunately contracted smallpox on the journey here. I have kept her quarantined in the retreat house."

Apparently, the Empress admitted defeat in private. The old palace maid would later reveal this to me.

But that was not the end of my misery. Enraged by the Empress's clumsy attempt to plot against her, Consort Tian dumped her wrath on the lowly tramp from Qinhuai. One day, when the Emperor had gone on his hunting trip, she summoned me into her presence.

"So you are the most beautiful courtesan from Qinhuai? Lift your head so that I can see your face," she snorted, thrusting her blade-like glance on me.

"Venerable Highness, people don't really.... mean.... what they say," I whimpered, lowering my head again in trepidation.

"Do you realize that you are not worthy to be my lowliest maid? Beauty is fleeting. All girls grow old. But courtesans are branded with the word *shame*," she said with spite, trying to come up with the most hurtful words. After a pause, she squeezed a foxy smile into her heavily painted face and scoffed, "You are only a man's plaything. Any man can use you, isn't that true?"

When I kept silent, the Consort snapped, "Isn't that true? Answer me!"

"I didn't become a courtesan by choice." At last I plucked up courage to answer back, and added, "Besides, I have never let any man use me." But alas, I was not mindful of the dire consequence of a pert rejoinder. Unwittingly, it gave the jealous Consort a wicked idea.

"Oh, is that right? I see. But I thought a courtesan's sole purpose is to let men expend their lust on them." She shot a venomous glance at me and then turned to her maid. "Get the chief eunuch to come here now," she said.

When the wobbly lump of flesh appeared, the Consort said to him with a reptilian smirk: "Take this cheap whore away and let your minions strip her of her pride. That will show her her proper place. I am in a good mood today, or else I would have her slapped a hundred times for daring to answer back."

For the next three months, I was to go through a living hell in the eunuchs' lecherous clutches. During the day, they would force me to wear a flimsy robe and would play all sorts of bawdy games with me. Each night they would take turn to come into my chamber. If I resisted, they would slap me into submission, and then starve me and make me clean their chamber pots as punishment.

One day, in a fit of crushing despair, I slashed my wrists with the shard of a broken porcelain bowl. I would have bled to death had the old palace maid not appeared in time. While dressing my wound, the kind old woman came up with a bright idea and dotted my face with the spilled blood. She then went and told the eunuchs that I had contracted a contagious skin disease. One eunuch came, stood at the threshold of my chamber and flashed a hasty glance at me. No eunuch ever came near me again.

Another ten days passed before the palace maid drummed up the courage to help me escape from the retreat house. She asked her nephew to put me in a boat bound for Nanjing. Two months later, I finally arrived at the Villa, broken both in body and spirit.

When the time came for the three of us to meet, Jingli and Xiangjun had nursed me back to reasonable physical health, but I was still feeling like a pile of wreckage. How could I ever face Xiang again? How could I even go on living in this shame? No doubt Consort Tian would try to fan the flames of lewd gossip about me. My career as a performer was in all likelihood over. I couldn't think of any way forward except to sink into prostitution, or face death.

Rushi had learned through Xiangjun's letters what happened to me. The moment she stepped into the dressing lounge where we had all gathered, she put her arms around me.

"My dear Yuanyuan, I am so sorry this happened to you," she cried. "I know no words can console you right now. But in time, the bad memory will fade, I promise you. Girl, you must not blame yourself! You are not at fault!" Shaking her fist, she hissed in a fit of explosive rage. "I curse Consort Tian with the vilest of curses! May the heavens make her pay for this!"

When Rushi calmed down, she murmured, "Does it give her pleasure to see others suffer?"

Xiangjun, who had been sitting quietly in a corner, twisting a loosened strand of hair around her finger, sniffed with distaste. "At the heart of it all, it's jealousy," she said. "As consorts, they should know they are little different from courtesans like us. At least we can have our pick of men."

"If only they could see that. Jealousy is a woman's worst enemy," said Rushi in an agitated tone. After a short pause, she said in a huff, "The eunuchs are a pitiable bunch, always seeking to work off their shame and anger on those weaker than themselves."

"Many are sold as small boys by destitute parents to the palace to be castrated," Xiangjun said in a sad voice, always sharp in her observation but soft-hearted. "Wiles and schemes become their tools of survival. It is this cruel custom that should be blamed."

"Yes, the inhuman customs of the imperial court breed venom that spreads to all levels of society," Rushi sighed. "It's just not right for one supreme ruler to build his pleasure on the pain of so many others."

"Girls, Yuanyuan is not entirely safe here," Jingli reminded us in a hushed and urgent voice, as if afraid someone might eavesdrop on us. "Consort Tian's eyes and ears are probably on the hunt for her now. There's no way she'll let her off that easy."

"Has Mao Xiang been around?" Rushi asked after a while, remembering my admirer.

"He came twice. But Yuanyuan wouldn't see him," Xiangjun said.

"He may not be able to take the truth well, unless he is open-minded about these things. Well, let this be a real test for his so-called love." Rushi sounded a little cynical. But she was not wrong.

"Things probably will never be the same again between him and me. I had fancied that we would someday become man and wife. Now the last shred of hope has snapped. That dream will always be just a dream." Tears had long been spent, and my eyes were dry with grief.

Rushi was trying hard to come up with something that could comfort me. After pacing for a while, she suddenly remembered that she had brought presents for us. From her sleeve pocket she pulled out three exquisitely embroidered white silk kerchiefs. Then she came up with an idea and announced:

"I worked on these for months and I hope you like them. You girls have been on my mind and in my heart these past two years. I have never doubted that it was fate that brought us together in that teahouse. You girls don't have sisters and neither do I. So, may I suggest that the three of us swear an oath of sisterhood? These silk kerchiefs will be the tokens, and Jingli our witness."

Surprised as we were, Xiangjun and I were more than happy to accept the kind offer. Having long been deprived of family, we were like wild flowers in the meadow. People stepped on us without even looking. No one cared if we lived or died.

I always counted it a blessing to have met Xiangjun and Rushi. Rushi's timely offer moved me to the core. I couldn't be prouder to have these lovely souls as my sisters. Suddenly, life seemed brighter with new hope. The earlier dolorous mood at last loosened its grip on me.We went out to the garden, knelt down and bowed three times to the open sky, swearing solemnly that we would love and care for each other like blood sisters until death.

Jingli brought out cups of wine and served them to us when the oath-taking was over. We all drank heartily to our new sisterhood. Merry singing drifted from the flower boats outside to suffuse the garden, as if to celebrate us.

Then Jingli, misty-eyed, tentatively said, "If you girls don't mind, I would like to formally adopt Xiangjun and Yuanyuan as my daughters."

Neither Xiangjun nor I saw that coming, close as we had always felt to Jingli. We were left speechless at her golden-hearted gesture, and dropped to our knees before her and bowed three times to complete the rite. Rushi refilled our cups and we happily drank another toast on our adoption. Mother drew from her pocket two red packets to hand to us to mark the occasion. It showed that she had planned ahead for this. Her kindness touched my very fibers. Xiangjun was blinking back her tears.

Then we all moved to the dining lounge in the west wing, where we sat down like a real family around a marble-topped table, laden with fragrant dishes. Mother had specially prepared savory foods to celebrate our reunion as well as the Lantern Festival. We had roasted goose, duck and taro pot, spicy prawns with pine nuts, steamed dace with spring onions, fried rice wrapped in lotus leaves and braised noodles. All were delicious home-made festive fare and our favorites.

The meal ended on a high-note with glutinous rice balls filled with red bean paste, the standard dessert for Lantern Festival. The sweetness and roundness of the rice balls symbolized family reunion and wholesome happiness. Love filled our hearts.

Then on Mother's suggestion, we all stepped back into the dressing lounge to take a closer look at Rushi's beautiful kerchiefs.

I held one in my hand and couldn't help admiring the exquisite three-bird design: a hovering green parrot, a purplish nightingale and a blue magpie perched on a bough of pink plum blossoms. "No wonder Rushi is called the goddess of needlework," I exclaimed in awe, having previously heard her work widely acclaimed.

Mother, also an embroiderer, chimed in enthusiastically: "Not only is the needlework exquisite; the design is a class of its own.

A less gifted painter couldn't have sketched birds as lively as these."

Rushi handed Xiangjun another one, keeping the last one for herself, all of the exact same design. To Mother she gave a scroll of her best peony painting, knowing that the peony was her favorite flower.

"You two are the lovely songbirds, and of course I am the chatty parrot! This design of birds is a symbol of freedom. May we all be free like birds! And you know how much I love your singing too." Rushi held our hands tightly, then added in a serious voice:

"From now on, I am your Big Sister. I want you to know that you can always count on me for help whenever you need it. Let's make a solemn promise to meet here every Lantern Festival, and each year I will embroider that year's Zodiac sign onto all the three kerchiefs to mark the anniversary. We'll stay in touch by letters at other times. Agreed?"

Xiangjun and I just kept nodding at her words, our eyes glazed over with tears. I silently gave thanks to the heavens for this good fortune of gaining two sisters and a mother in one day.

Turning to me, Rushi half implored, "My sweet sister, wouldn't you say that a change of scene is best for you now? You know I would love for you to come and stay with me in Songjiang. What do you say?"

I was really grateful for her kind thought. But despite what I had earlier said, I was clinging with all my heart to the hope that I would patch things up with Xiang one day. Leaving Nanjing would mean dashing that hope altogether. I was not ready to give up hope on Xiang yet. So I thanked her and gently declined her well-meant offer.

As I would later find out, sometimes a casual choice one makes can have a bitter consequence.

It is surprising that after all these years that I can still remember clearly every word we said that day. It was a special day in a way that defies time, and has remained fresh in my memory to this very moment.

*Jingjing saw fatigue creep up on her aunt's face and suggested to end the session for the day. The narrative made her shudder with dismay and she was emotionally enervated. Just like her mother's memoir, it was about an unfamiliar world, a world so dark with pain and despair. She felt like she was wading across a cold, desolate and murky pool, but she was determined to get to the other side.*

*When her mother was alive, she had mentioned that her two sworn sisters, together with Xu Fo and Jingli, were her closest family. Now she began to have a better idea of their background and relationship to each other. Intuitively she felt deep compassion for the hapless girls. At the same time, she was heartened to see the five women brought together by fate.*

# NINE

Upon their retreat *to the Temple of the Three Sages fourteen years earlier, Yuanyuan and Xiangjun had become Taoist novices while Jingli had remained a layperson. Three years into the retreat, Xiangjun had given up her fight with chronic illness, and had died on her sickbed with a broken heart.*

*Three years after Xiangjun's death, Wu Sangui, the Feudal Lord of Yunnan, built Anfu Garden especially for Yuanyuan as a token of contrition, to make up for a wrong he had done her. Jingli and Yuanyuan had been living here for the past eight years. "Jingjing, your Jingli Po Po would very much like to meet you," Yuanyuan said in her usual sweet voice when she brought the girl a night snack of almond soup. "She had gone to the Temple of the Three Sages up in the hills for a ten-day Taoist immersion retreat when you arrived, and has just come back."*

*"I would love to meet Jingli Po Po! My mother had nothing but praise for her."*

*"If you want to hear Aunt Xiangjun's story, Jingli Po Po is the one who can tell you everything about her. It's getting late now. You two can have a nice long talk tomorrow."*

*"That's so wonderful, I can't wait to meet her. Thank you, Aunt Yuanyuan, and good night."*

*Aunt Yuanyuan was a habitual early riser, and had already finished breakfast when Jingjing stepped into the rear lounge this morning. Jingjing was both nervous and pleased to see the slightly-hunched back of a white-haired woman sitting at the table. When the older woman turned around, Jingjing was looking at a matronly and kind face that wore the furrows of hardship. But her eyes radiated childish mischief and wisdom, tempered only by affectionate warmth.*

*When they finished eating, Aunt Yuanyuan cleared the table and discreetly stepped out, leaving the two to some privacy.*

Ah, young maiden, you're even prettier than I imagined! Aiya, what a sad end your mother came to! But that is by no means out of character of her. She always had an iron will and a fiercely independent mind. I dare say she didn't make that sad choice for nothing; she made it to achieve an end.

Girl, do not worry about your future. I'm sure your mother would want you to have a happy life here with us. I was one of your mother's great admirers and I understood her way of thinking.

Life was unkind to all the three sisters when they were young, each in a different way. Or maybe not so different.

You've seen how my Yuanyuan has defied age and still look so deliciously attractive. Even now, Lord Wu Sangui still adores her like a goddess.

My precious Xiangjun was another unique beauty, and full of wit too. It's a great pity she lived such a short life. But life is never fair.

She had a small, willowy frame, and luminous, talking eyes set under arched eyebrows in a heart-shaped face. Oh, she could ensnare any man's heart on a whim! Her nickname was "Fragrant Fan Pendant". No doubt you know that a fan pendant is a small ornament dangling from a folding silk fan. It refers to her dainty and graceful figure. Fragrant, because she always carried a small pouch of jasmine inside her robe.

Both Xiangjun and Yuanyuan were gifted pipa players. You probably remember these lines from Bai Juyi's narrative poem

*The Song of the Pipa Player:*
> The bold strings rumble like tumbling sheets of rain,
> The fine strings hum like lovers' whimpering.
> Rumbling and humming, humming and rumbling,
> Like big and small pearls tossed in a bowl of jade.

How I miss their pipa playing! Those lines describe so well their skilled performance. I'm not giving them praise just because they are my daughters. I'm merely telling you a fact, one that can be verified if you ask anyone who has heard them play.

But perhaps no one could match my sweet Xiangjun's crystal singing voice. She was also such a natural fun-loving person who could tease without offending. The heavens played such a dirty trick by heaping ill fortune on my lovely girl.

When she was nine years old, her father, a widowed Donglin Academy scholar, was arrested and imprisoned on a fraudulent charge of treason, as his outspoken criticism of officialdom corruption had stung some officials with powerful court ties.

It is always unwise to provoke the authorities, I would say. But that's me and my survival instinct talking. Girl, you have to make up your own mind as to matters of right and wrong. I am sure your parents taught you well on this.

In Xiangjun's case, I think I should probably have known what kind of fate would befall her, because she grew up to be just like her father, always stubbornly upstanding and proud, unable to stomach depravity of those wielding power. Old timers often say: "One's destiny is written when one is three years old." There must be some truth in that saying.

Anyway, the Li family's fortune quickly declined after that and when debtors knocked on the door two years later, Xiangjun's aunt had no option but to sell the eleven-year-old to a thin horse breeder in Suzhou City. That was where she met Yuanyuan, also sold by her relatives. They received one year's training at the procurer house, and were then put on display in public teahouses to attract buyers.

Jingjing, you were raised in the respectable Qian family and you would probably never have had the chance to hear of the sorrowful tales of courtesans, had your mother carried the secret to her grave.

People look upon these women as livestock. Legally, they are classed as *jianmin*, meaning worthless people. Once a bond contract is written on you, you will have little chance of regaining freedom, unless someone with a Buddha's heart comes along, buys it out and tears it up. Countless slave girls go to their deaths as slave concubines or slave prostitutes.

I, too, once belonged to this caste and suffered inhumane treatment at the hands of a cruel brothel owner. At that time, I was only thirteen years old.

Several times when I failed to bring in a customer, I was flogged and not given food for days. Mercifully, the gods did not forsake me and one day a scholar named Chen Zhenhui came out of nowhere to lift me from the fires of hell. With his help, I turned a new page in life and bought the Villa of Alluring Fragrance in Qinhuai.

But once you've been subjected to that kind of debasing hell, the soreness never wears off and will always live in the bones.

So, when I saw Yuanyuan and Xiangjun being displayed for sale at that Suzhou City teahouse, my heart truly ached for them. Somehow I felt confident that I could turn them into the most famous performers in Qinhuai.

It was by a mere stroke of luck, as much for me as for them. I had won a large windfall sum of money at a gambling salon just the day before I stumbled on that teahouse. Otherwise, I wouldn't have had the big sum needed to beat the other ogling brothel owners. But I ought to tell you that I lost big money on several previous occasions. I wasn't proud of my addiction to gambling. Jingjing, I hope you won't judge Jingli Po Po too harshly.

My addiction was once my die-hard weakness. You probably can never understand this. Much as Zhenhui breathed new life into my dead soul, a haunting voice still constantly badgered me, "You have no value." In a struggle to stop that voice, I tried to let the heady rush of making high-stake bets numb my senses.

But happily that began to change when I took the girls to my salon. Sometimes, fortune does make a double. I was so pleased that your mother came out of nowhere and offered to be the girls' sponsor. You see, when you run a business, you have to count every last copper coin, and every windfall helps.

Being my wards, they provided me with a solid goal for me to work towards, accidentally bringing out the best in me. My maternal instinct found an outlet, and I was able to enjoy and reciprocate their warm affection. All of a sudden, that pestering itch was gone. I was no longer plagued by abject fear and self-abasing urges. It didn't matter what the world thought of us. We had each other and we loved each other, and that seemed enough. When I say "us", I always mean the four of us, your mother included. Of course, I was also aware how Xu Fo had helped your mother.

Now back to Xiangjun. I still remember well what Su Kunsheng, the *kunqu* master whom I had hired to teach the girls, had once said to me, "I have never had a more gifted pair of students than Xiangjun and Yuanyuan, nor more beautiful. You are a fortunate foster mother."

It was so true. After about half a year's training in opera singing, my two girls already turned out to be brilliant performers. Each evening, my salon was packed with scholars and officials who came solely to watch their performances. Soon their fame spread to the whole of Nanjing, and far beyond.

It was at that time that the aristocrat and Revival Society member Mao Xiang began to breathlessly pursue Yuanyuan. But wretched fate wouldn't leave her alone even after her palace ordeal, and something vile occurred shortly after the sisters' first anniversary. I'll leave her to get on with her story.

After that nightmarish incident, another young, dapper and learned Revival Society member, Hou Fangyu, paid a visit to the Villa of Alluring Fragrance for the first time, introduced by his friend Mao Xiang, who had persuaded him to come and watch Xiangjun's performance.

The Revival Society members consisted of the young literati from all over the country who were engaged in the anti-eunuch political movement. They wielded influence on state affairs through recommending their members to fill ministry posts. These scholars were all genuinely concerned about social ills and championed efforts to stamp out corruption and reform the state and provincial governments.

That first time he came, Fangyu appeared shy and reserved, and he sat quietly beside Mao Xiang in the front row throughout Xiangjun's entire performance of arias from *The Purple Hairpin*. I had heard from Zhenhui, also a Revival Society member, that Fangyu was in Nanjing to sit for the civil service examination.

That night, from an obscure corner in the backstage, I peered out and saw the young man's eyes trained on Xiangjun all through her show. I could also tell that his bewitched stare didn't escape her.

Two days later, Xiangjun was scheduled to perform the main aria from *The Peony Pavilion*. This being by far the most popular opera aria at that time, tickets had sold out ten days earlier.

I'll just briefly describe the layout of the Villa of Alluring Fragrance.

It is a spacious two-storey timber building and is one of the largest and plushest riverside villas in the Qinhuai district.

On the ground level, once you step inside the entrance gate and through a small peony garden, the front porch landing is just two stone steps up and leads into the entrance hall behind a curtain of purple bead strands. This is where patrons can relax on pearwood chairs ranged in a row on the left and right, and wait to be served. On a suspended perch by the east latticed window sits my pet parrot with bright red and blue feathers. At the sight of guests, it would shout "Serve tea, serve tea!"

Past the entrance hall, and separated by a scarlet velvet curtain, is the audience hall in the center with a soaring ceiling. This area abuts a raised stage, brightly lit by ceiling-suspended lanterns, where nightly performances of opera singing or pipa playing take place. Each padded seat is separated from the next by a wide armrest which serves as a side table to hold drinks and plates of sweetmeats.

On the west side is a large dining lounge and on the east, two rehearsal chambers and a dressing lounge. Tucked away in the backyard are maids' and servants' quarters and the kitchen. On either side of the stage, a flight of stairs leads up to a wrap-around corridor. Private chambers on the east, west and south wings open onto this corridor, which commands a full view of the audience hall and stage below.

On the north side, above the front porch and visible through lilac silk gauze curtains, is a verandah adorned with jasmine climbers looping the balusters and railing. The verandah looks out on the misty Qinhuai Canal teeming with colorful flower boats. On the nights of Dragon Boat Festival and Moon Festival, endless queues of lantern-lit boats used to wind along the river like fiery dragons, making quite a spectacle.

That evening, near the starting time of the performance, when the ticketed audience members had all taken their seats,

I stepped out into the entrance hall to see if there were any disgruntled patrons who could not get tickets. There were five of them, and Fangyu, who came on his own, was among them. I signaled for one of the servants to take the four customers inside and seat them on temporary seats placed in the two aisles.

Then I said to Fangyu: "Would you like to have a special seat on the upper level?" He was so surprised that he couldn't respond, and blushed to the roots of his hair. "What an innocent!" I thought. Without uttering a sound, he followed me through the audience hall and up the flight of stairs. Two of my apprentices were seated on chairs placed on the east corridor, and I sat him down on a chair behind the two giggling girls. Then I hurried down the stairs to see to other chores.

On his third visit two days later, he came in the early afternoon and, apparently emboldened by his good friend Yang Longyou, a painter from a wealthy and well-connected family and a regular patron of ours, he asked to have tea with Xiangjun, who was not performing that night.

Both young men were neatly attired in loose-fitting pale green cotton robes with wide sleeves, their hair covered in a dark blue square cloth cap with two long bands streaming down the back, the most stylish clothing for scholars.

Our salon practice was that guests were free to make such tea meeting requests, but it was always up to the performer to accept or decline. Xiangjun, now sixteen and impossibly sweet and pretty, was known to have rejected out of hand all such requests. Scores of beguiled officials and scholars had been turned away from her chamber door.

"Master Hou and Master Yang, you honor us with your presence! How can we serve you today?" I said in my usual congenial tone as I stepped out to greet them, having been told of Fangyu's request by a servant. Yang rose up from his chair and

ALICE POON

spoke glibly:

"My good friend here saw two of Lady Li's performances and has been most impressed by her extraordinary talent. He has a sincere and honorable wish to make her acquaintance. I had already warned him, out of personal experience, of the lady's aversion to such requests, but he remains adamant. I've been mulling over a proposition... I was thinking that if we make a joint request, perhaps such a notion could assure the lady that there is no ulterior motive and could thus persuade her to grant two of her doting fans the pleasure of her company? All we want is a chance to express in person our sincere admiration of her artistic talent."

"Master Yang, I must say I am stumped for words. But you see, even I do not have sway over my daughter's decisions on such matters. The best I could do is to convey your message to her. Would you kindly wait here and let me be the messenger?"

"We are much obliged for your kindness, Madam Li." He clasped his hands together and made a deep bow as I turned to leave the front hall.

From the corner of my eye, I could see his lips turn up in a smug look. Fangyu, who was standing nervously behind his friend, remained pale-faced and awkward, not knowing where to put his hands. For some reason, I took a liking to this modest and reserved young man.

Just as I had suspected, Xiangjun did notice Fangyu on both nights of her show and his looks and disposition made quite an impression on her. When I relayed the message to her, she blushed a deep pink. She said she would receive the two guests in her private chamber and requested my presence for propriety's sake.

Of all the private chambers on the upper level, the ones occupied by Xiangjun and Yuanyuan were the largest and were next to each other on the east corridor. Each of these had its own lounge.

Sadly, Yuanyuan had not been with us since early spring and I had been staying in her chamber. Xiangjun's lounge was modestly furnished. A marble-top round table stood in the center surrounded by rosewood stools, and a side table leaned against one wall, set between two rosewood chairs. Painting scrolls hung on this wall gave artistic accent to the room. Opposite the wall were latticed doors opening onto the verandah.

Now dressed in a pale pink silk robe patterned in orchids, tied with a tasseled waistband, and a same color pleated silk skirt, her hair twisted into a long braid and tied at the back with a purplish ribbon, she emerged from her inner chamber looking like a dewy lotus bud. A waft of jasmine fragrance trailed her into the lounge and pervaded every corner. Her person arrested all eyes.

A maid came in to serve jasmine tea to all, now seated at the round table. Fangyu's eyes were drawn to one of the paintings. He rose from the stool to take a closer look, just as Xiangjun was exchanging pleasantries with Yang. The painting happened to be Xiangjun's own work, entitled *Sailing at Dawn on a Wintry River*, with her poem inscribed on it that read:

The rustling west wind has cleared the distant sky,

Hills and rivers feast the eyes, like a scroll in a mirror.

Through the mist of waves an old man drifts,

Calling on his son at dawn to go on a fishing trip.

Apparently in awe of the lines he was reading, he kept bobbing his head, and mumbled to himself, "Excellent verse, excellent verse." Xiangjun was too shy to lift her eyes as the blush on her face deepened. But she was also too curious not to steal furtive glances his way, while pretending to be interested in what Yang was saying to her. I had always thought that she had talent in poetry, and was glad that someone from the literati now affirmed my view.

Long aware of his friend's infatuation, Yang tried to be supportive and joined in the accolade:

"I know a good painting when I see one, and I absolutely love yours, Lady Li. Our Fangyu here is one acclaimed expert when it comes to poetry. He doesn't easily praise others' works. If you want a teacher, he would be a perfect choice."

"If Master Hou doesn't mind my lack of intelligence and can spare the time, I would be most honored to take lessons from him," Xiangjun said timorously, mustering her courage and grasping at the chance of getting to know Fangyu better.

"The honor would be all mine, Lady Li. I am quite convinced that you have the gift of words. To be honest, I hadn't expected the author to be you. Then I saw your signet chop. In four lines, you have captured all at once the stillness, the moving and the ambience; the rhyming is done right too. That's a marvelous piece of work, one that complements the painting. I have no doubt you would make a delightful student." His look was one full of genuine admiration. I saw his blush spreading to the back of his ears as he struggled to offset his natural shyness.

"My sweet Xiangjun would be lucky to have Master Hou as her teacher!" I exclaimed. "Now if you Masters are not otherwise engaged, I would urge you to stay for a humble meal to celebrate the new apprenticeship." I wanted to give the pair more time to talk with each other, and as expected, the young scholars agreed with alacrity.

With this student-teacher arrangement, there would be ample time for Xiangjun to find out what kind of a person Fangyu truly was, and whether her feelings for him were more than just fleeting. A man's real worth is not his family status or his wealth; it is his character and moral sense. I would hate to see my precious daughter fall for the wrong man, especially as I had been powerless, yet again, to help the other daughter escape her ill fate.

*At this point, Aunt Yuanyuan peered into the lounge to announce that lunch was ready. Jingjing had been so immersed in the story that she hardly noticed time passing. It was only when Jingli Po Po rose from her chair that she realized the mid-day sun was streaming in to warm up the lounge.*

*The whole time she was eating, her mind dwelled on this comment that Jingli Po Po made, "I dare say she didn't make that sad choice for nothing; she made it to achieve an end." At the same time, her mother's plea rang in her ears, "I chose death to shame the people who scorn and bully women whom they call 'jianmin' and regard as inferior and worthless. Please try to spread my message of protest."*

*As all three stories got her deeply invested now, she began to feel the pull of a new energy. A sense of responsibility was growing within her undetected.*

# TEN

WHEN THE NEW YEAR came around, I couldn't bring myself to visit Yuanyuan and Xiangjun at the Lantern Festival as promised. Crushed by a pain that snuffed out the joy in life for me, I surrendered to lassitude and apathy throughout that whole year. Still, a restless part of me was looking up from the bottom of the abyss, trying to reach for the ledge above.

Perhaps it was this that kept me breathing. It pushed me to spend my latent energy on a tangible interest of mine – the craft of embroidery. In six months, I finished embroidering a dress with pictorial renderings of the twenty-four paragons of filial piety. Did I do it to mock my bleeding heart? I cannot tell. All I knew was that my love had been prostrated before the shrine of filial obedience. Who did I think I was? Was I ever anything more than just a cheap whore from the *jianmin* caste that Peony had reminded me of?

Knowing what I was going through, Fo said gently to me one day,

"I know Zilong is bound by his filial duties. But, Rushi, your humble birth and your brush with the lowly caste does not define you. You must never let anyone make you doubt your own worth. You are a prodigy, and your talents are already recognized."

Her soothing words were a balm to my hurt pride and a timely reminder that it was I who willingly cut ties with Zilong. I bowed out so that each of us could move forward. Fo was always a flicker of wisdom.

During that year, whenever dark moods assailed me, she was always there to tell me fables of jest, or indulge my sweet tooth by making my favorite red bean soup. I couldn't imagine carrying on with life without her loving care.

By early autumn, my fits of depression became less frequent and my thoughts whirled constantly around Yuanyuan and Xiangjun. Guilt was poking at me for reneging on my promise to visit them, and I wanted badly to do something in expiation.

Then an idea dawned on me. I had heard from Fo that within the community of Qinhuai courtesans, there was a custom of exchanging kerchiefs as a way of cementing friendship between intimate friends. They were called kerchief sisters. Why don't I gift the girls with kerchiefs that I embroider? I was thinking I should work on three kerchiefs with the same design, so each of us could own one.

I chose a common design of three lovely birds conversing with each other: a hovering green parrot to represent me, a purplish nightingale to honor graceful Yuanyuan and a blue magpie to extol sprightly Xiangjun, the latter two nestling on a branch of plum blossom. On an abstract level this was a way to share with them my long-cherished fantasy of living the free life of birds.

Fo urged me several times to take the trip to Nanjing with the New Year just round the corner. A month before I set out, Xiangjun's letter arrived to let me in on Yuanyuan's odious torment at the Palace. Great anxiety rose within me. The poor girl had barely escaped death, and her flight was no guarantee for safety. The person she had rubbed the wrong way was none other than the vindictive Consort Tian. There was no holding me back from the trip.

On my arrival at the Villa of Alluring Fragrance, one look

ALICE POON

at Yuanyuan's sickly wan face, distraught with despair, was enough to break my heart. The idea of forming a sisterhood, using the kerchiefs as our token of oath, came to me on the spur of the moment. She was still just an adolescent. How crushed she must feel! Just the thought of Consort Tian's wicked wiles and the beastly eunuchs laying hands on her made me cringe in disgust.

It was fate that had drawn us together in that Suzhou City teahouse, and since then their hapless images lodged tight in my mind. Perhaps it was Fo who inspired me to be a big sister to them. For all I knew, I might well be the needier one emotionally, and was grateful that they accepted me as family.

After our sisterhood oath-taking, I drew comfort from seeing a little color return to Yuanyuan's face, and Xiangjun flutter about like a restless butterfly.

Then Jingli came up with her big-hearted proposition to adopt my two new sisters as her daughters. Tears flowed freely as familial joy pervaded the house. People who had not tasted the dual scourge of poverty and orphanage might never understand what this bonding meant for us. But Fo and Jingli could.

After dinner, I had a chance to talk with Xiaowan and was glad to see her settled in her new home. It seemed to me that she was now stuttering less. But her old forlorn expression did not escape me. Her father's debts still weighed heavily on her.

Yet Yuanyuan's precarious situation had me more worried, especially when she declined my offer for her to stay with me in Songjiang. Consort Tian was someone who could tear her to pieces if she so wished. Her malice towards Yuanyuan brought back nasty memories of how Gold Flower and Orchid had treated me at the Zhou household. But anyone with a heart would understand Yuanyuan's reluctance to leave Nanjing. She had her heart set on seeing Mao Xiang again.

On my return to Songjiang, I felt content, having achieved something in untangling Yuanyuan from the knot of despair. When I shared with Fo what had happened in Nanjing, she said with pride, "That was a very thoughtful and kind gesture, Rushi! I am so proud of you. The bond will give new meaning to all your lives, I am sure."

I knew as the eldest sister, I had to assume responsibility for the two girls. It would anchor my rootless life. From now on, they, together with Fo and Jingli, would be my dear family.

The year passed more quickly than I had anticipated, as I tried to immerse myself in the new role of a *guqin* performer, while carrying on with my editing work.

In the deep recesses of my soul though, the shadow of Zilong still stirred. From time to time, I would yearn for the dreamy days we had spent together, which now seemed a life-time away.

Around the middle of the year, I got a letter from Yuanyuan saying she had patched things up with Xiang. I murmured heartfelt thanks to Guanyin for putting my sister in safe hands.

At the first anniversary of our sisterhood, I was ecstatic to hear that Yuanyuan and Xiang would soon be betrothed to each other. The bloom on her beautiful face was hard to miss.

Before I left, I had embroidered pairs of mandarin ducks with gold and silver threads on her pink silk wedding garments, to invoke good fortune and happiness. My work fell short of excellence though, as my mind was preoccupied with Fo's illness and the menace posed by the mobster Xie Sanbin, who had literally been stalking me in recent months.

As Fo's 'Music Cruise' program had become more and more popular, some roguish patrons had also started showing up in the audience. Since separating from Zilong, I had begun putting on bi-nightly *guqin* performances on Fo's boat to help boost revenue for her salon. Perhaps my looks had something to do with it, but my performances always sold out well in advance. But in solitary moments, my mother's stark warning that "beauty is a curse" would often prick my nerves.

To match the boat's curtain color, I would always dress in a plain violet silk robe, cross-collared and tied at the waist with a purple sash, and a matching violet pleated skirt, which Fo had made for me. I would braid my hair into a long loose plait, weaving it with a purple ribbon, and would insert behind one ear the green jade hairpin that Fo had given me as my wedding present. Now the hairpin was just a sore reminder of a love union not meant to be. It was a bit like rubbing salt into a raw wound, but it also presented me with the message that life had to go on.

My signature performance was the tune set to the main aria from the play *The Purple Hairpin*. Somehow the dolorous mood of this aria seemed to echo mine. The story of the ill-starred lovers in the play closely mirrored my own, save for the happy ending. People say that happy endings are only for novels. They are probably right. Passion and happiness was ephemeral like a bird's footmark on snow.

Shortly after I returned to Songjiang from Nanjing, Fo said to me one day, her brow furrowed:

"That rascal Xie Sanbin was pining for your performance the whole time you were in Nanjing. He has come twice since your return, asking to see you in person. I told him both times that our new season would start in a month, but he insists on meeting with you. I thought I should warn you. When he comes again, I won't be able to turn him away. He's a brutish type and is hard to deal with."

"Don't worry, Fo. I'll see him next time he comes for me."

I didn't want to give Fo any unnecessary trouble, and thought the best way would be to face the man, unwilling though I was.

Except for three scrawny boy servants, who doubled as our

boatmen, all members of Fo's household were frail women. I had seen Xie several times in the audience, and he looked like a grumpy, ugly giant, always accompanied by two or three goons. He had sent me expensive jewelry, but I returned all to him, untouched. On one occasion, he had accosted me while I was on my way back to the villa, but I had managed to slip away after a short polite greeting, making up a random excuse.

It was said that he had fought and won in a major battle against the Manchus in Liaodong Province, and had thereby been promoted from foot soldier to the rank of deputy captain. Rumor also had it that he was immensely rich, having smuggled military supplies into enemy territory. Everything that I heard about him told me he was depraved and unreliable.

Soon thereafter the new season of performance opened. That evening was my first performing session to start off the season. Fo was happy that the session's tickets had long sold out. Our usual practice was to have our boatmen pole the three boats to the center of the waterway and align them side by side. One performer would be on board each boat with five or six patrons. A low table inside the cabin was laden with plates of sweetmeats and cups of rice wine. In the center was placed a small sandalwood incense burner. All the lanterns on the exterior of the cabin were lit, throwing mellow light onto the surrounding waters.

The three girls, including me, would take turn in performing, playing the *guqin* either solo or with singing accompaniment. As I didn't have a good singing voice, I would usually only play tunes on the instrument, and my boat would take the center position.

The evening started out perfect with a waxen full moon suspended in the velvety folds of an indigo sky. The night air was thick with the hypnotizing scent of the early spring narcissus. As I stepped onto the boarding plank at the jetty, a voice bellowed behind me. "Lady Liu, let me help you!" Xie grabbed my arm roughly and hustled me into the boat cabin, as if he owned me. Indignation and fear tugged at my nerves, but I couldn't possibly show displeasure. He was a patron after all.

I was on edge the entire evening, much as I believed he would not dare do anything brazenly indecent in public.

That night, as usual, all three boats were packed with patrons, but as I looked around, I did not see any familiar faces in the audience.

Xie spread himself out on the divan to my right, his two guards sitting on the bench facing me. To my left were three young ruffians in a row. Xie's leering eyes never left me alone for one moment. I avoided looking at him and pretended to be busy tuning my instrument. From the corner of my eye I could make out his swarthy pock-marked face with thick, black, bristling eyebrows. But throughout the session, I kept calm and ignored him as best as I could.

When the last aria of the night's session ended, he moved closer to me and, picking up a cup of rice wine, handed it to me, and offered a toast, "Let's drink to Lady Liu's health! May she be young and beautiful forever!"

Everyone raised the cup. Out of courtesy, I accepted and gulped it down.

By now, dark clouds had half veiled the moon, and the night breeze grew blustery, flapping the curtains and ruffling the water. Tossed by waves, the boats grated against each other, making loud sqeaking sounds. The girl in the boat on my right screamed as she lost her balance and slipped, knocked by a sudden jounce of the boat. I was getting impatient for the boatmen to turn the boats to shore.

Once back at the jetty, the boats started offloading their passengers. A strange feeling arose in me. My limbs seemed to have lost all energy and my knees were buckling. Xie saw this and he put his gigantic palm round my waist to keep me from stumbling.

After alighting from the boat, I saw things whirling around me and lost all sense of direction. The path we were walking on felt different from the one I would usually take to get back to the villa, although I couldn't tell. It was dark. After a few paces, the noise of the crowd was falling away.

The servants and the girls probably thought I was in Xie's escort and knew better than to intrude. Stumbling along disoriented, I sensed danger closing in on me and tried to scream, but to my heartstopping horror, no sound came from my throat! Through my hazy vision, I saw Ah Luk trying to intervene, but he was roughly shoved away.

Xie grabbed hold of me and carried me in his arms, his two goons following behind. All this time, I felt drowsy, but was still conscious, which made the experience all the more bone-chilling. He approached a waiting two-wheeled carriage, with me pressed against his chest. His two men lifted the thick front flap of the paneled enclosure to let us in, and then climbed onto the driving seat in front. The enclosure interior was pitch-dark and oppressive. The horses started at a canter, and then broke into a gallop. I clung desperately to the belief that Xie was trying to seek help for my ailment, but my guts knew better. Moments later, the carriage drew to a stop at the front gate of a large mansion.

I was carried to a bed chamber on the upper level. He laid me down on the canopied bed with silk coverings. I pleaded with him with my eyes, but he answered with a triumphant grin.

"Whatever I desire, I get," he said. "So lady, just submit to me. Even though you are just a whore, I will treat you right. I'm pissed that Chen Zilong got ahead of me."

Fetid fear choked me as I strained futilely to wriggle from him. My recoil of abhorrence probably provoked the primitive animal in him. His eyes were blood shot with lust as he roughly peeled off my robe and skirt. Tears gushed from my eyes. Time seemed to have frozen dead.

I bit my lower lip and shut my eyes for I didn't know how long. When at last he rolled off me, panting heavily, my whole body convulsed in disgust. His sweaty odor stank and nauseated me.- He took one salacious look at me and stomped out of the chamber.

The next morning, he came into the chamber and sat on the edge of the bed, looking gratified. With a sickening chuckle he said,

"I'll send a matchmaker over to Madam Xu tomorrow morning to make an offer. You will be my sixth concubine. A sedan and my guards will pick you up in the afternoon. You'll have the best food and the finest silks in my household. Now I'll send for a carriage to take you home, so you can prepare for the happy day…"

Before he could finish, I leapt up on impulse and, with the whole force of my body, slapped his face twice. He made no effort to dodge, and laughed a shameless, squawky laugh, "Hahaha, you're a feisty one! I like it!"

Shivers rattled me the whole journey home. The moment I saw Fo in the rear lounge, I rushed up to her, drowned in tears. She gasped in alarm and embraced me. I said between sniffles, "I have to pack immediately and leave for Hangzhou right away. Xie Sanbin is sending his people here to take me by force." Pausing to let the news sink in, I then continued in a fit of mad rage, "The bastard laced the wine to paralyze me and raped me last night."

I showed her the bruises on my forearms and thighs. She

shook her head in exasperation. "I couldn't sleep the whole night after hearing Ah Luk's account," she said. "That swine is an expert in using poisons. How could I have forgotten to warn you beforehand? I'm such a useless fool!" Pain and guilt flitted across her face, tears trickling down her cheeks. "You better take some herbal medicine to prevent pregnancy."

She climbed the stairs to her chamber and, after a while, came back down and tottered to the kitchen.

When the herbal drink was ready, she poured the dark liquid into a bowl, fanned it cool and handed it to me. After gulping it down, I went to the bath nook next to the kitchen, where she had a tub of hot water ready for me.

Not all the water in the world could cleanse me, I thought wearily. I could still smell his foul breath on me. My stomach churned and I threw up.

When I was done scrubbing and drying myself, she gently administered some minty balm onto my bruises and helped me dress. Then she handed me a piece of paper and said:

"Rushi, you must leave here at once. Go and find Wang Wei in Hangzhou. Here's her address and my letter of introduction. She's a retired courtesan also known as 'Straw Cloak Taoist'. Her generosity is well-known among our lot and she will be happy to put you up for as long as you need."

At this time, Fo was getting sicker every season. She did take the herbal medicine regularly as set down in the prescription Jingli had given me, but it seemed to be only a palliative. Once in a while her coughing fits would be violent, and she tired easily. I would not leave her at this time if I was not in such great peril. She sensed my hesitation and said, "Don't worry about me. I have the girls to look after me. You stay safe, and remember to write."

While in Hangzhou, I spent a lot of time wandering around the scenic West Lake, sometimes alone, sometimes with Madam Wang.

Her residence was near the Broken Bridge that straddles the eastern portion of the Lake. The lodge was modeled after a Taoist nunnery with sparse bamboo furnishings and an annexed garden filled with weeping willows and osmanthus bushes. It nestled inside a dense bamboo forest and right beside a crystal clear brook that fed into West Lake.

Floral scent filled the air. It was a perfect healing retreat for people with a wounded soul. Inspiration for writing poetry beckoned me all the time and spurred me to furiously spin out quatrains evoking the otherworldly scenery. My art was my time-tested refuge.

My host, middle-aged and blessed with a youthful face, was part of the much needed distraction for me. She was in every way as kind, considerate and generous as Fo had said.

During the day, she was never inquisitive. She knew exactly when to leave me alone, and when to strike up a casual conversation, spiced with mordant humor. Her measured companionship, while not in the least intrusive, was cozy enough to give me comfort.

But beneath that deceptive calm there still rumbled a howling storm. Several nights, I screamed aloud in my disturbed slumber, and each time, she responded without fail to my loud wailing, scampering to my bedside to wipe my perspiring forehead and neck, and coo me back to sleep.

One day, she saw on my writing table a quatrain that I had earlier written, picked it up and gave an impromptu recital in her honeyed voice:

East of the curtained window, lithe willows grace the court;
Birds nestle on nude branches, butterflies in the breeze cavort.

On the spring-scented path by West Lake,
Peach blossoms and beauties relish a friendly taunt.

When she finished, she exclaimed: "Exquisite verse, Rushi! Why don't you brush this poem in your lovely wild grass script? I'll have it mounted and it will make an elegant addition to the displayed scrolls in my lounge."

A month later, Qian Qianyi, the old poet and courtier, came to pay Madam Wang a visit, saw my poem, and took such a liking to it that he wrote a repartee on the spot. After he left, she came in to my chamber and handed me his poem, telling me that he was most impressed with the last line of my quatrain.

The Straw Cloak Taoist lives east of the Broken Bridge;
A good verse refreshes like a breeze from the pond.
I've lately commended Liu's talent by West Lake,
Peach blossoms and beauties relish a friendly taunt.

She then added, "He also left a personal note for you." The note was an invitation for me and Madam Wang to join him on a boat cruise on West Lake two days later.

"He's one of the few learned men who never look down on courtesans. He treats us like humans," she said.

The name of Qian Qianyi was by no means strange to me. I remembered having seen him once at a meeting of the Songjiang poetry club, but we had never been formally introduced to each other. In fact, I was a bit flustered that he, venerated poet and eminent historian that he was, deigned to praise a trivial work of mine. But his polite adherence to proper etiquette impressed me.

It was a drizzling afternoon when the three of us climbed onto the pleasure boat. Late spring mist hovered above the lake and birds' trilling echoed mysteriously in the opaque air. Raindrops speckled the limber willows draping the banks. Every now and then the sun would peep from behind clouds and play with the water drops on the willows, interlacing them into starry lattices.

When the mist skittered away, downy white clouds glided in the sky-blue water.

Scholar Qian's white hair and goatee told me his approximate age, but what caught my attention were his gentle, amusing eyes. His face was an earthy brown, like one that belonged to a peasant, but it had the patience and kindness of a seasoned man.

Still trapped in the rut of self-pity, I was not able to enjoy his company, but could still feel he was training his curious eyes on me. Even in that frame of mind, I did not let the magical ambience of West Lake escape me. I was glad, though, that Madam Wang was there to keep the polite conversation going.

After the boat ride, I excused myself to take a walk alone on the Broken Bridge, only to have the drizzling rain stir me into deep sadness. My sense of loss and emptiness suddenly broke to the surface and shattered me. How was it possible to sever the emotional chords with a man whose soul had become enshrined in yours? How could you separate the blue from the red when they had melded to become purple? His sonorous voice seemed to come at me from all sides to envelope me, and just as suddenly, faded and subsided into distant echoes. A cold gust woke me. Upon return to the lodge, I spilled my feelings into an elegiac regular verse:

Smoke rises above the crimson lodge by Broken Bridge,
Spring scent dreamily lingers in the flowery shades.
My love, who keeps you company now on North Bank?
Here, by West Lake, my heart aches pining for you.
How we loved to banter till late under the peach bloom!
All alone, I'm a broken willow sprig, yearning for that spring.
If a courtesan's life is slated to be a cold blustery dream,
Won't you, Wind and Rain, be kind and swaddle me in warmth?

This poem was etched deep in my memory and remained one

of my favorites. I gave it the title *A Walk in the Rain on Broken Bridge*. Rain had once given me hope. I was wondering if I could count on it again.

One late summer day, while writing a poem in my bed chamber, I learned from Xiangjun that Yuanyuan had been forced into slavery at the Tian household. What I had earlier dreaded had come to pass.

For those in our lot, disaster could strike whenever it pleased, without warning. Walking a thin rope was a daily feat for us. One could always pretend it would never happen, to make life a little easier, until that moment arrived. And when it did, there was no dodging it. You either face and bear it, or sail into extinction. Such was our reality.

Soon after the Moon Festival, I heard about Mao Xiang's botched attempt to rescue her. The news weighed like lead on my heart. It also forced me to put aside my own troubles to try to come up with a plan to help my ill-fated sister.

I was thinking that perhaps it would be best for Yuanyuan to give up on Xiang, as there was no way that the tyrannical Tian Hongyu would willingly give her to him. The best outcome would be for her to be given away to another household.

When I talked this over with my kind host Wei, who by now had become a good friend, she agreed with me, and came up with an idea. "General Wu Sangui is my former patron and a good friend of the Tian family," she said. "I just might be able to persuade him to play hero and rescue a girl in distress. If anyone could persuade Tian to give up Yuanyuan, it would be General Wu."

I thought that was an excellent idea, as I imagined that Yuanyuan, with her alluring beauty, would stand a good chance of charming the general once they met. So I entreated Wei to proceed and get in touch with the general with a portrait of

Yuanyuan, which I immediately set about sketching for her.

I just couldn't see the slightest possibility of Yuanyuan having a future with Xiang. Rather than hanging onto a false hope, might it not be better to be rid of it and face reality? Sometimes a practical approach could be the only path to a new life. I thought I should have a good talk with Yuanyuan at our upcoming second anniversary.

In the somber depths of winter, one snowy afternoon I got a letter from one of Fo's girls. It was to tell me that Fo had just passed away and had left her will for me.

The news caught me off guard and hammered me hard. Her chronic sickness had worried me for a long time, but never had I thought death was right at her doorstep.

I slumped onto the floor. Clutching the letter to my chest, I bawled and howled till I lost my voice. I owed her so much, and now I could never repay her. Guilt and pain scored my heart as I banged my head repeatedly on the floor. I was her closest family, and she had no one else she could talk to. When she needed me most in her last hours, I was not there to hold her hand and hear her last words. Tears gushed down my face like a cascade, but could change nothing.

When they finally dried up, night had shrouded my chamber. My eyes stayed wide open until dawn arrived. Time rushes forward and never back, oblivious of human joy or pain. We cannot but be driven by the tide of life.

I glumly packed my things and said farewell to Wei. She patted the back of my hand and said soothingly, "For your own safety, you may want to return to Songjiang in a man's disguise. When you've done what needs to be done there, come back to stay if you so wish."

Without a second thought, I changed into men's clothing,

donned a scholar cloth cap to hide my hair, and set out for home.

As soon as I arrived at Fo's villa, I got hold of and read Fo's will, written in a shaky hand, but in her typical light-hearted tone:

"My sweetest dumpling, I'm leaving you to go to my Buddha. Please do not shed tears for me. You know I always wanted peace. Now I will be in eternal peace. Be happy for me! But of course, I will watch over you from my new world!

"I'm bequeathing to you the villa, the boat and the operation of the salon. If you find your love and plan to marry, please do not hesitate to sell these, provided you find a new home for my girls. If you possibly could, please try to see to it that Xiaowan's bond contract is redeemed from her father's creditors.

"I have no complaints about my life. Buddha took good care of me, and he gave me the most precious gem - you. You must always remember that you are a genius. Never let the few setbacks in your life make you eschew your goals. Fortunate is the man who finds, loves and keeps you. I know how hard it is to break free from the cage of social scorn. Rushi, you are one who just might change the fate of our wretched lot.

"You have probably been wondering why I chose to keep my distance from Wen. My intuition told me that I had not much time left, and I just couldn't bring myself to indulge selfishly in a short spell of pleasure, leaving him to suffer a lifetime of pain and grief. He is a good man and deserves a nice woman who can be at his side and make him happy through old age. My reason is no different from yours for leaving Zilong.

We just want the best for those we hold so dear and close to our hearts. Sometimes love means having the courage to let go. I know you would agree. Farewell now, my precious. Your doting Fo."

# ELEVEN

ANFU GARDEN'S *pastoral settings and the sweet, cool mountain air laden with pine scent acted like a salve to Jingjing's riven heart. She had come to savor the morning strolls in the front and side gardens.*

The front garden boasted a large, round, lotus pond, where sturdy young stems of white lotus buds and wavy green leaves danced gracefully on water. On the far side of the pond, two supple weeping willows, in a courteous bow to each other, draped over a square stone table surrounded by stone benches. A winding pebble-stone path on the left led to a secluded side garden filled with cherry trees, peach trees, silk wisteria, sweet osmanthus, rose and lilac bushes. A small creek chattered through the lush garden, drawing flocks of songbirds to dip for a drink or blissful bath. She could sit all day on the low stone bench by the creek just watching the birds. No wonder Aunt Yuanyuan called this sanctuary her Shangri-La.

Recalling what her mother had said about the magical healing power of Nature, she now understood what that meant. The dulling pain that had beset her was whittled down bit by bit.

She had just finished her morning stroll when Yuanyuan came out to the front garden. She was really eager for her aunt to continue her story. The previous night she had read further passages of her mother's memoir. Some parts shook her to the core. Glimpses into all the sisters' lives tugged at her heartstrings in a way no novel or literary work ever could. She was getting a better grasp of their world of silent suffering.

Yuanyuan now took to pampering the young girl. She would wait

*till the girl got up from bed to eat breakfast with her together, bring*
*her fresh flowers everyday and make her afternoon tea delicacies such*
*as stewed pears and apricots with cane sugar, and pastries made with*
*honey and rosewater.*

*With her arrival, Jingjing had brought a breath of fresh life to the*
*otherwise sleepy abode. Yuanyuan could not be more pleased with her*
*vivacious company. Most of all, she was anxious to distract the girl*
*from the pain of her loss and to build rapport with her. Now that they*
*were both at ease in each other's company, her burden was gradually*
*easing. She was just thankful that Jingjing was always eager to listen.*

I came away from the sisterhood ceremony like someone in
the latter stages of recovery from a grave illness. No longer
bedridden, the invalid was trying to walk a few feeble steps. My
mental anguish seemed to have finally receded after paralyzing
me for months.

I talked to Mother about resuming my performances on stage,
but she was somewhat hesitant. She was worried that my public
appearance might attract unnecessary attention from Consort
Tian's eyes and ears and would prefer that I keep away from
public eyes. I knew she was right and did as she asked.

Having nothing to occupy me, I turned my attention to a
new apprentice named Dong Xiaowan, who had just joined our
salon from Songjiang on Madam Xu's recommendation. She was
the same age as Xiangjun and had a sweet heart-shape face like
hers, but in terms of personality, was the complete opposite. She
appeared very withdrawn. A forlorn air always seemed to hang
about her. Since the day she stepped into our salon, she had not
spoken one word to any of us except Mother. She alone could
understand the girl's stuttering speech. But when she started to
sing, even the thrushes would stop their warbling to listen to
her. She had brought a *guqin* with her and showed her mastery

with it.

Then it came to my attention that Mother had arranged for her to fill in for me and let her take up a leading *kunqu* singing role. After only a couple of months on the stage, she began to attract a large audience who loved her high-pitched voice. Her favorite *kunqu* aria from *Dream Under the Southern Bough* quickly became popular and she made a name for herself as one of the best novice performers in Qinhuai.

I would admit that all that excitement she created made me a little jealous. I tried not to allow the sour sentiment take hold and to let Xiangjun's friendly attitude toward her rub off on me. I felt so ashamed when Mother explained to me on one occasion, "I'm glad that people have shifted their attention to Xiaowan, because that throws your hunters off the scent."

Now that my emotional state had become more stable, I started to ponder my own future. I was nearly fourteen, a marriageable age. The Villa of Alluring Fragrance was obviously only a temporary hideout for me. My only hope of finding permanent protection would be to come under a household with powerful court ties. Consort Tian would know the limits of her reach. She would not want to escalate things so much as to draw the Emperor's attention.

I knew only too well that Xiang and his family would be able to offer me that protection. Whether he would be willing was another matter, now that I was no longer "pure". From a desirable *kunqu* talent, I had sunk to the nadir of being a molested flower. Would he ever be able to look past that? I was getting desperate and wanted to have a meeting with him, but did not know how to go about it. Since my last refusal to see him, he had never showed his face again. Now I was regretting my foolishness.

Finally, I drummed up a last shred of courage and asked a servant to deliver a note of invitation to him. I prayed and prayed that he would come.

On the day of my proposed assignation, I braided my hair into two plaits, looped each into a knot over one ear, and fastened them by hairpins and silk ribbons, leaving wisps around my temple to give accent to my large dark eyes. I dusted my face with crushed pearl face powder and brushed a little rouge on my lips and cheekbones.

Having changed into an ensemble that Xiang used to love, a pink silk robe, embroidered in plum blossoms and tied at the waist with a tasseled sash, paired with a pearly white silk skirt, I was at last satisfied with the reflection in the bronze mirror. I could still picture him in awe when he had seen me in it for the first time. Lastly, I stuck a fresh pink rose into one knotted plait for a finished look.

When he arrived in mid-afternoon, a servant announced him and I went down to the front lounge to greet him.

He looked pale, ill-at-ease and appeared not to notice my ornate coiffure or my costume. I invited him up to my antechamber on the upper level, and when he seated himself, served him a cup of hot jasmine tea. He took two sips of the fragrant tea and seemed somewhat calmed. The blare of silence was deafening. Neither of us knew how to pull aside the thick veil of awkwardness that hung stiffly between us.

At length, I spoke, straining to sound impassive, "It has been a long time since we last met, Master Mao. Have you been busy with preparations for the civil service examination?"

He did not answer my question. His face changed from pallid white to blushing pink. Another bout of strained silence. Then he suddenly let loose a torrent of emotive words.

"Why did you refuse to see me, on both occasions? I was going mad worrying about you. I thought you were sick, or something. Madam Li had said the Empress wanted you to join the inner court as a musician. But when you came back a few months later, Xiangjun only told me that you were not fit to receive guests, and she refused to say anything further. Yuanyuan, what had really happened to you while you were in the Palace? Why have you been avoiding me? I'm heartbroken! Will you please tell me the truth?"

Faced by his barrage of questions, tears welled up and my old nightmare of the palace scenes seized me once again. Sobs sent me into a convulsive quiver.

When he saw me melt in tears, he rose from his seat and put his arms around me and stroked my hair. His tender touch on my skin threw me into a fit of shame. Torn between my desperate need for his love and the necessary evil of baring the truth to him, I was roiled with shame. He was my last hope of salvation. What if he could not bring himself to accept the ugly truth? His touch was already weakening my resolve to tell the truth.

"If I tell you the true story, will you promise you will forgive everything?" I forced the words out of me.

"Don't be silly! What is there to forgive?"

"It was something vile...... Neither the Emperor nor Empress had a chance to meet me. Somehow I was brought before Consort Tian. She said the wickedest things to me. I said something in reply that pricked her and she ordered to have me locked up... I was made to wait on.... the eunuchs."

"You mean as their maid?" He looked puzzled at first, then, after a pause, seemed to get what I was trying to say. Too taken aback to say anything, he staggered towards one of the two side chairs and slumped into it, his face reddening. "So what they say is true," he muttered to himself.

I threw myself down at his feet and hugged his legs. "You have to forgive me, Xiang. I tried to kill myself.... An old palace maid saved me from the brink of death and helped me escape.

Consort Tian's men are still hunting for me. My fate is in your hands...." I broke into a helpless wail. "Please take me as your concubine. I will do anything for you and your family. Only you can deliver me from my wretched destiny."

Raising my tear-stained face to him, I saw sadness and compassion in his eyes. As much as our love for each other was genuine, I was aware that the situation called for seductive skills. A part of me was staking my future on his sentimental and generous nature. If my judgment was wrong.....

"Yuanyuan, I love you so much... Don't you know you have long stolen my heart and soul? You are the very fountain from which I draw life. Without you, there'll be no life for me."

He lifted my chin to stare into my eyes. "It was ill fate that you had to go through this cruelty. I understand. You did nothing wrong. I will take you as my concubine after I have obtained my wife's consent. Don't worry, everything will work out fine. I won't let anyone hurt you again."

He leaned forward to kiss away the tears on my face. Words failed me, as I gazed feverishly into his eyes. I pulled the hairpins to loosen the plaits, letting my hair fall. Then I unfastened the sash to let slip my silk robe and skirt. There was nothing else underneath. His eyes glistened in excitement and he carried me to my bed. Our thirst for each other took a long time to quench.

Following that meeting, Xiang and I took up where we had left off. He made frequent visits to me at the Villa. Words could not describe how relieved I felt. My mood brightened with the passing of each day. I now had a secure future to look forward to, not to mention that my husband would be the man I loved with my whole heart.

Mother fussed over Xiang whenever he came. She served him her precious Snow Orchid tea and cooked delicious meals for him. That was the way she showed her delight with him.

Now, instead of watching me perform on stage, he took pleasure in having me sing and dance for him in the privacy of my antechamber. But sometimes when he came in the evening, he couldn't help making a stop in the audience hall to hear Xiaowan sing. I told him her story, as relayed to me by Mother, and he seemed to feel pity for her. To keep his attention from straying, I would sometimes dance the seductive fan dance for him, dressed in an embroidered *dudou* and a flimsy skirt.

Very soon, it was Lantern Festival again, the first anniversary of our sisterhood. At our reunion dinner, Rushi told us that Xu Fo was quite ill with a chronic cough and that a mobster called Xie Sanbin was stalking her. I thought that was just one of her secret admirers, and didn't take it to heart.

Mother went up to her chamber and came back with some herbal prescription for coughs, which her own mother had passed down to her, and she gave it to Rushi. She thanked Mother and told us she was thinking of hiding away in Hangzhou to avoid the mobster. I could tell that she had not recovered from the painful separation from Zilong, as hard as she tried to hide her feelings. My heart ached for her. I would feel this way too if my beloved Xiang and I were forced apart. In the matter of love, women are as brittle as porcelain, whether we admit it or not.

When dinner was over, Mother announced, not without a dash of pride, that Xiang had asked for my hand in marriage and that the betrothal would take place in a month, followed by a formal wedding in late spring.

Xiangjun squealed in delight and gave me a big hug, thrusting a piece of pink jade tasseled hairpin into my hand. My sweet sister had emptied her hard-earned savings to buy this wedding gift for me. I hugged her back, all choked up.

Rushi also came over to me to embrace and congratulate me.

She offered to embroider my wedding dress before her departure. I thanked her from the bottom of my heart. She didn't forget to collect our kerchiefs so she could embroider the New Year zodiac sign onto them.

Never had I felt such bliss in my entire life, and I prayed to the heavens that Rushi and Xiangjun would also find their own love.

Earlier, Mother had told me that Xiang had tried to get my name struck off the register of entertainers, but had run into a snag as he did not hold my bond contract, it being still in Consort Tian's hands. The chief eunuch had somehow managed to filch it from the Empress and given it to the Consort. And the municipality requested to see the annulled contract before it would allow the entry to be erased. The fact that the Mao and Tian families were not on friendly terms with each other did not help, and Xiang's efforts were thwarted. When the worst came to worst, he might have to bribe the chief eunuch into persuading Consort Tian to release the contract.

Xiang promised Mother that he would, upon our betrothal, give her three hundred taels of silver with which to set up a nice dowry for me, plus a gratuitous amount to her for having taken care of me. She was not a money-grubbing kind of person, but that didn't stop her from being delighted by his kind gesture. She also found great comfort in having him as her son-in-law, knowing that he could give me the protection I needed.

I could not have been more grateful to Xiang for his gracious help and was eagerly looking forward to the betrothal and wedding. My only wish now was to make him happy with my whole heart and soul. Time was not passing quickly enough. But, hope as I might for an ever after happy life, my fate had been written differently.

The day before the scheduled betrothal ceremony, loud and

urgent banging on the entrance gate wrecked the early morning peace. The parrot was shocked into a stupefied squall "Help, help, somebody!" It flapped its wings hard in frantic warning.

Mother and I were the only ones who were up. She was in the dressing lounge sewing seed pearls on my new robe, which I was to wear the next day at the betrothal dinner. I was lounging about in my sleep garment in a chair near her and reading a novel.

Hearing the commotion, she stepped out to the garden to see who was at the gate. I raced upstairs to the verandah to take a peep.

When she opened the gate, four armed men in private guard attire burst in, followed by two palace eunuchs. My heart leaped to my mouth when I saw the lumpy eunuchs, and on reflex, sprinted back into my antechamber, almost stumbling on the threshold. I banged the doors shut and bolted them.

Even in my chamber I could hear one of the eunuchs yell in a squeaky voice: "One of the Palace musicians, Chen Yuanyuan, escaped from custody. By order of Consort Tian, she is given as a slave to Minister Tian's household, as her punishment. The minister's guards are here to take her to the Tian residence now."

His shrill voice cleaved through the morning stillness to rattle the entire villa. Minister Tian Hongyu was Consort Tian's father and a former military captain in Yangzhou, now promoted to the post of Minister of War. No one in court was more powerful than he. Mother had previously warned me that he was notorious in his abuse of concubines and slaves.

Before Mother could react, the boorish men were stomping up the stairs to the private chambers to search for me. Helpless as she was, she cried out desperately to alert all the servants, but none of them dared to go near the ferocious guards, let alone try to bar them from the chambers.

The four armed men rammed open the doors of one chamber

after another, letting the eunuchs peer in to check the girls. I was trembling like a leaf when the doors of my antechamber crashed open and the eunuchs poked their heads in. I recognized their faces immediately. With ugly grins, they shrieked like hounds baying for blood, "Here she is! This is the runaway to take to your master! He'll be pleased. The whore is still crispy fresh..." Two burly guards came forward to pinion me. My head was in a wild spin. I fainted.

When I came to, I was already on a boat bound for Yangzhou. Tears trickled down my cheeks, as wicked reality struck. My heart sank to my feet. There was little chance that I would ever see Xiang, Mother or my sisters again. Despair was eating into my soul. Thank Guanyin, I had remembered to grab my birdie kerchief before I fainted.

Upon arrival at the Tian residence, the guards bundled me into a luxuriously furnished bed chamber and left. The chamber was illuminated by a tasseled silk lantern dangling from an ornately carved wooden stand. The bed sheets and quilt cover were of plush crimson silk, as were the bed curtains. For all the lavish trimmings, the chamber felt cold and eerie to me.

In my disoriented state, I heard two female voices drawing near. The more high-pitched voice said, "I've never seen such a beauty before. I'll bet Master Tian will be busy with her for a while." The other voice with a hoarse edge said in an indifferent tone, "Just as long as his fancy lasts. There are always younger and prettier girls to be had."

They came in, saw me standing awkwardly in the middle of the chamber, and said fawningly, "Mistress, we are here to serve you. Master Tian sent us to help you bathe and change. He is waiting for you in his bed chamber."

There was no escape from my destiny now. Somehow I had to prepare myself mentally for what was going to happen. My only way out was to try to dissociate my soul from my body, and to blunt my senses. I had to let my body play dead.

Before I had time to ponder further, the two maids shoved me into the alcove behind a silk screen. I was disrobed and given a wash in a tub of steaming perfumed water. After patting me dry, they dressed me in a new blush pink satin shift and brought me to my new master.

When he saw me, he raised his thick-set bulk from his seat and swaggered towards me. He lifted my face with one finger and said in a raspy voice, "You are indeed a rare beauty, just as they say. I have my daughter to thank for passing you to me. Pity you are tarnished goods. But if you please me, I might make you my private courtesan."

As soon as the maids stepped out, he roughly tore off my shift, pushed me onto the bed and forced himself on me. My heart thrashed sharply. The image of gentle Xiang flashed through my mind. On impulse, I kicked and screamed under his dead weight. But that only provoked him into a bout of violent frenzy. He bared his unsightly teeth while mauling me. I bit my lower lip and pretended the body was not mine. When he pulled himself off me and saw me wincing, he said gruffly, "Don't try to be coy with me. You're no virgin."

As the father of the Emperor's favorite, Tian was known to have used the imperial relationship to hoard a massive fortune through power abuse and extortion of commoners. His mansion was by far the most opulent in Yangzhou. Still in his prime, he kept a harem of nine concubines selected from gentry and merchant families plus three private courtesans seized from brothels, two of whom had just been downgraded to the *jiaji* status. A *jiaji* was required to entertain and bed the master's guests.

Now he was to spend his lust on me. I endured the abuse for months and waited stubbornly for news from Xiang. Never for a moment did I give up hope that he would come to my rescue. After the Palace throes, my emotions seemed to have taken on a steely armor. I was not going to look to suicide as a way out.

Whenever I ran my fingers over the birdie kerchief, into me would come some spirit too subtle to be force, too light to be strength. Yet that feathery spirit would incant in my head, "Hang on for your sisters and your mother. They are your family and they love you and want you to live!" Grasping at that faint voice, I secretly vowed to suffer my torments with stolidity. One day I just might take flight like a bird.

Two days before the Moon Festival, Xiang managed to smuggle through a letter, hidden inside a box of mooncakes which Mother sent to me.

In a few sentences he told me his rescue plan. On the day of the Festival, I was to dress in men's clothes and wait by the backyard gate on the stroke of the second night-watch gong. He knew that the Tian family had a habit of celebrating the Festival in the front garden, which would provide the distraction. At the signal of a bird call, I was to open the postern gate and he would be waiting in a cart to take me away.

That morning, I was all nerves. My worst fear was that Master Tian might want me to entertain the guests or to bed him that night. There was no problem in getting a male robe and cap, as a boy servant whom I had befriended agreed to help.

Then, my worst fear came to pass. In mid-morning, Master Tian came in and said to me,

"I have invited three court ministers to come and join us in our Festival celebrations tonight. I want you to sing two folk songs and the opera aria from *Romance of the Western Chamber*. I had earlier ordered new garments made for you. Take your pick and make yourself beautiful." Apparently, he was eager to show off his new plaything to his court peers.

He leaned closer and pinched my cheek. "The other three girls are to serve the ministers tonight. You will wait on me as usual."

I knew I had to wriggle out of this somehow. So, I pleaded with a little coyness, "I would be happy to do your bidding, Master. But, unfortunately... it's that time of the month..." His face wrinkled into a scowl, and with ill humor he said, "Then I will go to the ninth mistress tonight."

After dinner, the whole Tian family and the three guests moved to the front garden for moon viewing, refreshments and music performance.

The two *jiaji*, the other private courtesan and I were to take turn in singing, accompanied by pipa. Each of them had to sing two songs. I was to be the last performer. Cold sweat made my hands clammy as I waited for my turn.

I went through the two folks songs as hurriedly as I could. When I came almost to the end of the aria, I heard the second night-watch gong, and my fingers slipped on the strings. To my relief, no one noticed the wrong notes. At last, my singing was done.

As the reveling crowd began to mill around the tables laden with sumptuous food and drinks, I slipped quietly from the garden and scurried to the backyard. There was no time to change into men's clothes. I paced anxiously in front of the postern gate, waiting for the bird call. I opened the gate to take a peek outside. There was no cart. Aiya, I must have come too late. Xiang probably thought his letter never reached me.

But a much nastier shock was yet to come. It turned out that Master Tian had caught sight of my stealthy exit and had trailed me into the backyard. In a way it was fortuitous that Xiang and I had missed each other. Otherwise, he would have been caught too, and the consequence unthinkable.

Leaping from the shadows, he grabbed me from behind and

dragged me into his chamber. Banging the chamber doors shut, he shoved me down to the floor and began grilling me severely as to who it was that I was expecting to meet.

When I kept silent, he seized a horse whip from the shelf where he kept his riding gear and ordered me to strip. I slowly removed my robe and skirt, and knelt trembling in my undergarments. He took one look and thundered, "That time of the month, eh? How dare you little bitch lie to me?" With a savage scowl he poked the whip handle into my ribs, and bawled, "Tell me the truth, bitch!" Then lashes rained on my back.

I yelped in pain and tears. "I wasn't going to meet anyone." More lashes. To distract myself from the blistering pain, I tried to fasten my eyes and mind on the flower embroidery on the silk lantern.

Going nowhere with his questioning, he pinned me down and had his way with me. When he was done, he ordered his maid to take me back to my chamber and lock me in. I shed inward tears as despair throttled me. There was in all likelihood no hope of another rescue attempt.

As it happened, I had to stay put in my slave life for two more years.

That first whipping had probably stirred the evil in him, and my helplessness had spiked his sinister instinct to abuse me. The two months after the Moon Festival incident were the worst.

In time, though, I learned that my best weapon was faked submission. I gave up resisting, fantasized myself to be a cold-blooded snake covered in scales, and wore the expression of a statue. Then mercifully he turned his attention elsewhere. He found another young and pretty woman. I was at last allowed greater freedom of movement.

He even gave me leave to visit Mother on New Year's Day and stay to attend the second anniversary of our sisters' reunion.

During my stay at the Villa, my heart melted when Mother handed me a short letter that Xiang had left for me a few months earlier. It said something along these lines:

"My sweet Yuanyuan: Fate is a knavish ghost. But it has done nothing to blight my spirit or my love for you. Our trials have only strengthened my resolve to wait for the day of our reunion. It won't be long before Tian gets the punishment he deserves. The day he is thrown into prison will be the day we see light. You must take care of yourself and keep well. Believe that your ordeal will end soon. With undying love, Xiang."

On the day before the Lantern Festival, I had an argument with Rushi that nearly severed our relationship. Jingjing, I will go into the details of that sad day in another session.

I had never told Mother, my sisters or Xiang about Tian's perverse abuse of me. It was hard for me to say these things even to them. Jingjing, this is the first time I have let it out, and you are the first one to hear it. I think no one can speak frankly about bone-deep pain until we no longer suffer it.

*Yuanyuan stared at the swaying willows, her eyes dry and unseeing, as if emptied by suffering.*

*Jingjing kept wiping her tears with her sleeve. Aunt Yuanyuan's incredible strength of character bewildered her and tugged at her soul. A strange affinity began to bind her to this hapless woman whose very bones seemed to be drenched in pain. Yet something faintly sardonic and knowing in the set of her chin suggested that beneath the tense frailty lay a spirit as unyielding as it was pliant.*

*But, as Jingjing suspected, Yuanyuan's miseries did not end there.*

# TWELVE

*Too absorbed in Aunt Yuanyuan's story, Jingjing didn't realize it was already past noon time. At that moment, Jingli Po Po was calling out to them to come inside for lunch. Both were glad to take a break. Jingjing was looking forward to another session with the affable old lady after lunch.*

Where was I last time? Ah, I remember. Xiangjun was starting her poetry lessons with Fangyu.

Those two were really fond of each other. Since Fangyu's courtship began, Xiangjun was always skittering about like a butterfly, pink and glowing. Happy magpie would best describe her. With Fangyu's devoted tutoring, her poetry writing also began to take on his poetic tone and shades. Meanwhile, her fame as an opera aria singer grew at a gallop.

Xiaowan had her own fans, but her popularity still paled in comparison. Many young scholars were flocking from all over Jiangnan to come to hear Xiangjun sing, or just merely to gain a view of her on stage. Some wealthier ones were willing to pay me one thousand silver taels just to have tea with her. But true to her nature, she declined all such offers. One time she said to me when I told her of another such overture:

"Mother, you don't have to ask me. No amount of money is ever going to move me. My heart belongs to Fangyu alone and I will never, ever set eyes on anyone else."

"My child, I understand. When it comes to a matter of the heart, the heart knows what it wants. Now I am dreading the day when Fangyu asks for your hand in marriage," I said with a sigh, anxious at the prospect of losing a gem of a performer.

"Mother, I am just over fifteen. I promise you that I will stay at least two more years, even if Fangyu makes a proposal now."

"Whatever makes you happy, my child. I'm just glad that you and Fangyu are so devoted to each other."

While I took a liking to this shy lad, I harbored some doubts about his best friend Yang Longyou, brother-in-law of the sycophantic Ma Shiying, who was a key leader in the Ruan Dacheng cabal. Ruan was the foster son of Wei Zhongxian, the power-mongering and corrupt chief eunuch of the previous reign. Although the Chongzhen Emperor had forced Wei Zhongxian to commit suicide, the cabal remnants like Ruan were still like hungry ghosts on the prowl, waiting for the right moment to make their vicious presence felt, and they were feared. I was a bit worried that Yang Longyou might have a bad influence on Fangyu. This eunuch faction could do nothing but harm to the country.

One summer day, Fangyu came to the salon with Yang, Ma and Ruan to watch Xiangjun's performance of arias from *The Peony Pavilion*. After the performance, as usual, she left the stage to go upstairs to her chambers. Ma's and Ruan's ravenous eyes trailed her, and they started to make a rowdy scene, drunk on the rice wine which they had been downing.

"Look how seductively she sways her body!" Ma said with a thick slur. "I would pay five hundred taels of silver just to play with her little feet. Why did she leave so quickly? She should at least come and greet us. Isn't that right, Master Ruan?" Fangyu was put in a spot.

Yang hurried to explain politely, "Lady Li is habitually

disinclined to meet with the audience, because there are just too many invitations, and she doesn't want to offend anyone by selectively accepting some."

"But Fangyu is our good friend and Lady Li is his lover. I am sure Lady Li will not mind meeting her lover's friends," Ma insisted, not letting it rest.

Ruan, bleary eyed, pressed in a hoarse voice, "Fangyu, Master Ma is right. We're your friends, aren't we? I was even thinking if you would mind sharing your beautiful lover with us? Good things ought to be shared, right? Hahaha.... You can take a joke, my friend, can't you?"

The shy lad was not prepared for such teasing and was left tongue-tied, his face and neck flushed red.

"Fangyu, I'll talk straight with you. Master Ma and I know you are a literary talent. We are trying to recruit learned scholars such as you to help us build up our power base in court. The Emperor obviously needs our sound advice, and we need a good scribe to pen memorials." Ruan paused to gauge Fangyu's response. Then, clearing his throat, he continued, "He is too soft on the Revival Society traitors. For your own good, you should distance yourself from that group. If you are willing to help us, we can guarantee you a prosperous future."

Apart from being thoroughly corrupt, both Ma and Ruan were notorious lechers, keeping countless concubines and always seeking out young courtesans in the Qinhuai brothels. These good-for-nothings, if they ever laid claim to power, mercy be on us all!

I purposely avoided showing my face but I was standing behind the half-opened door of the small rehearsal chamber, to eavesdrop on their conversation.

Ruan's out-of-the-blue proposition caught Fangyu off guard, and for a moment he was stumped for words. In a diffident voice he stuttered, "Master Ruan, you flatter me too much... I'm hardly worthy... of your high praise."

At this time, Yang came to Fangyu's rescue and proffered, "This afternoon the opera *The Swallow Letter* is on at the restaurant theater down the street. You don't want to miss Zhu Chusheng's performance now, do you? Act One is starting even as we speak." The opera was adapted from a play written by Ruan himself, and he wouldn't have missed it for the world.

The two clowns heard that and, with arms round each other's shoulder, stumbled after Yang. Halfway through the audience, they mimicked in a buffoonish antic the actress's water sleeve dance, falling clumsily over each other. I almost let out a giggle.

It seemed to me that Yang genuinely wanted to help Fangyu out of a sticky situation. Maybe he had a good heart after all.

In late autumn, Fangyu came to the salon one morning with Yang, having earlier finished his examination. They didn't come inside, but only paced in the garden, as if waiting for someone or something. A little while later, Xiangjun came out to the verandah and started playing the pipa tune of an aria from *The Peony Pavilion*. The lads probably had found out somehow this was her habit. When she finished, Fangyu raised his head and addressed her in a quavering voice:

"My sweet Xiangjun, I have worshipped you from the first moment I saw you. Please indulge me and allow me to propose to you! Will you deign to be my betrothed? I'm throwing to you a token of my love, and I won't leave until you give me your answer!"

It was a customary betrothal rite in brothels for the courting man to throw to his lover a love token, and for the courtesan, if she was agreeable, to answer by throwing back some fruit.

Giggles rang out from the verandah. Other girls had gathered around Xiangjun, cheering her on. I was thinking aloud, "At last he has the good sense to propose!"

The lovesick Fangyu, looking pale and excited, was pacing back and forth, while his companion looked on good-humoredly. After a spell of what must be to him excruciating silence, I heard a girl shout: "Scholar Hou, here comes your answer!"

Then I saw him catching a small bundle wrapped in a white silk kerchief. He untied the bundle and found inside a bunch of red cherries. His face at once flushed with joy. I would later find out that his love token was an exquisite fan pendant carved from fragrant sandalwood, to match Xiangjun's nickname "Fragrant Fan Pendant". That was a thoughtful betrothal gift.

One thing that distracted me at this time was that Mao Xiang seemed to have recently softened his heart towards Xiaowan. If he became serious about her, that would kill Yuanyuan. But the problem was that Xiaowan desperately needed help to repay her father's debts. That was the reason why she was almost begging Xiang to take her as his concubine. Fate is so fond of playing bad jokes.

Soon it was the New Year. At this year's Lantern Festival, the three sisters would be celebrating their second anniversary. Strangely, I had been having an ominous feeling about this year's gathering. But festive activities kept me distracted.

Having gotten permission from Master Tian, Yuanyuan arrived on New Year's Day and stayed for the reunion, which was just two days away. Rushi would be arriving any time now.

It was our customary practice to close the salon from the New Year's Day to the day after the Lantern Festival fifteen days later. Many of our performers and apprentices would, as a matter of custom, go back to their hometowns for New Year family reunions.

"Big Sister is here! Welcome! Serve tea! Serve tea!" The parrot announced in a cheery squeal. "There are five more guests! Serve tea! Serve tea!"

I was in the dining lounge making ready for our afternoon refreshments. On one of the smaller tables I laid out plates of lightly fried turnip cakes, taro cakes and red bean cakes.

"I'm in the dining lounge," I shouted, while heating up water to brew my favorite Snow Orchid tea. One of our patrons, Master Zhang Dai, grew this specialty tea in his Happiness Garden at the foothills of Dragon Mountain. He was kind enough to indulge me with gifts of the precious tea leaves every year.

As soon as Rushi came in, I sensed that something was wrong. She was wearing all white and had a white flower in her hair. Her face was haggard and tear-stained. My heart sank. I knew it must be Xu Fo. I went up to her and hugged her, which touched off a flood of tears.

I understood well how intimate the bond was between her and Fo. It must be such a crushing blow to her. But she looked more broken than I imagined she would be. I had a hunch she had gone through something unspeakable, other than deep grief over Fo's death, but then it didn't feel like the right moment to ask.

In a dispirited and hoarsened voice she said, "I have brought Fo's girls here in the hope that you would be kind enough to take them under your wing. They are in the reception hall. I have been trying to sell Fo's villa and her more valuable belongings, but haven't found a buyer yet. For your trouble, I will give you all the proceeds from the estate sales." She paused to take a breath.

With a deep sigh, she sniffled, "If I am ever to have a normal life, safe from Xie Sanbin's reach, I have to make a clean break with my past and forge a way out of the rut."

Noting her plight, and knowing the young girls were

excellent *guqin* players, I gave no second thought to her request and immediately agreed to accommodate them in my salon. I instructed a servant to help them set up pallet beds in the larger rehearsal lounge and serve them our festive food.

I understood well Rushi's way of thinking. Seeking a safe refuge from Xie's predatory claws must be first priority now. And this would be impossible if she remained a courtesan in Songjiang. She desperately needed a man's protection.

At this moment, Xiangjun and Yuanyuan came in together, and after being told the sad news, each hugged Rushi in turn. As devastated as I felt about Fo's passing, I was determined not to let sadness ruin the little time we could have together as a family.

To lighten the mood, I told Yuanyuan and Rushi the sweet story of how Xiangjun and Fangyu had met, become teacher and student, and had just become betrothed.

"Ah, I've heard of the name Hou Fangyu," said Rushi. "He's an up-and-coming icon of the Revival Society. I'm really happy for you, Xiangjun." She tried to sound as upbeat as she could.

"I am dreading the day that my dear Xiangjun will leave me. She's sweet to have promised that she would stay for two more years," I said.

"But Mother, you still have Xiaowan as a lead performer even if Xiangjun leaves. I've heard that she's getting more and more popular," Yuanyuan said with a palpably sour note.

From the day she had arrived, she had been keeping much to herself and would not even talk to Xiangjun, let alone me. I had asked her whether the Tian family had been treating her well, and she had given a curt and blunt answer, "As well as could be expected," her face rigid like marble.

"That's true," I replied. "But Xiaowan will never be another Xiangjun. Talking of Xiaowan, she's become quite distracted lately, like she's after someone... Oh, that reminds me, Yuanyuan,

I have a letter for you from Xiang. He left it with me three months ago. Let me go and get it for you."

As soon as I handed her the letter, she devoured it, blushing a pretty pink. Xiangjun, who was in a playful mood, snatched the letter from her sister, jesting: "It's family time. No man is allowed in our company!"

Yuanyuan, almost in tears, snapped in a raspy voice, "Give it back to me! It's mine!" She sounded as if someone had pinched a raw nerve in her.

"Alright, I was just teasing you. No need to be so serious!" Xiangjun protested.

"Come now, Yuanyuan, Xiangjun didn't mean any harm.... Look what delicious food Jingli is serving us! I have been craving for her famous taro cakes. Let's show our appreciation and dig in!" Rushi tried to divert attention to the food. She, too, seemed taken aback by Yuanyuan's over-reaction.

That night, while alone with Rushi, I told her about Xiaowan's plight and her desperate appeal to Xiang for help. Her father's creditors were now threatening to sell her to a brothel.

In response, Rushi disclosed her plan to persuade Yuanyuan to give up Xiang, leaving an option open for General Wu. I could see her reason for doing this. It sounded like a sensible solution to the present triangle between Yuanyuan, Mao Xiang and Xiaowan.

Rushi said she was going to talk to Yuanyuan the next morning, requesting my presence. When I looked into her eyes, they betrayed a melancholy that was too deep to fathom.

But I could never foresee that her well-meant suggestion to solve the love triangle would nearly rupture her sisterly bond with Yuanyuan.

Jingjing, Aunt Yuanyuan will tell you what was said between her and Rushi that morning.

*At this point, Jingli Po Po stopped and yawned a big yawn, her eyelids half drooping. The sun's oblique rays through the latticed window announced it was near supper time. Jingjing didn't want to tire the old lady unduly and said, "I'm famished." Earlier, she had already had rose-flavored pastries made by her aunt for tea. She had come to love Jingli Po Po's cooking so much that she was always ready to eat. The old lady was only too happy to indulge her.*

# THIRTEEN

*THINGS NOW FELL into a pattern with the story-telling. Aunt Yuanyuan would run morning sessions while Jingli Po Po would take up the afternoons. In their respective free time, Jingli would work in her vegetable and fruit patch in the backyard, and Yuanyuan would tend to her flowers in the side garden.*

*In the evenings, the three would have a light supper, usually of rice, stir-fried eggs with bean sprouts or chives, fried taro patties and stir-fried mushrooms and vegetables. Jingjing always savored these simple dishes cooked by Jingli. After supper, they would either do needlework together or retreat to solitary reading in their chambers.*

*This morning, Aunt Yuanyuan had breakfast laid out for two when Jingjing stepped into the rear lounge. They would usually have congee and stir-fried noodles for breakfast. Jingli Po Po would often skip breakfast. After eating, as usual, aunt and niece took their seats under the willows.*

*Facing the older woman, Jingjing noticed for the first time the mesmeric beauty of her aunt's big dark eyes, eyes so incandescent that they seemed to have drunk in all natural light around her. It was easy to get lost in their luster.*

The morning following Rushi's arrival, Mother prepared and served a simple breakfast of rice congee and deep-fried wheat dough.

Having read Xiang's letter the previous day, I had had a good night's sleep, which was a rare luxury for me these days. As long as Xiang was willing to wait for me, I would not give up hope. But a part of me was still mired in anguish.

Over breakfast, the four of us chatted about the garden's newest addition, a beautiful blossoming peach tree in a large clay pot placed just outside the lounge entrance. It was a New Year gift from Fangyu, now Xiangjun's betrothed.

I thought of my would-be betrothal the previous year. What a hugely divergent fate for me and her! In one or two years she would be happily married to the man she dearly loved. What I had in front of me was an eternal grind of demeaning servitude. Could any of them understand what I had to endure?

You see, Jingjing, it is not that I had anything against Xiangjun being happy. But at that moment I just resented the heavens for playing me such an unfair hand.

"Fangyu is coming to take me for a boat ride, so I have to excuse myself," Xiangjun beamed. The exhilaration in her voice almost grated my ears. However hard I tried, I just could not squeeze a smile on my face.

After she left, Mother said to me softly, "Yuanyuan, there is something Rushi would like to talk to you about."

"Yuanyuan, while I was in Hangzhou, I met a retired courtesan named Wang Wei. She knows General Wu Sangui very well and she told me that he, being a good friend of the Tian family, is the one who might be able to persuade Master Tian to give you up. She has recently shown him a picture of you and he appears interested. He has agreed to consider Madam Wang's suggestion. This could be a good chance to get you freed from Tian's clutches." Rushi looked at me and waited eagerly for my response.

My emotional state being jittery as it was, I took her words badly and said in a grumpy tone,

"I don't care if General Wu is interested in me or not. I am not interested in him. Xiang is my only love and unless he tells me to my face that he doesn't love me, I will not give him up."

Rushi looked at Mother for a moment, as if to ask for help. Then Mother said to me,

"Yuanyuan, I know this is going to hurt, but I have to let you know the truth. Xiang has indeed indicated that he doesn't see a future with you, the situation being what it is. He realizes there is no way that he could wrest you from Master Tian."

That was a hard punch on my stomach. I could not believe my ears. "But what about his letter?" I almost screamed. "He said he would wait for me!"

After a while, Mother said cautiously, "He wrote that three months ago, right after the failed rescue attempt. The purpose of his letter was to keep your spirits up. But Xiaowan took seriously ill a little after that, and then Xiang felt...great compassion for the poor girl."

At the mention of Xiaowan, I couldn't keep it down any more. I felt like a hurt animal being cornered.

"What are you all conspiring to do? Do you mean to break us up? Why are you taking Xiaowan's side? Xiang loves me! He is the best thing that has ever happened to me." Then I aimed my vitriol at Rushi, trying my best to prick her, "Didn't you say you loved Zilong? How could you give him up? You think you can trade up, don't you? Do you even know what love means?"

At the mention of Zilong, Rushi's eyes immediately turned red. Mother was piqued and said severely, "Stop saying what you don't mean, Yuanyuan!"

"Yuanyuan, we are not taking Xiaowan's side. She is in a pitiable state. If she can't find a way to repay her father's debts, the creditors will seize her and sell her to a brothel." Rushi tried to explain the situation to me. But I couldn't take it in.

"So I should be sacrificed in order that she may be saved? Rushi, I am your sworn sister. She is not. Does our vow still hold?" As soon as I spurted out the barbed words, I regretted them.

"It's not like that at all, Yuanyuan. Rushi means well. She was hoping her suggestion could solve at once Xiaowan's problem and yours. And you are too rash in judging Rushi. You don't understand things between her and Zilong..." Mother tried her best to straighten things out, but to no avail.

In truth, I understood full well Rushi's pain at losing Zilong, but I was just too embittered to care what I was saying.

"Yuanyuan, only General Wu has the power to give you a new lease on life. Think about that! I was only thinking of your welfare as your big sister... And you could at the same time be a life-saver to Xiaowan if you just let Xiang rescue her." She chose to ignore my puerile verbal assault on her.

I wish I had had the courage to tell them of my fiendish sufferings at the Tian household, but shame held me back. A deep sense of isolation swallowed me up whole. I blurted out the most hurtful words I could think of,

"So you think you can play the Goddess of Mercy now? There is true love between Xiang and me. But what do you care? You lost your love, and you want to see me lose mine!"

On hearing those bladelike words, Rushi turned her head away, to hide her tears.

"Stop it!" Mother raised her voice in anger. "That is the most unfair thing to say of Rushi." She had never raised her voice to me before.

I felt so trapped and unloved that the thought of slitting my wrists crossed my mind for a flicker of a moment. My treasured hope, or fantasy, was shattered. Who else could I lash out at?

As things stood then, the three of us were totally drained

from the emotional outbursts. There seemed no way out. So we retreated to our own chambers with hearts wounded.

Yes, words can cut like a knife. How I wished I could take back the brutal words I said that morning. But I was not to have a chance to apologize to Rushi until the night before her wedding. And I would not find out about the Xie Sanbin rape until that night, which fact would heap more guilt on me and make my apology appear almost trivial.

On the Lantern Festival day, the three of us had more or less collected ourselves. But pride and shame kept me from offering an apology there and then. I let the chance slip by when Rushi approached me to ask for my kerchief to embroider the new Zodiac sign. Xiangjun could probably sense that something was wrong, but was in too happy a mood to let it bother her.

With Mother's permission, she had invited Fangyu to our reunion dinner.

Now that I was my calmer self, I could see what a handsome couple they made. Xiangjun and I had gone through thick and thin together and she was like my twin sister. As dejected as I felt, I held my chin up and wished them a happy life together. Remembering that I was wearing a sapphire butterfly hairpin in my hair, I unclasped it and gave it to Xiangjun as her wedding gift.

Thanks to Mother, who was always the affectionate glue among us, we were able to enjoy our excellent reunion dinner, over which our warm familial ties were once again renewed. I knew very well they had forgiven me, even if I did not have the good sense to apologize to them.

The next morning, while packing my clothing to get ready to return to Yangzhou, someone knocked lightly on my chamber door. I opened the door, and there stood Xiang, looking florid and elegant in his impeccable scholar attire, but in a sullen mood.

It felt like we had separated for a lifetime, and he might as well be an apparition in that instant. The veil of tension between us was as thick as a wall, as each tried hard to find appropriate words to say. I hardly knew how I felt. Surprised? Excited? Heartbroken? Desperate? Or all those feelings mixed together?

At long last, he broke the silence:

"Yuanyuan, I am so happy to see you again. How have you been?"

Those simple words unhinged me, like letting loose a herd of wild bulls. It took a while for me to settle down. Then I looked him in the eye and said in as coherent a manner as I could manage,

"I read your letter. Please tell me if you meant what you said. I need to know."

His face turned red as he faltered, "Yuanyuan, the love I feel for you will... never change. If I had any means of....... tackling Tian, do you think I would not try? But he happens to be the Emperor's father-in-law. My family is not even close to being a match for the Tians, in power and in wealth. Did you think I would willingly let you go? But we must face reality. We are stuck."

I took in every word of his with smarting pain. The reality was hewn in stone. My mind was clearer this morning and I knew it was time for me to accept it, for everyone's sake.

"Can you hold me one last time and tell me again that you love me?" I said slowly, my eyes begging him.

He took me into his arms, breaking down in tears. "You will always be the one I love, Yuanyuan! You have to believe me," he whispered in my ears. Then he kissed me feverishly on my mouth. I led him by the hand to my bed.

As I yielded to him, I tried hard to etch on my memory his every facial expression, his every caress, his smell and his sound.

The impressions would be saved in the storehouse of my mind, to be used as a salve for all my future sufferings.

"Please don't forget me, Yuanyuan! I will never forget you in this life, I swear! I will find you and make you mine in our next life." His soft whisper sounded like a balmy chant, and was what I would give my life to hear. There was nothing more that I could ask of him.

Looking deep into his eyes, I said, "My love, you will always reside in the temple of my heart, for as long as I live. You don't know how eternally grateful I felt when you accepted me even when dishonor had ruined me. No one else can ever take your place. If you want to take Xiaowan as your concubine, you have my blessing. Do whatever you can to help her." Those were my last words to him before we parted that day.

Once back at the Tian mansion, I resumed the life of an imprisoned snake, cold blooded and unfeeling.

In early summer, Master Tian demoted me to *jiaji* status, which meant that I was no longer free to leave the house, especially during the busy New Year festivities, as all *jiaji* were expected to stand by at all times to entertain guests.

The demotion was something I had expected, and it neither irked nor agitated me. I just accepted it as a part of my ill fate. If anything, I was actually feeling thankful that Master Tian had finally tired of me.

But, as someone no longer in his favor, I had to tread even more carefully. If I displeased him or his guests in any way, punishment would be a dose of flogging and demotion to housemaid status. I had heard the chilling story of how one of his *jiaji* had played a wrong note in front of an esteemed guest and been flogged half to death.

I wrote to Rushi and Mother and Xiangjun telling them about

the demotion. Rushi replied asking me to be patient, as General Wu was busy with a military campaign and would most likely come for me around the New Year.

The remaining months of the year passed more quickly than I had expected. Soon, it was the New Year. I asked a servant to deliver a note to Mother to say I could not join my sisters for reunion this year, as domestic duties kept me from going. I wouldn't want them to worry about me.

On the day of the Lantern Festival, a profound sense of homesickness crept up on me. I took out my birdie kerchief and fingered the lovely birds, as my mind dwelled fondly on past gatherings. Lost in nostalgia, I didn't realize my maid was at the door. She blurted out with a lisp that Master Tian wanted me to perform for a General Wu at dinner time, and bolted away.

At the mention of the General's name, I jerked into alertness. I had waited for him for so long that I had nearly given up hope. My heart thumped wildly as vague flashes of a new life ahead wakened my senses.

I immediately went about preparing a perfumed hot bath. Much as my present status afforded me the service of a maid, I would always do menial tasks myself as far as I could, just to avoid arousing ill feelings among the maids.

After the bath, I stood in front of the bronze mirror and took a good look at my face and body. I would soon be sixteen and my body was a ripe womanly form, rounded with smooth curves. This face had arrested the heart and soul of the most handsome and talented scholar in Jiangnan. Would I be able to capture General Wu's heart? That was a question that I did not have the nerve to answer. Yet my one chance of escape from bondage rested on my affirmative reply.

Having dressed in a light pink silk robe paired with a pale blue pleated skirt, I carefully applied rouge to my cheeks and powdered my face, highlighting my eyebrows with *qingdai*, and stained my lips with cherry paint. To achieve a more mature look, I coiled my hair into a knot at the nape of my neck, leaving tendrils around the temple. Finally, I inserted the pink jade tasseled hairpin into my hair for good fortune, as I was hoping this gift from my cheerful sister could bring me a better fate.

When I appeared in the dining lounge, Master Tian and General Wu were already downing their second round of rice wine. From the sumptuousness of the dishes being served, which included birds' nest soup with ginseng, steamed garoupa with black fungus, roasted quail, spicy prawns, and stewed partridges, I could tell that General Wu was an honored guest. Apparently I was the only *jiaji* summoned to perform for this venerated guest.

Usually when Master Tian received important guests like the general, the women in his harem above *jiaji* status would not be allowed to join the meal. That was why I had never had a chance to meet him on his previous visits.

Seated on a wooden stool placed a few steps from the table, I began to strum my pipa and sing a light-hearted folk song. I would always sing folk songs during the meal, and reserve the popular aria from *Romance of the Western Chamber* for the end of the meal, when the guests' attention was no longer on the food.

During the intermission between two songs, I couldn't help stealing quick glances at the general. One time, my eyes met his as he was taking a sidelong gaze at me, which sent a deep blush to my cheeks instantly. I lowered my head at once. Master Tian detected the guest's interest and said to me, "Sing your aria for the general now! It's his favorite!" So I did as I was ordered.

As I went through the lilting tune, I infused it with passion. People like Tian couldn't tell one song from another, let alone appreciate the artistic value of one. For him, the most sublime tune and lyrics would probably be no different from a dish of roasted duck.

I was wondering what effect my song might have on the general. He seemingly knew the aria well, as he kept time with the tune by tapping his feet, while continuing to eat. The host was obviously more absorbed in the food. When I came to the end, I noticed a softness creep up on the general's angular face. His eyes glistened beneath his bushy eyebrows.

As a valiant general, he had fought numerous vicious battles, a fact easily gleaned from the scars both old and new on his face. Music would be the last thing such a brawny man would care about. Yet he appeared deeply touched by the song I sang, which was about thwarted love.

As I was musing, a round of hand-clapping broke my train of thought. Hazily, I heard Master Tian speak fawningly to his guest,

"Sangui, don't flatter her. It's her duty to sing well. If you like, I'll have her dance for us later. But come, let us have more food and wine." He waved the maid to refill the wine chalices and insisted that the guest take another helping of steamed fish.

"What is her name, Hongyu?" the guest asked casually.

"She's called Yuanyuan, surnamed Chen. One of my *jiaji*. She had the gall to offend my daughter, and so ended up being my slave," the host said in contempt. When the guest kept silent, he sheepishly changed the subject, "Let's talk about more serious things. Sangui, do you think the peasant rebels will reach Yangzhou any time soon?"

"As far as I can tell, the mob will probably target Luoyang and Kaifeng in a few months. I would say Yangzhou is safe for now."

"Ah, my sentinel's report tallies with your estimate. Those damned peasants! I wish I could get the Emperor to send me more troops. I have already petitioned His Imperial Highness several times, but he is just playing deaf."

"I always thought you had enough troops at your command..."

"Numbers are no use when it comes to fighting battles. Unlike your troops, mine are untrained, and we lack weapons."

"It is true that our various skirmishes with the Manchus have sharpened my Liaodong garrison. My soldiers are all devilish combatants. But I've heard that Shi Kefa is a brilliant general, and he will be put in charge of Yangzhou. Why don't you request help from him?"

"I wouldn't think of it. Aiya, Shi is a stubborn blockhead who does everything by the book, and he doesn't care one whit about court politics." Tian paused and leaned over to the guest, continuing in a low voice, "Actually, I was hoping to drill my private troops so that they are up to the task of protecting my properties. If you could be so kind as to lend me some weapons and a few of your veteran captains to train up my men, I would be forever indebted to you."

"I see.... I'll see what I can do....that should not be a big problem..." the general replied with a slight grimace, appearing bored. He then cocked his head and set his burning gaze on me. Tian saw that and quickly went off on a tangent.

"Ah, to hell with the peasants and the Manchus!" he said. "Come, General, have another cup of wine, and let's enjoy the rest of the evening. Yuanyuan can do the fan dance really well. You'll love it!" He then clapped his hands to signal his order to me, and bade the maid to serve wine and sweet red bean paste dumplings.

I had expected to be asked to dance for the guest, and had brought with me two purple folding silk fans with fluffy down borders. The other *jiaji*, who was standing by to play the pipa accompaniment, sat down on the stool that I had vacated and started strumming.

Timed to the music, I started to twirl slowly in front of the two spectators, and flutter the two fans in a semi-circling motion, hiding and showing my face in a mildly coquettish way. I wavered the silk fans like I was guiding two large butterflies around me, while pirouetting and spinning around the room. From time to time, I would bend my waist to strike a seductive pose.

This was one of the dances that Xiangjun and I had been taught at the thin-horse breeder's, and I was acclaimed the best fan dancer. Poor Xiangjun had bound feet and had dreaded the dancing lessons. I had escaped the ordeal as my mother had died when I was a toddler.

As the music came to an end, I did one final swirl and dropped to my knees, bowing my head low. My stealthy glance at the general fell on his hypnotized gaze. He looked much like a life-size bronze statue, if not for his rubicund complexion.

I threw him a quick smile, which I knew he caught. He responded with a bright smile: "You have a nightingale's voice and dance like Zhao Feiyan!" I blushed, keeping my head down, lest he might find me too eager to throw myself at him.

The signs seemed to say that he did bite the bait. But I still couldn't help dithering between hope and doubt. Did it bother him that I was a lowly *jiaji*? Did he see me as damaged goods? On my part, I would not care a straw if he was to make me as his slave courtesan or *jiaji*. All I cared was that he was willing to take me away from Tian.

From what I had earlier eavesdropped on, there was little doubt that Master Tian would be ready to exchange me for General Wu's help with fortifying his private troops. But would the general find the deal attractive enough to accept? This tormenting toss between a vague triumph, premised on my flimsy vanity, and deeply ingrained low self-esteem, kept my mood in flux in the following months.

By mid-year, Tian's harem abounded with gossip that the Master would soon be casting me out of his household. The hearsay circulated with the slightest hint of jealousy, though, as it was also rumored that he was planning to give me away in a wedding, complete with a dowry.

One month before my formal wedding to General Wu, Master Tian adopted me as his foster daughter in a prominent ritual, so that my marriage would make him a foster father-in-law. During the adoption rite, Tian ceremoniously signed the annulment of my bond contract in front of the whole household, and ordered a house servant to go to the magistrate to have my name erased from the entertainers register. He even asked his wife to plan the wedding feast and send invitations to Mother and my sisters.

In the wake of the General's promised help to protect his estates, all this trouble would have been well worth it. But obviously, outsiders would need to know that charity was at the heart of his fuss over me.

That night I stayed awake until dawn. At last my jitters of the past months were laid to rest. But, as if lost in a strange Shangri La, I teetered between adventurous excitement and too-good-to-be-true fear. What would life be like with General Wu as my husband? Would he treat me well? Somehow I couldn't bring myself to believe that I was going to be the primary concubine of this military dignitary. I dared not fall asleep, lest I should wake from my magical dream.

I got out of bed, lit the oil lamp on the dressing table, and began writing to Mother and Xiangjun and Rushi telling them about the good news and the arrangements for the wedding day.

Both the tea-offering ceremony and the wedding feast would take place in the main lounge of the Tian residence on the fifteenth day of the sixth lunar month. Mother, Xiangjun and

Rushi were to come one day before the wedding to help with the ritual of "combing the bride's hair", and to stay the night.

On the wedding day, Mother would preside over the tea-offering ceremony, along with Master Tian and his wife. On the third day after the wedding, General Wu and I would go back as a wedded couple to the Villa of Alluring Fragrance to bring Mother bridal gifts. He and I would be staying temporarily in his resort lodge in Yangzhou. A new three-bay house was under construction on his Beijing property, which would be our permanent home.

In my letter to Rushi, I mentioned that I would be wearing the wedding garments on which she had embroidered pairs of mandarin ducks for me. I just wished that the groom was Xiang.

As my brush flew up and down the sheet, I didn't forget Xiang. My next letter was to him, telling him that finally I could look forward to a free life, and wishing him and Xiaowan a happy life together.

*At this point, Jingjing shed a tear of joy for Aunt Yuanyuan's hard won break. She wished with all her heart that General Wu would treat her aunt well, even as she sensed more hazards still lay ahead. Yuanyuan took a sip of jasmine tea to moist her throat. Then they heard Jingli Po Po's lunch call. It was time for recess.*

*As Jingli Po Po was having a visitor in the afternoon, her session would be cancelled.*

*After lunch, Jingjing continued with reading her mother's memoir.*

# FOURTEEN

AFTER READING Fo's will for a second time, I stared into the space before me, my thoughts whirling and wheeling. There was such a lot to be done. Finding a burial ground and setting up a tombstone was among the priorities. On top of the chores at hand, fear constantly taunted me. I prayed that no one from Xie Sanbin's household would take notice of my return.

Vaguely conscious that the other task was to find a buyer for Fo's villa and her more valuable belongings like her paintings, because I needed to raise funds to pay Jingli for taking up Fo's girls, I thought of writing to Zilong for help. I was hoping that when the Lantern Festival came around, I would have the proceeds to take to Jingli, along with the girls.

I took up the brush, and then put it down. Was it wise to make contact with him? I ruminated for a long time. Finally, prudence suppressed my emotional urge. I knew that if I got so much as even a few words from him, they would kindle the flame of desire again.

He was as much shackled by Confucian duties as I was pilloried by social scorn, which sadly arose from the same mountain of millennia-old class and gender biases. A pedantic scholar family would loathe accepting a courtesan into their household as a proper concubine. This proved true with both Song Zhengyu and Chen Zilong. The only difference between the two affairs was that there was genuine passion and respect between myself and Zilong, whereas it was absent with Zhengyu.

On the third morning after my return, with the help of the girls, I bought an expensive coffin made with the finest Liuzhou sandalwood. That was the least I could do in Fo's honor. But a pang of guilt and shame pricked me at the thought of having buried my own mother in only a straw mat. After brooding in sorrow for a long time, I was eventually resigned to the fact that what had been done could not be undone.

In the afternoon, with a burial land broker's help, we found and bought a small piece of burial ground on which two graves could be accommodated – one for Fo and one for my mother. For a small fee, the broker agreed to handle the inscription engraving for both tomb tablets. The land was on a quiet hillock shaded by a bamboo thicket, within walking distance of the villa.

Two days later, in late morning, the girls and I attended a simple burial rite conducted by two Buddhist monks. I knew Fo would have wanted this.

The long-missed winter sun smiled down on the hard frosted earth, melting away some of the bitter cold of the previous day. All dressed in white, we burned incense sticks and joss paper as coffin bearers lowered the coffin into the pit. Each of us scooped up a handful of loose soil and threw it on top of the coffin. The coffin bearers filled the pit with mounds of earth while the monks chanted the Lotus Sutra.

Into the shallow pit of my mother's grave I threw the lock of her hair that I had kept all these years. Then I filled up the pit using my hands. I lit three sticks of incense in front of the tomb tablet, knelt and bowed three times. The girls also came up to pay their respects. I prayed that both Fo and Mother were now resting in peace.

That afternoon, I went to Fo's chamber to go through her stuff and found among her writings a pile of unsent letters, all addressed to Wen. It suddenly dawned on me that Wen had not been informed of Fo's passing. Then I took a look at her fine paintings, among which I found a small portrait of myself in sketch. I was thinking that perhaps I should not sell her paintings and should give Wen all of Fo's letters and paintings for him to keep, except for my portrait.

After wrapping up the paintings and letters and putting them in a cloth sack, I went to my chamber to don a scholar's robe and to put on the cloth cap.

I waited till dusk to set out on foot for Wen's cottage, which was about mid-way between Fo's villa and Zilong's South Villa, off the main carriageway on the quiet rustic side of town. On the way, I looked over my shoulder every now and then to check if I was being followed. In less than half a joss stick's burning time, I was at the doorstep of Wen's sparsely-furnished home.

He recognized me at once, as he had seen me in scholars' clothing before.

"I haven't seen you for a long time, Rushi!" Wen asked in his usual good-natured voice, "How has life been treating you? What wind has brought you here?" He seated me in the more comfortable of two chairs, the padded one made with wicker. The two flickering candles on the single table in the dingy lounge threw undefined shadows on the bare clay walls. He busied himself heating water to make tea, in a small alcove off the lounge that he used as kitchen.

"I am afraid I bear sad tidings, Wen," I proceeded cautiously, not knowing when he and Fo had last seen each other. His hand rested still on the lid of the earthen jar of tea leaves.

"Fo passed away seven days ago. I heard the news five days ago while I was in Hangzhou, and I rushed back at once." In the dim light, his gaunt silhouette seemed to freeze in a heartbeat into a stone sculpture. Moments later, he came out of the daze to continue with the tea-making. When he served me a cup of hot tea, his face was contorted with grief and his eyes glistened with tears.

I was wondering, had Fo gone all out with her love while alive, would he have suffered more, or less, now? With that thought, my tears welled up.

Having somewhat regained my composure, I retrieved the contents from the cloth sack.

"Fo is now in repose in the hillside bamboo copse a short distance from here, to the north," I said tearfully. "I think she would like you to have these."

On the sight of the familiar handwriting, tears began trickling down his cheek. I waited patiently for him to collect himself.

When he calmed down, I said softly, "I have a favor to ask of you, Wen. Only you can help me now. I am trying to find a buyer for Fo's villa. Do you know anyone in your circles who might have an interest? My plan is to ask Jingli to take up Fo's girls, and as compensation I'll give her the proceeds from the property sale, and then I will probably go back to Hangzhou."

"I know a wealthy merchant by the name of Wang Ranming from the poetry club. He lives near the West Lake and is known for his generosity and philanthropic deeds. He was the one who donated a lodge to Wang Wei when she was so depressed. I think if you go and approach him in the right way, he is sure to lend you a helping hand."

"Actually I was staying at Wang Wei's lodge while I sojourned in Hangzhou. I could ask her to introduce me to Master Wang then."

"Ah, that's perfect. Why did you stay in Hangzhou for so long, if I may ask?"

"You've probably heard of Xie Sanbin. Well, he had been a stalker and a pest at Fo's salon operation for nearly a year. I had no other option but to go in hiding for a while." Close friends that we were, I still couldn't bring myself to reveal to him the sordid part of the story.

"I hadn't been in touch with Fo for over a year. She seemed…. so determined….. to keep her distance. But I just couldn't get her out of my mind," he said with a lump in his throat.

"I am sure whatever misunderstanding there had been between you and Fo, you will be able to find your answers in Fo's letters. Know this, Wen, she loved no one but you, and deeply, right up to her last breath. She confided that much in her last letter to me."

On hearing those words, his eyes brimmed with tears again. Then something dawned on him and he said with spirit, "Oh, I almost forgot to tell you. Wang Ranming is the publisher of your collection of poems to which Zilong wrote the preface. Did Zilong tell you that? Now I'm sure Old Wang will be pleased to meet you."

"He may have, but I didn't pay any attention. Wen, as always, you are such a big help to me. I can't thank you enough for this."

As the New Year was just a month away, I decided to delay my trip to Hangzhou until after the Lantern Festival. First I needed to persuade Jingli to take up Fo's girls. So I traveled with them in tow to Nanjing for the Festival.

Jingli consented to sheltering the girls, and I felt like a big rock had been lifted from my mind. But I never for one moment dared forget Fo's last wish for me to help Xiaowan. All the time I had been thinking that Wang Wei's suggestion was the perfect solution, as much for Yuanyuan's sake as for Xiaowan's.

Obviously, my optimism was misplaced. The day after my arrival at Jingli's villa, I revealed Wang Wei's plan to Yuanyuan, in the presence of Jingli. I must say I didn't see it coming. Yuanyuan's irascible reaction to the plan caught me by surprise.

I could understand her commitment to Mao Xiang, but how I wished she could see that that was a dead end. There seemed to be something that was gnawing her insides but she couldn't bring herself to utter it. It was not hard, though, to conjecture that being a slave courtesan at Tian's could be anything but misery.

So I tried to ignore her cutting words and just put the case before her as plainly as I could. But that is not to say I didn't feel hurt. Nothing mattered more to me than her well-being, which was her freedom from slavery. But somehow she seemed dismissive of my good intentions. Still, I was hopeful that she would eventually come round to realizing what was best for her future.

Fortunately, with Jingli's careful handling, our reunion dinner still turned out to be a joyful occasion. We were all so happy to have Fangyu join us as Xiangjun's betrothed.

The next morning, both Jingli and I were pleasantly surprised by Xiang's appearance. As the saying goes, the one who ties the knot is the one who can untie it. If anyone could persuade Yuanyuan to face reality, it would without a doubt be Xiang. By the time he was ready to leave, we saw a much more relaxed expression on Yuanyuan's face. I prayed to Guanyin that General Wu would take up the good cause to deliver her from slavery.

I returned to Songjiang with a much lighter heart than when I had left it. To make the villa more presentable to buyers, I spent the next few days clearing out junk and cleaning the spaces. Then I dismissed two of the three servants, keeping Ah Luk as my boatman. I packed my personal belongings and headed to Hangzhou in my boat.

As soon as I stepped inside Wang Wei's lodge, she told me that Master Wang Ranming had left an invitation for me to pay him a visit, as he had received a letter of introduction from Li Wen.

"Master Wang is one of the wealthiest and most charitable merchants in Hangzhou." She then said in a burst of energy, "I am forever indebted to him for this lodge, which he had gifted me when I was homeless and most of my patrons and friends had deserted me. His one obsession is beautiful pleasure boats. Several years back he built himself a large craft with lush trimmings. It's moored on the bank of West Lake, near the West Bridge, and he has since lived in it. He has named it 'Untethered Villa'. Qianyi is a very close friend of his."

I lost no time, and on the next day went to Master Wang's floating abode to pay him a visit. His opulent pleasure craft was about four times the size of my boat and was fitted with three large cabins, the middle one serving as the sitting lounge, the one at the prow as the dining area with an annexed kitchen and the one at the stern as the bed chamber and study.

I was received in the ornate lounge furnished with silk-quilted divans and a red wood table with beautifully carved legs. White silk gauze curtains billowed over the carved railings and the cabin front. A light aloeswood scent pervaded the whole cabin. A housemaid sauntered in and served me Snow Orchid tea, fresh plums and sweetmeats.

When Wang saw me, he appeared delighted and greeted me warmly. For his advanced age, he moved with the agility of a forty-year old and he wore a jaunty grin on his white-bearded face. I could glean from the paintings hung on the back board of the cabin that he was a connoisseur. He looked at me steadily and said with a glint in his eyes,

"I have heard so much about you, my dear child, and I finally have the pleasure of meeting you!"

"The pleasure is all mine, Master Wang! I should have paid you a visit long ago to thank you for publishing my poetry. I owe you a big debt of gratitude!"

"I should thank you and Zilong for the business you brought me. How I admire the talent of you both! But I have also heard of the sad news of your separation. Sorry though I am, my advice to you is to let bygones be bygones." Pausing, he picked up his cup of tea and gestured for me to take mine. "We have to get on with life somehow, true? Beautiful women with brains like you are rare. Don't you worry about suitors! I would be most happy to do match-making for you! In fact, let me tell you that you have one smitten secret admirer!" He beamed with a good-natured guffaw, smoothing his long white beard with one hand, his eyes gleaming with mischief.

I could not deny that his natural disarming ways were quickly winning me over. I blushed as I replied,

"Thank you so much for your very kind words, Master Wang. I'm not sure that I deserve your praise. But right now I have a more urgent matter to deal with than thinking about suitors, and I was wondering if you could possibly oblige me with a favor."

"I've learned from Li Wen's letter that you would want to find a buyer for Xu Fo's villa, is that not true? That's just a triviality. Consider it done. I'll have my book keeper take care of that in a couple of days, if you would just let me have the key to the property. I don't mind having another riverside property to rent out. If you need the funds urgently, I could even advance the money to you right now."

"Oh, no, it's not that urgent! I can't thank you enough for your help! I am really, really grateful! Here's the key to Fo's villa."

"This is just a business deal. Please don't consider this as a great favor from me. I hate taking credit when it's not due. Now, back to the matter of your suitors. How do you feel about Qianyi, I wonder?"

His out-of-the-blue question stumped me, and I was at a loss for an answer. I was thinking, for a marriage prospect, Qianyi was certainly a good choice, being a highly-ranked court official and a renowned member of the literati. He could in all likelihood offer me protection and a secure family life. But I had only met him once and... Before I could utter a reply, Master Wang rambled on, as if he could read my mind.

"You must be worrying about the age difference, true? Listen to me, Child. I will tell you something... I know about the Xie Sanbin incident... He is such a loud mouth, and has been bragging about that shameful deed. I wouldn't be surprised if he's still on the prowl for you. But I will also tell you that that is exactly why you should accept Qianyi, because Sanbin happens to be one of his old-time students. No matter what a brutish outlaw he is, he won't have the guts to offend his former teacher. Besides, Qianyi is in your thrall, and let me assure you: he is mentally and physically more nimble than a lot of young folks. My child, if I were you, I wouldn't pass up this golden opportunity!" The sixty-three-year-old kindly man blinked his eyes like a lad who was up to all sorts of impish pranks.

I was hanging on every word of this street-wise and golden-hearted man, and I knew he was right. He was not only right, but was out-and-out thoughtful and genuinely caring. No wonder Wang Wei had nothing but deep respect for him. A short pause later I said:

"Master Wang, words cannot express my gratitude to you. Your advice is sound and sensible, and is obviously offered in my best interests. There is no reason not to accept it."

"Haw haw haw! You are a clever girl, just as I thought! I'll give you Qianyi's address in Changshu. Why not pay him a surprise visit? That should please him!"

"Is there any way I can repay you for your kindness?"

"Just let me publish more of your poetry. I know a prodigy

when I see one. So does Qianyi! He is your big fan. If only I were ten years younger, I would be his deadly rival!"

"You are making me blush…"

"Seriously, I just hate uncouth rogues like Xie Sanbin. For that matter, I hate all men who treat women like dirt. Confucius was dead wrong to have classed women as inferior humans. Just think of all the female talent that has gone to waste over the past several millennia because of that stupid gender discrimination! Aiya, too tragic! And our society is so depraved to exploit girls from poor families and allow the thin horse trade to thrive! Why aren't learned men ashamed at just ignoring it and do nothing about it? Let me tell you this: Qianyi and I have always shared the same view on this issue. We have even planned to jointly petition the Emperor to ban the slave trade. That's why we are great friends!"

"Ah, now I understand why you call your boat the 'Untethered Villa'! You are a freedom lover, true? Wasn't it the Song poet Su Shi who had used the term 'untethered boat' to portray his freedom from the burdens of officialdom?"

"Hahaha, you nailed it! My child, we are all fellow travelers in this world, and from birth each one is tethered to death, no matter the class or race or gender. So why fetter ourselves with spite towards others? Life is only a very short trip. Making others miserable doesn't make us any happier. That's why I try to practice Lao Tzu's First Treasure, compassion."

"I have never heard wiser words, or kinder! You have opened my eyes, Master Wang! I wish all men and women were as broad-minded as you."

"Now you are making me blush!"

By now, my mind was made up: I would do whatever was in my power to win over Qianyi. I simply couldn't afford to lose this one chance to turn a new page in my life. He was one with the ability, and willingness even, if there was any truth in what Wang said, to lift me from the muck of degradation. Whether or not I could love him was immaterial. At twenty-two, I was no longer young. At this point in my life, the security of family life could not be more tempting.

Once back at Wei's lodge, I told her all that had passed between Master Wang and myself, and she said: "Go and grab this chance, Rushi. The stars are aligned to work for you! I wish you all the best."

Back in my chamber, I gathered together a collection of the poems that I had written during my stay and asked Ah Luk to deliver the package to Master Wang.

About a couple of months later, Master Wang sent word to me that he had closed the transaction on Fo's villa and that I could collect the proceeds from him any time, along with copies of my newly-published book of poetry, entitled *Poems Drafted by a Lake*. I was so overwhelmed that I wrote a long emotional letter thanking him for all his help and care, and asked Ah Luk to deliver my letter and collect the money and my new books.

Since then, Master Wang and I went into regular correspondence with each other like old-time friends, right up to the time of his death. Being friends with this eccentric senior was one of the best things that ever happened to me in my life.

# FIFTEEN

IN LATE SUMMER, I received news that Yuanyuan had been demoted to *jiaji* status and thought that was probably a small relief for her. I spoke to Madam Wang and asked her to apply her charm in wheedling General Wu into paying Tian a visit. She told me that the general was fighting a battle in Songshan and it looked like the earliest he could make it to Yangzhou would be around the New Year. So I wrote to Yuanyuan asking her to be patient.

One early autumn day, I set out with Ah Luk at dawn in my boat for Changshu, attired like a Confucian scholar, carrying with me one copy of my new book of poetry, the repartee poem that Qianyi had left for me, and my little portrait that Fo had sketched.

On arrival at midday, I left the boat in Ah Luk's care and hired a horse-drawn cart to head straight to Qianyi's famous "Sweeping Water Villa" in the foothills of scenic Mount Yu. I climbed a long flight of stone steps up a small hill and when I reached a clearing, I stood in awe of what came into sight.

Right in front of me towered two steep crags covered with sweet osmanthus bushes, separated by a narrow ravine. A hanging cascade tumbled down the ravine in force, fed by heavy rain the previous day, carrying with it a dense spray of white flower petals. An occasional sweep of southern gusts tossed up the sheet of water to swirl the petals, turning them into a flurry of dancing butterflies. The whole scene was drunk with sweet floral scents.

The sights and fragrances were so mesmerizing that I could not help lingering and feasting my senses.

About thirty paces to the left of this empyrean scene stood Qianyi's two-storeyed villa. Now I saw how the villa's name had come about. Then I noticed there was a narrow flagstone path to the right of the waterfall, half-hidden by a tangled web of overgrown morning glories and other climbers.

Tempted to find out what lay at the end of the path, I tip-toed carefully along the mossy path, pushing the snarled climbers to one side as I advanced. Cicadas chirped happily amidst the muted sounds of the waterfall tinkling and splattering, joined at times by a cacophony of frog croaks. The path became wider near the end, as sunlight peeped in through the foliage of mulberry, haw and cassia trees that spread out on the leeward side of the crag.

Suddenly an expansive green meadow came into view, with a small creek gliding through the middle. The north side of the creek teemed with peach trees that looked a little sad with their barren thin branches. But rosy finches and thrushes resting on their perches were belting out their tunes with glee, unfazed by the visit of autumn. In my mind's eye, the springtime scene was almost palpable, with peach flowers in full bloom. This hidden grove seemed like a place that could exist only in the imagination. Tao Yuanming's narrative prose *Peach Blossom Spring* immediately leapt to mind.

Moments later, I was in the reception lounge of Qianyi's home. I asked the housemaid to announce me as Scholar Liu, referred by Master Wang Ranming.

I seated myself down on one of the two rosewood chairs placed against a latticed window on the east side, separated by a rosewood marble-top side table. The afternoon sun was streaming in through the opposite window, which looked out onto the waterfall. Another housemaid served me a cup of Rain Flower tea. I was fidgeting a bit as my mind frantically searched for the appropriate things to say.

At last he came out. He was congenially disposed and bowed slightly, bringing his palms together in a courteous gesture, entirely deceived by my guise. I cordially returned the bow and said in a low sonorous voice:

"Master Qian, I am honored to make your acquaintance, and thank you for sparing the time to see me. Master Wang has graciously directed me to you for help with a literary matter."

"Ah, Master Wang and I are very good friends. Master Liu, how can I be of help?" When I saw the serious expression on his face, I almost wanted to giggle, but managed to check myself.

"I don't know if you've come across this recently published work of poetry. The author of this work is a lady and a friend, and she has requested me to ask if you would do her the honor of writing an appraisal." I retrieved the book from my sleeve pocket and showed it to him.

"I wonder why the author herself didn't come and make the request personally..." he said with a slight grimace, taking the book from my hand. No sooner had he read the name on the book cover than his face lit up, his jaw relaxing into a softer outline.

Then curiosity took hold as he scanned me with his squinting eyes. "Ah, I know the author. So you are a close friend of hers?" I could detect a tint of edginess in his voice, subtle as it was, and decided to have a little fun with him.

"Rushi and I grew up together. We are actually second cousins. I'm sure you'll appreciate that it would not be becoming for her to pay you a visit. Could I leave the book with you and come back, say in three days, to get your written appraisal? She is very eager to promote her book at the Songjiang poetry club."

It was customary for an acolyte poet to get a written appraisal of a new work from a respected poet, and circulate it to the club's members.

"Of course, I would be glad to appraise her work. I had the honor of meeting her once at West Lake. Your cousin is quite a talent, for a woman."

"Do you mean to say that women in general have less poetic flair than men?"

"Oh no! I didn't mean it that way. I just wanted to say that Lady Liu has an extraordinary gift, as I know that she has perfected her writing skills mostly through her own efforts, with little help from others. She is probably one in a million!" I didn't think he was lying, and appreciated his clarification.

"That is indeed a fact well-known to me. I have adored Rushi since we were children, and I am so blessed that she has agreed to be my betrothed." I was having so much fun that I didn't want to stop. On hearing those words, his brow wrinkled into a deep frown and he remained sulkily silent.

Then I thought of my golden lotuses and wanted to use them as a hint. I shifted in my seat and lifted my robe just above my ankles, trying to reveal my bound feet. Unfortunately, he was now so stuck in misery to notice anything. I decided it was time to leave.

"Master Qian, may I offer you sincere thanks on behalf of my cousin. I don't want to take up any more of your precious time. In three days I will return. I would like to take my leave now!"

When he turned to order his maid to see me out, I quickly inserted the folded sheet containing his repartee poem and my portrait into the book.

When I appeared again in that room three days later, I was dressed in my violet robe and skirt, and he wore a smile so wide and for so long that it made me fear his jaw might stiffen.

"Lady Liu, I have to ask for your forgiveness for failing to recognize you the other day," he said awkwardly, his unblinking eyes riveted on me, as if afraid I might vanish.

"When I saw your portrait and my poem inside your book, I was so... stunned, but elated! Let me just say what a pleasure it was to read your new work. Here is the appraisal that I've written for you. If your need me to change anything, please do tell me." He gingerly handed me the sheet of appraisal. I took a cursory glance at it and said with feigned remorse,

"Master Qian, thank you so much for this. About the other day, I was so afraid that you might take offense at what I did... I hope you don't mind my prank. Will you accept my sincere apology?"

"Apology for what? You think that an old man like me can't take a joke? I am surrounded all the time by people too serious for their own good, and then you came along and put a smile on my hardened face! That night I could think of nothing but your handsome look and chuckled at my stupid expression of jealousy... Won't you take a seat and make yourself comfortable?"

Then, over fragrant osmanthus tea and sweetmeats, he and I gushed about our love for Song and Tang poetry like two rivaling kids.

In the end, his passionate love for Song lyric poems rubbed off on me and I started to appreciate his adoration of the relatively free style of expressing emotions and sentiments, with less regard to form imposed by the classic Tang style. He thought that Song lyric poet Su Shi was a prodigious talent who employed such style in the most fluid and artful manner, thus making his unparalleled mark on literary history. I had to agree. Very soon, under his influence, I switched the focus in my poetry writing from the rigid Tang style to the more spontaneous and relaxed

Song lyric style.

With the vivacity of an adolescent and the pride of a veteran collector, he took me by the hand and led me on a tour of his vast library, named "Half Rustic Hall", which housed the rarest collections of old classical imprints dating from the Yuan and Song dynasties, including *Histories of Han and Later Han Dynasty*. He told me with unconcealed zest about how he was embarking on an ambitious project of compiling a collection of poetry written under the various reigns of the Ming dynasty.

By the time I had sated my eyes with just a part of his book collections, dusk was at hand. He pleaded with me to stay for dinner and I agreed without a thought, but wished that I hadn't.

His primary wife Madam Chen had already passed away. He introduced me as Master Wang's student to his two concubines, Madam Wang and Madam Zhu, and they responded with an impassive nod and an unfriendly gaze. His son Sunyi and daughter-in-law greeted me with a cordial smile.

Neither of the two concubines said a word to me. Perhaps in their eyes, I had breached the proprieties, because a young maiden from the gentry should never dare to visit a male friend's home without an escort, let alone stay for dinner. Evidently for them, I was most likely from the uneducated lower classes.

What appeared even more puzzling to me was that they treated the old man almost like a stranger. I sat through the meal like a fish snatched out of water. Qianyi sensed my unease and directed all his attention on me, as if to protect me from his disdainful women. He piled one serving after another into my bowl, but I could eat no more than a few bites.

Finally the ordeal was over and I rose to take my leave. Qianyi saw me to the front entrance and bade a servant to escort me in his private carriage back to the pier where my boat was moored.

At the top of the flight of stone steps, he said to me, slightly abashed, "I apologize for my concubines' discourteous behavior. Please don't mind them. Rushi, I was hoping to have another chance to talk with you, and would love to have the pleasure of your company on a boat cruise on Lake Tai in a couple of days. Please do not say no. I'll meet you at the pier at noon the day after tomorrow, if that is alright?"

I nodded my consent, convinced that he had a genuine interest in knowing me better.

That night, my mind whirred over whether I should be frank with Qianyi upfront about the rape. I really didn't want to go further in the relationship without knowing how he might feel about that ugly reality. If he couldn't swallow this fact and live with it, then trying to win his affections would be pointless.

Fo had told me that many men had a blind spot about such issues. They would take it as an ignominy that reflected badly on a woman's character, however unjustified that assumption might be. I was not sure whether Qianyi was aware of the incident. But the fact that even Master Wang had known about it meant that it could also have reached his ears. After careful contemplation, I decided my best option would be to raise it with him at the first opportunity. When I thought about his concubines, a sense of foreboding touched me.

The day of our rendezvous was a bright autumn day with a vivid blue sky. After picking me up at the pier in his carriage, he instructed the coachman to head for the Wuxi pier on the lakeshore, where his pleasure boat was berthed.

On arrival, we boarded his single-cabin boat, which was a little larger but less ornate than mine and was manned by a boatman using a single oar harnessed at the stern. After serving us osmanthus tea and almond cakes, the boatmen steered us away from the bustling noise of the peddling hawkers on the shore, and moments later we were sailing leisurely on the expansive Lake Tai.

I had heard of the beautiful islands and vistas on the famous lake but had never before had a glimpse of the much-acclaimed scenery. I could not remember the last time I had felt as light-hearted as on this day.

Qianyi seemed to be in a buoyant mood, which made him look considerably younger. His alert eyes shone with a curiosity that was at once disarming and amusing.

"Did you know that people in Suzhou like to collect limestone rocks in all sizes and shapes from some of those islands and use them in decorating their gardens?"

"Yes, I've heard they are called 'scholar's rocks', is that right? Were you planning to get some this time?"

"Only if you are interested in accompanying me."

"Oh, I would love to take a look at them."

"I'll show you where there are abundant choices." He called out to the boatman to head to the Jade Flower Islet.

On the way, we saw a couple of fishing boats with great cormorants on leash. I felt sorry for the poor enslaved birds. To prevent them from swallowing the fish, the fisherman would run a tight noose round the throat of each bird, which seemed cruel to me. He saw me frown and said: "The fishermen treat those birds well. Once they finish their job, their nooses are taken off to allow them to feed."

"But in Chinese society, it is the patriarchal system and class distinction that strangle the lives of the weak."

"I know what you mean. Our society has historically been most unfair to women. The *jianmin* class should not even exist. What gives one person the moral right to call another person worthless? It's just not right. A human is a human, regardless of high or low birth."

"Master Qian, this is the first time I have ever heard such an enlightening statement. I can never understand why entertainers and courtesans or prostitutes deserve to be classified as *jianmin* and be scorned for life. What woman would of her own volition sell her body to numerous men in order to live? You have a broad mind, Master Qian, if I may say so..."

"Please do away with the Master appellation and call me Qianyi. It's most unfortunate that not many of my peers agree with my eccentric views. Rushi, in my opinion, you are a perfect role model for all women. If only other women followed your example, maybe things would start to change for the better for the weaker gender. Having said that, I am also aware that many women are just not motivated enough to learn. My two concubines have absolutely no wish to read literature or history. They would rather spend their time talking about clothes and jewelry and in idle gossip. I've given up trying to persuade them."

"Maybe that's because in their upbringing they were never encouraged to learn to read and write. It always puzzles me how people can turn down a chance to learn. I was fortunate, though, to have a kind scholar to teach me in my childhood, and to have Master Zhou Daodeng as my tutor for a short while. After that, I learned on my own. The more I learn, the more I come to realize how ignorant I still am. Now that you've shown me your library, my interest is so piqued that I wish I could devour every book in it."

"Haha, Rushi, you are welcome to use my library any time.... Ah, here we are. We can alight here and try and find some rare rocks."

We landed on the islet where the entire shore was covered with perforated colorful rocks in all shapes and sizes. Some were submerged in the shallow water, and most were of a greenish or yellow-brown color. A few were like red coral. Some had edges all smoothed out by long-time water corrosion.

We saw a group of enthusiastic collectors crouching on the edge of the water poring over their finds. After browsing around on land for while, I decided to wade into a small wave-swept cove. There I stumbled upon a light pink lump shaped like a big rabbit and picked it up. In the sunlight, the rock looked opaque and as smooth as jade. Its beauty put a smile on my face.

Nearby, Qianyi, bare-footed, found a white rock shaped like a horse rearing up and he couldn't let go of it, exclaiming: "I've always wanted a horse! What a fortuitous find!"

We were both thrilled with our new found treasures and returned to the boat in high spirits.

Having dried ourselves with cotton cloth, we continued our cruising. I saw that the moment was right for me to broach the embarrassing topic. I took a deep breath and said timorously, averting my gaze:

"Qianyi, can I ask you a question?"

"Of course, ask away!"

"…If a housemaid of yours was unfortunate enough to get… raped…. by say, a male servant, and become pregnant, how would you deal with her?"

He fixed his probing stare on me for a long while, and then said with firmness:

"I would first try to pressure the offending male servant into agreeing to marry the maid, and if that failed, I would dismiss him, and try to arrange a marriage for the maid. If no marriage prospect was likely, I would send the girl to a Taoist nunnery as a last resort. I know such incidents can be sticky, but my sympathy would always lie with the girl." On hearing those words, I was satisfied that Master Wang had not exaggerated his praise for Qianyi.

Before I could utter a response, he moved closer to me and, with a knowing but tender look, said gently,

"Rushi, I think I know what is on your mind. You see, as soon as I was apprised of what Xie Sanbin had done to you, I gave him the harshest tongue-lashing I have ever meted out to any of my students. I told him that he had brought the greatest shame upon me and on his fellow students. I banned him from my lecture hall and home. But you mustn't feel ashamed, my sweet girl. It is not you who are at fault. You hold your chin up!" He took my hand and patted it lightly.

After a pause, he resumed with a twinkle in his eyes, "If you allow me, I will use the coming days and months to help you erase that most unpleasant memory. I will take you to visit the most beautiful mountains and lakes that Suzhou has to offer. Also, I was thinking of enlisting your assistance in the editing of the anthology of Ming poetry, a huge compilation project that I have only just started to work on. Your previous editing experience can be put to good use."

I was not surprised that he seemed to know quite a bit about me, as he was friendly with Zilong and Wen, all fellow members of the Revival Society and the Songjiang poetry club.

"That is so flattering, Qianyi. I don't see how I can refuse such a kind offer."

Master Wang was right. Qianyi had the agility of mind and industry of a young man, despite his fifty-eight years. But it was his embrace of unconventional thinking, at his advanced age, which earned my deepest respect.

At that moment, I wasn't sure how I felt, except that I was thrown off balance. Never before in my life had I felt so tongue-tied as then. I looked out the boat cabin and trained my eyes on the large and small islets ranged with sunlit green mountains, a relief from the sapphire water vanishing into the distant sky.

I asked myself: could Qianyi be the answer to my life-long quest for inner peace?

That evening, on his invitation, I went to his home for dinner again. He ordered for the meal to be served only to us in the library. This time I got to enjoy the wonderful dishes prepared by his discerning cook.

Over the next three days, I visited his immense library to read Ming poetry to my heart's content, staying for early dinner before returning to my boat. On the third evening, he said to me during dinner:

"Rushi, I think you know how much I'm in your thrall and I'm going to be straight with you. I was hoping you would agree to live with me, because I don't want to suffer your absence any more. If you would permit me, I will build a temporary cottage in the peach tree grove, so that we can live and work in it and begin our life together immediately. You see, after reading your first book of poetry, which was three years ago, I felt that I had come to know you. When I met you in person in Hangzhou last summer, you looked so heartbreakingly lost and forlorn. I felt sure that you needed me as much as I wanted you. All I am asking is that you let me take good care of you. I promise I will build you a beautiful permanent home with a huge library, and I will take you as a primary wife in formal nuptial rituals. What do you say?"

He riveted his ingenuous and expectant gaze on me, which made me a bit nervous. For a moment, I was lost for words, because what he said sounded like sugary sentimental fiction to me. Yet there was nothing that made me fear any slyness or insincerity on his part. Returning his gaze, I mustered up my courage and said:

"Qianyi, you've accorded me with more kindness and respect than a woman of my station can ever hope to gain, and I am truly grateful for your affections. Your offer is no doubt so generous that it would be foolish of me to even hesitate to accept. I will, however, also be very honest with you: I like and respect you very very much and I know you and I are kindred spirits. It's just that at this moment I don't feel I am in love with you. But I promise you that I will learn to love you and make you happy. That is what I desire to do, because as you said, I do need a spouse and a safe home. You mustn't think that I am being crafty. These are words from my heart. If you are not offended by my honesty, then my answer is yes."

He gave a sigh of relief. "I was expecting much worse," he said. "Rushi, thank you for being honest with me. I do understand that you and Chen Zilong had an intimate past, and it is natural that you need time to get over him. But I am content with what you are offering. You probably don't realize how happy you've made me! I'll have our cottage built in ten days. Meanwhile, please feel free to use my library."

Ten days later, Qianyi and I moved into the hastily-built but cozy cottage in the tranquil peach tree grove. He named it "The Heart Sutra Study", as he knew I believed in Guanyin. We spent the next few months traveling to and relishing all the famous sights in Suzhou.

When I learned that Yuanyuan would not come to Nanjing for the upcoming Lantern Festival, I suggested to Jingli and Xiangjun that we cancel our third anniversary celebration.

Shortly after the Festival, Yuanyuan wrote to announce her upcoming mid-year wedding. I was so thrilled for her. At long last, things were looking up for both me and her!

Qianyi happily escorted me to the Yangzhou wedding in the sixth lunar month. We both enjoyed our two days at Yuanyuan's nuptials. I felt gratified when I saw the handsome couple.

Yuanyuan's luminous smile told me at least she was happy with her new-found freedom.

At the tea-offering ceremony, Qianyi quietly proposed to me. Then later at the wedding feast, we announced that our wedding would be in the ninth lunar month.

# SIXTEEN

THIS MORNING, Jingjing found her breakfast laid out on the table where she would usually sit, but her aunt's place was empty. While she was eating alone, Jingli Po Po came in, grim-faced, and said under her breath, "Jingjing, please come with me at once to the backyard shed. I'll explain later." Jingjing was puzzled to see the old lady all tensed up, but followed her quietly.

Once inside the shed, which was used as a barn for storing rice and millet, Jingli closed the door. They sat themselves down on wicker chairs inside a small room, partitioned off in one corner near the entrance. The morning sun stole through a high window, tossing in a ray of dusty light. "Your Aunt Yuanyuan is receiving General Wu in the front lounge. He mustn't see you here with us," said she in a low, tense voice.

Jingjing wondered why her presence would upset the general. But that question didn't pique her interest as much as her aunt's love story. With a mindless tilt of her head she asked,

"Didn't Aunt Yuanyuan and General Wu live happily ever after? He was the gallant hero who rescued her from the monster Tian. Why aren't they together now?"

"For a short while after her wedding, yes, she was content, or tried to appear so. But I guess it was gratitude for her freedom more than anything else. Then the war changed everything, or rather, hastened the inevitable. Aiya, child, things are never as simple as they look in life! Your aunt will tell you what happened during and after the Manchu invasion. If you like, I'll continue with Xiangjun's story now."

*Jingjing nodded absently, still dewy-eyed over her aunt's tale of chivalrous love.*

Last time I told you how the shameless Ruan and Ma pair wanted to lure Fangyu to join their clique. Xiangjun, with her sharp wits and deep sense of integrity, had no trouble seeing through their plans. The problem was that Fangyu was by nature a man with not much of a spine. Being a pampered son living far away from his family in Henan and with scanty financial resources, he found it hard to resist the juicy offer dangling before him. Fortunately, this became known to my Zhenhui, and he asked me to warn Xiangjun to be vigilant of any trap that Ruan and Ma might be laying for Fangyu.

Having been betrothed to Xiangjun for nearly two years now, Fangyu was getting restless and had his mind set upon formalizing the union as soon as practicable.

This year, we had already attended Yuanyuan's and Rushi's weddings, in the sixth and ninth lunar month. We were now settling down into a quiet early winter.

Having seen her two sisters enter a new phase in life, Xiangjun was itching for her big day to arrive. It was a natural dream for any young girl. So, with a little nudge from me, she and Fangyu decided that they would hold their wedding at the upcoming Lantern Festival, to make it a double celebration along with the sisters' fourth reunion. I thought it was a good idea, as it was the best way to make up for the lack of a third anniversary.

Nothing could make me happier than to see my precious daughter and her true love finally going to seal their bond. I would have thrown myself wholeheartedly into making preparations for Xiangjun's wedding, if not for the nagging worries about Xiaowan's father's creditors. They were now given to harassing us constantly.

ALICE POON

By now, Mao Xiang and Xiaowan were a steady couple, but Xiang seemed to have fallen into a habit of reckless spending. This spurt of folly was possibly a venting of his repressed grief over the severing of love ties with Yuanyuan. At least that was how I saw it. But all it did was to worsen an already dire situation. Xiaowan's father's debts had now ballooned to three thousand taels of silver, and the creditors were threatening to seize Xiaowan and auction her off to brothels. Obviously, Xiang realized a little too late how bad things really were. And he now chose to avoid his troubles by not showing up at all.

"I've heard from Fangyu that Mao Xiang has been depressed lately," Xiangjun said to me on Winter Solstice Day, while helping me in the kitchen with preparations for a big festive dinner for the whole salon. "Unfortunately Fangyu is in no better shape than Xiang where money is concerned."

"If Xiang didn't let his whims get the better of him, he could at least repay a good portion of the debts. But he had to fling away his money as if he owned a gold mine!" I said with plain exasperation, cursing under my breath. I must admit that at that time I was not aware of Xiang's penchant for charity.

"If those debts are not soon repaid in full, Xiaowan will end up in a brothel, that's for sure. Xiang has probably come to realize that the situation is beyond salvage. The poor girl has been like an ant in a hot cauldron. The slightest thing can provoke her into endless tears. Mother, we must do something to help her."

Xiangjun was slicing a bunch of taro roots into strips and I was braising the seasoned cut-up pieces of two ducks in the big clay pot. The salivating aroma of warm spices filled the whole kitchen. All my girls loved this taro root and duck hotpot. My culinary secret was the blended powder of pestle-ground star anise and Sichuan peppercorns. This condiment was a concoction that Master Zhang Dai's family cook had inherited from his ancestors. Master Zhang had filched a pouch of it from his cook to bring to me. Bless that good man!

Xiangjun's wedding news had cheered me up and made me want to splurge a little on this important family meal of the year. So I had planned to prepare savory dishes such as stir-fried spicy prawns, steamed carp with ginger and scallions, braised lotus roots with pork, and roasted goose.

My cook had earlier done all the cleaning and chopping and slicing, and had roasted the goose. The taro and duck hotpot was now on the stove. I was getting ready to cook the remaining dishes.

"I wish I could, Daughter. Since taking on Fo's girls, the salon has been saddled with extra expenses. The price of fabrics has gone crazy this year, and I've already spent a lot on make-up, dress-making and accessories in order to initiate them onto stage. All this has used up nearly half of what Rushi sent me from the sale of Fo's villa. The other half is set aside to pay for their upkeep while they build up an audience. I'm already stretched thin."

"Mother, I know you've been struggling hard to keep your head above water. But this is not a good time to dwell on these problems. The girls have been looking forward so much to this festive meal, so let's not spoil it over the debts. I'll think about it some more tomorrow. There's got to be a way out."

I had to agree with her. It was only at festive times that we allowed ourselves such indulgence in food. Normally we would have simple meals of rice, steamed eggs, salted fish and stir-fried bean sprouts.

That evening we all dug into the dishes with relish, except Xiaowan. She just pushed her food around, hardly eating it, much as she tried to act appreciative out of courtesy. I couldn't blame the poor child, with such a deadweight swinging over her head, and Xiang hiding away like an ostrich ducking in the sand.

The other girls, new and old, loved festive meals in my salon and were eating with hearty gusto. I had long made it a habit to cook on Moon Festival Day, Winter Solstice and Lantern Festival Day. You see, Jingjing, I am not one who is good at expressing feelings. Cooking for my girls on festive days was my way of thanking them for their hard work. I've always believed food is the best glue to bind people together.

From the day I took the girls in, I had treated them like family, but I had also allowed time for our mutual trust to develop naturally. No human bond can form without trust. You can only treat people with your heart and hope they will come to like you. The new girls' happy chirps and their smiling faces around the table told me that I must have done something right. It warmed my heart.

I knew they all craved something sweet at the end of a festive meal, and nothing pleased me more than to indulge them. How their eyes shone when they saw me bring out bowls of glutinous rice balls with red bean paste! We all had quite a bit of rice wine to drink. Two girls got up to fetch their pipa and sang a few light-hearted folk songs for us. By the time we retired to bed, it was well past midnight.

The next morning, loud bangs in the garden shook the villa. I had already risen and was on the verandah gazing into the silvery glints of the calm waterway ahead of the start of its daily hustle and bustle.

Looking over in the direction of the noise, I was aghast to see five brawny thugs trying to pry open the bolted wooden gate with spikes and axes. Before I could make sense of it all, they were already storming the front lounge, shouting crude obscenities.

I almost tripped as I raced down the stairs. Steadying myself, I scurried through the audience hall to the front lounge. There I saw my pet parrot curled into a ball, whimpering "Help! Help!" pitiably. Their scar-faced leader bawled at me when I turned to face them, still slightly bleary-eyed from a hangover:

"Tell Dong Xiaowan to come out at once, or else we'll turn this place upside down!"

All sleepiness was pushed out of me. The galling scene in which Tian Hongyu's guards had snatched away Yuanyuan darted through my mind. My legs went weak. I pinched myself hard to focus my brain on the crisis before me. A voice inside my head whispered, "Stay calm, stay calm! Try to look collected and confront the situation."

"Please Big Brothers, please don't frighten my girls. I have to tell you that Lady Dong is the betrothed of Master Mao Xiang, the eldest son of the noble Mao family. As long as she is with us, I have a duty to protect her." I figured that calling their bluff was probably the best bet.

"That bitch's father owes our master three thousand taels of silver. We don't give a fart who Mao Xiang is. We want to see money! If she can't show us the money, we'll have her person instead!"

"I'm afraid Lady Dong is still asleep. But I had better warn you. If you so much as harm one hair of the lady, you should know to whom you will be answering! The Mao family is known to have powerful ties in court. As far as I know, the lady owes nobody anything. Anyway, what makes you think you have a right to force your way into people's homes?"

"What home? Is this not a public brothel, Old Witch? Our master holds Dong's bond contract. We are under orders to deliver her to him because her father couldn't repay his debts. Whether our master wants her for himself or to sell to a brothel, we couldn't care less!" The leader broke into a lewd, rasping laugh.

"If money is your only concern, then don't you worry about it! Who in Nanjing doesn't know the Mao family is one of the wealthiest? The young master has just written to his mother asking her to courier money here. His family lives in Rugao County, so it will be at least ten to twelve days before the money arrives. Now, I am asking that you please be reasonable and leave. You are scaring the ladies of this salon."

I tried to look as unfazed as I could, but cold sweat was already trickling down my back. Were I to say anything more, the intruders would most certainly be able to find holes in my made-up story.

After a tormenting spell of silence, the leader and his henchmen finally backed down. They muttered in low voices for a while, then the scar-faced coughed up and spewed a gobbet of phlegm into the nearest spittoon. He jabbed his finger at me:

"Old Witch, you know what will happen to you if you're making this up! Half a month is all you have. We'll be back when the time's up! And don't you dare try any tricks in the meantime. We have eyes and ears all over town."

I drew in a deep breath, knowing they were sold on my bluff. As the last of the gang filed out, the poor parrot became bold and yammered in a high pitch: "Farewell! Farewell! Don't come back, you craven rotten eggs! Rotten eggs!" Its shrill gibberish tickled me into a good chuckle. I picked up a dried apricot from a plate on the side table and fed it to the indignant bird. It bobbed its blue-feathered head a few times, wheedling a stroke from me. I loved it to bits.

Now that my nerves were calmer, I began to wonder where I had gotten the gumption to drum up such a sham. The truth was that Mao Xiang had earlier written to his father asking for money for his wedding but had been coldly rejected, because the old man was angry at his choosing a courtesan. So that was already a known dead-end at the time I blurted out my bluff. Now I had to race against time to come up with a real solution, or be ready to be fed to the wolves.

As I was lost in thought, Xiangjun came tiptoeing into the front lounge and, covering her mouth with her hand, said in a muffled voice, as if afraid any louder sound might bring back the thugs:

"Thank heavens they're gone! Mother, you amaze me sometimes, the way you can act!" She had hidden behind the curtains to listen to the whole conversation.

"If only you could see how I was shivering," I replied. "Now we really have to think hard on how to deal with this."

She lowered herself into the chair beside me and said, unruffled as usual,

"I've given it some thought, and I think the person who is best placed to help us is Rushi. Wasn't it her plan in the first place to persuade Mao Xiang to help Xiaowan? Now that Xiang has lost the means to help, I just think Rushi need only be told the truth and she will not rest until Xiaowan is freed. She would walk on fire to see that Fo's last wish is fulfilled. And the person she can now rely on for help is naturally her new husband. If she could persuade the well-heeled Master Qian to lend a helping hand, then we're all saved."

"You are quite right, Xiangjun. That had somehow slipped my mind. Rushi being Rushi, I am certain she will give her all to honor Fo's last wish. Anyway, she is our best hope of getting this snag out of the way. I would have asked Zhenhui for help if I hadn't already been in his debt for the salon's set-up cost. Being only his kept mistress, I can't possibly ask for more favors from him."

"I know, Mother. All these years running the salon on your own hasn't been easy for you. Even in hard times, you just slogged away in silence and never troubled Master Chen, and he respects you for your courage. I do think Rushi is our best bet.... Let me write to her explaining the quandary we're in and hope for the best."

"I can't think of a better option, my dear child. Talking about her, I felt so bad for her on her wedding day........"

"Yes, I felt really sorry for her too. It should have been her happiest day, and yet... Aiya. the vicious things those rascals said! I can't imagine her taking it well. It was heartening though to see Master Qian take a manly stand for her."

She paused for thought. Letting out a sigh, she said with her face clouding up, "Just the thought of the havoc that day makes me balk at the idea of having a formal wedding. It's never good to draw attention."

"I don't blame you for wanting to keep things simple."

"Fangyu is not even going to tell his wife and his parents. Frankly, I don't mind in the least. Formalities are just for show. Mother, if you don't object, we would like to have a simple family-style wedding meal with just you and Master Chen, my sisters and their husbands, and Yang Longyou, as our guests. I must also invite Xiang and Xiaowan, as Xiang was the one who had first introduced us. I hope Yuanyuan wouldn't mind this...."

My Xiangjun was always practical, compassionate, honest and considerate.

"I'm sure she won't... My child, I don't object to a simple wedding. But I do worry about Fangyu choosing to keep the news from his family. After all, you are a virgin and he should have respected that by at least volunteering to hold a formal wedding, so that you are accepted into his household with all the proprieties. That would be the proper thing to do. I was not even going to require him to provide bridal gifts."

"Well, Mother, you know he is short of funds. As for his

family, he told me that he wanted to make it a done deal before
he writes to announce it. Hopefully, they will then see that it is
pointless to object."

"I do hope that will work.... But he had better not be stingy
with the feast! It is your most important day. We must celebrate
with the best food and wine. If he comes up short on funds, he
must let me help! Oh, let's not get carried away with this now.
You had better get started on writing that letter to Rushi. We
can't afford to lose time. Don't forget to send her the wedding
invitation."

From the way I had seen Qianyi doting on Rushi, I felt quite
sure that she would have little problem in coaxing him to help
us. The amount involved should be quite within his means, and I
had often heard how he had taken to helping the poor and needy.

In fact, I was so happy that Rushi had found someone who
worshipped her so much and could give her a safe nest. Qianyi
would never be Zilong, for sure. But this union was the best
match she could ever have hoped for, not to mention she was
given primary wife status! No woman from the courtesans' lot
had ever had that good fortune!

I must say that Yuanyuan looked just stunning on her
wedding day. I couldn't hold back tears when I saw her radiant
smile. Rushi's ingenious plan had worked out perfectly for her!
Not only is General Wu handsome, but he seemed helplessly
smitten with her. The important thing was that she finally broke
free from slavery.

I would say that both Rushi and Yuanyuan could not have
found better spouses.

All said, I still found the fracas on Rushi's wedding day
unsettling. Qianyi's concubines seemed to take wicked pleasure
in watching her being humiliated. My gut told me it was not
beneath those two to conspire to hurt her.

As expected, Rushi replied in the affirmative. Qianyi had thankfully agreed to fork out the entire sum of three thousand taels of silver. No doubt Rushi had worked her magic.

Without further ado, I set out to have the debts repaid and Xiaowan's bond contract torn up. As for the removal of her name from the entertainers' register, she insisted on using her savings to pay the fee. I much admired her backbone. Fo, wherever she might be, could now feel consoled. In our circle, it was rare for something as fortuitous as this to happen.

Complete relief came when I learned that Xiang's primary wife, Madam Su, had graciously consented to accept Xiaowan into the Mao family. Her decision even won over his stubborn father, and the couple were finally joined in proper nuptials.

I spent the remainder of the winter days working hard on Xiangjun's and Fangyu's wedding garments, something which I enjoyed doing to the fullest. My embroidery skills were nowhere near as good as Rushi's, but still not too bad by ordinary standards. I had secretly put aside an amount of savings and had used it to buy a bolt of high quality Suzhou pink silk for making Xiangjun's bridal garments. Pink was the customary color for a concubine's bridal dress, but it was also the perfect color for my delicate and fair-skinned daughter.

Rushi had sent, along with her reply to Xiangjun, a separate note asking me to buy a wedding gift for her sister on her behalf. As Yuanyuan had given her a sapphire butterfly hairpin, I thought to have a matching hairpin custom-made, to make a pair of them. The jeweler down the street happened to be one of our regulars. He was good enough to give me a generous discount.

Before I knew it, the Lantern Festival was just round the corner.

Two days before the big day, the Ruan and Ma pair paid an

unexpected call to my villa. I was not particularly interested in seeing them. At the time, Xiangjun and I were in her antechamber and Fangyu was reading in the dressing lounge downstairs. So I shouted to him to receive them in the front lounge. I then carried on with helping Xiangjun try on the newly-made bridal dress, on which I had labored over the butterfly embroidery.

When I was doing the needlework, all I cared about was the pretty shapes of the butterflies. I never gave a thought to the superstition that butterflies were a portent of ill-starred love.

Jingjing, I'm sure you are familiar with the folktale where the star-crossed lovers Zhu Yingtai and Leung Shanbo were reincarnated into a pair of butterflies after they died. This poignant story would only surface in my mind much later, when misfortune had struck out of the blue.

Moments later, Xiangjun and I went down to the dressing lounge to look for Fangyu. He was coming in from the front lounge, dragging along a beautifully carved sandalwood casket. As if nothing was out of the ordinary, he said absently,

"This is your dowry, Xiangjun. It is a special gift from Master Ruan and Master Ma."

"What dowry?" I said with an angry hiss. "They are not related to my Xiangjun. If anyone is in a position to give her dowry, it would be me." I never had anything against Fangyu, but at times he got on my nerves when he acted like a witless spoiled kid. Today, he was at it again. I didn't know whether to laugh off his naivete or to give him a good tongue-lashing.

"Oh, they mean well. They know I can't afford to buy Xiangjun all the lovely jewels and clothes…" He seemed unperturbed by my snub and turned to his bride-to-be. "They say they know how special you are to me, and that if you don't have a few luxury trinkets to show, it would reflect poorly on me. Besides, you are a renowned opera singer and you can't let your admirers see you looking drab. They also said that this is the least they could do for you as your devoted fans."

Out of curiosity, I opened the casket and scanned the contents. There were bolts of silk of the finest quality in light green, blush pink and crimson, a brocaded velvet cape with sable fur trim, dainty lacquered boxes filled with all kinds of exquisite jewelry like pearl earrings, green jade bracelets and all shapes of hairpins inlaid with kingfisher feathers. Xiangjun cast one glance at the contents and frowned.

"Mother is right," she said. "Fangyu, you shouldn't have accepted any of these. I dare say it is not out of kindness that they are doing this. Even if it is, we would not want to be in their debt. Why would we? Besides, I don't need these things. All I ever wanted is to live a simple life with you by my side. I already have the most precious gift from Mother. She made it with her hands, stitch by loving stitch. This is the best dowry I could ever hope to receive." Xiangjun pointed to her bridal robe with unconcealed pride. At that moment, I felt that all the affections I had lavished on her were paid for.

"But they wouldn't have it any other way. I just thought it would be rude to reject their kindness," Fangyu said falteringly, realizing that he had not thought things through. His one redeeming trait was that he trusted Xiangjun and could easily be swayed by her perceptive words.

"Fangyu, listen to me. We must return the whole casket to the two Masters. There is something that they want from you, and make no mistake, they belong to the shameless eunuch faction, whose foul play caused our patriotic General Yuan to die an unjust and cruel death. Would you be prepared to side with this treacherous clique? I would hope not. After all, you are a member of the Revival Society, the eunuchs' arch-enemies. But once you are in their debt, they can and will make a turncoat of you."

"No, I wouldn't think of it. Frankly, I haven't involved myself in the political activities of the Society. I joined mainly for the pleasure of meeting and befriending literary icons…"

"That's what I thought. When you return the casket, just say that it is not proper for us to accept such luxurious gifts. If you like, and if Mother agrees, you may invite them to our wedding feast and let them share our joy, since they are friends of your good friend Yang Longyou, who is on our guest list."

"I guess a couple more guests wouldn't make any difference…." I said, giving my grudging assent.

"They asked me to consider a position in court. I thought they did it as a matter of goodwill on account of my friendship with Longyou. Honestly, I was tempted by the generous pay." He was abashed, as he had earlier hidden this from Xiangjun.

"Zhenhui has told me that the eunuchs' plan is to try to weaken the Revival Society's influence in court by luring top scholars to take their side." I told him what I knew to be common knowledge among the patriotic literati.

"Now that I know their real motive, I will definitely turn down the offer. They are too presumptuous if they think I can be bought. Nothing would make me sell out my friends at the Revival Society. I'll return the casket right away. Mother, Xiangjun, you know I would never do anything dishonorable."

It was as if he had just awakened from a dream. Xiangjun and I breathed a sigh of relief.

On the Lantern Festival Day, the simple wedding went ahead as planned and everyone had a good time. Much to my relief, those two characters had the good sense to stay away.

But when things go too smoothly, you can almost always feel that dark shadows are lurking in the corner. The seeds of hatred were sown the moment Fangyu returned the unwanted gift. Our rejection of it, though with no ill-will on our part, caused the senders serious loss of face. For them, our snub was viewed as a deliberate insult. At least, that was what they would want people to believe. In truth, they were offended for only one reason: our rejection completely foiled their plans to win over Fangyu. If we were not their friends, naturally we must be their enemies.

*Now Jingjing was beginning to appreciate Aunt Xiangjun for her strong sense of right and wrong and her kindness. No wonder her mother had loved this little sister.*

*At this point, Yuanyuan came into the shed. Jingli asked her daughter, "What does he want now?"*

*"The same," replied Yuanyuan with a slight shrug. "He wants me to move into his Palace. My answer was still no. But maybe at some point I'll have to accede. Who knows? Perhaps my presence in his life could help ease his tortured conscience."*

*"He's now the Vassal King of the West, but even that doesn't seem to satisfy him! I dare say one day he's going to sell out his Qing masters, no matter that he is already a Ming traitor!" Jingli mocked with keen perception.*

*"If only he could see that greed is often a person's undoing!" said Yuanyuan with a sigh.*

*As it was nearing time for the midday meal, Jingli got up and went to the kitchen to prepare congee with mushrooms and dried conch.*

*Jingjing, now alone with her aunt, noticed a light frown on her face. But what had happened between the couple, she wondered to herself.*

*Unable to restrain her quest for the truth, she asked softly, "Aunt Yuanyuan, would you mind telling me why my presence here would upset General Wu?"*

*Yuanyuan looked into the girl's eyes with tenderness. "Jingjing, can I ask you to be patient please? I know you must have many questions in your head. But you'll eventually have your answers as I move further along in my story, and as you continue reading your mother's memoir.*

*I would like to skip our session today though, as I'm feeling a bit tired."*

*After lunch, Jingjing spent the afternoon devouring another chunk of the memoir.*

# SEVENTEEN

HAVING RETURNED from Yuanyuan's wedding, Qianyi and I immediately set about drawing up a list of guests and sending out wedding invitations. We planned to hold our ceremony on a pleasure cruise on West Lake.

Master Wang, who owned several pleasure boats aside from his plush floating abode, kindly offered to lend us the largest one for the happy occasion. He had said in his letter, "Just leave it to me to get the cabins and the hull decorated in bridal trimmings. It makes me happy to do you this small service. As the person who helped in the match-making and who can claim to be your mentor, may I impose on you my wish to be your guardian on your important day?"

Impose? This kind man had no idea that his offer literally sent me straight to heaven!

The reason for choosing West Lake was a sentimental one. That was where a chance had allowed Qianyi and myself to meet for the first time. It was the place where that chance meeting was fated to give me a new lease on life.

Besides, there was probably not another place in the world that exuded such magical charm. The place was the poetic muse of nature, with the understated luster of a pearl.

What really pleased me was that no sooner had the venue suggestion left my lips when Qianyi nodded his head vigorously in approval.

About ten days prior to our big day, Qianyi received a letter from Song Zhengyu. Apparently it was a response of sorts to our wedding invitation. It had been Qianyi's idea to invite Zhengyu, along with Zilong and Wen, as their three names were always inextricably tied together, being the celebrated Three Geniuses of Songjiang. My idea had been to invite only Wen. But Qianyi had thought it rude to invite one but not the other two. I had acquiesced and had said nothing further.

Zilong had written to decline and offer his apologies, which was within my expectations. His decline set my mind at ease, as I wouldn't trust myself to keep calm in his presence. Wen had sent us his exulted acceptance, along with his brush painting of a pair of mandarin ducks as our wedding gift.

Qianyi would have torn up the letter had I not been quick in snatching it from him. Zhengyu's rambling letter read thus (I had kept the letter, as a reminder of a friend's treachery):

"Honorable Master Qian,

I am writing to acknowledge receipt of your wedding invitation. I must admit, though, the occasion came as a total shock to me.

Having always held you in high esteem, both for your distinguished place in the literati and for your official rank, I reckon I can be forgiven for expressing disbelief over your unfortunate decision.

Rumors had abounded about your amorous dalliance with a seductive courtesan, but no one from the respectable literati had expected the affair to amount to anything more than casual philandering. My fellow scholars and I are most concerned that you, probably under ill-meaning influence, are setting a regrettable example in our class. We are afraid you are making the biggest mistake of your life.

As your friend, I am distressed to see you lose your head at your golden age, and let a lowly woman befuddle your judgment in a matter of social moral code. It is sad that you seem to have forgotten the high moral standard our scholar class is held to.

A whore will always be just a whore. Wasn't that obvious enough when she brought ignominy on herself by inviting Xie Sanbin's leer?

We would have no objection to you buying her as your house maid, which would have been the proper thing to do. That would not even tamper with your right to seeking pleasure with her. But taking her as your primary wife will make you the biggest laughing stock of Jiangnan for a long time to come.

As your fellow scholar, I will also say this: I had once philandered with the same woman you are calling 'wife', as had countless others of our class. I will say she is a seductive beauty. But that does not change the fact that she is from cheap stock. She would serve men best as a courtesan, I can assure you.

I hope with all my heart that you will try to remedy things while there is still time.

Yours truly,
Zhengyu"

Tears prickled my eyes when I finished reading it. What an acrid piece of diatribe! Whatever had I done to him to deserve such invective? Hadn't he once felt love for me? Words could not describe how his cruel letter made my skin crawl.

"My sweet girl, don't give this garbage another thought," Qianyi said. "He is just a sour and jealous man. Frankly, I feel flattered. I'm sure he's not the only one who envies my good fortune." He released a good-natured guffaw, as he gently wiped away a tear from the corner of my eye.

"Maybe it's because I had refused to become his kept mistress. His vanity was pierced and he has never been able to forgive me for snubbing him. Yes, that explains the bitter rancor."

Unknown to us then, it was to be the fuse that would set off an embarrassing wrangle on our wedding day.

An autumn breeze wafted in through the half-opened latticed window, letting in a wistful mood that this season of falling leaves often evoked. The creek in front of the cottage was chiming its usual jingling tune, but it now sounded mirthless.

I had been living in this tranquil retreat for six months. Much as I savored the painting-perfect sea of pink this past spring, the scene had only stirred fond memories of time spent with Zilong in the South Villa peach garden. I was there again, we were holding hands, he was cooing in my ears, his touch burning on my flesh, his sweet breath on my neck. How I thirsted for that feeling again! That shameful pulsating pleasure that felt as natural as drinking water. All ashes now.

But suddenly another thought rudely intruded. Were we to meet again now, would he see me in the same light as before? Would he, like so many others, despise me as a fallen woman stained with the stigma of rape? Would his love and respect for me crumble to dust? I didn't even want to guess.

The past is always a wayward ghost that defies prediction. It couches in shady crevices of the mind and will jump out to trip you up when you least expect it to.

Coming out of my trance, I sat down opposite Qianyi at the working table in the unadorned small lounge. I felt I had no reason to hide my past liaison with Zhengyu from my husband-to-be. So I slowly recounted the whole story from the time I had met him right up to our parting.

"When I refused to be his kept mistress after he married a rich girl, he bore a deep grudge. Then his mother forced Fo to take her salon operation away from Songjiang. I asked him for help, but he saw that as an opportunity to punish me. After that incident, I vowed I would never see him again."

"I did not know him well, but this letter tells me all about his character. I can see clearly that it's more about venting his anger at you than caring for my reputation. No self-respecting man would ever bad-mouth a past lover in such a way." He looked at me with ardent sympathy and typical curious wonder. It was hard not to like this man.

I couldn't help asking him a straight question that had been nagging me for a long time:

"Qianyi, if I hadn't made the first move of coming to you, would you have taken the initiative to come to me?"

His face drew taut as he replied in a tense voice, as if his integrity was challenged:

"Of course I would! Did you not find out from Master Wang how I felt about you? With your cutting wit, you wouldn't have thought what he said was purely guesswork, would you? He was the only friend I had confided in about my true feelings. As I said before, my mind was made up at our first meeting on that West Lake cruise. You had such a desperate look in your eyes, as though you were drowning. Since then, my only obsession was to save you. I was only waiting for the right moment to make contact. Good for me, you beat me to it!"

To his artless answer, I could not think of a rejoinder. If there was any flaw in what he said, it was that it fed my vanity over the brim.

"What is it about me that you love most? I want to know the truth. You must be very honest."

Slight bafflement fleeted across his face, and he said with a glint in his eyes:

"Your lustrous silky hair and soft white skin."

I was a little taken aback by his reply, which sounded at once flattering and shallow. It was not what I had expected to hear.

So after all, he was no different from any other man, young or old. Beauty and youth in women is what all men truly desire. I was thinking of my mother's warning again. Maybe she was wrong. Maybe beauty is not a curse if you can use it as an aid to get what you need.

Then the pragmatic side of me thought of how I could help Qianyi leave a mark on literary history through his massive project of compiling an anthology of Ming poetry. Together we could select the best quality works written in the wide span stretching from Hongwu Emperor's reign to Chongzhen's. After all, poetry was a second life to me. And being a part of this colossal effort would give me a much-needed distraction to help keep my tormenting demons at bay.

While I was lost in thought, Madam Zhu's maid from the main household came in and said to Qianyi, "My mistress would like Master to join her for lunch." Qianyi's two concubines were now in the habit of taking turns to make him stay in the main mansion for as long as possible each day.

Before I moved into the cottage, they had not bothered at all to know his whereabouts, according to my maid Begonia.

Madame Zhu, whom Qianyi called Spring Flower, was the mother of his only son, Sunyi, and was the more overbearing of the two. Madame Wang, or Orchid, though more soft-spoken, was Spring Flower's trusted ally and would parrot anything she said. My only allies in the main household were young Sunyi and his wife, who were fans of my poetry and painting.

Drawing lessons from my previous experience at the Zhou household, I was mentally prepared to tolerate with greatest patience the little wiles that these querulous women used in their efforts to malign me. I would just try to stay out of their way as far as was possible, if only to keep the peace. I couldn't but credit Qianyi for his foresight in giving me a home separate from the main mansion, in order that he and I could enjoy our time together away from their prying eyes.

From a sidelong glance, I caught the maid training her eyes on the letter which was lying on the writing table. At that moment, I didn't pay any particular attention to it.

A short while after Qianyi left, I bade Begonia cook some congee for lunch, and continued with my embroidery work on my wedding garments.

Begonia was the daughter of an old servant couple in the Qian household whom Qianyi had assigned to serve me. It wasn't long before I took to the fourteen-year-old round-faced, round-eyed girl, who was endowed with a jaunty sense of mischief. It was a joy to see her get along well with Ah Luk, who couldn't resist her teasing ploy and girlish charm. Ah Luk was three years older and now stayed in the cottage to help with tending the peach trees and my small patch of flower garden. I thought they would make a perfect pair.

When Begonia served the congee, I realized the letter was no longer on the writing table. As if she could read my mind, she said, "I think I saw Madame Zhu's maid take it. But I didn't dare stop her." A sense of foreboding came over me when I heard that. But then I thought since I had already come clean with Qianyi about my past with Zhengyu, there should not be any harm even if the letter fell into Spring Flower's hands. So I didn't bother myself unduly with it, as there were just too many wedding chores to attend to. Anyway, the letter reappeared the next morning, and I stashed it away among my correspondence.

Qianyi and I had decided to keep our guest list short, and

apart from my foster family, other guests included my good friends Master Wang, Wang Wei and Li Wen, Qianyi's two colleagues from court and his favorite young student Zheng Chenggong, who was later to make an attempt at salvaging the fallen Ming Court.

As soon as I had told Wang Wei about my wedding, she had offered to let me use her lodge as the bride's home. I would need to arrive a day earlier for the bridal hair-combing rite, which would be performed by Jingli on me, as she was to be my guardian at the wedding.

I had already written to her and my beloved sisters asking that they and their respective partners come to Hangzhou on the same day as I, in order for us to have a nice get-together. Master Wang was to be my other guardian and he was also invited to this pre-wedding gathering. By custom, the groom was not allowed to attend the bride's hair-combing ritual.

On that day, my family and Master Wang arrived in early afternoon. We had light refreshments while catching up on each other's latest news. In the evening, we had a delicious vegetarian dinner that Wei kindly prepared.

Then, witnessed by all present, Jingli combed my hair with a fine-toothed sandalwood comb while chanting auspicious wishes: "First combing to wish the new couple a long harmonious marriage; second combing to wish them abundant offspring; third combing to wish them longevity." When the ritual was over, Wei served everybody jasmine tea and sweet soup with lotus seeds and red figs. Just before the second-watch gong, Master Wang said farewell, and the rest of us were ready to retire to bed.

The sleeping arrangement was for Yuanyuan and Xiangjun to sleep in my chamber, Jingli to sleep in Wei's, and the men were to bed down on pallets set up in the lounge.

By the time Yuanyuan and I entered my chamber, Xiangjun

was already fast asleep on the pallet set up near my bed, which I was to share with Yuanyuan.

Yuanyuan tugged lightly at my sleeve and asked softly if she could chat a little with me. Nodding my consent, I led her quietly back out through the lounge into the garden, closing the lounge doors lightly behind us.

The garden was flooded in a silvery sheen under the bright autumn full moon. Seated on the cool stone bench under a weeping willow, we were drunk with the osmanthus-scented night air and the sweet lullaby of cicadas and crickets.

The entrancing aura relaxed us and put us in a chatty mood. We had seen each other at her Yangzhou wedding three months earlier, but had not had a chance to talk.

Now I saw the same wondrous glitter in her large dark eyes, like those of a startled fawn, wary but guileless. I could sense that years of sufferings had taught her to hide her true feelings deep behind those two shiny black pearls that drank light from the moon but gave nothing out. This night was an occasion when that wall of sangfroid crumbled to reveal her naked fragility, and more.

"Rushi, I have wanted to have this conversation with you for so long, and I couldn't find a chance to talk to you at my wedding. I wanted to thank you for all that you've done to help me regain freedom. If it hadn't been for your well thought-out plan, I would have been stuck forever in my misery. I owe you so much...." Her voice trailed off as she fidgeted and lowered her head, like a criminal waiting for a verdict.

Then, lifting her gaze to meet mine, she went on, "It turned out that Sangui was born and raised in the same Suzhou village as I, and once we began to talk to each other, we found some common ground. He makes me feel protected. But he seems a complex person."

"Oh, Yuanyuan, it's such a relief to me to see it has all worked out for the best. You found it in your heart to persuade Xiang to help Xiaowan, and that set everything on the right track. Of course, if Sangui wasn't attracted to you, all my efforts would have gone to waste! But I made a judgment and staked on it! Your freedom was worth ...." Before I could finish, she interrupted me in a choked voice, her face flushed,

"Rushi, you have to forgive me for the terrible things I said to you at our second reunion. You had my interests at heart and I didn't even have the decency to show appreciation. I was such a fool! I didn't mean to be bitchy, much less to hurt you. It's just that...I felt so trapped...that no one understood me... And then afterwards I couldn't find the courage sooner to beg for your forgiveness. I knew in my heart that you had forgiven me, but I can't be at peace until I hear you say there's no bad feeling between us!"

"Come now, my sweet girl. There's never been any trace of bad feeling between us. No one understands better than I how hard it was for you to give up Xiang. I had walked in the same shoes with Zilong. But letting go does not mean the end of our love. We love in a different way, that's all. I could also see how isolated you must have felt, drudging all alone under Tian's thumb. Yes, I'll admit that your words did graze my heart at that moment. But by the next morning, I had already forgotten all about it."

"Oh, Rushi, you don't know how much your words mean to me! I love you. Nothing will change that love. You will always be my Big Sister and my idol." She paused to wipe away a large teardrop that was rolling down her cheek.

With a deep frown that betrayed her inner struggle, she stared without seeing into the space before her. "I don't know if I'll ever be able to forget Xiang. But life has to go on and we have to make hard choices just to survive. And there are things that happened during my wretched time at the Tians' that I wish I could forget....."

Breaking into heaving sobs now, she let her unfinished sentence hang in mid-air, her face livid with bruising sadness. I thought it best not to press her to continue, and circled my arms around her. Whatever it was, I had a feeling that it had gashed her soul.

"If you don't want to share anything, you don't have to. It's alright. We are sisters for life, and we will help each other, no matter what. We swore on it, remember?"

"Rushi, if you, Xiangjun and Mother had never entered my life, I could easily have already stepped into the other world. From the time we were sold to the procurer, no one cared one whit if we lived or died. Even now, Xiangjun and I often talk about the kindness we saw on your face when you offered to be our sponsor. It melted both our hearts. Your genuine concern let us see hope again. Since we became sisters, every time I slipped into despair, just one look at the birdie kerchief, and I knew I must wait it out." Tears were cascading down her cheeks. I leaned over to wipe them away with my sleeve.

The way she was opening herself up to me made my eyes prick with tears. I blinked them back and faked a chiding, "Now, now, you shouldn't have made me cry. Have you forgotten I have to look beautiful tomorrow?" An awkward smile darted across her tear-streaked face. She then took both my hands between hers, looked me in the eye and asked a straight question,

"Rushi, are you happy with Qianyi?"

The simple question stumped me and it took me a while to come up with a coherent reply, unconsciously moved to share my secret of shame.

".... I couldn't have hoped for a better spouse than Qianyi...

given my status, and above all, something that had happened to me in Songjiang. You see, Yuanyuan…. I was… drugged and raped two years ago… It was that stalker… Xie Sanbin I had told you about. Out of meanness, he went around bragging about it. The men I used to know at once distanced themselves from me, except Qianyi, Li Wen and Master Wang. Qianyi doesn't seem to mind it one bit…He is so determined to affirm his stance that he is giving me primary wife status."

Her face twitched in a pang of guilt.

"Oh, Rushi, I didn't know… I am so very sorry this dreadful thing happened to you… And you still had the heart to worry about my future after that….. I'm so ashamed now!" She faltered as she struggled to compose herself. "But I feel happy for you that you've found Qianyi! He is a real man with a spine and a generous heart. Such men are really not easy to come by. You should treasure him." She moved closer to wrap her arms around me in an affectionate embrace.

"To tell you the truth, Yuanyuan, I don't know if I can be…. intimate with him….. in bed. He's old enough to be my grandfather!" I finally let her in on my true feelings.

"It can't be all about the age gap. Is it because of the rape or because of Zilong?"

"I don't know…. Maybe both! Zilong is still very much a part of me, whereas the violation seems to have killed off my sense of worth… The very thought of being touched by a man, any man, gives me shudders. Sometimes I'm puzzled as to why guilt and shame never cease to torture me."

"Rushi, you mustn't let shame have a hold on you. You are a beautiful, talented and kind soul with nothing whatsoever to feel ashamed, or guilty of. What happened to you is foul, but it should be blamed on our unkind and bigoted society. Don't ever forget your outstanding literary and artistic achievements. You have every right to feel proud of yourself."

"My reasoning tells me the fault does not lie with me. Yet something in my blood prevails to strip me of my defenses. Perhaps that something is a stigma internalized through centuries of women's meek submission to men's bullying."

"Rushi, in our culture, girls are born with a curse, and girls born into poverty are cursed ten times over. Most men want us to feel inferior and shameful, just to make us vulnerable and easy to overpower and enslave. But few men are above leching after women's looks and bodies. If we can use ours as bait to get what we need, it is our best revenge."

I looked closely at her features in the pearly moonlight, and for the first time noticed a barely perceptible new hardness on the set of her mouth. She was still deliciously tender and beautiful. Yet there was something else that I couldn't immediately put my finger on. Something that smoldered beneath her tense frailty, formless and unyielding..... Yes, defiance! That's what it was!

"For the life of me, Yuanyuan, I would never have imagined such hot-headed words would come out of your mouth. I can't argue with the points you make. Sister, I don't mean to pry, but I would like to know how you coped with..... giving yourself to your husband when your heart is still filled with Xiang?"

"At one time I did fear that Sangui might find me frigid. It is because during my time at the Tians', I steeled myself to feel nothing. The first two times in bed with him were difficult for me. I was so tense I couldn't give him any pleasure. But I was able to make him think it was due to my inborn shyness. The third time I went to him prepared. I had earlier had a bit to drink and was able to relax. In my tipsy state, I started to dance an erotic dance for him. Afterwards, things went smoothly in bed, at least for him...."

It was clear to me that my sister was trying hard to make

her conjugal relationship and her new life work. The last thing she would want was to lose that status and safety that she had fought for with her youthful beauty, which was sure to diminish with age. The next throw of the dice might not be this favorable.

"Ah, so drunkenness and seductive dancing can do the trick. That's good advice, Yuanyuan. I must keep that in mind. So all things considered, you are content with him?"

"My only complaint is that on the days he is at home and not away in the battlefield, he can never keep his hands off me. And if I so much as even mention another man's name, it is enough to send him into a squall of jealousy. I could not imagine what would happen if he found out about Xiang."

She and I both understood only too well that the pursuit of love was like giving chase to a treacherous tempest. Catching up with it could, in a wink, land you in wreckage. And when you were confronted with a choice between survival and love, by instinct it was not even a choice. The pathos of it was that even with foresight, you would still pant for the deadly trap like moths for the flame.

Among the three of us, Xiangjun seemed to be the more fortunate one at that point, and her love life appeared set on a smooth path. But that assumption would unfortunately prove to be grounded on wishful thinking.

We let ruminating silence strike the final note to our hearty chat. I saw her eyelids droop with fatigue and so ushered her to bed at once.

"I'm so very glad that we've had this chance to talk, Yuanyuan," I said as I lay down by her side, feeling closer to her than ever. A part of me wanted so much to take her into my arms and hug her.

"As am I, Big Sister. Sweet dreams! I hope you will find happiness with Qianyi," she said in her dreamy voice.

# EIGHTEEN

As DAWN BROKE, my bed chamber bristled with excitement. The three of us had risen together and just eaten a light breakfast of congee.

My two sisters first fussed with my coiffure, braiding my hair into a double knot and securing it with hairpins. With care and dexterity, Yuanyuan dusted my face with pearl powder, applied rouge to my cheeks and rose paint to my lips. Xiangjun shaped and painted my eyebrows with *qingdai*, applying the same expertise that she had flaunted with Yuanyuan's three months ago.

"Big Sister, both you and Yuanyuan have the most exquisite eyebrows I've ever seen on women," she chimed in her musical voice. "They have the same willow leaf shape and the same lushness." This sister could sweet-talk in such a way as to lure the most flighty birds from their perch to peck from her hand.

When my make-up was done, Begonia helped me to put on the red silk brocaded robe and red silk pleated skirt. I had brought along the green jade hairpin that Fo had given me, and the pair of pink jade bracelets, gifts from my sisters. I took those from my small jewelry box and inserted the hairpin into my coifed hair and put the bracelets on my wrists. Then Yuanyuan deftly fitted the pearl-studded bridal headdress on my head, and draped a large red silk veil over it. Finally, I was all set to go: ready to turn over a new leaf.

At midday, the eight-bearer bridal sedan chair arrived on time. Leaning on Begonia's arm, I climbed into the sedan. Preceding the bridal sedan was a band of cymbal and flute players, playing the loud ceremonial music that attracted a crowd of curious onlookers.

My host, the guests, Begonia and Ah Luk trailed behind the sedan in two large horse-drawn carriages. Following proper wedding formalities for a primary-wife bride, the sedan chair and the carriages were decked in bright red hanging bands and patterned skirts with tassels. Eight small silk lanterns were hung all around the sedan chair, a custom for a primary-wife bride. Having eight sedan bearers was also part of the primary-wife etiquette.

Inside the sedan, excitement initially buoyed me up. Then, a mercurial shift of mood almost unnerved me. The sense of doom I had felt on that fateful day when I was taken in a sedan to the Zhou mansion suddenly raked my mind. Instinct warned me I had to drive out these gloomy thoughts before they had a chance to ruin my day. I reached for the birdie kerchief in my sleeve, and was calmed.

Upon arrival at the West Bridge pier, Qianyi came up to the sedan to take me by the hand and lead me onto the grand nuptial boat, where other guests were waiting. When the guests from the carriages had all come on board, the tea offering ritual began.

To give face to Qianyi's two concubines, who were my seniors, I began by offering bridal tea to them. Begonia was by my side holding a red lacquered tray and passing me one cup at a time. When they took the cup from me, each was supposed to give me a red packet just as a token of blessing, but neither of them did. Under the veil, I couldn't see their faces, but could feel their scathing stare. My maid was quick-witted and, averting an embarrassing moment, said aloud, with a deliberate inflection:

"Our bride thanks the mistresses for their *good wishes!*" She gave me a nudge and bundled me to Qianyi's side.

Next Qianyi joined me in kneeling down and offering tea to Master Wang and Jingli. They each gave us separate red packets, uttering heartfelt blessings and good wishes.

I lifted a corner of the veil to steal a glimpse around and caught Jingli dabbing the corner of her eyes. Without actually seeing, I could visualize Master Wang's eyes narrowed into slits in his cheerful guffaws.

Then Qianyi and I went to the prow of the boat and kneeled and bowed three times to the open sky. When that was done, he lifted my red veil and smiled sheepishly at me, holding my hand tightly in his.

Yuanyuan and General Wu, Xiangjun and Fangyu, came up in pairs to convey their good wishes. I saw Wen's smiling face and Wei's reddened eyes. Tears of gratitude slid down my cheeks.

Ah Luk was lighting up firecrackers at the stern to mark the completion of the ritual, and Begonia went around the boat serving guests Rain Flower tea and sweetmeats.

The wedding feast was to be served up in the early evening from two catering carts which would be stationed on shore. Now the boat was being steered away from shore to cruise around the lake for an afternoon of leisure sight viewing.

It was a crisp, bright day and all our guests drank in the natural beauty of West Lake. The brittle blue sky smiled dreamily in the glinting water. All around the shore, flaming golden ginkgos embraced fiery red maples in a graceful dance, cheered on by the autumn breeze. In the misty distance, mountains were brushed green and gray, giving accent to the raging blaze in the foreground. Nearer, limp remnants of white and pink lotuses idled close to the banks, cooing summer to sleep. Sweet osmanthus scent hung over the lake, in praise of the change of season.

Su Shi was the poet who had likened West Lake to the ancient-era beauty Xi Shi. Whether dressed in rich court regalia of gold and crimson or in wispy gossamer of pink and green, her goddess charm was never lost on spectators.

Reading our guests' enraptured faces, Qianyi and I took pride in having made the perfect choice of venue. I was not surprised when I saw Wen itching to capture it all on paper, but sorely regretting that he hadn't brought along painting brushes and paper.

By the time the boat returned to the West Bridge pier, the sleepy sun had lost its glare and shone without warmth.

The efficient caterers began to serve up course after course of sumptuous fare. The feast boasted of birds' nest soup, roasted piglets, steamed garoupa, deep fried prawns and scallops, roasted ducks and salt-baked chicken. At the host table, Qianyi busied himself with serving me the best of every dish. His attentions became almost embarrassing, as I saw Spring Flower and Orchid pull a long face. Sunyi was sweet to distract them with jokes.

The double-paneled back board of each of the three cabins had been left open to allow unobstructed views from prow to stern. All curtains over the railings had been pulled aside to give open breadthwise views.

The host table covered in red cloth occupied the larger middle cabin, and in our company were Master Wang, Jingli, Spring Flower, Orchid, Sunyi and his wife. The other guests were seated in tables set up in the front and end cabins. A couple of hired flute players were playing merry wedding tunes at the stern. Jovial conversations and laughter blended with the clinking of porcelain cups and dishes.

Just as the last course of lotus leaf fried rice was being served, an onshore commotion became apparent, drawing ever closer. I looked up and saw Orchid's lips curled up in a malevolent smile.

Moments later, a crowd of rough-looking men gathered near the nuptial boat, shouting in rehearsed rhythm: "Liu Rushi belongs in the brothel!" "A whore has no right to be a scholar's wife!" "Liu Rushi is a family wrecker!"

Some men in the crowd were carrying buckets filled with stones and they began pelting them at the boat. Some hit the dishes and bowls and wine cups, spattering the tables and floorboards with blobs of food and porcelain shards.

Our guests were as aghast as we were, and we tried to dodge the flying stones and shards by sprinting to the other side of the boat. In a heartbeat, the air of gaiety curdled into alarm and distaste. Qianyi's complexion shifted from earthy brown to steel green, his face muscles taut as drawn bowstrings.

When I turned around, he was already stepping onto the boarding plank. Raising his hand, he motioned to the men to stop the stone-throwing, shouting at the top of his lungs: "Hey! Stop! Stop! What on earth are you people doing? If you don't stop at once, I'll call the magistrate's guards and have you all arrested! This is a private function. You are breaking the social order!" Then Master Wang also left the host table, jumping ashore to stand beside Qianyi.

Someone dressed in a scholar's robe emerged from the crowd to give a strident retort. "You must be Master Qian," he called. "As a respected scholar-official, you should know that it's against social code for scholars to take courtesans as concubines. If you want to go to the magistrate to file a charge against us, by all means go ahead. We would be eager to hear who the magistrate says has broken the social order."

Qianyi opened his mouth but no words came out. Master

Wang leaned over to whisper something into his ear. His shoulders drooped and he kept silent. Master Wang drew himself up to face the man and said with placid poise,

"Young master, there's no need to embarrass Master Qian. I am sure you did not mean to spoil his happy day. Let's face it. You know as well as I that it is common practice for scholars to take courtesans as concubines these days. Is that not true? Now, would it make you happier if I invite you all to a good feast at the Sanbo Restaurant just down the street? I would even make it worth your while to go. Let's see. There are about ten of you. Here's a bill for fifty taels of silver for you to share. How does that sound?" The kind-hearted Master Wang fumbled in his sleeve pocket and took out a folded bill of exchange.

The bill instantly drew the leader's greedy stare and he grabbed it without thinking, blurting out in his husky voice, "In that case, it would be discourteous to turn down your offer. We don't want to be difficult, just working to make a living!" He turned to address his followers, "Fellows, let's call it a day! The old master here has offered us a good fee. And we've been invited to a free meal at Sanbo. Now follow my lead!"

Qianyi came back to the boat cabin, his face contorted with smoldering rage. For a moment I was too distressed to find soothing words for him. With difficulty I forced myself to come out of the befuddled daze and to face down the situation. There was no doubt in my mind that Spring Flower and Orchid were behind this crude spectacle designed to humiliate me, taking their cue from Zhengyu's letter. But I knew I must not go down that path now. The immediate task was to appease our startled guests.

Thankfully, the buzz of consternation began to quiet down. Begonia and Ah Luk had already started cleaning up the spilled mess and broken porcelain in the host cabin. I went up to the caterers and tucked into their palms the red packets I had earlier received, and asked them quietly to clean up the two guest cabins. In a flash, all the cabins were tidied up, and the guests returned to their seats.

By now, Qianyi appeared somewhat collected. He waved to the caterers to serve the dessert of snow fungus and lotus seeds soup.

Master Wang came back just in time for this sweet delicacy. As he sat down and tasted the soup, he blinked at me playfully, then stood up and said aloud in a cheerful voice: "This is the best sweet soup I have ever tasted! Let us drink to the new couple! May they share a life just as sweet!"

He raised his wine cup, and everyone else in the boat followed and echoed him, except Spring Flower and Orchid, whose faces were grimly set like clay effigies in a temple. The sweet soup drew resounding praises from the guests and salvaged the day. Qianyi and I went the rounds of thanking the guests for the pleasure of their company and urging them to have more rice wine.

A bright yellow full moon was peering shyly from behind the opaque gauze of clouds, and attracted everyone's admiring gaze. Both Yuanyuan and Xiangjun came up to me to squeeze my hand in unspoken consolation, and Wen flashed me a wide supportive smile from his table. Qianyi busied himself with chatting with the male guests in the two guest cabins in turn, while Master Wang engaged Jingli and Wei in light banter. I threw my loyal friend a grateful glance.

Begonia, in her usual nimble gait, served plates of sweetmeats and hot Rain Flower tea to all the tables. Qianyi and I were at last able to exchange a smile.

With farewells said, guests began to disperse. Qianyi and I, my foster family, his family, Begonia and Ah Luk all headed to a nearby inn to stay the night.

It could have been a perfectly blissful day for me if not for that farcical interruption. But then I counted my blessings. Things could also have turned out much worse. Qianyi, probably exhausted, sank into deep slumber as soon as he touched the bed. I was relieved that he did.

The next day we arrived back at our cottage by the afternoon. With as much equanimity as I could muster, I told Qianyi about the mysterious disappearance of Zhengyu's letter, hinting that Spring Flower's maid might have filched it and then stealthily returned it.

A look of relief crossed his face, as though he had found the denouement to a tangled scholarly dispute. He patted my hand.

"I am aware that Spring Flower has always harbored animosity towards you," he said. "I will question her, and if indeed it was she who had concocted the stupid show, I will reprimand her, but I doubt that will change what's in her nature. My dear wife, if there is anything I could do to make up for your displeasure, I will gladly oblige."

"Qianyi, I wasn't expecting you to stir up a storm, because that would only deepen the bad feelings in this household," I said. "As long as you know the truth of the matter, I can put my mind at ease." The last thing I wanted was to fan the flames of hostility in the household, but then I was thinking that since he offered atonement, I might as well hold him to it. So I said with a smile, "As a new bride, I think a little pampering is not too much to ask of my husband.... I'm holding you to your promise."

"Madam Rushi, my heart, body and soul are all yours now. If I don't pamper you, who else will I pamper?"

That night in the bed chamber, the vicious calumny of the previous day crept up and scraped open the scab on my old wound, making my heart bleed anew. I needed to numb the pain before I let it spoil the night for my new husband.

Remembering Yuanyuan's advice, I gulped down three cups of rice wine and made Qianyi down two cups. Then I struggled to dance a slow butterfly dance for him, dressed only in a white silk shift and silk underpants. His eyes were glued to my little feet, shod in red embroidered silk slippers. By the time I hit the bed, I was unconscious.

The next morning, I found myself without clothes underneath a silk quilt. Qianyi was sitting at the end of the bed, fondling my naked feet. He wore a smug smile on his face. He looked at me as if in an intoxicated daze. I knew he had claimed his right as husband. It was almost a comfort that I didn't remember anything. That thought had barely passed when he saw that I was awake, and he lifted the quilt and took me again.

My thoughts wandered off to those dizzying nights of pleasure with Zilong, which made my face burn with shame. Qianyi had no clue what was running through my mind, and thought I was feeling shy. How could I tell him that I was clinging for life to those images of aching passion, so as to escape the here and now? But I knew that there was no escape from the fact that I was now his woman. He appeared anxious to prove that, as he practically kept me bound to the bed for the next three days.

On the south side of the brook, construction of a three-storey lodge was ongoing on the clearing. The new lodge would accommodate a large library on the uppermost level, a painting gallery and work studio on the middle level, and living quarters on the ground floor. Qianyi and I had decided to name the new abode "Crimson Clouds Lodge".

I was gradually attuned to a routine of reading Ming poetry and editing Qianyi's annotations to the poems to be included in his anthology. He had moved a great number of his books to our cottage from his library to save me the trouble of shuttling to and fro when he and I needed the books for reference. My impeccable memory awed him time and again, as I effortlessly showed him the accurate source of literary allusions every time he requested my help. I would take breaks from my work now and then to paint and write poetry.

Shortly after the Winter Solstice, I got a wedding invitation from Xiangjun along with a letter explaining the predicament that Xiaowan was now in, and how Mao Xiang was now too destitute to offer her any help.

When I brought this up while having a chat with Qianyi the following day, I told him the whole story of how I had tried to maneuver between Yuanyuan, Mao Xiang and Xiaowan in order to arrive at the best outcome for everyone. He looked at me with his typical captive wonder and said:

"Ah, Mao Xiang is a talented and kind-hearted young man. He and Yuanyuan would have been so perfect for each other. How sad that harsh reality forced them apart! But my dear wife, what you did was a kindly act. At one stroke you saved two women from living hell. I can't be prouder of you."

"Well, one of those women is my beloved sister, and as for Xiaowan, I do have an obligation to fulfill my best friend's last wish. Sadly, for every enslaved woman who is pulled back from the brink of hell, there are thousands others who are pushed off the cliff. Qianyi, I was going to ask if....."

"Our society has traditionally been unfair to women. But every bit of our effort to help them counts. I know you want me to help with repaying those debts. You and I are husband and wife now. Your problem is my problem, and I have a duty to solve it." He paused for breath, and, looking me in the eye, he came clean with me about his finances.

"But I will also be honest with you," he said. "I was going

to use my savings on the building of our new lodge. If I dole out the three thousand taels of silver to help Xiaowan and Mao Xiang, it means that I will be left without a copper and will have to sell my only valuable property: the old classic imprints of *The Histories of Han and Later Han,* in order to foot the construction bill. To tell you the truth, those imprints came into my possession as Orchid's dowry when I took her as my second concubine. Her father loved to collect rare imprints. I guess I will just have to do the sale behind her back."

"My dear husband, yes, I was hoping you could help to repay the debts. But I wasn't aware of the financial situation. Now that you've told me that solving my problem would cause you trouble, I don't think it right to impose on you...."

"Frankly, those historical imprints have neither sentimental nor academic value to me – there are cheaper print versions. They have a high market value mainly because they are sought after by collectors of rare items. Don't worry, if I don't tell Orchid about the sale, she will never even notice it. In all these years, she has not once visited my library."

Before I could say another word, he moved over to his writing table, sat down and wrote out a bill of exchange in the amount of three thousand taels of silver. When he handed the bill to me, he said:

"I gave you my word that I would make amends for the defects of our wedding. I'm only making good my promise. Besides, I am happy to help Mao Xiang. He has a good heart. Last year, the farms in some remote villages were ravaged by locusts, and many peasants were starving to death. When he heard the news, he led a charity movement to raise money for the peasants. To set an example, he donated all his savings to help."

"Qianyi, I don't know what to say.... Xiang is respectable. Xiaowan is fortunate to have him as her husband and I'm very happy for her. But you, my husband, have my adoration for wanting to help a downtrodden woman who is a total stranger. Words are beyond me...." I stepped up to behind his chair to circle my arms around his shoulders and peck lightly on his cheek, which pleased him a lot. He took my hand and kissed it passionately.

"Haw haw, my sweet wife, you've made me the happiest man in this world. Thank you."

To show him my gratitude, I ushered him into our bed chamber and submitted to his erotic whims, using some techniques I had learned from *Jin Ping Mei*.

Later that day, I wrote back to Xiangjun enclosing the bill of exchange, with a separate note to Jingli and ten silver pieces for her to purchase on my behalf a wedding gift for my sister. Then I bade Ah Luk deliver the correspondence and money to Nanjing.

My heart was now filled with genuine respect for him, because my gut told me he had really done this for me. In accepting this massive favor from him, I felt I would forever owe him my loyalty.

I was praying to Guanyin that when the time came for him to sell the historical imprints, that Orchid would not have cause to find out. As things stood, she already hated me for taking the primary wife status. I couldn't imagine her wrath were the secret to see the light of day. Somehow, the very name Orchid had an unpropitious ring to it, as a former friend with the same name at the Zhou household had heartlessly sold me out.

After a few months, I began to notice Qianyi's manhood was fast failing him, and by instinct I knew we would not be blessed with a child.

# PART THREE

## The Secret

# TALES OF MING COURTESANS

# NINETEEN

J*INGJING HAD SPENT* the previous afternoon immersed in her mother's memoir.

She always knew her father had adored her mother, who, as her doting mentor, had impressed her as a spirited marvel. Having now read a big chunk of the memoir, which at times wrung her heart, she came to appreciate her character much better. Deep down, she could not but worship her.

But when she came to that line "I noticed his manhood was fast failing him and by instinct I knew we would not be blessed with a child", she was thunderstruck. Her heart raced like a wild horse. It took her a long while to come out of her bafflement.

"Who is my birth father, then?" The deeply troubling question had boomed in her head all night and kept her awake till the fourth night-watch gong. She had then drifted in and out of sleep through to dawn.

This morning, her mind cleared somewhat and a deep sense of emptiness engulfed her. She yearned to snuggle up to her mother, embrace and comfort her, and be hugged and coddled in return. But that was not going to happen now, or ever again. She tried to reassure herself that the answer to that question must lie in the rest of the memoir. No matter what the answer turned out to be, her mother's place in her heart would never change. That much she was certain. She decided it was best not to mention the shocking discovery to her aunt yet.

When she entered the rear lounge, Yuanyuan was already at the table waiting for her. After eating breakfast, they stepped out to the

*front garden as usual to take their places under the willows. Jingjing*
*tried her best to concentrate.*

Last time I stopped at the point where I was about to be married
to General Wu. The wedding went smoothly as Master Tian's
wife had planned everything perfectly. I was happy that my
sisters and Mother had a most enjoyable time both on the hair-
combing day and the wedding day.

When the wedding feast was over, Sangui took me in a
carriage to his resort lodge in the quiet outskirts of Yangzhou.
The lodge was a modest one-storey cottage, simply furnished
but kept sparkling clean. The servant Ah Seng and the maid
Azalea came out with lanterns to greet us and led us to the bridal
chamber, decorated in red, with a pair of bright red wedding
candles flickering by the latticed window.

That night, Sangui and I got into conversation while we lay
in bed, holding hands. I was surprised to learn that he had been
born and raised in the same Suzhou village as I. Then we began
reminiscing about those childhood days in our home village. He
started teasing me when I told him how, at the age of five, I fell
into the lotus pond near my cottage when I tried to pluck a white
lotus blossom.

"In your former life, you must have been that great beauty
Xi Shi from the Spring and Autumn period," he said to me
with a disarming smile. "Did you know she was a reincarnated
Goddess of Lotus Blossom? I will set up a marble statue of her
in the courtyard of our new home, to honor you." I must say this
art-loving side of him pleasantly surprised me. Letting down my
guard, I told him about my early past.

"My mother had died when I was a toddler and by the age
of nine, I was orphaned. My maternal widower uncle took me
in. But he was already having a hard time feeding his own two

children, as the small vegetable farm he owned was destroyed by locusts. So after living in his run-down home for a year, I was sold to a thin horse breeder in Suzhou City. That was where I met and befriended Xiangjun. A couple of years later, Jingli took us in as new performers. She then became our foster mother on the day Rushi, Xiangjun and I swore our oath of sisterhood. You already know the rest of my story from Master Tian."

"So it was at the thin horse breeder's that you learned your singing and dancing?" His eyes squinted as he asked. He looked so severe that it would be impossible to tell him a lie.

"Yes, I learned the basic skills there. Then at the Villa of Alluring Fragrance I learned opera singing and pipa playing from the eminent Master Su Kunsheng. For my dancing, I improvised my own moves and steps as I became more experienced in the art."

"You have music in your fibers and fluid grace in your dance movements. It is your natural gift. That is something no teacher can teach."

"You are flattering me!" I said, blushing. "It was a good thing that I escaped the ordeal of foot-binding. Otherwise, I would never have become a good dancer."

"But I hate those men who have seen you perform your delicious dancing. The thought of it riles me; it makes me want to gouge out their eyes! I don't want you to ever again dance before another man. You will dance for no one but me. Do you understand?"

I flinched at the sudden savagery of his voice. While talking, he peered at my face with an intensity that was almost animalistic, as though he wanted to swallow me whole. I changed the subject and urged him to tell me of his past, which he did with blunt candor:

"My mother died young and I grew up under the austere guidance of my father, who drilled me into being a cunning military man. My childhood training under him was harsh. Whenever I made a mistake or when I showed any slackness, he would beat me with a cane till I bled. At a young age I enlisted with the army, and through my father's connections, rose fast in the ranks. My father taught me one cardinal rule: that winning is all that matters, in life as much as in the battlefield, and that scruples are only a hindrance that mess things up."

As far as I could make out, Sangui was a two-faced man. He was basically brutal and devious, as he had never been taught love or morals. But if he willingly opened up to a person he trusted, he could be forthcoming and decent. Strangely though, as much as his crudeness was to my distaste, his ferocity didn't frighten me.

This night and the next, I felt tense and awkward lying in the big canopied bed with silk coverings. I couldn't seem to shake off my habitual charade of frigidity. Fortunately he was gentle with me and never doubted my excuse that it was due to my innate shy nature.

On the third day, he and I took the morning boat to Nanjing with Ah Seng and Azalea tagging along, carrying basketfuls of bridal gifts like silk fabric, fresh fruit, wedding pastries and candies. From the Peach Leaf Pier, we went by carriage to the Villa of Alluring Fragrance. There, we offered tea and gifts to Mother. She was very excited, seemingly proud of the fact that the illustrious General Wu Sangui was now her first son-in-law. On her insistence, we stayed for lunch. Before we left, she reminded us that Rushi's wedding in Hangzhou was only three months away.

That night, before preparing myself for bed, I gave Sangui two cups of rice wine and downed a full cup myself. Remembering how he loved my dancing, I got up to dance the fan dance for him.

Next morning, I was awake before dawn. In the dim natural light, I saw him smiling in his sleep. When I tried to get out of bed, he suddenly grabbed my waist and pulled me up against his chest, demanding more pleasure.

I would soon find out that he had a big appetite for bed pleasures. But I could not complain. As his concubine, I was expected to please him, in bed or otherwise. At least I did not loathe him like I loathed Tian, Compared with the debasing way Tian had abused me, his treatment could certainly count as kindness.

So now, on top of faking contentment, I had to try to appear cheerful and willing to serve his carnal needs. It was a small price to pay for a little dignity and a normal life. But whenever his touch evoked images and memories of Xiang, my heart would freeze and crack, and I would be vigilant to blink back tears, or pretend they were tears of joy.

At the end of the first month in my new home, I came to realize that in my husband's view, I was a talisman that he possessed. And it was with jealous obsession that he guarded me. The mere mention of Tian or any other man's name was enough to make him fly into jealous rage.

One time when I casually mentioned the name of a childhood friend from our home village who was now living in Yangzhou and working as a junior ministry official, he frowned and grilled me for a whole night to see whether or not the friend and I were still in contact.

By now, I knew his soft spot well enough to easily divert him. He simply could not resist my seductive dancing, especially when I dressed in my skimpy *dudou* paired with the billowing white silk skirt. Such teasing could bring him to a high point of excitement, from which only an abrupt descent was possible. At other times, singing his favorite song from *Romance of the Western*

*Chamber* on pipa accompaniment could tame the lustful beast in him.

By the start of the eighth lunar month, I was relieved to learn that he had been summoned by the Emperor to fight the Manchu army at Songshan under General Hong Chengchou's command. He was not to return until the start of the ninth lunar month. It was a welcome break for me.

I was pleased that Sangui accompanied me to Rushi's wedding at West Lake, because it at least showed that he had respect for my foster family.

Jingjing, the wedding and the unfortunate fracas are probably all described in your mother's memoir, so I am not going to repeat them. I would just say that Rushi and I grew closer than ever after that night's intimate chat. We now understood each other's feelings perfectly, and my heart went out to her during that unfortunate incident. Mother had said she was sure it was Qianyi's concubines who had plotted it. I was a bit worried about Rushi too, knowing what a proud person she was. She would think it beneath her dignity to tangle with small-minded people.

There was one pleasant surprise for me, though. During the hair-combing ritual, Mother had quietly slipped a folded envelope into my palm, and just a quick glimpse at the familiar handwriting made my pulse quicken. I had it well hidden all the while in Hangzhou and didn't dare read it until after Sangui left again for the battlefield.

This was what Xiang wrote:

"My sweet Yuanyuan:

Knowing that you'll be coming to Hangzhou to attend Rushi's wedding, I've entrusted your mother with this letter to pass to you.

I received your letter telling me about the big break you had been longing for: a new life with General Wu.

It pleased me to know that you gained your freedom at last. But at the same time this piece of news skewered me in my weakest spot.

It is with a bleeding heart that I say this to you. Not a day goes by without my pining for your delicious scent, your silky soft skin, your fragrant tresses and your heavenly singing voice. Above all, I miss the wise listener in you. No one in the entire world understands me better than you. Since our parting, I've been only going through the motion of living. There's hardly any life left in me. Visualizing you in the arms of another man cuts me to pieces. The pain defies words.

Xiaowan is good to me. For her, I only feel pity and charity. There has never been any passion between me and her. Your lovely shadow that resides in my heart leaves no room for her or any other. But I will keep the promise I made to you. I will take her as my concubine in order to rescue her from ruin. Before I can do that, there is the problem of repaying her father's mountainous debts. I've donated all my savings to the starving peasants in the locust-plagued villages. Maybe it is not the wisest thing to do. My head is all muddled up these days. But please don't worry for my sake. I'll have the issues sorted out somehow.

Yuanyuan, if ever you need my help in anything, please do not hesitate to come to me. The doors of my heart will always be open just for you. Let us use your mother's villa as the hub for our exchanges. I'll pay regular visits there to leave my letters and collect any mail from you. I must hear from you, my love, or I shall die. Take good care of yourself.

With undying love,

Your Xiang"

After reading the letter over and over, I moved my finger slowly over the written words, hoping to feel through them his gentle touch, while trying to draw from my mental store his odor, the chiseled outline of his face, and his low-keyed timbre. In that solitary moment, my long repressed tears poured out furiously like a rainstorm. After the emotional purge, I actually felt a lot better.

On Winter Solstice day, I got word from Xiangjun that her wedding would be held on Lantern Festival Day. A little later Mother wrote to me to say that Qianyi had helped to repay Xiaowan's father's debts, and Xiang and Xiaowan had just held their nuptials. I knew it was wrong for me to feel jealous. But I couldn't help it. The thought of another woman in Xiang's arms was driving me off the ledge of sanity.

Meanwhile, life went on. Fortunate for me, Sangui's battle stints were becoming longer, which meant that I could enjoy longer spells of peace.

One day, Ah Seng came back from his daily scouting and, all excited and panting, told me in gasps what he had read on the Yangzhou city notice board: "Mistress, Commander Hong Chengchou….. was captured by the Manchus at the Battle of Songshan… He has now defected to the Qing court. Our Emperor has promoted…. our young master….. to fill the commander position at Ningyuen! He has just been sent to Hubei to quell peasants' riots."

I secretly felt immense joy at hearing the news. The promotion and the riots would most likely keep Sangui away from home for an extended stretch, and any home leave he could take would probably be short.

As expected, I got a message from him telling me he would

not be home for the New Year as he was stuck in skirmishes in Hubei. He bade me take Ah Seng as my escort for the trip to Nanjing for Xiangjun's wedding. I could not be more pleased. I was so looking forward to the wedding and our sisters' fourth reunion on Lantern Festival Day. Xiangjun had mentioned that Xiang and Xiaowan were on her guest list.

I spent the few days preceding the Lantern Festival at Mother's villa longing to see Xiang, while pretending to be engaged with the festive and bridal preparations. I wanted so much to see with my own eyes whether there was any hint of love between him and Xiaowan, whether or not Xiang had lied to me in the letter. A woman can tell these things.

Xiangjun was looking resplendent. She and Fangyu made a beautiful couple. True to her nature, she let her gaiety rub off on everyone around her. She was a jaunty sight to behold. But when Mother told me about the story of the dowry rejection, an ominous feeling quietly stalked me. I couldn't help worrying about how those ruthless people from the eunuch faction would react to what they would deem an insulting rebuff. I could only pray that my sister would not incur their wrath.

Worries aside, I was determined to enjoy Xiangjun's and Mother's company as much as I could during my stay. Who knew when we would see each other again, with the winds of war now blowing hard.

During the day, I busied myself with helping Mother make wedding pastries with lotus seed paste filling and wedding candies. At night, I chatted with Xiangjun and told her about my new life and shared with her my most intimate feelings.

The day before Xiangjun's hair-combing day, Rushi arrived. She told us that Qianyi was delayed by work and he would be joining us on the wedding day. As soon as supper was over, the three of us disappeared into Xiangjun's bed chamber to have a girls' talk.

"Yuanyuan, how has Sangui been treating you? You look a little slimmer than the last time I saw you." Few things could escape our Big Sister's eyes.

"Poor Yuanyuan! It seems to me she has escaped one cage only to be trapped in another," Xiangjun volunteered her keen observation, with empathy.

"What can I do? I have no choice but to make the best of my new life. Sangui values my artistic skills and is protective of me, but he and I don't see eye to eye on a lot of things. As his concubine, I cannot refuse his demands in bed. But, when he touches me, my body repulses it, and my mind wanders off to Xiang. Xiangjun, you and Fangyu are a fortunate pair. I'm truly happy for you! For most women in our situation, marrying someone for love is pure fantasy."

"I know how you must feel, Yuanyuan. I wish things were easier for you..."

"Xiangjun, I'm really happy for you too. Yuanyuan, I am so sorry that you are not happy in your marriage. I had a hand in this and I really hoped you'd find happiness. But, like you said, love is an elusive dream in our lot. My marriage is no better than yours. Nothing can make me forget or yearn any less for Zilong."

"Rushi, you mustn't feel any guilt about my situation. For all my complaints, I'm still in a far better situation than at the Tian's. Submitting to my husband's demands is a small price to pay. At the Wu household, I am at least a human."

"I guess I am a bit more fortunate than you. Thank heavens Qianyi is losing interest in physical love-making, and we are like spiritual mates now. But I recently got a letter from Li Wen telling me that Zilong had fallen seriously ill around the time of my wedding....." Her voice trailed off, as though words were clotted in her throat.

"Rushi, to be honest, I cannot completely cut ties with Xiang...."

"Yuanyuan, Rushi, it makes me feel bad that I seem to have it so easy. But the truth is, something weighs heavy on my heart. I am far from sure that Fangyu's family will accept me. His idea is to make our marriage a done deal before announcing it to his family. Ai, what if they reject me anyway? My gut tells me that we are in calm waters before the storm." Xiangjun batted her wet eyelashes.

Both Rushi and I felt for her. All courtesans and performers, even if not in bondage, were classed as *jianmin*. Unless and until someone took them as concubines, they would be stuck with that status, which was for life. It might sound beastly unjust, but this was how our society worked. We knew there was little we could do, but still tried our best to console her.

"My maid Azalea told me that in the last five years, Sangui has failed to get any of his concubines pregnant. So, in all likelihood, I won't have a child by him. You can't imagine how relieved that makes me feel. Honestly, I have no feelings for him and would hate to carry his child." I paused and looked into my sisters' bewildered eyes, then decided to be frank with them.

"With every day my soul dies a little more yearning for something I cannot have. It's only in fiction that you see a woman fall in love with the hero who saves her. It doesn't happen in real life. I don't know how much longer I can put up with this hollow charade. I've been wondering if there might be a way out...." I faltered, choked by welling up tears.

After a moment of meditation, Rushi said with grave concern in her eyes: "Yuanyuan, I hope you won't try anything foolish that you will later regret."

The burden of my secret had weighed me down for so long

that I felt an urgent need to unload it.

"Rushi, Xiangjun, if I am ever to have a child, I want it to be by the man I truly love. Having Xiang's child is the only way I could feel alive again, and his child would be my ray of hope, something to live for."

"But how are you ever going to do that, while your husband is alive?" Xiangjun asked, her eyes growing round in puzzlement.

"I know this may sound like wishful thinking, but I'll wait for the chance. With all the peasant revolts in progress and a big war at our doorstep, who knows what will happen? Perhaps the heavens will give me a chance."

"Yuanyuan, I can feel your pain. I just hope you are aware of the risks in even contemplating such a plan, let alone carrying it out. Having said that, if you feel it is a matter of life and death to you and your heart is set on it, then your goal has my blessing and support. I won't even question your reasoning. You have gone through hell and you deserve to have what your heart most desires. When the time comes for you to act on it and you need my help, just come to me."

Rushi looked steadily into my eyes with a solemnity I had not seen before. When she squeezed my hand with firmness, I knew she meant every word she said.

Xiangjun put her hand on my arm and echoed Rushi's support with equal resolve, "Yuanyuan, you are so like Lady Du in *The Peony Pavilion*. She is my idol for daring to love and stand up to the tyranny of social codes. In the same way, you are my idol for your courage, and I promise I will help you in any way I can to realize your dream."

They probably had no idea how much I loved them just for their consoling words. I hugged each tightly in turn, and then said,

"Xiangjun, enjoy your time fully with Fangyu while you can.

Happiness is like a slippery eel. It is hard enough to catch, and even harder to hold onto."

At last Xiangjun's big day arrived. At midday, Qianyi, Xiang and Xiaowan arrived just in time to witness with us the bridal tea offering inside the cozy dressing lounge, which held so many fond memories of our past sisterly reunions.

Xiangjun, dressed in her finely made pink wedding garments embroidered with blue butterflies, had her hair knotted and prettily decorated with a pair of sapphire butterfly hairpins. Pink suited her ivory skin perfectly.

She and Fangyu offered tea to Mother and Yang Longyou, who stood in as the groom's guardian. In the background a hired band of flute and lute players were playing wedding tunes, giving life and gaiety to the ceremony.

A contented smile lit up Mother's face when she held the cup of bridal tea in her hands. Handing out red packets to the bride and groom, she muttered in a choked voice: "May Guanyin endow your union with harmony, longevity and offspring."

The noise of firecrackers prodded the parrot into cackling its rehearsed chant: "Good fortune... Good fortune to the new couple!"

It was a good thing that they would be making their home in the villa, as otherwise Mother would feel too abandoned when the wedding was over.

But no one present at the wedding could have guessed what was to befall the couple only about a year later. No one except, perhaps, Yang Longyou. As Ma Shiying's brother-in-law, he naturally had a key role in the Ruan and Ma farce, and I noticed a palpable sense of unease on his florid face.

Rushi and Qianyi appeared relaxed enough. The calm smiles on their faces seemed to indicate they were comfortably in sync.

When my gaze fell on Xiang, wistful longing spilled across his face, as he stood at an arm's length from his new concubine. His fiery gaze darted across the lounge to lock with my eyes. That instant felt more precious than a lifetime. Then, as if struck by sudden acute pain, he abruptly averted his glistening eyes.

Xiaowan was fixing her stare on her new husband, who looked like he was hardly aware of her presence. At that moment I felt a sharp sense of pity for her. I had the answer I was looking for. He had not lied to me. I still held his musical soul captive. The spiritual bond between us, which had sprouted from our love of music, was something that would transcend time. That meant more to me than being in physical contact with him. I had planned on having a secret assignation, but now thought better of it. He was not going to give me up.

After attending Xiangjun's wedding, I felt a little more light-hearted, having slipped my deep dark secret to my sisters. Their vow of support was like a vicarious glimpse of spring flower buds in the numbing cold depths of winter.

In the second lunar month, Sangui came home one morning and told me the new house in Beijing was now ready and that we would be moving there by boat on the Grand Canal in a couple of days. He told Ah Seng and Azalea to start packing at once. I wrote a brief note telling Mother of our imminent departure, leaving her our Beijing address, and asked Ah Seng to put the note in the mail.

*Jingjing now had no doubt that in Aunt Yuanyuan's heart, only one man mattered, and that man was Mao Xiang. She just wondered if Sangui's love for her aunt would ever change her heart.*

*The aroma of fried rice with shrimps that wafted from the rear lounge told her it was time for the midday meal. She was eager for Jingli Po Po to continue with Aunt Xiangjun's story afterwards.*

# TWENTY

*It was late spring and the days were becoming longer. Jingjing was in a lighter mood. This time of the year always put a spring to her step. But there was something else. For the first time since her arrival here, she now found herself at peace. Solace and security had replaced grief and pain. She had no doubt that it owed much to the loving company of Aunt Yuanyuan and Jingli Po Po. These women were the kindest souls she had ever met in her life.*

*Light breezes were whisking heady fragrances from the flowering side garden to the lotus pond garden, now warmed to a golden hue by the early afternoon sun. Jingjing had no trouble persuading Jingli Po Po to come out to the inviting front garden for the storytelling session. Aunt Yuanyuan was in the side garden cooing her precious, lovely blooms.*

On the day of Xiangjun's wedding, I was quite surprised and moved by a little incident during the wedding dinner. When the last course of sweet soup was being served, Fangyu's friend Longyou tried to poke fun at the groom, in a good-natured way:

"Fangyu, now that you and Xiangjun are man and wife, don't you think it's appropriate for you to show us what you've given her as wedding gift?"

At the unexpected tease, Fangyu's face flushed deep red. His friend had accidentally touched a sensitive nerve in him. He was always self-conscious about his lack of means. My quick-witted daughter immediately sprang to his rescue.

Retrieving a folded silk fan from her sleeve, she said in her musical voice,

"My husband gave me the most precious wedding gift. It is a poem dedicated to me that he wrote on this silk fan." Veering her half-mocking gaze to Longyou, she teased, "But this poem would only speak to people who read with their heart."

Then everyone around the table clamored for a recital of the poem. Longyou laughed a hearty laugh and said, "Why don't I read it aloud for everyone to hear?" He flipped open the fan and recited fluidly in his sonorous timbre,

Crimson villas line the sloping path,

Wealthy princes in their fancy carriages ride from afar.

Noble magnolias by the Green Brook abound,

They pale beside the breeze-blown peach flowers.

Rushi and Qianyi were the first to clap their hands in cheery applause, followed by others. I had to admit that Fangyu's poem excelled in its subtle elegance. I could certainly see why Xiangjun was so touched. She never lacked for wealthy and powerful suitors, yet wealth and privilege meant nothing to her. And she never let her low social status define her. His nuanced confession to being her dedicated admirer was rendered to perfection.

For half a year after their wedding, Fangyu and Xiangjun lived a happy though frugal life at my villa.

Then in the summer, nasty news struck. Though not entirely a surprise, it still wrecked her.

When Fangyu wrote to his family in Henan to inform them of the wedding, not only did his primary wife respond with an acrimonious letter, but he also got a good carping from his strait-laced father. The verdict was unambiguous: the Hou family was too prominent a family to accept a courtesan into the household, even as an unworthy concubine.

My poor Xiangjun cried for two whole days in her chamber. I had almost seen this coming. It was all-too-common for the scholarly gentry to put up a snobbish front for the sake of face. I was sure that Xiangjun was just as cultured as Fangyu's primary wife, if not more. As for looks, it was a known fact that she had few rivals. Her only sin was her wretched childhood and the *jianmin* status that fate thrust on her. Those who could best afford to be generous in heart were often the stingiest.

Now that the Hou family had rejected the union, it was clear that Fangyu could not expect financial help from his father.

To make matters worse, when he sat for the civil service examination again in autumn, he wrote an essay that was highly critical of the Chongzhen Emperor's court. It came as no surprise that he failed the exam. His hopes of finding a job in the local municipality were also now totally dashed. Xiangjun decided not to give up her profession because she needed the money for both of them to live on.

Towards the end of that year, one day Longyou paid us a visit out of the blue, bearing bad tidings. As soon as he saw Fangyu and Xiangjun, he said in a tense voice,

"Fangyu, you must leave here at once. Ruan made a big fuss about your examination essay and persuaded the court to have you arrested for treason. The imperial guards may show up any time now. My brother-in-law warned me against tipping you off, but I couldn't stand by and watch them play dirty on you. It's clearly out of spite that they are doing this."

Both Fangyu and Xiangjun gasped at hearing the news, their faces pale. The news shocked me too, and I could only think of asking, "Where can he hide? This is so sudden!"

"I've thought this through. Here's a letter of introduction from me addressed to the General Secretary of the War Ministry,

Master Shi Kefa. Take it with you and head straight to Yangzhou. Master Shi is Ruan's archenemy and can give you the protection you need. He could also use a literary talent like you."

"I don't know what to say, Longyou. You're a real friend..." Fangyu stammered in confusion.

"Longyou, I thank you from the bottom of my heart for saving my husband. We are forever in your debt. I'm sure Master Shi will take good care of Fangyu. If you will now excuse me, I'll go and pack a few things for my husband."

As usual, Xiangjun was the cool-headed one of the two, although the tremor in her voice betrayed her grief. I could see her trying hard to hold back her tears as she turned and rushed upstairs.

"I'm so sorry to see you in such hot water. But hopefully you can come back after this has passed. Have a safe trip, Fangyu, and don't forget to write. I must go back home now."

As soon as Longyou left, Fangyu went upstairs to bid his Xiangjun farewell. When I passed by her chambers, I heard her sing the song *Pipa Story*, while strumming on her pipa. This song was her favorite of favorites, and as a habit, she would not perform it for any of our customers. The lyrics were adapted from Bai Juyi's narrative poem *Song of the Pipa Player*, which told the sad life story of an aging courtesan whose husband abandoned her. It was Xiangjun's way of hinting to Fangyu never to forsake her. I couldn't help shedding a few tears for my poor girl.

When the couple emerged from their chamber, Fangyu was all set to depart. Xiangjun's tears had dried and she put forward a stolid front.

As we walked Fangyu to the Peach Leaf Pier to see him off, our hearts were too heavy for conversation. Silence was in our company.

When we passed by the Long Chant Pavilion, the largest

brothel in Qinhuai right by the Pier, lusty laughter, sing-song voices and scraps of ribald dialogue streamed from the verandah. Whoever they were, those pleasure seekers didn't seem to care a whit that our country was teetering on the edge of a cliff. Already a growing number of starving vagrants were seeking refuge in Nanjing, fleeing from rebellions and famines in their home towns.

As I was lost in thoughts, we found ourselves already at the dock. Neither husband nor wife knew for how long they were going to be apart. It could well be for years in these unsettling times. Pleading for her husband to write often, Xiangjun finally released her clasp of his hand and said her reluctant farewell. Even in the bright winter daylight, I saw night fall on her spirits, inexorably as it fell on the hills. The tragic butterfly folktale surged into my mind.

When the Lantern Festival came around, Rushi and Yuanyuan arrived one after the other for the sisters' fifth reunion. Having heard what had happened to Fangyu, they went up to say comforting words to Xiangjun, which only set off rivulets down her face.

On the Festival evening just before dinner, Yuanyuan gave us the latest news about the war at the northern border, which made our hearts sink. Rushi told us that the Revival Society members were preparing to take up arms under Zilong's leadership. She looked tired and wan that evening, probably worrying about Zilong's safety.

Then I remembered Xiang had dropped off a letter for Yuanyuan a few days ago. I hurried upstairs to get it for her. When I handed her the letter, I couldn't help blurting out,

"Is it a good idea for you to keep up this liaison with Xiang? You are both married!"

Before she could answer, Rushi jumped to her defense.

"Jingli, I think Yuanyuan has her reasons. The heart wants what the heart wants. A heart thwarted of love is like a plant denied water. It will wither and die. In *The Peony Pavilion*, Lady Du dies not from illness but of a deadened heart."

"I understand what you mean, Rushi. The heavens are cruel to force you lovers apart. Ai, what right do I have to judge you girls? I was just worried about the danger that might beset Yuanyuan, the danger of being found out. That's all."

"Mother, I will take every care to keep our liaison secret. Please don't worry on my account. Xiang is my only glimpse of hope in life, but I won't do anything stupid. I hope you don't mind us exchanging letters through you."

"Why would I mind? What kind of silly words are those? What wouldn't I do to make you a little happier? You are my beloved daughter! It already pains me so to see Xiangjun so alone and sad and I can do nothing to help her.... Aiya, enough of misery. We must not get so pessimistic. Let us have our dinner now. After dinner, let's get out to Banknote Vault Street to watch the display of lanterns and then come back for sweet soup. I have made your favorite rice balls with red bean paste. A little sweetness on the palate will perk us up."

None of us knew that this was to be the last reunion dinner for the sisters before the onset of war.

Six months had passed since that reunion. Now that Fangyu had fled to Yangzhou, the Ruan and Ma pair started to set their sights on their even-more defenseless prey.

There was a Canal Transport Minister named Tian Yang, who had been one of Xiangjun's covetous admirers. He had once offered to pay five hundred taels of silver just to have tea with her, but she didn't even bat an eyelid, and shut him right out.

After her wedding, he became resigned to reality.

Being from the same hometown as Tian Yang, Ruan soon heard about this and felt it his duty to stoke his old pal's flame.

One day in the seventh lunar month, he paid Tian a personal visit to deliver a message: that Fangyu had fled to Yangzhou to evade arrest, and that his concubine was now living in what amounted to widowhood. Longyou happened to be with Ruan on that visit. It was from Longyou that I later came to learn of this.

It seemed that sometimes the heavens liked to play tricks on mortals. No sooner had one odious Tian exited our lives than another Tian made a rude entrance.

One rainy day towards the end of the following month, Tian Yang led a band of armed guards on horseback, two carriages filled with bridal gifts, servants and maids, and a bridal sedan chair to our doorstep.

Earlier in the month, he had twice tried to woo Xiangjun by sending betrothal money and gifts through a sweet-talking matchmaker. Both times she had rejected him. It was probably Ruan who gave him the idea that if he couldn't succeed by persuasion, he had every right to resort to force. Who were we lowly women to dare to disobey His Lordship's orders?

Just before Tian's group arrived, Longyou had rushed ahead to alert us, but by then it was already too late. Tian's servants and maids were in the front lounge setting down bolts of silk and satin, urns of rice wine, basketfuls of cakes, fruits and candies.

In Xiangjun's antechamber now, Longyou and I were wracking our brains on how to deal with this disaster. Profound sadness shrouded Xiangjun's face and she didn't utter one word. Longyou paced back and forth, his fine forehead deeply creased. Suddenly he glanced at me and eyed me up and down with a strange expression:

"Jingli, you're about the same height and build as Xiangjun. Under a veil, the bride's face is not visible...." Before he finished, I knew exactly what he was thinking. I considered the idea for a moment, and then made up my mind. Love is innocent. It was something that meant everything to Xiangjun, and I was the only one who could help her in this situation.

"Longyou, I know what you're thinking. I'll stand in for Xiangjun. Why don't you go downstairs and engage Tian in talk, while I go and get changed?"

Just as I finished donning Xiangjun's bridal garments in my bed chamber, I heard a violent bang and a heavy thud, followed by what sounded like muffled moans. I dashed to her antechamber and found her lying prostrate with blood spattered on her face and hair. The silk fan with Fangyu's love poem lay limply on the floor, mottled in red.

Words could not describe my shock! I leaned down and saw a horrible gash on her forehead, with wood splinters lodged in the flesh and still oozing warm blood. The angled corner of the side table was chipped and stained red.

"My poor child, stay with me! Xiangjun, please don't drift off! Heavens, what have you done to yourself?"

She strained to lift her eyelids on hearing her name and whimpered in a daze,

"Mother, I'm so sorry.... But I'd rather die than have my honor stained.... I couldn't let you take the risk..."

"Hush, hush, precious. There is no risk. They can't do anything to me. I promise you we can get through this... Aiya, you mustn't move. Let me get some *sanqi* root powder to stop the bleeding first."

At that moment, Longyou came back up and appeared at the threshold. His mouth fell wide open at the sight and he couldn't speak for a while. I asked him to keep an eye on Xiangjun so I could go and get the herbal powder.

Using pincers, I carefully picked out the splinters one by one, then used a piece of cloth soaked in warm water to clean the wound before spreading the *sanqi* root powder on it.

While I was dressing her wound, Longyou took up the blood-stained fan and stared at the poem wistfully. On the side table were scattered a painting dish, a few brushes and a teapot. Quietly, he took out the tealeaves from the pot, pressed out the excess water and then squeezed the remaining greenish liquid onto the dish. A few graceful strokes by his hand magically became the leaves and twigs to a blooming branch of peach blossoms.

At that moment, beauty itself struck me as a kind of painful sorrow. I wondered if my pretty magpie would ever sing happily again.

When the wound dressing was done, I helped Xiangjun to lie down on her bed. She motioned Longyou to come nearer and show her the fan. Forcing a smile, she whispered,

"Longyou, your work is so lovely. Thank you! Would you mind.... taking the fan with you? Please... when you happen upon Fangyu, please hand it to him.... and say that I will always belong to him alone."

"Don't worry, Xiangjun. I promise I will get the fan and your words to him. Now you rest. Jingli and I have to go downstairs. I'll get the girls to look after you."

Longyou went out and alerted one of my girls to keep an eye on Xiangjun. Then he called one of Tian's maids to come to the bed chamber door. I covered my head with a large pink veil and allowed myself to be led by the maid downstairs.

I found it hard at first to suppress my pulsating fear while in the sedan. As always, my common sense eventually won over and I thought, "The worst they can probably do is to make a housemaid out of me as punishment. I wouldn't mind the free food and abode. If I don't care a whit about it, nothing can hurt me."

My greatest worry was Xiangjun and the other girls. But then they were old enough to take care of themselves in my absence. I was certain they could get by without me.

It turned out that my fate was not as bad as I had feared. But I always giggle when I recall that dumbstruck look on Tian's puffy face when he lifted my veil. At that moment, though, I was afraid that he might strike me on the face or something. You can imagine how relieved I was when he simply screamed like a girl and bolted out of the bridal chamber.

After a while, he came back. He scanned me from head to toe and smiled.

"For your age, you still look beautiful, I must say. It's not such a bad deal after all."

The thing was that all his guests had witnessed our wedding ceremony earlier, so he couldn't go and tell people that he had been tricked, because that would make him lose a great deal of face. Neither could he go back to the Villa of Alluring Fragrance to make another claim on Xiangjun, as that would only make him a laughing stock.

I was more or less mentally prepared that I would become his concubine. My mind had been set to save Xiangjun from dishonor and I had no regrets. As for my Zhenhui, I didn't belong to his family and so was not breaking any code of conduct.

Thus began my life as the fourth concubine in the Tian Yang household. Soon I came to know that Tian was a timid man, also a little short on backbone. He treated me well enough when he found out that I was literate and well-read. For a while, life sailed along smoothly. I was well-fed, well-clothed and pampered. But good things usually don't last long.

As my husband got into the habit of staying with me night

after night, neglecting all his other women, his wife couldn't tolerate me anymore.

One day when Tian was out working, she waddled into my bed chamber with the other concubines and falsely accused me of having stolen a bracelet of hers. She had a vicious look on her face and held a bamboo rod in her hand. It was her word against mine, but none of the concubines dared take my side. She gave me a good beating that made me wince. I bit my lip and tried to conjure up funny toad-like images of her. She had warty skin and a big, loose mouth, and she did actually sound like a male toad when she spoke. I tried to suppress my laughter.

The next day, the toad insisted on banishing me from the house and selling me to one of Tian's retired guards. Tian's mousy protests were useless and I had to leave. The old guard, surnamed Tang, now made his living as a fisherman near the Xuanwu Lake in the north-eastern part of Nanjing, and he came to claim me a couple of days later. Tang turned out to be a soft-hearted human being, and after being told the whole story, he showed great admiration for me. We got along well.

It was a frugal life as a fisherman's wife, but misery-free nevertheless. When the Lantern Festival arrived, I wondered if the sisters were meeting for their sixth reunion. Then two months later, the Manchu army breached the Shanhai Pass and took the Forbidden City and the capital.

Destiny arranged for me to be reunited with Xiangjun and Rushi shortly after the establishment of the Southern Ming court in Nanjing, under the reign of the Hongguang Emperor. He was essentially a puppet under the control of Ruan and Ma. This was bad news for Xiangjun.

*When this session came to an end, Jingjing felt hearty respect for Jingli Po Po for her incredible selfless act. Aunt Xiangjun also impressed her as a noble soul.*

*Jingli rose from her seat and went into her bed chamber. When she came back out, she showed Jingjing that painting scroll with Xiangjun's poem that had attracted Hou Fangyu's attention at their first meeting, The impressionistic painting and the dainty calligraphy gave Jingjing a better sense of this aunt's delicacy and her artistic flair.*

She had never known until now that there was a sub-commoner class known as "jianmin". The label of this lowest stratum literally meant worthless people. It was probably the meanest label that society could tag a person with.

As taught by her mother, she always treated the bonded servants Begonia and Ah Luk as part of the family. They were her childhood playmates and were at no time deemed beneath her. It was beyond her comprehension how such a stratum could even be allowed to exist. She winced just thinking of all those poor girls being stuck in that class for life.

# TWENTY-ONE

As usual, Yuanyuan was already waiting in the rear lounge when Jingjing showed up for breakfast. When they finished eating, Yuanyuan held the girl's hand and asked her tenderly, "Jingjing, do you feel distressed by these stories that we are telling you?"

"Not at all, Aunt Yuanyuan. I never knew much about my mother's early life until I began reading her memoir. But even as a child I could feel how much she loved you and Aunt Xiangjun. Very often she would sit alone and gaze wistfully into her birdie kerchief. Now from your stories I begin to see how much the sisterhood meant to each of you. That loving bond is so precious. I'm really, really touched."

Strangely, Jingjing had a vague feeling that the rest of the stories might even unravel the mystery about her birth father. She just couldn't wait to get to the end.

As much as she still missed her mother terribly, she gained a new perspective on life from these stories. A sense of purpose was taking root. There must be something she could do to make the future better for the downtrodden, she thought.

The boat trip to Beijing took over a month and a half. Also traveling with us was one of Sangui's `military captains. As Sangui and this captain seemed preoccupied with discussions about the ongoing border war, I knew better than to bother them. Ah Seng and Azalea were engaged in their jokes and banter as usual.

To distract myself from the sadness of parting with my sisters and Mother, I spent my free time on board reading *Romance of the Three Kingdoms*. I was moved by the story of the Oath of the Peach Garden, which extolled the unflinching loyalty between three valiant warriors sworn to brotherhood. It got me into musing why sworn sisterhood was never the subject of novels or of any kind of writing. But then again, that was hardly a surprise.

Upon arrival at the main wharf of the capital in mid-morning, the captain left us to go on his way. A horse-drawn carriage was waiting to take the four of us to our new home.

We headed straight for the Inner City, where senior court officials and military generals lived in large mansions with their families. Once inside this affluent but austere part of the capital, we came upon a criss-cross of wide, cleanly-swept streets that sprawled in all directions. After taking several turns, the carriage halted in front of a large courtyard mansion with red pillars and green-tiled roofs, guarded by a pair of grim stone lions at the gates.

Sangui had built a new three-bay single-storey house in the inner courtyard especially for me. The main household took up two-storey blocks fringing three sides of the front courtyard. His first wife, son, five concubines, his father and his three concubines all lived in those front buildings, while servants' and maids' quarters and the kitchen were crammed in the backyard.

After settling in, Sangui reminded me that I had to offer bridal tea to his primary wife, Madame Zhang, and his father. So as soon as Azalea had the tea tray ready, Sangui and I stepped into the inner courtyard.

In the center of the courtyard nestled a round stone pond. Gold fish and carp jostled merrily with each other in the water, basking in the lukewarm sun. To the right of the pond, a beautiful Xi Shi marble statue rose behind a scattering of decorative rocks and fragrant lilac shrubs, and to the left, a stone table and four porcelain stools were couched under three pear trees bearing white flowers. The charm of spring soothed my senses and made me feel less jittery.

Once inside the main household lounge, Sangui and I knelt down and offered tea to my new father-in-law. After taking a sip of the tea, he fumbled in his sleeve pocket to fish out two red packets and gave them to us, uttering his blessings in a gruff tone. When I offered tea to the wife, I lowered my eyes in demure obedience. The ensuing silence was deafening. My outstretched hands that held the cup began to shake.

Sangui became impatient and couldn't help raising his voice, "Yuanyuan has had a tiring journey. Hurry up and drink your tea. She needs to take a rest."

I looked askance at the woman and saw a painted face with a snub nose. She shot me a biting glance after grabbing the cup from me. With a shrill inflection, she sniffed, "Don't you ever forget your position in this house. There are five mistresses who are more senior, in case you let a few special favors go to your head! We have strict house rules. Don't let me catch you breaking any of them."

I was fully expecting such hostility because of the way Sangui was doting on me. So I just kept my peace.

As Azalea helped me rise from my kneeling position, Sangui's voice boomed out.

"What rules are you talking about?" He shouted, brows drawn tight and eyes spewing fire. "When did I permit you to make rules? What I say are the only rules in this house! Now I will say this only once. Don't you forget that Yuanyuan is very special to me. She is now as much a mistress of this household as you, and she takes no orders from you or anyone. Is that clear?"

Madame Zhang's face blanched at this outburst. Then in a

subdued voice she said to me, "You are the primary concubine. There is no need for you to offer tea to the other concubines. My husband must be exhausted. Why don't you both take a good nap. When dinner is ready, I'll send a maid to call you."

"Thank you kindly, Elder Sister. I have much to learn from you and will seek your guidance in matters of household duties." I hurried to utter a courteous response. Tugging lightly at Sangui's arm, I nudged him out into the courtyard, Azalea trailing behind.

Passing by the statue again, I suddenly recalled the sad story of Xi Shi. Because of her exquisite beauty, the courtiers of her home state placed her as a pawn in the enemy state to seduce their king. Her story somehow stirred a sense of foreboding in me.

Three days later, Sangui had to leave for the battlefield again. I was left alone to adapt to my new home and its occupants. Fortunately, Ah Seng and Azalea were always eager to help me out.

In that entire year, Sangui only took leave one time in the summer, for a period of ten days. He was now charged with commanding the garrison at the defense stronghold Ningyuan Fort, near the Shanhai Pass. Probably his full-time presence there was deemed vital to maintaining army morale.

During those ten days, I tried to pander to every whim he had an appetite for, taking every care not to show my distaste. The knowledge that my loathing would need to be suppressed for only a short stretch made it much easier to bear.

After his departure, the rest of the year ambled past in relative peace, except for unsettling moments when I read his letters telling of the loss of one border town after another.

A dark pall hung heavy in the air of the capital. Prices of rice and grains were spiraling out of control as many rice farms in the south had been ruined that winter either by drought or by locusts. Folks were starting to stock up in case of famine. Every day I would send Ah Seng out to collect the latest news from the battlefront and for an food prices update.

Since moving to Beijing, I missed Mother and my sisters terribly. I thought that perhaps by refreshing my cooking skills I could be freed from some of my smarting homesickness. My brain told me that the Wu household was my home now. Yet my heart was a universe away.

At the start of the twelfth lunar month, I spent one morning teaching Azalea and the family cook to make festive food for the New Year. I had learned to make a variety of Jiangnan delicacies from Mother, such as taro root cakes, water chestnut cakes, deep fried pastries with coconut shred filling, glazed lotus root candies and sugar-coated lotus seeds.

Ah Seng told me that recently a lot of starving vagrants from rural areas hit by drought were swarming the city streets, begging for food from door to door. So we made an extra batch of everything to feed them.

That afternoon, Azalea and I served the whole family Jiangnan festive delicacies with jasmine tea. Everyone including Madame Zhang relished the refreshments. Yingxiong, her eight-year-old son, set upon the candies with gusto. The doe-eyed boy peered at me shyly as he nibbled away. For a while I had been sneaking sweetmeats to him and teaching him to make lanterns with paper coated in crushed sheep horn. He was fast becoming my secret admirer.

A few days later, with Ah Seng as my escort, I traveled to Nanjing for our fifth reunion. With Sangui's arrangement, we took one of the War Ministry's courier boats for the trip, which was faster and safer than merchant boats.

When Mother, my sisters and I met for tea upon my arrival,

I reluctantly told them the bleak news of what looked set to be an inevitable all-out war with the Manchu aggressors. Rushi, looking wearied and frayed, confirmed my tidings, based on Qianyi's contacts.

I was distressed to find out that Fangyu had been forced to flee to Yangzhou. The Hou family's rejection of Xiangjun left a bad taste in my mouth. It looked like she would not escape the sad fate of being trapped in *jianmin* status. I wished so much that there was something I could do to help her. But how could I change people's bigoted attitudes?

At the reunion dinner, Mother handed me a long letter from Xiang. It was an elixir that I had been craving day and night! I fought to hide my excitement and forced myself not to read it until I got on the boat, where I could savor it in private.

As soon as Ah Seng and I boarded the boat bound for Beijing, I sent him to the pantry to make tea for me. With him out of sight, I ripped open the letter and devoured the words with ravenous hunger. He repeated what he had said before, and poured his feelings for me into three lyric poems that he wanted me to match with suitable *sanqu* tunes, the way we used to do when we were together, in happier times.

Once back in Beijing, I immediately set out to find the tunes that would be the best fit for his lyrics. His favorite *sanqu* were mostly derived from opera arias of *Romance of the Western Chamber*. It was easy enough for me to guess which songs he had in mind.

In the following days and months, I practiced singing the songs with Xiang's lyrics while playing on my new pipa that Sangui had given me. His lyric poems also prompted me to respond in writing, which I jotted down in my reply to him. I was so glad that I could dive into a project with Xiang in my cozy nook of solitude.

Sangui had been out with the Ningyuan garrison for almost a year without leave, as the Ningyuan Fort's situation looked more precarious by the day. It appeared his absence from home would continue for an unknown period of time.

By autumn, a courier arrived from Nanjing with Xiangjun's letter telling me about the dreadful Tian Yang incident, her attempted suicide and Mother's standing in for her as an imposter bride.

I had always known there was an unbending character hidden under that deceptively brittle façade of my sister's. It was no surprise to me that she would try to use death to defend her honor for Fangyu's sake, and thanks to Guanyin, she cheated Fate this time. The question in my mind was whether Fangyu was worthy of her sacrifice. But as an outsider, I was in no position to judge Xiangjun's heart. The only thing that mattered was that Fangyu was the love of her life. With all my soul I prayed for the couple's early reunion and for Mother's safe return to the Villa of Alluring Fragrance.

To the waiting courier I handed a reply to Xiangjun, chiding her lightly for forgetting our sisterhood vows, along with a letter to Xiang with my three love poems. In my letter to Xiangjun I also mentioned that I would probably not be able to attend our upcoming sixth reunion, because boat travel these days had become hazardous due to rampant piracy on the Grand Canal.

The New Year came and went quietly. Our family festive fare this year was reduced to a stingy selection as a result of food scarcities in the capital. To keep Yingxiong happy, I still made him candied lotus roots, replacing honey with cheaper cane syrup. By now, his mother's attitude towards me had mellowed a great deal. She would respond to my morning greetings.

One morning at the start of the third lunar month, Ah Seng

came in from his scouting and told me in a dejected voice, "Li Zicheng's peasant army is only a few *li* away. I've heard that wherever they passed, they left a trail of chaos. The Forbidden City only has a handful of imperial guards to defend it. Things are looking bad."

The news distressed me. The best thing I could think of doing was to get the eight man servants to arm themselves with kitchen knives and axes and to take turn keeping night watch at the front and postern gates. This I immediately set out to arrange with no fuss.

A couple of days later, I went into the lounge in mid-morning with Yingxiong's torn paper lantern, which I had promised to mend for him. The lounge was the best-lit chamber in the whole house and I would usually use it as my work place. Barely had I sat down at the table when I heard loud noises filtering through from the main house, noises of things being knocked down and smashed.

Moments later, Madame Zhang staggered through the courtyard, tugging the frightened boy along, her face ashen with fear. As soon as she saw me, she squealed,

"Yuanyuan, please help us! The rebels have rounded up all the men in the house.... They are going upstairs to get to the women.... Can you hide Yingxiong somewhere?"

At first I could hardly make sense of what she was saying. Then a mix of frantic shrieks and raucous laughter rolled across the yard and stung me out of my torpor. Peering out through the half-opened panel doors, I was stunned to see a thug with a stubby beard chasing Azalea around. He tumbled her down to the ground and tried to straddle her. I jumped up and shouted at the top of my lungs, "You beast, get off her now!"

He spat out a ribald epithet and started ripping off her

clothes. Her pleas for mercy only spurred him on. Madame Zhang covered the boy's eyes while the struggle was going on.

My entire body bristled with rage. In a blinding flash, the scene of Tian Hongyu forcing himself on me shot through my mind and jangled my nerves.

Then something that Sangui had told me rang in my ears. The Emperor had on the occasion of his promotion granted him a sword crafted by a renowned swordsmith. I looked over at the wall near the east window, and there it was, hung on a silk-braided cord in a shiny jeweled scabbard. I dashed over to unsheathe it and raced out to the courtyard.

Creeping up silently on the hateful man, I raised the sword with both hands and slashed down with the whole weight of my body. He was too engrossed in his act to detect approaching danger before it was too late. When I saw blood spattered all over my face and clothes, I didn't even realize that I had shorn off the man's right upper arm. The only thing I could make out was a blurred form thrashing and writhing on the ground. Madame Zhang came up from behind, picked up a porcelain stool and banged it on his head several times. When he screeched and wiggled back and forth in agony, I saw the ground redden and his severed limb trembling in a dark pool. The girl pulled her clothes about her and scampered away to her quarters in the backyard.

I felt faint from the exertion and shock and my arms and legs couldn't stop shaking. Just then, a towering, brawny man in metallic armor, followed by a gang or five or six, walked into the courtyard. He clapped his hands in mock applause.

"What courage, Lady! You have my respect! You must be the famous Chen Yuanyuan, if I'm not mistaken."

"Who are you people?" I shouted. "What have we done to offend you? Why are you seizing our folk? If you have a complaint against our master, let us hear it." I tried hard to give an impression of composure, still clasping the blood-stained sword firmly in my hand.

"You are not very well informed, are you now, Pretty Lady? My name is Liu Zongmin, and I am the Deputy Commander of the Shun army. Our great leader, Li Zicheng, has just declared himself King of Shun. We are a group of fighters with one great common goal, which is to topple the Ming court, beat back the Manchus, and to give every peasant a plot of land to farm. But you needn't worry your little head about that!" He sneered at me insolently, and then, clearing his throat, continued in a brassy tone,

"This is what you need to know: your husband Wu Sangui has made the grave mistake of rejecting our King's invitation for him to join hands with us. But our sovereign is a big-hearted man. He is willing to give him a chance to rectify his mistake. So here we are, taking his household members as a guaranty."

"Deputy Liu, we women are never involved in our master's military affairs," I replied. "Whatever he does, right or wrong, it has nothing to do with us. If you must take our folk by force, we are powerless to stop you. But it is a shame that your men are treating the good women of this house like whores. They do not deserve this. I beg of you to please stop this savagery."

A silence descended, tempered by his raspy breathing. Madame Zhang was fidgeting nervously next to me. The wolf pack leader swiped his narrowed eyes up and down my body. Then he flicked his glance to the sword I was holding and softened his tone a notch.

"Hmm, I'll make you a deal, Lady Chen. I think our King would be very pleased to welcome a beauty like you into his camp. If you yield yourself up and come with us peacefully, then I will order my men to spare the other women's honor."

ALICE POON

I knew I had little choice but comply with his demand, if the concubines and maids were to be spared. There was also no question that I was stepping right into a wolf's lair.

"I would be willing to do your bidding, if you will also let go our mistress here and her young son." I felt I must try to save the innocent child and his mother from this peril, if only out of fondness for the boy.

"We have no use for old hags and kids. It's a deal! You better get yourself cleaned up and put on something pretty."

Liu blew a sharp whistle to summon his lusty brutes. Once outside, they filled four mule-drawn carts with thirty-nine men and women, including myself and Sangui's father. Liu and five of his men rode on horses that clopped alongside the carts through the frosted streets, followed by others on foot. Light snow drifted down, whispering a mournful dirge.

Anguish and misery overwhelmed me when I overhead a muffled conversation between two of the horse riders.

"Only ten days more and we'll be raiding Forbidden City! Can you imagine our great King sitting on the dragon throne?"

"I'm thinking of all the treasure I could take away, and of course, all those fragrant women.... hahaha!"

"You're making me drool!" Then both of them broke into profane laughter.

Chills ran down my spine. So this was it! The end of Chongzhen! Fifteen reigns after the first peasant Emperor, Zhu Yuanzhang, another peasant was about to take the throne! I had never followed politics or learned history like Rushi did, but even I could tell by instinct that nothing good would come from violent outlaws taking over the country.

I took a look around the city and it appalled me to see the wide streets teeming with military tents like bamboo shoots, their "Shun" banners brazenly flying in the spring breeze.

One brute was pushing a half-naked young woman onto the ground and another one forcing her legs apart. Nearby, three ruffians were waiting in turn to mount a girl. Common folk robbed of their homes, fraught with desolation and shock, were wandering around with vacant stares. Little children separated from their parents were racing about screeching, their faces caked in dirt.

A staggering sense of helplessness overwhelmed me. I clutched the sheathed sword closer to my chest. My thoughts jumped to my only family and to Xiang in Jiangnan. I prayed and prayed for their safety.

The procession stopped just outside a large fenced-in marketplace in the Outer City. In the center stood a large felt tent, tightly guarded on all sides. Liu came to my cart and motioned me to step down. Then he ordered the horse riders to lead all the carts to the city prison.

He told me to wait outside while he entered the tent. A few moments later, he came out and signaled me to go inside.

Seated on a high-back, tiger-pelt-covered chair was a middle-aged man with a swarthy and pockmarked face. He was reading some documents and didn't lift his eyes as I stood before him, a low wooden table between us. On one side was a bed covered in layers of brown beaver fur. On the other, a maid crouched by an exquisite wooden brazier stand with carved aprons and curved legs, and was pouring hot tea from a dainty porcelain teapot. The luxury trimmings were completely out of place in an army camp.

The maid stepped towards me with a nervous smile and handed me a cup of tea. I smiled back and thanked her. The man flicked his hand to wave her out.

I was wondering what was likely to happen. The moment I had climbed onto that cart that carried me here, I had already accepted my fate, which I reckoned could not be worse than what I had endured at Tian Hongyu's hands. So I tried to lull myself into calmness by singing softly in my heart.

At last he looked up. He stared at me for a long time, as if transfixed.

"You are more beautiful than I imagined. I don't blame General Wu for falling head over heels for you. But I have often pondered on a question. Would you say.... that you love your husband?"

"Does it really matter to you?"

"There is something I want from you. It would be in your interest if you were to oblige me willingly."

"What woman would of her own free will submit to a total stranger?" I tensed up and shifted my glance to the sword I was holding.

"Do you submit to your husband of your own free will? Perhaps with Mao Xiang it is different, it would be for love, I suppose?"

His bluntness made me blush. I was shocked that he held such information on me.

"Haha, don't you worry! I am not going to ask you to sacrifice your honor. In fact, what I'm asking of you will benefit your husband and the whole of China. I want you to write a letter to General Wu convincing him to join forces with the Shun army. The Ming court is ours to take in a matter of days. Our combined armies will be able to repel the Manchus and enable us to restore peace to our nation. You're an intelligent woman. I'm sure you can see the great benefit of your involvement."

"I don't see how my letter would make any difference. You have already taken General Wu's father hostage. Everyone knows he is a pious son, and he will do whatever you ask of him."

"Oh, I think you are far underestimating your worth to

General Wu. I am a cautious man. Your letter would be like a double surety."

"If you think it is so important, I shall write the letter. But can you promise me that once General Wu agrees to do your bidding, that you will at once release all of us?"

"I don't usually make a promise to a woman. But with you, I'll make an exception. The day I receive General Wu's written confirmation, I will set all of you free."

At that moment, I was still clinging to a fantasy that things would work out and that very soon all thirty-nine members of the Wu household would be returned to safety. Later, a flash of insight would slap me back into sobriety.

That night, I was housed in a small tent in a far corner of the guarded compound. As I blew out the single candle on a side table and was about to lie down on the quilt-covered pallet, a dark shadow slipped in through the canvas flap. I gasped in terror.

In the opaque darkness, I could make out the shadow of Liu, Li Zicheng's deputy. I tried reaching for the sword on the floor, but he leapt over just in time to kick it away. He pinned me on the bed and then tore open my robe. He was far too strong for me to put up an effective resistance. I spat in his face and lay still like a corpse. His reeking breath made me want to retch. I strained to turn my face away.

But it was what he said to me next that truly turned my stomach.

"The letter you wrote will never reach your husband. Instead, I will write him another one telling him how much pleasure you give Li Zicheng and me. That should be enough to goad him into turning against Li. When they are done killing each other, I will then step in to reap the spoils…. Hahahaha…."

Li was hoping to use me as a chip to barter for Sangui's

allegiance. I too nurtured a fancy that there was a fair chance Sangui might acquiesce to Li's request in exchange for his father and family.

But now Liu's depraved treachery forced me to open my eyes to harsh reality. Sangui once told me how he had made a scapegoat of one of his subordinates in a military investigation so he could get off the hook for a decampment charge. He and Liu were birds of a feather! They were the kind of men whose only loyalty is to himself. There was no greater cause or higher code of conduct than serving their own ambitions.

Sangui's only motivation would be whatever could give him the most benefits. I remembered clearly what he had said to me on our wedding night in Yangzhou: that winning was everything, that scruples were nothing but a hindrance. Certainly his odds of winning would be much greater if he sided with the powerful Manchu army. Also, he had too much vanity to want to share power with a low-class peasant, let alone stoop to accept him as his king.

Reason convinced me that Sangui's plain choice would be to join forces with the Manchus rather than with Li Zicheng. Neither his father nor I would figure in his deliberations; we were both dispensable. My letter of persuasion would have been useless even if it had reached him, and Liu's attempt to rile him up was in fact unnecessary.

So even if Liu Zongmin didn't send his letter, the outcome would still be a confrontation between Li and Sangui, only that Liu didn't foresee Sangui joining hands with the Manchus and his own interests would be jeopardized because of that.

Li's hope was based on a faulty assumption — that taking hostages of Sangui's family would induce him to submit. It was a strategy doomed from the start. I silently lamented the grisly future that awaited common folk like us, wedged as we were between the alien Manchu army and these dissolute outlaws.

My prediction would turn out to be accurate. But it didn't change my wretched time in Liu Zongmin's lecherous hands. For four days he kept me confined and ravished me constantly. During that time I tied the birdie kerchief round my arm to sustain my spirit, which was fast waning.

On the fifth day, thanks to Guanyin, Li's good-hearted maid came to my rescue. With her help, I managed to sneak into Li's camp and expose Liu's subterfuge. Li had the decency to assign his personal guards to protect me at all times. After that day, a murderous look would visit his face whenever Liu's name was mentioned.

A few days later, on Li's orders, the Shun army invaded, ransacked and set fire to the palaces of the Forbidden City. He gave his men explicit permission to loot and rape as their rewards. In the frenzied carnage, Empress Zhou hanged herself with a silk rope in her chambers, and the Chongzhen Emperor went about stabbing and killing his daughters and consorts with his sword in order to protect their honor. Finally, with the help of a hemp rope that his chief eunuch handed him, the Ming Emperor ended his life on a hill behind the imperial garden.

As expected, Sangui chose to surrender to Regent Dorgon of the Qing court and opened the Shanhai Pass gates to the Qing army. In no time, their combined forces defeated Li's peasant army. One of Li's loyal henchmen ambushed Liu and hacked him to pieces in the battlefield.

Out of sheer vindictiveness, Li ordered that all of Sangui's family members, except for myself, should be executed by beheading. Maybe I could still be a useful chip or pawn in some future scheme, or because I had alerted him to Liu's treachery. Regardless, all I felt was abomination at the senseless brutality. What kind of an emperor would he make, were he given the chance? I shuddered at the thought.

Some people believed that Sangui made that flagrant choice out of love for me. They misunderstood the circumstances. If he had cared one bit about my safety, or for that of his family, he would have had second thoughts about antagonizing Li in the first place. I didn't understand why this wasn't obvious to everyone. Regent Dorgon rewarded him with an honorable title and promises of wealth and power. Those were the things that he truly cared about.

*Jingjing was quite speechless. She had not expected the story to turn out the way it did. She now understood Aunt Yuanyuan's woeful role in the cataclysmic dynastic change. For the first time, she felt a distinct repugnance towards Wu Sangui. Yet public opinion tended to put the blame on her aunt, maligning her as the jinx who inspired him to betray his country. If only people could see! Her aunt was in a totally powerless position throughout the entire series of events! She let out a long sigh.*

# TWENTY-TWO

SINCE RETURNING from our fifth sisters' reunion in Nanjing, I wallowed in a kind of nostalgic melancholy.

The letter I had earlier received from Wen disturbed me a lot. The news about Zilong falling sick several times after we parted devastated me. Then Qianyi told me that Zilong would be heading the Revival Society's resistance movement. That piece of information unhinged me. He was a gentle scholar, untrained in combat, and further had a weak constitution! How could he cope with fighting on a battlefield like a warrior? Was he not tempting death? But knowing him as I did, I realized that no one could possibly make him change his mind. He was a stubborn patriot, and his unflinching loyalty was to his Ming sovereign and Confucian principles.

Unconsciously, I revisited the scene where we said our final farewell. The glimmer of dawn was peeking in on us, to herald our imminent parting. How we wished the night would never end! His eyes were swimming with hot tears. They drizzled down his cheek, and soaked my kerchief. Poring through my prose poem *Parting* that I had dedicated to him, he chanted these lines in a grievous voice:

In this century, we meet, we bond, in sadness.

Life is never calm, fate all too wild to harness.

You and I, kindred as we are, our paths must run apart;

Parting ways, even if brief, would be a thorn to our hearts.

I wish that we'll enter the next life together;
I wish our will never yield, our hearts one forever.

He looked at me with tender eyes, lit with a fleck of flame, and improvised on the spot a verse entitled *Forever In Love*, nimbly brushing the words on a parchment:

As we say farewell, your scent wafts from your sleeve;
If your scent has passion, it will find its way to me.
I only wish your heart will hold your old love dear,
Then it matters not even if you're not near.

My blood, my flesh, my bone, drank in every word as if it were nectar. Those lines would sustain my soul in the coming empty days. Our separation meant I could no longer feel his touch, but I could still refuse to forget the artful curl of his fingers around a brush. How could I ever forget the flicker in his eyes, the honey in his voice, even if I tried?

Not long after my return, something that had hung over my head like a grouchy raincloud finally burst open to dump its ire.

Qianyi had a distant cousin named Qian Chaoding, who was also Orchid's brother-in-law. He was a well-connected and wealthy merchant in Changshu, and was a frequent guest in the Qian household. Whenever he came, he would first help himself to Qianyi's cache of fine osmanthus wine, and then would lounge about in the library, now neatly set up on the top level of our newly-finished Crimson Clouds Lodge. This cousin was one of those vain philistines who likes to brag about books that he has never read but only knows them by the titles and author names.

One day, whether by careless slip of tongue from drunkenness or with malicious intent, he bragged that he was the brains behind Orchid's and Spring Flower's scheme to ruin my wedding. I confronted him and we had a few sparring words. After that, I gave up all pretense of social grace, and whenever he showed up in our lodge, I would retreat to my own chambers to avoid him.

Then, out of the blue one day, he brought Orchid over and led her straight up to the library. I could sniff trouble brewing. Before I had a chance to gauge their intent, Orchid stormed into my antechamber, her face splotched red, and yelled at me:

"What did you do with those valuable history books? How dare you lay hand on my precious dowry?"

"You have to ask Qianyi. He is the master of this household and owner of all the books," I said a little diffidently, not without feeling a certain amount of guilt. But my meekness only brought out the worst in her.

"Don't you try to be sharp-mouthed with me! Qianyi wouldn't have cause to dispose of those imprints if you hadn't pushed him to build this lodge for you. To think of this abode... this... this whore house having been built with my dowry. It makes me sick! You have a nerve to insult me like this! We knew from the day you seduced your way into this family, the Qian family's reputation would sooner or later be ruined by you, you lowly whore and thief!"

Her hurl of invectives sent me scrambling for self-defense.

"Please mind your words," I replied. "I came into the Qian household as Qianyi's primary wife, complying with all proprieties. Believe what you want to believe, but the truth is, I never asked him to build this lodge. It was entirely his idea. Ask him if you like."

She was taken aback at my fearless response. At this point, her relative egged her on:

"Let's go and ask Qianyi himself. Dear sister, you are from the scholar gentry and it's beneath your dignity to reason with cheap whores from the *jianmin* class. She's not worth it. If Qianyi doesn't have a good explanation, you just write this into your ledger as a debt owed by this tramp."

From that day on, I knew there was never going to be peace between these two and me.

By the end of Spring, Qianyi got promoted to the post of Minister of Rites in Nanjing, and in early summer, we moved to our new residence there, near the Rain Flower Terrace in the southern part of the city.

I was so happy to have left Changshu, to get away from those pugnacious people, and to be living in the same city as Jingli and Xiangjun. It was a pleasant surprise to me to learn that Zilong was also living in Nanjing now.

Then came the distressing news that Tian Yang had tried to seize Xiangjun as his concubine and caused her to attempt suicide. Jingli, true to her selfless spirit, stepped in to save her honor, and shouldered whatever fate was to befall her. In my heart, Jingli was as much my heroine as Fo had been.

Right after the incident, in order to nurse Xiangjun back to health, I made daily trips to the Villa of Alluring Fragrance by carriage, with Ah Luk as my escort and driver. I changed her head wound dressing everyday and gave her ginseng soup and pig liver broth on alternate days to boost her energy. On most days, all I got from her in return were a vacuous stare and these scant words: "Thank you, Big Sister."

Seeing a little color return to her wan face was a comfort, but her unnatural indifference, with emotions congealed underneath, wrenched my heart. Who could blame her? She waited day after day for a letter from Fangyu, and still no word came. All I could think of to say was: "Sweet sister, we are in turbulent times; obviously the post is disrupted." I honestly couldn't tell whether that was the truth, but for her sake I prayed it was not something else.

Apart from caring for her, I also helped with running the salon on Jingli's behalf, taking up chores like scheduling performances, putting up posters, selling tickets, checking the costumes and make-up supplies, inspecting the musical instruments, taking dinner orders and manning the receipt register. Knowing that Jingli was likely somewhere in Nanjing, I asked Qianyi to use his resources to search for her.

One late night when the salon was emptied of guests save for one gentleman in the dining lounge, I went to the counter at the hall entrance to do the sums of the day's receipts. That diner, dressed in a light green cotton Confucian scholar robe, came up and stood silently a few paces from me. He had come in rather late and had gone straight into the dining lounge and ordered his food. There were guests who would come in just for late night meals. I had been busy with mending an opera costume, so one of the girls had taken his order.

When I lifted my eyes from the silver pieces that I was counting, I found a skeletal white form, almost like an apparition, right in front of me! I stared wordlessly at this bony husk that had appeared from thin air, with a scrawny face fringed with straggly grey strands. Only his agate-like eyes remained recognizable, still aglow with life.

"Zilong! Is that you?" I cried, with a voice that struggled to come out of my throat.

He gave the faintest hint of a nod, his eyes locked on mine. "How are you, Rushi?" He swept his gaze quickly around the hall, and, after a pause, said, "Can I talk with you?"

I knew the dressing lounge would be empty at this time and quickly led him into it, closing the door behind me. When he seated himself, I lit the brazier by the side of the dressing table and put a pot of water on it. Then I sat down on a chair by his side, my pulse quickening to a dizzying pace.

"It's good to see you, Rushi. I've missed you, so much…" He

couldn't finish his sentence, his voice also lodged in his throat.

"I've missed you too, Zilong! If only you knew how much!" I couldn't let my eyes stray from his face, fearing I would lose him if I did.

"Look, I've come for a purpose. We have had news that Li Zicheng has declared himself King of Shun, and is laying siege to the capital. They will probably capture the city in a matter of months. When he does that, the days of the Ming court are numbered. The Revival Society must act now to set up Nanjing as the emergency capital to counter Li's claim to the imperial throne. We must also take it upon ourselves to resist the Manchu army's onslaught. I was wondering if you could help to convince Qianyi to join our cause. He has connections that can get resources the Society urgently needs, like military manpower and supplies."

"Zilong, are you sure this is what you want to do? I'm thinking of your safety. Why are you risking your life? You are not a warrior. I know the Ming court is doomed, and we will have a new ruling class. Why not just let things be? We might be getting a better sovereign and court, for all we know. Life goes on. Don't forget we are just little people trying to eke out a humble living...."

"Rushi, do you still remember what I once told you, that if we lose our country to aliens, we lose our lives, our future and our dignity. Our families and loved ones will be ravished and enslaved. Every man has a duty to protect his family and fellow countrymen from alien invaders and bandits."

"At least the Qing Emperor has treated Ming defectors with respect," I replied. "Our esteemed scholar Fan Wencheng and General Hong Chengchou are good examples. Who can say for certain that the Qing court will not rule with benevolence? Haven't we suffered enough under the last few Ming Emperors?"

"The Qing court will try to supplant our customs and beliefs.

We will become slaves with no dignity. Losers always have to pay dearly."

We were on our old battleground again. I knew where this was going and it made me mad that he was not wrong. Scattered thoughts wheeled and whirled in my head, "Who can we common folk blame except our own rotten Ming court? War means there will be winners and losers, and losers are routinely subjected to harm and indignities, leading to endless hatred. The Manchus will be no winners in the end unless they prove to be benevolent rulers worthy of respect."

Yet all those thoughts paled alongside my chief concern, which was Zilong's safety. My emotions got the better of me and I vented my frustrations on him,

"Chen Zilong, you never change! You and your high principles! What if something happens to you? How can I go on if, heavens forbid, you are killed in the battlefield? Do you think you can solve anything by dying?"

"Death can be lighter than feather, it can also be weightier than Mount Tai. I would want to die with honor behind me. My love, I know you understand me and you will feel proud of me. My death will not change our love. Love alone can transcend time. Dying with your presence in my heart would make that moment a glorious one." He knelt down before me, took both my hands into his and kissed them with frantic intensity.

I hated his sweet-talking. He always sugar-coated everything. Tears pooled in my eyes and cold anger kept me from submitting to the urge to embrace him. Just before my tears had a chance to spill, I said, "I'll make Rain Flower tea for you," and went over to the brazier to weep. I was thinking about how I could ask Qianyi to help without making him suspect my motive. I thought of Mao Xiang, whom Qianyi adored and trusted.

"I'll talk to Xiang and make him persuade Qianyi, because

that would be better than for me to bring up the matter with him on your account. I don't want him to harbor any suspicion."

"Rushi, you've always been more adept than I at human relations..." Zilong paused, then said as if in apology, "Truth be told, I abhor the very name of Qian Qianyi.... I could never bring myself to talk to him...."

"Wen told me you fell sick several times, that you became seriously ill when you heard of my wedding. You must take better care of yourself. Do you know how worried that made me?"

"How do you expect me to react to your 'good' news, that Qian Qianyi was going to own you for life? My grandmother passed away a month before I received your wedding invitation. I would have had the chance to have a life with you, if that man hadn't barged in. You don't know how much I loathe him!"

I didn't see this coming, and was struck dumb. Gazing into his stubborn eyes, I saw remnants of pain that tore at my guts. How willful of Fate to have kept us apart!

"And if I ever run into that stinking bastard Xie Sanbin, I swear I will tear him to pieces with my bare hands!" A vein throbbed in his pale forehead. I had never before seen him so agitated.

"You mustn't even try, Zilong! He is a bully and a sly crook, and you would just be putting yourself in harm's way. Please promise me that you'll stay away from him."

"If that's what you want... You must also beware of Qianyi; he is not exactly a scrupled man."

Now that I knew he never faulted or slighted me for the rape, my heart was finally at peace. I snuggled up to him and said,

"You know very well that my heart doesn't belong to Qianyi. I was desperately looking for a safe home, and he offered it to me. There's nothing to it except a debt of gratitude. Zilong, on the day I set eyes on you, I gave my soul to you. You alone own my heart, in this life and in the next. Nothing will change that. Please, not another word. Just hold me now."

He used his finger to brush a straying strand of hair from my face. Then he bent to kiss me passionately on the lips, clasping me to him with a brutish energy that at once surprised and excited me. We clung to each other as if for life. Time and the universe were reduced to a sublime instant of our souls touching. Our shared memory, singed with that bone-deep jubilant sorrow, would be our shield against time.

A few days later, Mao Xiang came to the Villa to leave a letter for Yuanyuan. I grabbed the chance to speak to him about Zilong's plea, and was surprised when he said, "At Zilong's request, I have already spoken to Qianyi. But he doesn't appear enthused."

Only then did it dawn on me that Zilong had come to me solely to bid me farewell. His plea for help was merely a convenient excuse. It suddenly struck me that we might never see each other again in this life.

As Yuanyuan once said, we needed a shred of hope to keep us going. As abstract as it might sound, for me, life was more worth living now. My heart was filled with the desire to fight like a loyal comrade beside him. Our spirit would be one, no matter what happened.

After that last encounter with Zilong, my trips to the Villa of Alluring Fragrance became less frequent, as Xiangjun's wound was completely healed and she was able to take over the day-to-day chores at the salon. She even resumed her opera singing so as to keep the struggling salon from going under.

Very soon it was Lantern Festival. As Yuanyuan had told us she wouldn't be able to join us for our sixth reunion, and as

Jingli still eluded our search, Xiangjun and I decided to cancel the celebration. The general mood did not call for celebration anyway. The number of customers to the salon was in sharp decline, as the men's preoccupation was now with war news rather than pleasure-seeking. Besides, heavy military taxes were taking a toll on everyone's finances.

One evening towards the end of the third lunar month, Qianyi came home with a crestfallen look on his face. When he saw me, he seemed relieved to find an audience for his pent-up grief.

"Our Emperor hanged himself several days ago," he sad. "The peasants have control of the Forbidden City. Ma Shiying and Ruan Dacheng have just put Prince of Fu on the throne in Nanjing, naming him the Hongguang Emperor. The Revival Society is opposed to this Southern Ming court, but we can do nothing to stop the opportunists. Ma has made himself Chief Minister, and has appointed Ruan as the Minister of War."

My heart sank when I heard the news. Ma and Ruan were notorious sycophants and power mongers, and the Prince of Fu was widely known as a wanton profligate.

"How is Wu Sangui holding out at the Shanhai Pass?" I asked, fearing for the worst, for Yuanyuan's sake. Somehow I sensed Qianyi was holding something back.

"The latest I've heard is that... Rushi, this is bad news. A little while ago, Li Zicheng wanted to force Wu Sangui to submit and he ..... abducted.... Yuanyuan and other members of the Wu family. Please don't panic..."

I felt like a heavy hammer had bludgeoned my heart. The news was far worse than I expected. In all honesty, I didn't care about Sangui half as much as I did my ill-starred sister. She, a young and defenseless woman, in the hands of the ruthless rebels! I could only assume the worst, and tried hard to push away ugly images.

"And you are just standing here, doing nothing!" I shouted. "Do you have a clue how dear she is to me? I only have these two little sisters..." My nerves snapped and I didn't give a whit whose head I was biting off. Qianyi was unfortunate to be near at hand at that moment.

"I know, I know. But she's a long way off from us, Rushi. My informants are out gathering the latest news from the capital every day."

"Please forgive me, Qianyi. I didn't mean to be unreasonable. But I'm worried sick... I want to take a trip to Beijing."

"No, no, that's not a good idea. The Grand Canal is crawling with pirates and rebels. You mustn't take that risk."

"I'm praying that Sangui will do something to rescue Yuanyuan. But my gut tells me he is not dependable." Despair was wrapping its tentacles around me. I tried to choke back my sobs, but without success.

"Rushi, you must calm yourself. Begonia, please bring your mistress some hot ginger tea.... My precious, please, let's just wait for more news. Chief Minister Ma has kept me in my post. I promise I'll pull all strings available to get news faster."

After waiting forever, around the start of the fifth lunar month, we heard that Wu Sangui had surrendered to the Manchus and opened the Shanhai Pass gates to their army led by Regent Dorgon. After defeating Li Zicheng's peasant army, they had then marched into the Forbidden City.

According to Qianyi's source, in the midst of the pandemonium, Yuanyuan somehow managed to escape from her captors in Kunming and was later seen inside Sangui's military camp. Hearing this, I was finally able to let out a breath of relief.

How I yearned to see her! I was hoping she would turn up in Nanjing in the New Year.

On the day following Moon Festival Day, at last word came

that Jingli had returned safely to the Villa of Alluring Fragrance. But barely had I had time to enjoy our reunion when another wretched blow hit Xiangjun and Jingli. It happened around the New Year, the year we were hoping to have our seventh reunion, and to see Yuanyuan back among us.

# TWENTY-THREE

*HAVING READ ANOTHER portion of her mother's memoir, Jingjing recalled how Qian Chaoding and Orchid had been pestering her mother for years, and then upon her father's death, had slapped on her a bill of debt for three thousand silver taels that they claimed she owed. Jingjing was aware that her parents had used up their savings in financing Zheng Chenggong's anti-Qing campaign, a cause that her parents had taken up to honor Chen Zilong. Those two wicked relatives literally hounded her mother to death. In her adolescence, she had not understood that class snobbishness was the reason for their spite, but even as a child, she had sensed their viciousness. Tears rolled down her cheeks. She could never understand why some people would cling to meanness and hatred.*

*She had no doubt now Chen Zilong was her mother's one and only love. She couldn't help but wonder if he might be her birth father. Having grown quite fond of him, she was hoping it was true. But a voice at the back of her mind nagged at her. Something was amiss.*

*While mulling over the question, she joined Aunt Yuanyuan and Jingli Po Po for lunch. They had a light meal of congee with dried conch, shrimps and mushrooms. She was now ready for Jingli Po Po's afternoon session in the warm breezy garden.*

With the Southern Ming court now in place, we common folks in Nanjing were more or less resigned to the prospect of another corrupt regime, with the Hongguang Emperor on the throne. We had no way of knowing which was the more evil: this Nanjing court or the Qing court in Beijing, occupied by the Manchu Shunzhi Emperor. We only knew there was a distinct possibility that Regent Dorgon would sooner or later come south with his army. So war was still lurking on the horizon.

Two days before the Moon Festival, my husband Tang came home and said breathlessly to me:

"I saw a magistrate's notice in the fish market just now offering a reward for anyone who can locate Li Jingli and bring her safely back to the Villa of Alluring Fragrance."

"So, you want to exchange your wife for the reward?" I teased him, knowing full well he was not the greedy or selfish kind. His face turned red with embarrassment and stammered,

"I wouldn't have told you this if I didn't think... I thought you might like.... to return to your home..."

He was not wrong. I couldn't wait to get back to my old life. But even if that was true, I still felt guilty about my wish to leave this kind old man. He seemed able to read my thoughts.

"I know you'd be happier back at the Villa. Don't worry about me. I can stay with my son and daughter-in-law. They would be pleased to have me help look after their children." His eyes were red with tears.

It was the hardest decision I ever had to make in my life. But in the end, I could not fight my heart's call. On the Moon Festival Day at break of dawn, he put me in a mule cart and drove me back to my old sweet home in Qinhuai.

When I stepped into the front lounge, my parrot almost went berserk. Its feathers stood up and it kept fluttering and squawking, "Mother is back, mother is back!" It only calmed down when I went up and took it into my arms and stroked it.

It was late afternoon, and the performance hall was quiet and empty. The girls were probably gathered in the dressing lounge to make ready for their evening performances.

Xiangjun was alerted by the parrot's yowl and came out to see who it was. We rushed at each other in great excitement and embraced, as if a lifetime had intervened between us. Then all the other girls came out to greet me with shrieks of joy and warm hugs. They all looked the same as before. I couldn't help but notice a barely visible pinkish scar on Xiangjun's temple. Otherwise she was as attractive as ever.

It felt so good to be home, and on this Moon Festival Day too, a day for celebration of family reunion.

Later that night, when all the customers had gone, the girls and I enjoyed a late-night reunion dinner that went on until midnight. Afterwards, Xiangjun came into my antechamber with a pot of my favorite Snow Orchid tea to sit and talk with me.

I told her in detail my dramatic story in the year-and-a-quarter since I left. She then recounted all that had happened during my absence, including the bad news about Yuanyuan's abduction. I thanked Rushi in my heart for helping to nurse Xiangjun and running chores for the salon.

The sorrow of being separated from Fangyu was written all over Xiangjun's face without her uttering one word about it. The longing for the letter that never came could be read in her wistful brow. When it came to matters of the heart, I was just another outsider. No one but she alone could feel the love she felt. No one but she alone could judge whether he was worth it.

I was also wondering what Yuanyuan had been up to after her reunion with Sangui. My heart ached for her for having suffered another wicked slap of ill fate. Not exactly sure from where I got encouragement, but I nonetheless felt an uncanny optimism that she would pull through, whatever evil might have befallen her. She was no longer the fidgety weakling she had been years ago.

Not long after my return, news circulated that Ruan was searching for beautiful opera singers from Qinhuai to perform *The Swallow Letter* for the Hongguang Emperor. Ruan was the writer of this play and he was eager to show off his literary skill while grabbing the chance to pander to the Emperor's lust for pleasure and beauties.

When I heard the news, an ominous feeling rose in me. Ruan and Ma knew Xiangjun was skilled at singing the main aria of *The Swallow Letter* as the female lead. Ruan was now a powerful courtier in Nanjing and was definitely aware that she had wriggled her way out of Tian Yang's clutches. Our livelihood, scrimpy as it had become, was entirely in Nanjing. There was nowhere to hide.

Finally the evil wind caught up with us two days before the New Year Day.

In late morning, when the girls and I were finishing our breakfast in the dining lounge, four armed Imperial Guards from the Fengxian Palace clacked insolently into the front lounge. Their head guard shouted with a disdainful smirk on his face:

"Li Jingli and Li Xiangjun, kneel to receive His Imperial Highness's Order."

Xiangjun and I went out to the front lounge and knelt down.

"By order of His Imperial Highness under Heavenly Mandate: The imperial opera troupe of Fengxian Palace is soliciting singing and dancing talents. Li Xiangjun and Li Jingli have been selected to join the troupe as opera singers. You are to serve without leave in the troupe for as long as His Excellency, Minister Ruan, deems fit. Your first performance is scheduled for New Year's Day, to celebrate the festive season. Make ready to depart at once."

Xiangjun and I had no doubt that vindictive Ruan had arranged this entirely in retribution, to punish us for the trick we pulled on Tian Yang. But there was no way out this time, and there was no telling how long this bout of imposed servitude would last. If Guanyin decided to abandon us, there was little we could do to reverse our ill-fortune. We heaved deep sighs and went to our respective chambers to pack a few things, and then followed the guards to our destiny.

Upon arrival in the newly-refurbished Fengxian Palace inside the Nanjing Imperial City, we were led to a small palace in the inner court, where the imperial opera troupe leader, a pretty and exquisitely-attired court lady, awaited. The palace maids told us that she was the renowned *kunqu* opera actress Jade from Suzhou City, and that Ruan's men had kidnapped her from her home a couple of months before. Ruan had forcibly pimped her to Hongguang as an imperial consort.

Without fuss, she whipped us into rehearsing the most popular aria in *The Swallow Letter*, assigning the male lead role to me and the female lead role to Xiangjun. As I was also familiar with the aria, we had little problem with the rehearsal. When she saw that we were skilled singers, her mask of self-defense fell away to reveal a warmer personality.

In the evening, we were given a stingy meal of vegetables, salted fish and rice, and then were ushered by palace maids to separate bed chambers.

The next morning began with a frugal breakfast of thin rice gruel, followed by the same rehearsal routine. Having eavesdropped on the palace maids' chat, I learned that our meals were different from those served to other troupe members. Ours were deliberately kept stingy, and we weren't served lunch with the others.

In the afternoon, an old palace maid brought stage cosmetics and richly-brocaded and embroidered opera costumes for us to try on. We were told to get to bed early for next day's performance.

Again, thin rice gruel was all we got for breakfast. Xiangjun and I had to huddle around the ornate celadon brazier in the rehearsal lounge to keep from shivering with cold. Before the rehearsal began, Consort Jade came near us and passed a hot pork bun each into our hands.

Xiangjun was silent the whole morning and her face muscles drew taut. As soon as Consort Jade stepped out after the rehearsal, she whispered into my ear, "I've changed the lyrics for my part." Hardly had I time to make out what she meant when the palace maids showed up to take us to the performance hall in the Fengxian Palace.

The dome-shaped hall was gaudily decorated in gold and bright red. A raised stage with red velvet curtains occupied one end, flanked by two musician nooks. In front of the stage lay a plush audience area furnished with rows of cushioned sandalwood chairs.

In the backstage area, the maids helped Xiangjun put on make-up, dress her hair with hairpins and dangling buyaos, and don the opulent costume. My male lead outfit was just a simple embroidered scholar robe and a square cloth cap with two hanging bands, and I managed to dress without help.

When the maids left, Xiangjun quickly thrust a piece of paper into my hand. A quick glance at the content was enough to rattle me. The musicians were already playing the introductory cue for our stage entrance and it was too late for me to say anything other than: "Are you sure you want to do this?" She nodded with firmness. For the life of me, I hadn't seen this coming. This daughter had a way of astounding me every so often.

We went onto the stage and saw there were about twelve people in the audience: the Hongguang Emperor, Ruan, Ma and, thanks to Guanyin, our friend Yang Longyou in the front row, and eight other unknown faces in the rows behind.

In this aria, the female lead parts were much longer than those of the male lead. The verses that Xiangjun was singing were a biting tirade obviously aimed at Ruan and Ma. Words strung together told of their corruption, treachery and their shameless bullying of powerless women.

I just couldn't keep my eyes off their faces. When she came to this line: "Some ministers have opened my eyes; they sell their honor for gold and silver, more readily than we courtesans," their eyes literally bulged and their faces darkened from greyish pink to fiery crimson. It was a better show than the one onstage!

Abruptly Ruan bounced up from his seat, jabbing his index finger into the air, blue veins heaving in his temples.

"How dare you insult court ministers! You worthless whore! Stop at once! You are asking for it! Guards, take that young one outside and give her twenty strokes of the large rod!"

"Minister Ruan, I beg for your mercy!" I pleaded. "You can see how delicate my daughter is; even ten strokes will kill her! Surely you don't want to see death on New Year Day; it will provoke the heavens and bring ill fortune for the whole year. The heavens will reward you for showing mercy, Minister!" I mustered up all my courage and betted on his superstitious leanings. He faltered, his breath labored, his murderous look not letting up.

At this point, Longyou interceded for us in the calmest of voices:

"Your Imperial Highness, if I may say a few words. I have known these performers for a long time, and I assure you they are good, honest people. The girl was merely trying to poke some fun. She didn't mean any harm at all." Indeed, the good, honest part was true.

The Emperor was smiling a foolish smile and bobbed his head. Longyou then turned to Ruan and said,

"Minister Ruan, you are a venerable courtier. Why let yourself be riled up by a silly girl's pranks? You surely don't want to ruin the first day of the New Year. Come now, please don't take such a triviality to heart and forgive the girl on my account."

Ma, who had kept quiet all this time as he did not want to spoil the Emperor's mood, now said to Ruan,

"My good man, why don't we ask the performers to sing another aria. I'm sure His Imperial Highness would like that."

"Alright, on your account and Master Yang's, I'll spare her the corporal punishment this time. But I'll demote her to a laundry maid just to rub off her arrogance."

"Yes, yes, that's what she deserves. I approve," said Ma.

I let out a sigh of relief and blessed Longyou in my heart. I asked the musicians to play another aria of the same play, just thankful that matters didn't get any uglier.

After we returned to the backstage, Longyou came in looking for us, with tidings for Xiangjun.

"Xiangjun, I just wanted to tell you that I found Fangyu in Yangzhou about two months ago and told him about that dreadful incident, and gave him your fan and your message. It turned out that he had long resigned from the job at Minister Shi Kefa's workplace. He appeared downcast, and just asked me to say this to you: 'Please take care of yourself.' Those were his only words. I now spend most of my time working for Minister Shi in secret. I only came back to Nanjing a few days ago on a family visit."

"Longyou, thank you for telling me this…. I must say I am rather saddened by Fangyu's strange response…." Her eyes glazed over with tears.

"What an ungrateful bastard! Whatever is wrong with him?" I couldn't hold down my simmering anger when I thought of how much Xiangjun had sacrificed for him.

"According to what Minister Shi told me, it seems that Fangyu was looking for a better-paying job, and Shi couldn't afford to raise his pay and had to let him go."

"Yes, that must be what's bothering him. I can understand that. He got cut off by his family because of me. Mother, we mustn't be harsh on him. I'm sure he's only trying to stand on his own feet."

Maybe Xiangjun was right. These were hard times for all of us. Anyway, we were in our own hot cauldron and could only wish him well.

"Longyou, when, in your opinion, will the Manchu army come south?" I was thinking that our only chance of escape would be when tumult began to take over.

"Minister Shi is of the view that they will target Yangzhou first. If Yangzhou doesn't hold, then the rest of Jiangnan including Nanjing will not have a chance. He is doing everything he can to conscript soldiers from neighboring cities to beef up the Yangzhou garrison, but sadly he is obstructed at every turn by the corrupt Hongguang court. It sickens me to see the Emperor and his ministers here still obsessed with pleasure in such times."

Thanks be to Guanyin that we had Consort Jade on our side. She asked the Emperor to let her have Xiangjun as a chamber maid, to protect her from Ruan's wrath and the Emperor's lechery.

Thankfully, our hard times in the Palace were about to end. But what was going to come did come at last. Yangzhou was razed to the ground in the fourth lunar month when Dorgon's army unleashed brutal violence there in a ten-day massacre. Minister Shi refused to surrender and was killed by the invaders. I knew in my heart that the days of the Hongguang reign were numbered.

As predicted, the Qing army laid siege to Nanjing one sweltering day in the fifth lunar month. The Emperor fled to the outskirts but was later caught, imprisoned and taken to Beijing to face execution. Ma was killed by Qing soldiers and Ruan fell over a cliff to his death while trying to escape. Could it be that karma was at work? I certainly believe so.

On that fate-changing day, Consort Jade appeared in mid-morning in my chamber to announce that the Emperor and his court ministers had all fled. Without delay, I went with her to look for Xiangjun in the maids' quarters. Thankfully we found her without much effort. At this time, the whole inner court was drowned in wails and general chaos as the frenzied beating of war drums outside the South Gate unhinged each one of us.

Then amidst the turmoil, I saw Qianyi. He was the only minister who was still in the Palace. When he saw the three of us huddling together in disoriented stupor, he shouted:

"You had better leave through the North Gate with the other court ladies. That's the only safe exit. I'm going to lead the court in surrender. There's no point in giving the Manchus reason to inflict more deaths and bloodshed."

Thanks to him, all women of the inner court were able to make an escape through the North Gate, which the Qing army purposely left unguarded. I thought Qianyi made the right decision. It couldn't have been an easy one for him, as Rushi and Zilong were always against surrender. But after the Yangzhou tragedy, who could blame him for bowing to reality? Ideals couldn't be more precious than human lives!

Consort Jade walked with us until we reached the Peach Leaf Pier, where we said farewell and she took a boat that was heading for Yangzhou, and from there she would take a connecting boat to Suzhou City. Xiangjun and I then trudged wearily along the familiar willow-fringed Qinhuai riverside. Only a couple of lonely flower boats idled along the shore. It was a far cry from the days when swarms of pleasure boats clogged up the river from morning till night.

At last, in the misty twilight we could see in the distance the lilac curtains fluttering over the Villa's verandah. It was like a long-lost friend was waving to us.

As we dragged our exhausted legs into the front lounge, my pet parrot flapped its wings frantically and shrieked with abandon, "Mother is back! Xiangjun is back! Oh, thanks to Guanyin! The whole family is here!"

While Xiangjun and I wondered what the parrot was yapping about, Rushi poked her head from behind the scarlet curtains and then rushed towards us. Behind her floated a silhouette as slight as a nymph, dressed in a pale color robe. Xiangjun was more sharp-eyed than I in the dim light and she squeaked with excitement, "Yuanyuan!" The four of us then wrapped our arms around each other in a long embrace and cried our eyes out.

In the candle-lit dressing lounge, while savoring precious Snow Orchid tea, we exchanged our stories in a sombre mood. When Yuanyuan told us her tale, we came to understand why she had never taken to her husband. What meets the eye is not always what lies underneath.

It felt so good to be back. Yuanyuan and the girls had kept the salon in pristine condition. While we were catching up with each other, the cook crept out to buy some fresh vegetables and eggs. I cooked a simple late-night meal with stir-fried greens and steamed eggs with dried shrimps. Everyone savored the meal.

With Rushi's financial support, Yuanyuan, Xiangjun and I were able to work together to bring the salon business back to life. Many of our old customers came back in no time. Sometimes I had to deal with some crass Manchu noblemen, but overall, business almost went back to normal.

Two days before the sisters' eighth reunion, to everyone's

surprise, Fangyu showed up. With the help of good old Longyou, he had fortunately escaped from Yangzhou before the massacre began, and had been living in Longyou's home. Xiangjun was of course delirious. But I chided him under my breath, "You could have at least written to let us know you were safe!"

On the Festival Day, Xiang also unexpectedly came for a short visit, to Yuanyuan's heart-throbbing delight. But he left in a hurry after getting my herbal mix for poor Xiaowan.

Not long after the couple's reunion, Fangyu made known his wish to seek a job with the Qing court. Xiangjun tried to talk him out of it.

"Fangyu, we've been through this before. You are an eminent member of the Revival Society. Even though you have played no active part in the resistance movement, it would still be treachery for you to work for the enemy, don't you think?"

It was apparent to me that the austere life was driving Fangyu desperate, even though Xiangjun did not mind supporting him with her meager performance income.

The ninth reunion was a little sad, as everyone seemed to be dragging a heavy heart along. Rushi, in particular, appeared still in anguish when she recounted the rough patch she had been through.

I tried to lighten the mood by suggesting we all go down to Banknote Vault Street after dinner to watch the lantern display. We noticed that cheaper paper lanterns far exceeded silk lanterns in number this year. Still, there were a few pretty silk gauze ones with tassels and festoons of beads. As usual, many lanterns had history texts and riddles written on them. We had fun solving the riddles. Afterwards, I served the girls sweet soup with rice balls filled with red bean paste, as was our tradition.

In the middle of the year, real tragedy hit Rushi. Zilong

heroically gave his life for the country. She took it badly and attempted to end her life. It was fortunate that Qianyi was with her and saved her.

By the time the tenth reunion came around, Xiangjun was ten months along in her pregnancy and gave birth to a boy on Lantern Festival Day. It was a double celebration for us.

You would think that that would change my precious daughter's fate. What parents would not want their son to take his devoted spouse and their newborn son into the household? But this was how Fangyu's father reacted to the news, in his letter to the son:

"....The whore would be presumptuous to think that she and her bastard son will ever cross the threshold of the Hou residence....."

Xiangjun didn't take this well. She fell very sick with consumption and was not able to breastfeed her infant. Rushi kindly offered to hire a wet nurse for the infant, but Xiangjun turned it down.

What made matters worse was that shortly thereafter, Fangyu accepted from the Qing court a clerical job in his hometown in Henan and decided to move back home. As he was secretly planning to reconcile with his family, he departed one morning at the break of dawn without facing up to Xiangjun, and only left a short farewell note for her.

By mid-year, the sickly child died. My poor daughter almost went berserk with grief on that tragic day. But she never blamed Fangyu. She just sucked it all up and went on with life.

A few days after that painful mishap, something blissful happened to Yuanyuan. Jingjing, you will hear it all from her.

Business at the salon went on for two more years, and then it was shut down by order of the Nanjing magistrate. I thought our best, or rather, only, option would be to retreat to the Temple of Three Sages in Kunming to live out our lives there. Very often, temple retreat is the only refuge available to retiring courtesans.

Yuanyuan used her influence with the Taoist monk, Master Yu Lin, and got the three of us accepted into the Temple quarters. So, after saying farewell to Rushi, we came here to the Temple to begin our life of retreat.

In the third year of our retreat, one rainy summer day, my precious Xiangjun gave up her fight with chronic sickness and slipped into the next world.

I can never forget her last words:

"Mother, Yuanyuan, thank you for taking care of me these years. I'm so blessed to have both of you and Big Sister as my family. I can only hope to repay your kindness in the next life. Mother, forgive me for leaving you.... Yuanyuan, your daughter will be the hope for our lot. You did the right thing!"

To that, Yuanyuan replied, "My sweet Xiangjun, I owe it to you. If it hadn't been for your spiritual support, my dream would never have come true."

She and I each held one of Xiangjun's hands until the last. Death finally freed my precious daughter.

*Wiping a big drop of tear from the corner of her eye, Jingli Po Po said to Jingjing: "You must be hungry by now. Let's go inside and make dinner."*

*This was the first time that Jingjing saw the old lady cry.*

*After dinner, she showed Jingjing Fangyu's short biography of Aunt Xiangjun. He died one year after her death. A few years after his death, a friend of his published a collection of his works which included the biography. In it, he lauded her for her upright character and unyielding loyalty.*

*Jingjing felt that his writing came too late and rang empty. What good do praising words do to a dead person? But she still took heart that at least her aunt's short biography, written by the man who had forsaken her and regretted it, would live on. Readers of generations to come would be able to make their own judgment.*

# TWENTY-FOUR

*This morning, Jingjing was looking forward to Aunt Yuanyuan's morning session. She had fantasized about the romance between her aunt and Wu Sangui, and now realized how naïve she had been. The lesson she learned here was that there could be no love without a meeting of minds; love could not be forced, just as marriage was no promise of happiness.*

*When she and Aunt Yuanyuan finished breakfast, thick sulphurous rainclouds hung heavy in the sky. It looked like a severe rainstorm was in the offing. The cozy rear lounge, warmed by a burning brazier, definitely looked more inviting than the garden this day.*

When I got word from Li Zicheng's guards that Sangui had surrendered to Regent Dorgon and that the Qing Manchu army had breached the Shanhai Pass and had almost annihilated Li's forces, I was torn by ambivalence.

I knew Sangui couldn't escape blame for betraying his countrymen in exchange for advancement in wealth and power. In the end, it was he who had to answer to his own conscience, and I didn't envy him for that. On the other hand, I couldn't but rejoice at the news that the peasant outlaws had been subdued, but at the same time I was full of anxiety about the new Qing rulers.

Li managed to flee from the battlefield near the Shanhai Pass and came scrambling back to his base camp in Beijing. His vengeful murder of thirty-eight members of Sangui's family was cruel and shockingly depraved. Completely at a loss as to why he spared me, I took fleeting comfort from the thought that at least Yingxiong and his mother were not among the poor victims.

The next thing Li did was to pack up and head for his old base in Xi'an, taking me and a handful of his surviving followers along.

For the next couple of months we traveled on horseback through rough terrains, as Li chose routes that were off the beaten path to avoid his pursuers. We rode by day and camped in the wild by night. I found out that Sangui had been ordered by Regent Dorgon to track Li down and capture him, dead or alive, and his army was never far behind us. For that reason, Li didn't dare go back to his redoubt in Xi'an, where traps might be set for him, and so we continued our journey to Kunming in Yunnan.

While in the Beijing camp, I had befriended one of Li's followers, named Ah Hong, who was from Suzhou. A few days ago, I made a pact with him to escape together. He was to lead me to Sangui's camp, and I would ask Sangui to reward him.

The previous day he had used his soldier's hunch to gauge how near Sangui's army was, and had determined that we should make our move this moonless night. I had earlier smeared my face with ashes taken from the brazier and dressed in men's clothing, and was now in my tent waiting for his signal.

As soon as I heard a dog's bark repeated two times, I slung the sword across my shoulder and quietly slid out of the tent. Latching onto Ah Hong's arm, I climbed onto his horse and sat behind him. We headed in the direction opposite from that which Sangui's men were taking, and in a matter of half a joss-stick's burning time, Sangui's camps marked by the fluttering "Wu" flags came into sight.

We dismounted in front of the largest camp. I showed the

guards Sangui's sword, the hilt of which was inscribed with his name, and they let us through without further questions.

Once inside the brightly-lit camp, I called out his name in a full-throated wail. He was flabbergasted. It had been more than a year since he had last seen me, and as much as he did recognize my voice, he certainly was not expecting to see his concubine with a dirt-smeared face and in a shabby ill-fitting robe. When the moment of astonishment passed, he said,

"Yuanyuan, I almost didn't recognize you! Where on earth have you come from? Who is this man?"

"He is Ah Hong, from Li Zicheng's camp. It was he who rescued me and brought me here. He only wants to stay alive. Please give him a reward and let him serve in your camp."

"Guard, give the man ten silver pieces and set him up with a junior rank. Take him away now," he ordered in a peremptory tone. Then, turning to me without looking me in the eye, he said with barely concealed irritation in his voice,

"You better get yourself cleaned up. This is no place for a woman." The curt manner in which he spoke ruffled me. I had imagined he would at least be glad to see me after such a long separation.

"I'm very sorry about your father and your folk.... I couldn't do anything to save them. But I expect Yingxiong and his mother are in a safe place now...." He didn't even bother to ask how I had managed to deliver the two from near death.

"I wish I had torn that vermin Liu Zongmin to pieces. He had the gall to .... When I get my hands on that scum Li, I'll skin him alive. Did he take you too?" He ground his teeth in rabid rage, his bloodshot eyes still averted from mine.

"Li never touched me. What do you want me to do, Sangui? Are you not going to let the past rest? I am just a woman. I wasn't strong enough to fight Liu off. If I could somehow undo what he did to me, I would. Can you not find it in your heart to let it go? How I wish this had never happened to me!"

"Please don't talk about this anymore! I can't bear the thought... You are not that same woman...A lowly peasant has touched you...The whole world knows! How am I going to face my men?"

On the spur of the moment, I reached for the sword I was carrying. Had he been a twinkle late in seizing it from me, I would have slashed my wrist with it. But as soon as I calmed down, I cursed myself for acting so impulsively. Why? This man was not worth dying for! And I wouldn't let him fault me for a wrong that was not my doing.

"Why? Which part of me is different, Sangui? I assure you that you are looking at the same Chen Yuanyuan that you had met for the first time, her soul and spirit intact. But I see.... you think that I am blemished. But by that token, I was already stained when you first took me. You didn't mind it then. You made me think that you loved me. How come you now think that I'm somehow a shame? Can't you see that the shame is never on me?"

He remained mute for a long time. Now appearing more collected, he said in a less rigid tone,

"It's not convenient for you to live in a military camp. Maybe it's best for you to go and stay in a temple in Kunming until you figure out what you want to do next. I know a Taoist monk at the Temple of Three Sages who would be happy to shelter you. His monastic name is Yu Lin. The place is not far from here and I'll have one of my personal guards escort you there tomorrow morning. How's that?"

So he was now intent on discarding me like a piece of garbage just to coddle his male ego. As much as my heart ached over his vain and disparaging attitude, I felt a strange sense of relief, realizing that this was the most sensible option. Without another thought, I nodded my consent. What better place than a temple to find peace in?

That night, I refused his offer to let me sleep on his comfortable bed of beaver furs behind curtains, and insisted on sleeping on a wooden pallet set up in the screened-off corner where a wash basin stand affixed with mirror was placed.

Looking into the bronze mirror, I saw the plain and haggard version of me. The reflection was of a disowned woman who would be thrown right back into the *jianmin* lot. That thought depressed me. Self-loathing crept up on me like an old demon.

But when I took out the birdie kerchief and placed it on my lap, it seemed to be smiling kindly on me. I seemed to hear a light voice saying: "You still have your mother and sisters! They will always love you." And in the deep recesses of my soul, my cherished dream was still alive. When I lied down, I was able to sleep without nightmares for the first time in a long while.

Upon my departure the next morning, I handed the sword to Sangui, the sword that had saved his wife and son, and my maid Azalea.

For the next half year I lived at the Temple of Three Sages, the one sitting above our Anfu Garden here on Mount Wuhua.

Upon settling down, I started taking Taoist lessons from the kind monk, Master Yu Lin. The daily lessons pacified my inner self and helped me to accept, value and respect my own being.

Then one day I unyoked myself from my painful past, and he listened to my life story with patience and kindness. Afterwards, he led me outside to the sloping hillside and showed me a brook that ran down the hill. With a gentle smile he said,

"Look at the flowing water. Water is humble. It always heads to a low point. Water is soft, formless and flexible. It slides meekly and wittily around rocks, and it nurtures the plants on all sides.

That way, it is content and it sings. If you are humble, wise and nurturing in the same way as water, you will not feel shame. You will have peace."

Those words were like a lightning rod that rattled my soul. They would stick with me for the remainder of my life. I knew I still had to work at humility.

I was now really yearning for Mother and my sisters, and was certain they missed me too. By a stroke of chance, Master Yu Lin was planning to go to Nanjing on a pilgrimage visit to the Qixia Temple towards the end of the year. Knowing my heart's desire, he kindly offered to escort me back to Nanjing, suggesting that I disguise myself as a peasant. I couldn't wait to be home and to join my sisters for what would be our seventh reunion.

After half a month's tiresome travels by land and along waterways, we arrived at Nanjing on New Year Day. The kind monk and I said farewell at the Imperial City Southern Gate, and he went on to the Qixia Temple to the northeast, while I headed to the Villa of Alluring Fragrance in the city center.

As was usual at this time of year, the salon was quiet, as many of the girls had gone back home for family reunions. And I was surprised to see Rushi coming out at the parrot's alert. At first, she did not recognize me. When she came closer, she gasped in excitement. She told me that I had missed Mother and Xiangjun by two days. It was unbelievable that Ruan and Ma were still trying to seek revenge on them. These two spiteful knaves truly opened my eyes.

Rushi had come to see about the New Year Day festive meal for those girls who had no homes to return to. We were both worried about what Ruan and Ma might do to Xiangjun and Mother. But there was nothing we could do except pray to Guanyin for their safe and early return.

"Now that you're back, I have a good excuse to stay for

dinner!" Rushi said. She then sent Ah Luk out to buy a roasted duck and a salted chicken for our festive meal. Three of Fo's girls, who always stayed behind for the New Year, busied themelves in the kitchen preparing dishes of preserved sausages and stir-fried cabbages with dried mushrooms.

After we had eaten, Rushi and I went up to Xiangjun's bed chamber to catch up with each other. She told me in confidence about her encounter with Zilong here at the Villa. I marveled at their deep passion for each other and said to her,

"Apart from our sisterhood, nothing is more precious than having one true, passionate love in one's lifetime, even if intimacy cannot last. You, Xiangjun and I could say we have no regrets."

When I shared with her my Beijing abduction and everything that had happened thereafter, words flowed more easily than I thought was possible. But we both regretted that our seventh reunion was not going to happen, with Xiangjun and Mother absent.

She and Ah Luk left on the second-watch gong. While setting up a pallet in Xiangjun's bed chamber, I was thrilled to find that my old pipa, the first gift from Xiang, was lying under the bed, wrapped neatly in white silk cloth. I removed the wrap and hugged it tightly. It felt so good to be reunited with something from my happiest days! I fell asleep thinking of Xiang.

Four months later, on the day the Qing army descended upon Nanjing, Xiangjun and Mother thankfully managed to escape from the Palace and returned home safely. Rushi had got news from Qianyi and had come to the Villa earlier that day.

The joy on Xiangjun's and Mother's faces when they saw me moved me to tears! The four of us were rapt with emotions and bliss. It seemed a lifetime ago that we had last all been together in one place! We couldn't wait to tell each other our different stories, while lamenting the fall of Nanjing. We just felt glad that Qianyi had decided to surrender to the Manchus, as it prevented what would certainly have been a repeat of the Yangzhou bloodbath and carnage.

Rushi was in a wistful mood.

"The Qing court will try to impose their customs and beliefs on us once they have found a firm footing," she said. "Dorgon has already issued an edict commanding all Han men to shave their foreheads and wear Manchu-style queues. We can only pray that they won't destroy our culture altogether. It seems they are here to rob us of our lands. Their use of violence will only harden our resolve to resist. Scholars like Zilong, Xiang, Zhenhui and others from the Revival Society will never deign to submit to the Qing court."

We couldn't say she was wrong. But at least for now, Nanjing was intact and safe and we counted that as a blessing. All we asked for was to be left in peace to carry on with our daily lives.

"Rushi, I do understand what you're saying. But as long as we are breathing, we need to find a way to go on. We would just have to deal with surprises as they come."

Mother, always the practical one, nodded: "I agree with you, Yuanyuan. With your help and Xiangjun's help, I'll try to revive our salon's operation. I just hope the Qing rulers won't ban the pleasure business, and leave open this lifeline for us."

Rushi took the only hair ornament from her coifed hair, a beautiful green jade hairpin, and handed it to Mother, "Jingli, take this and pawn it. You can use the proceeds to get the business going again."

"Isn't that Fo's gift to you? Are you sure you want to part with it?" said Mother.

"Yes, I'm sure Fo would have wanted me to use it to help my dearest ones."

Mother thanked her profusely, "As soon as we have a surplus,

I'll redeem it and give it back to you."

Then she told us what had happened to Xiangjun and her in the Palace. We all exclaimed that Yang Longyou's appearance couldn't have been more opportune!

When I finished telling them the story of my torturous experiences, starting with my kidnapping in Beijing right up to my short retreat at the Temple of Three Sages, I let out a long sigh. Then I added,

"I wouldn't have the courage to tell you the kidnap part if I had never met Master Yu Lin. It was he who taught me to let humility and love drive out shame. That was perhaps the single most valuable lesson I have ever learned in my life."

When Rushi heard this, she said, "That is an inspiring but difficult lesson. Yuanyuan, I am so happy for you that you met the wise Master Yu Lin. I would really love to meet him some day." After a pause, she puckered her lips and hissed,

"But it's a real shame that Sangui didn't lift a finger to try to save you! It was a miracle that Li Zicheng spared your life. And afterwards Sangui had the gall to treat you with such insensitivity. He doesn't deserve you, Yuanyuan. I, for one, despise him for being a turncoat."

Xiangjun was listening without joining in our conversation. The only thing she had said was: "Yuanyuan, you should have slept in my bed." She appeared pale, withdrawn and desolate. Apparently, she was worrying about Fangyu. So many civilians had been killed in Yangzhou; it would be a real blessing if he survived. It was only after Rushi promised her to get Qianyi to help with making a search for him that she looked more relaxed.

Our happy mid-year reunion that day ended on a high note with a simple but delicious late night meal that Mother cooked for us.

With Xiangjun and I taking up our previous opera singing

roles, business at the salon began to grow again. As the Qing ruling class was still trying to set up their administration framework in Nanjing, our pleasure business was too trivial to warrant their attention and was allowed to go on as usual. But Mother was prudent to keep ticket and catering fees affordable in these unsettled times.

Very soon, our old customers, hearing that Xiangjun and I were taking the stage again, began flocking to our salon. New Manchu customers from the Qing noble class of the Eight Banners, on hearing about our salon, also ventured forth to become curious members of the audience. But some of these new customers were overbearing and would on occasion stir up trouble for us, mistaking our salon for a common brothel and our girls for whores. At such times, Mother's suave talking and diplomatic skills would come in handy.

By early winter, life settled into a routine, and my thoughts turned to Xiang. I was certain that he must have heard of my return by now, and it disturbed me that he had not shown his face. It was only when Mother told me that Xiang's family was now living from hand to mouth because he was out of a job since Nanjing fell, but stubbornly rejected any offer of a position from the Qing court, that I understood the reason for his absence.

So I put aside my slim savings and started to scrape together any surplus coins in the hope of building a relief fund for Xiang.

*Jingjing was not sure whether it was the inclement weather or this episode that depressed her. Sometimes, the truth stinks. She now understood why Aunt Yuanyuan had never been able to give her heart to Wu Sangui. He was a man with no love or compassion, only worldly wants. She pitied him for his withered soul! At the same time, her aunt's tenacious will to survive amazed her time and again.*

*By now, Jingjing had an idea of what she might do to help downtrodden women. Her half-brother Sunyi, whom her mother had loved like her own son, was a court official in the Ministry of Rites and was in a campaign to reform the class system. She thought she could team up with him to push for the ban of the 'jianmin' class.*

# TWENTY-FIVE

THE SEVENTH REUNION was not meant to be. The irony was that Yuanyuan arrived at the Villa on New Year Day all the way from Kunming yearning for reunion, only to find that Xiangjun and Jingli had been gone for two days. I was glad I happened to be at the Villa when she stepped in.

Yuanyuan's story made my heart ache. She went through unspeakable torments during her abduction in Beijing, but nothing abraded her more than Sangui's cold renunciation later. Yet her auspicious encounter with Master Yu Lin happily proved to be the counterpoint. She seemed a transformed person, thanks to him.

When Qianyi told me that he was going to lead the Nanjing court in surrender, I protested vigorously, because I would hate to see him turn his back on our country. But after he recounted to me the brutal Yangzhou massacre, I at once ceased my griping. I started to hate the Manchus.

On that fateful day, once the official surrender passed, Qianyi sent me a message telling me he had met Jingli and Xiangjun in the Fengxian Palace and that he had advised them to flee through the North Gate, which, thanks to Guanyin, they did.

I immediately headed to the Villa of Alluring Fragrance in the hope of meeting them. By this time, Yuanyuan was already settled in the Villa.

It was ironical that the four of us were finally reunited on the day when Nanjing fell into Manchu hands.

Yuanyuan and Jingli were certainly in the right mindset when they vowed to revive the salon business. Life had to go on somehow and I was happy to help them in any way I could.

After Nanjing's fall, Hangzhou and Suzhou also surrendered in tandem. But other cities that put up resistance to Dorgon's shave-head order, like Jiading and Jiangyin, went through hell as self-serving Ming defectors helped the Qing army suppress protestors with much violence. Such heinous incidents made me cringe, all the more because it was Ming defectors slaughtering their fellow countrymen to curry favor with the Manchus! I was just glad that I hadn't tried to stop Qianyi from surrendering to avoid another massacre. But I also grieved for our fallen motherland.

Zilong seemed to have gone underground with Zhenhui and other Revival Society members in their stubborn determination to stir uprisings against the Qing. Day and night I prayed for Zilong's safety.

When the time for our eighth reunion arrived, we all tried to have a good time. Jingli did the best she could to whip up a sumptuous meal on a limited budget. I couldn't have been happier for Xiangjun for having Fangyu back at the Villa after such a long separation. Xiang's sudden appearance certainly lifted Yuanyuan's spirits, although he couldn't stay for dinner.

When Yuanyuan approached me with the request for Qianyi to hire Xiang as an editor, I immediately relayed the request to Qianyi, and he agreed on the spot. It was one of the most heart-warming reunions we had ever had.

In the middle of the year, one day a messenger from Qianyi's ministry came with a shocking note. It was from Qianyi telling me that Imperial Guards had arrested him for allegedly writing a libelous document. In the note, he also asked me to try to raise three hundred taels of silver to pay the prison warden for his release. With petty crimes, paying for a prisoner's release was an acceptable practice under the code of law.

It turned out that Qian Chaoding had had an altercation with Qianyi a few months ago over the authorship of a certain book. When Qianyi proved himself to be right, Chaoding took offense and bore a grudge. He had the gall to forge a defamatory document and then accuse Qianyi of being the writer; the document spoke ill of a powerful Manchu aristocrat from the Yellow Banner.

This threw me into difficult circumstances. Qianyi was in the habit of spending most of his salary on buying books and we hardly had any savings put away. I had just given Fo's green jade hairpin to Jingli to get her salon going again, and the only valuables I had left were the two pink jade bracelets that were wedding gifts from my two sisters, and the gold necklace dowry from Master Wang.

Pawning the jewelry was the obvious choice, and I was more than willing, as this was an opportunity for me to repay Qianyi for his past favors. Knowing there would still be a shortfall, I asked Ah Luk to go to the pawn shop any way.

When Ah Luk came back, one look at his bruised and bloodied face sent my heart racing.

Falling on his knees, the usually stoic boy mumbled between sobs, "I couldn't fight them off... there were seven or eight thugs...Please forgive me!"

It was one of those times when mishap comes in pairs. I helped him up and tried to console him, "Don't blame yourself, Ah Luk. It's not your fault. Aiya, I should have cautioned you and taken preventive measures in these times. Come, let me clean up your wounds." While tending to his wounds with Begonia's help, I wracked my brains trying to find a way out of this mire.

Who could I look to for assistance? There was but one person who would have the heart to help, my generous old friend Master Wang! Immediately I set out to scribble a few lines and asked Ah Luk if he was well enough to take a boat trip to Hangzhou. The dare-devil nodded with a stubborn spirit. I must see to it that he and Begonia tie the knot soon, but that could wait.

I turned the house upside down looking for the most moth-eaten cotton robe that Qianyi had discarded. In the lining of the robe front I sewed a pouch securely, and then let the boy don the robe, secured with a waist band, and gave him a walking staff for self-protection. He was to wait for a reply once he delivered the letter to Master Wang. Anything that the old gentleman gave him should be put inside the pouch. He should ask for permission to stay the night and take the early morning boat back.

The whole night I tossed and turned on the bed. What if Master Wang was not at home? What if Ah Luk had an accident? If no money came, would I have to sell myself to a brothel?

Begonia and I went to the front yard at dawn to wait. Thanks to Buddha, at noon we saw him gamboling down the lane. Master Wang's heart-warming reply and the exchange bill for three hundred silver taels sent tears to my eyes. Without further ado, I set out with Ah Luk for the city prison inside the Imperial City.

We descended into the dark and dank prison by a flight of stone steps and groped our way along a slimy hallway. Immediately a miasma of stale food and urine rushed at our faces. A single naked flame torch held in a metal ring on the moldy wall threw light on a dark living form, hunched over a bowl of rice and steamed fish.

I explained the purpose of my visit and passed the exchange

bill into a scabrous hand. He snorted and trained his cloudy eyes on my upper body. I squirmed as I held fast onto Ah Luk's arm. Thanks to Guanyin he at last raised his heavy trunk from the chair, snatched the torch and led us down the corridor to Qianyi's cell.

I will never forget the look on his face when he saw me. Bewilderment gave way to catharsis. He probably could not believe he would see me so soon. Proud man that he was, he broke down and wept like a child. He was fortunate that the warden had heard of his name and had treated him with measured impertinence, believing his family was rich enough to ransom him. At least no torture was used on him. Nonetheless it was apparent that fear had eaten into his bones, wasting him away into a dried husk and turning his queue into a snowy white.

When Qianyi's health started to improve, I made a pact with him that he was to let me put aside half of his salary to repay the debt. After that prison experience, he was ready to do anything I asked of him. On my part, I felt I had to at least partially repay his favors.

Then in the New Year, we had our ninth reunion on Lantern Festival Day, which was a little off compared with the eighth, as everyone's heart was heavy. We did enjoy watching the display of lanterns on Banknote Vault Street and the sweet soup that Jingli made.

In late spring, we learned that Xiaowan had passed away. Qianyi and I attended the funeral at Xiang's family home.

In the midst of the rites, a thought raced through my mind. Would Xiaowan's death mean that Yuanyuan's cherished dream had a chance of coming true?

At the end of the fifth lunar month, I received a letter from

Master Wang. As I slit open the envelope, an ominous feeling assailed me.

In the first paragraph he told me that Li Wen, my good friend, had passed away on his sickbed a month before. Remorse pricked me for failing to visit him before his death and I made a mental note that I must pay respects to his grave in the upcoming autumn grave-sweeping season, when I would usually visit my mother's and Fo's graves in Songjiang.

Then the lethal blow struck. The passage cut me like a sharp blade.

"My dear Rushi, I hate to be the one to break this to you. Two days ago, while being transported in a boat to the city prison, Zilong unhitched himself from the cangue and jumped into the river. The soldiers watched him drown. They retrieved the corpse, sliced off his head to take to the magistrate as proof of death, and threw the rest back into the river. The Chen family later found the body and buried it."

The news turned my stomach; gall rushed up to my throat. The words rippled in a whirlpool through my head. My breath labored and I lost consciousness.

When I came to, I was lying in my bed, the collar of my robe drenched in tears, the letter in my clutch. Begonia was fussing over me when she saw me open my eyes, and tried to spoon-feed me warm ginger tea. I propped myself up against the bedstead and struggled to read the rest of the letter.

"After taking over Nanjing, the Qing court had been trying to lure Zilong to work as an official, but he had flatly rejected their offer. In order to avoid being harassed, he went to the Jiming Temple to become a novice Buddhist monk, and had all his hair shaved off. He thought it was better than being forced to wear a Manchu-style queue. Under this disguise, he was in constant contact with the anti-Qing groups, busily planning a full-scale uprising to take back Nanjing. Sadly, the rebellion ended in carnage, and he was captured."

Baneful reality stared me in the face. What I had always feared had come to pass. He had got what he wanted – honor after death. There was no doubt he would go down in history as a glorious martyr, having sacrificed his life as a resistance leader. I knew he wouldn't want me to grieve for him. He would only want me to take up where he had left off.

A plan was in the making in my head. I decided it was my mission to liaise with Qianyi's favorite student, Zheng Chenggong, and offer him any financial aid he might need for his anti-Qing campaign. Our debt to Master Wang was now repaid, and I would convince Qianyi to put aside our future savings to set up a fund for the campaign.

My head was telling me the future path to take, but my heart was a long way from being there yet. A high fever struck me and left me bed-ridden for almost a month. I could scarcely sleep or eat in the meantime. More than once I asked myself, "Why am I still here? Zilong is in the next world, and I had said I wished we could go there together. Shouldn't I be there with him?"

I couldn't even pay proper respects to my love, as his family made it clear that I would not be allowed to visit his grave. The pain would have annihilated me if it had not been for Yuanyuan's company and solace.

When the ninth lunar month arrived, Qianyi and I made a trip to Songjiang to visit my mother's and Fo's and Wen's graves.

After visiting the graves, we took a boat to cruise the once-familiar Songjiang River. While on the boat, memories of my first encounter with Zilong crept in to haunt my thoughts.

I could see Zilong, at his handsome best, gliding over the water towards our boat. His smile had a mocking twist, as if he was accusing me. A spasm of grief choked me and I said to

Qianyi, "We are Ming subjects. Why don't we pay our dues to our motherland and die for her?"

Before he could answer, I jumped off the boat into the inviting depths.

When I regained consciousness, Qianyi was looking down on me with a ginger smile, whispering: "Thank heavens you've come back. How could you leave me behind?" I had no words, but his gentle eyes were a comfort to look into.

Winter melted into Spring. At our tenth reunion on Lantern Festival Day, Xiangjun gave birth to a boy. We had a joyous double celebration at the dinner table. I also noticed that Yuanyuan was glowing with the life inside her.

Sadly, we later learned that Fangyu's family doggedly refused to take either mother or child into their household. Like many other unfortunate souls amongst the courtesans, Xiangjun couldn't escape the scourge of discrimination. My heart broke for her.

When I heard that Xiangjun couldn't breastfeed her child due to illness, I offered to hire a wet nurse for her. She said she didn't want to owe me too much. I wished I could have convinced her to accept my help. Tragically, her child died in mid-year.

One summer morning, Jingli made an unexpected call on me. She was carrying a new-born girl infant in her arms.

"Yuanyuan gave birth to this child three days ago. She can't keep her because Sangui is back in her life. She needs your help and says the child will have a better life with you. Her name is Jingjing."

I never forgot my promise to Yuanyuan. And I was more than pleased to raise the child as my own.

That scene where a well-groomed little girl enjoyed herself

in a garden, the scene I used to conjure up by the Songjiang riverbank when I was a child, came back to me. Now I could live that dream through Jingjing. She would grow up well-loved and well-educated, without a care in the world.

When I told Qianyi of my wish, he said happily, "How blessed we are to have this beautiful daughter! We'll shower her with all our love and will raise her to be a brilliant scholar."

This is the end of my memoir.

# TWENTY-SIX

*JINGJING HAD COME to the end of Rushi's memoir. The truth was now bared to her. Never had she felt as blessed as at this moment. Not only had her foster mother nurtured her in love, but both parents had endowed her with precious knowledge, along with their own distilled wisdom. For that, she would be eternally indebted to them. In all honesty, the truth actually made her adore her foster mother even more. She was now more determined than ever to do all she could to honor Rushi's last wish.*

*But before acknowledging the truth, she would wait for Aunt Yuanyuan to finish her story that morning.*

Time zoomed past and soon the first days of the New Year had come and gone, and the Lantern Festival was almost here. We were looking forward to an enjoyable eighth reunion this year, having skipped two reunions in a row due to the war.

Two days before the Festival, to Xiangjun's tearful ecstasy and our collective relief, Fangyou showed up at our Villa. He had cheated death by a hair's breadth and had managed to escape from Yangzhou unscathed, with the help of the good Yang Longyou, who had kindly put him up in his home.

That night I moved my pallet, my quilt and beddings and my pipa out of Xiangjun's bed chamber into the small rehearsal chamber near the hall entrance. As all the girls were now well-trained performers, there was little use for the chamber. Fo's girls had long taken up the bigger one as their bedding quarters.

On the Festival Day, while I was helping Mother prepare the big dinner in the kitchen, Xiangjun came in and said with a secretive smile,

"Someone is looking for you. He's waiting in the front lounge."

I went out to the lounge, and there he stood, in a slightly soiled and frayed pale green robe, looking excessively lank and fraught. Rapt with frantic joy and nettling anxiety, I could hardly move my limbs. He smiled and opened his arms. I threw caution to the wind and dived into his embrace.

"Why did you take so long to come to me? Don't you know I've been dying to see you?" I couldn't help chiding him gently.

"I wanted to come as soon as I heard of your return. But I felt ashamed that I couldn't afford to buy you even a tiny welcome gift.... So I hesitated. Xiaowan fell very sick in the autumn and her coughing has gotten worse and worse. The reason I've come today is to see if you could ask Jingli to give us some herbal medicine for coughing."

"You are so silly! Who can afford to buy gifts these days? Come, let's go to my chamber and I'll make you some Snow Orchid tea. Can you stay for dinner?"

"I'm afraid I can't stay for too long. Xiaowan is waiting for the medicine. She's really feeling bad."

"In that case, just make yourself comfortable in my chamber while I go and ask Mother for the medicine. I know she has a new prescription that uses dried fritillary bulbs and lily bulbs, which are very effective for curing coughs." After getting the herbal packet from Mother, I went into my chamber and handed it to him. I put a pot of water on the brazier to boil. Then I took five silver pieces wrapped up in a white silk kerchief from a small box that I kept near my pillow, and put it into his hands.

"Thank you for the medicine," he said. "But what is this? I can't accept your money."

"It's only five silver pieces. You can use it. Xiaowan needs nourishment to get well even if you don't mind going hungry. I insist you take it." Then I went over to the brazier and made tea. When I handed him the cup, he stared into my eyes with a fondness that melted my heart. "I will not forget this, my love," he whispered in his magnetic voice.

"Please promise me this: don't be a stranger. I'm back on the stage. Do come to see me perform once in a while. I'll sing for you your favorite songs set to the new lyrics you sent me."

"I promise I'll come whenever I can. But what of Sangui? Is he not in Beijing? I was going to ask why you are staying in Nanjing." He stared at me with eyes at once inquisitive and impassioned, while taking slow sips of tea.

"It's a long story. A lot has happened. I'll tell you everything next time you come. What are your plans for the future?"

"For me, working as a Qing court official is out of the question. I was thinking of setting up a street stall to offer letter and couplet writing services."

"I know your position. But that idea doesn't sound very promising – the fees you can charge would hardly be enough to feed your family of eight. Have you thought of working as an editor for Qianyi? Rushi mentioned that he was planning to compile an anthology of prominent Ming officials' biographies. Working for him personally is not the same as working for the Qing court. Do you want me to ask him for you?"

"I wouldn't mind working for Qianyi…"

"Leave it to me then. Now I'm not going to delay you any longer. Xiaowan needs you."

Throughout the rest of the year, Xiang came to see me a few times. On his second visit in late spring, when I told him what had happened to me in Beijing and in Kunming, he sobbed like an infant on my shoulder and said, "Life is too cruel to you, Yuanyuan!"

My eyes pricked with tears, as I knew he too had had a hard time fleeing with his family during the war from Rugao County to Nanjing, losing all possessions to robbers during the flight. On that visit, I also told him that Qianyi had agreed to hire him as an editor. That at least solved his most pressing livelihood problem.

The year passed without incident at the Villa, but Rushi had to tough it out. At our ninth sisters' reunion, we learned of Qianyi's earlier imprisonment. This reunion would have passed in a sombre mood had not Mother suggested we go out to watch the lantern display on Banknote Vault Street. We had fun solving lantern riddles.

In late spring, Xiangjun announced she was pregnant with Fangyu's child. But Fangyu didn't seem thrilled by the news, as he was still in financial distress.

Shortly thereafter, news came that Xiaowan had passed away as she lost her fight with lung disease. I went with the girls from the salon to attend the funeral in Xiang's home. He appeared calm and collected, with a wisp of sorrow in his brow. We were aware that his primary wife, Madam Su, had treated Xiaowan with generosity and kindness. So all in all, she had had a contented life in the Mao family.

Throughout the summer, Xiang came as usual to watch my performances.

In late summer, news came that Zilong had died a martyr. His death struck Rushi so hard that she was constantly delirious. I paid several discreet visits to her home to console her and keep her company. Her distraught mental state made me fear that she might try something drastic.

Around the Moon Festival in the eight lunar month, I found myself with child.

A month later, Rushi had a brush with death in Songjiang, but thankfully that was not her destined end.

At the tenth reunion, Xiangjun gave birth to her son right on Lantern Festival Day. But to our utter dismay, Fangyu's family still stubbornly refused to take her and her son in. She was so desolate that she fell gravely ill. Then Fangyu left her to head back to his Henan home to take up a job at the Qing court.

In mid-year, their child died. Xiangjun was inconsolable on that tragic day. At that moment, rage filled me to the brim. Compelled by the feeling that I had to do something, I sat down and wrote a scathing letter to Fangyu, lambasting him for his cowardice and for shirking responsibility. Other than allowing me give vent to my fury, the letter didn't change anything.

But I truly admired Xiangjun for her forgiving nature. Not once in her deep grief did she say a bad word about Fangyu. The mourning for her infant's death didn't last a long time, or maybe she learned to hide her pain. Soon, she picked up the pieces and carried on.

A few days after her infant's death, I gave birth to a girl. It was with the utmost awe and gratification that I welcomed this beautiful creature into the world. My dream finally had come true! From then on, it was for her that I would breathe.

Three days after her birth, Sangui appeared for the first time since our separation. When Mother came into my chamber to announce him, I was thrown off balance. Then the initial shock gave way to contemplation. I felt I must make a crucial decision.

Moments later, I bade Mother take my infant daughter to Rushi at once and said to her, "Mother, please take the child to Rushi and say that Yuanyuan needs her help now. The child will have a better life and future with her. She'll understand. You must leave by the postern gate."

Just as I was lifting the infant from the crib, Sangui was stomping in from the front lounge. He caught me passing the infant to Mother on the threshold. She was alert and quickly swept down the hall to the backyard. He barged into my chamber and seized me by the shoulders, demanding to know if that was my child and who had fathered it.

With a bland voice and a steely stare I said,

"Yes, it is my child. But you needn't know who the father is. I don't see how it concerns you. You abandoned me, remember? And why are you here today, anyway?"

Shame-faced, he took two steps back. But my glacial countenance was not enough to repel him. Before long he began cajoling and pleading for me to go back to him. In truth, the moment he showed up, an inner voice had warned me that my destiny with him was not over yet.

After he left, I wrote a letter to Xiang explaining my decision to put our child in Rushi's care. He wrote back to say that he understood that it was in the child's best interests.

Two years later, after closing the salon business, Mother decided that we should retreat to a temple. On the day of saying farewell, Rushi brought two-year-old Jingjing to the Villa for our farewell dinner. The feeling of the toddler's little hand grasping my fingers filled me with a magical sense I had never known before. I knew I would treasure my own life for her sake.

Two days after our last gathering, Mother, Xiangjun and I came here to begin our life of retreat at the Temple of Three Sages. Three months after our departure, Rushi, Qianyi and Jingjing also left Nanjing to return to Changshu. In that same year, Xiang took up monastic life at the Qixia Temple in Nanjing. He just couldn't bear the fact that Sangui was clawing his way back from his desertion of me.

Since then, Rushi wrote to me twice every year to tell me little anecdotes about you.

Jingjing, I hope by now you've got answers to all your questions.

*"Mother," Jingjing cried, and threw herself into Yuanyuan's longing embrace.*

*"Jingjing, you were born out of love, and I know that as you grew up, Rushi and Qianyi loved you with all their heart. But can you forgive me for leaving you back then?" Yuanyuan stroked her daughter's hair tenderly, as big drops of tear slid down her cheeks.*

*"Mother, there's nothing to forgive. I understand everything. I love both my mothers so very much! Also, I must make a trip to the Qixia Temple to visit my father."*

*"He would be so happy to meet you. All these years, I've been copying Rushi's letters to him. I'm sure he thinks of you every day."*

*Then Yuanyuan murmured in sadness,*

*"Rushi was a poet to the end. Death was her elegiac verse mourning people's deadened hearts. Jingjing, it is now up to you to make her death worthwhile."*

*"Mother, I've already made up my mind. I will work with my half-brother Sunyi to draw up a petition to the Emperor pleading for the ban of the jianmin class. We will not give up until we see it happen. I know this is what my foster mother would want."*

*Yuanyuan closed her eyes tightly as if she wanted to shield herself from the glaring pain and miseries of the world. Yet her frail form still shone with unrelenting hope.*

*In Jingjing's poetic soul, all the kerchief sisters were beautiful sheaves of water, soft, humble, pliable, yet capable of wearing away even rock.*

# AUTHOR'S NOTE

IN THIS NOVEL, the cast consists mostly of real historical characters. Many of the episodes in the protagonists' lives are based on or inspired by literary works. Literary writings and unofficial history (called "yeshi" in Chinese) are important research sources that throw light on these women's stories. On the other hand, numerous instances of artistic license pertain to the details and chronology of events depicted in this novel.

The sworn sisterhood between Liu Rushi, Chen Yuanyuan and Li Xiangjun has been inspired by a customary practice that prevailed in the brothels' sphere in Ming and earlier dynasties. Among courtesans, exchanging kerchiefs was a rite to cement a sisterly friendship. In real life though, Liu Rushi and Chen Yuanyuan were truly close friends and at one time lived under the same roof in Suzhou City.

Liu Rushi's story, as relayed in the novel, is largely based on the 800,000-word biography written by eminent Chinese historian Chen Yinke (1890 – 1969), titled An Ulterior Biography of Liu Rushi. This biography has been carefully reconstructed from literary works written by Liu herself, her husband Qian Qianyi, her lover Chen Zilong, and their contemporary peers. But details about her early childhood are skeletal. It is here that I've tried to fill the gap using my imagination. The generous help that Liu and Qian accorded Dong Xiaowan to free her from bondage is noted in the biography and various other literary writings.

As for Chen Yuanyuan, there are different versions of her

romance with Ming General Wu Sangui and of the role she played in his perfidious decision to join hands with the Qing army, causing the Ming dynasty to be supplanted. Such versions are nevertheless based on folklore. Qing poet Wu Weiye (1609 – 1671) famously wrote an epic poem titled Song of Yuanyuan, and it has remained a key source of her life story. Wu's poem is credible by virtue of his friendship with Mao Xiang, Chen's lover. In Zhang Dai's history tome Sequel to the Book of the Stone Casket (this sequel is entirely about the Chongzhen Emperor's reign), Tian Hongyu's forceful abduction of Chen and his abuse of concubines is well recorded. I've basically framed her story around these written texts and popular lore, with a few dramatic twists of my own creation.

In my novel, I have placed an accent on the love relationship between Chen and Mao Xiang. This has been inspired by the latter's published memoir titled Reminiscences of the Plum-Shaded Cloister, which gives an unmistakable impression of his deep attraction to Chen Yuanyuan.

The character Li Xiangjun is very well drawn in Kong Shangren's masterpiece historical drama The Peach Blossom Fan, which in fact is based on real history and her short biography written by Hou Fangyu, her lover. My novel closely follows that portrayal.

Regarding the character Jingjing and her identity, it is an instance of speculation and taking artistic license. In real life, Liu Rushi gave birth to a daughter in 1648, seven years after her marriage to Qian Qianyi, when he was sixty-six years old.

As regards the degrading social classification of courtesans and entertainers as jianmin, it was officially banned during the Yongzhen Emperor's (1722 – 1735) social reforms.

## Courtesan Culture in the Ming Dynasty

When Zhu Yuanzhang (1328 – 1398) began his reign as the first Ming Emperor, he made present-day Nanjing his capital. During his rule, he established an entertainer compound along the banks of the Qinhuai River for the purpose of hosting public functions, to which courtesans were summoned to perform music and dance.

However, the Emperor decreed that it would be a crime for scholar-officials to sleep with courtesans, and offenders would be slapped with a punishment only one degree below the death penalty. This became legislated as a criminal law under the Great Ming Code. But in practice, it was not uncommon for scholar-officials to flout this law. By the end of the Ming dynasty, the Qinhuai pleasure district had turned into an entertainment hub for the literati.

Historians have suggested that it was definitely in the late-Ming period that cultivated courtesans were highly extolled, as romantic association between the literati and cultivated courtesans normalized. Poetry often acted as a conduit in these romantic liaisons, and many courtesans were well versed in poetry writing, calligraphy and painting. In fact, many courtesans-poets/artists married into gentry families, becoming wives and concubines of prominent scholars. This phenomenon was unique to the late-Ming period.

In Sufeng Xu's 2007 dissertation entitled Lotus Flowers Rising from the Dark Mud: Late Ming Courtesans and Their Poetry, the McGill University scholar argues that the phenomenon owed much to the rise of literary-political societies throughout the region of Jiangnan (South of the Yangtze) during the troubled times of the Ming-Qing transition.

Elite and non-conformist scholars of these societies would

meet regularly and freely discuss poetry and politics. Through promoting and anthologizing poetry writings by cultivated courtesans, and through romantic involvement with them, these scholars were in fact championing a counterculture, which could be seen as open resistance to the prevalent Neo-Confucianism teachings. It was also a kind of protest against the officialdom examination system that valued solely the art of prose (called "eight-legged essays"), a relatively insipid form of literature compared to poetry.

Thus, it was this conscious effort on the part of the free-minded, poetry-loving literati that helped the unique late-Ming courtesan culture to thrive.

# ACKNOWLEDGEMENTS

FIRST, I WOULD like to give heartfelt thanks to Graham Earnshaw, publisher of Earnshaw Books, for his unremitting support and guidance. A big thank-you too, to his entire publishing team for their dedicated effort in bringing this novel to life.

A distinct debt of gratitude is owed to illustrious historian Chen Yinke for his seminal work An Ulterior Biography of Liu Rushi, to playwright Kong Shangren for his historical play The Peach Blossom Fan, and to poet Wu Weiye for his narrative poem Song of Yuanyuan. Without these illuminating works, the writing of this novel would have been a mission impossible. Also, Yu Huai's Banqiao Zaji (Diverse Records of the Plank Bridge), Zhang Dai's The Dream Recollections of Taoan and Jonathan D. Spence's Return to Dragon Mountain: Memories of a Late Ming Man have provided me with insight into the unique late-Ming courtesan culture. I am much indebted to these eminent authors/historians.

Last, a huge shout-out to book bloggers, reviewers, readers and author friends who have generously cheered me on in my writing career.

# FURTHER READING

Berg, Daria. Women and the Literary World in Early Modern China, 1580 – 1700, 2015.

Chang, Kang-I Sun. The Late-Ming Poet Ch'en Tzu-lung (Chen Zilong): Crises of Love and Loyalism, 1991.

Chang, Kang-I Sun (editor), Stephen Owen (editor). The Cambridge History of Chinese Literature: From 1375, 2010.

Chen, Yinke. An Ulterior Biography of Liu Rushi, Vol. I to III, 1980. 柳如是別傳.

Ko, Dorothy. Teachers of the Inner Chambers: Women and Culture in Seventeenth Century China, 1994.

Kong, Shangren. Cyril Birch (translator), Chen Shih-Hsiang (translator) and Harold Acton (translator). The Peach Blossom Fan, 2015.

Lee, Lily Xiao Hong (editor), A. D. Stefanowska (editor) and Clara Wing-chung Ho (editor). Biographical Dictionary of Chinese Women (the Qing Period 1644 – 1911), 1998.

Mao, Xiang. Reminiscences of the Plum-Shaded Cloister, 1651. 影梅庵憶語.

Peterson, Barbara Bennett (editor). Notable Women of China: Shang Dynasty to the Early Twentieth Century, 1999.

Spence, Jonathan D. Return to Dragon Mountain: Memories of a Late Ming Man, 2007.

Yu, Huai. Banqiao Zaji (Diverse Records of the Wooden Bridge), 1693. 板橋雜記.

Zeitlin, Judith T. Notes of Flesh and the Courtesan's Song in Seventeenth Century China - Chapter 3, The Courtesan's Arts: Cross-Cultural Perspectives (editors: Martha Feldman and Bonnie Gordon), 2006.

Zhang, Dai. The Dream Recollections of Taoan, 1646. 陶庵夢憶.

# About The Author

Born and raised in Hong Kong, Alice Poon steeped herself in Chinese poetry and history, Jin Yong's martial arts novels and English Literature in her school days. This early immersion has inspired her creative writing.

Always fascinated with iconic but unsung women in Chinese history and legends, she cherishes a dream of bringing them to the page.

She is the author of *The Green Phoenix* and the bestselling and award-winning non-fiction title *Land and the Ruling Class in Hong Kong*. She now lives in Vancouver, Canada and devotes her time to writing historical Chinese fiction.

http://alicewaihanpoon.blogspot.ca
https://www.instagram.com/alicepoonauthor
http://twitter.com/alicepoon1
https://www.goodreads.com/alice_poon
https://www.facebook.com/AlicePoonWriter
https://www.facebook.com/alice.poon.author